THE
RETURNING

The Saga of Davi Rhii Book 2

BRYAN THOMAS SCHMIDT

BORALI ALLIANCE

ALSO BY BRYAN THOMAS SCHMIDT

NOVELS
The Worker Prince (Saga of Davi Rhii 1)
The Returning (Saga of Davi Rhii 2)
The Exodus (Saga of Davi Rhii 3)
Simon Says (John Simon Thrillers)
The Sideman (John Simon Thrillers)
Common Source (John Simon Thrillers)
Milk Run (John Simon Thrillers, forthcoming)

CHILDREN'S BOOKS
Abraham Lincoln Dinosaur Hunter: Land Of Legends
102 More Hilarious Dinosaur Jokes For Kids

NONFICTION
How To Write A Novel: The Fundamentals of Fiction

ANTHOLOGIES (AS EDITOR)
Robots Through The Ages (with Robert Silverberg) (forthcoming)
Aliens Vs. Predators: Ultimate Prey (forthcoming)
Surviving Tomorrow
Infinite Stars: Dark Frontiers
Joe Ledger: Unstoppable (with Jonathan Maberry)
Predator: If It Bleeds
Infinite Stars: Definitive Space Opera and Military Science Fiction
The Monster Hunter Files (with Larry Correia)
Maximum Velocity (with David Lee Summers, Carol Hightshoe,
Dayton Ward, and Jennifer Brozek)
Little Green Men—Attack! (with Robin Wayne Bailey)
Decision Points
Galactic Games
Mission: Tomorrow
Shattered Shields (with Jennifer Brozek)
Raygun Chronicles: Space Opera For a New Age
Beyond The Sun
Space Battles: Full Throttle Space Tales

Praise for Bryan Thomas Schmidt's *The Saga of Davi Rhii* trilogy:

Honorable Mention for *The Worker Prince*, Barnes and Noble's Year's Best Science Fiction Releases—Paul Goat Allen.

"THE WORKER PRINCE breathes dynamic new life into the space opera genre. Rich characters, wild action, and devious plotlines collide in a thoroughly entertaining book!"
— Jonathan Maberry, New York Times bestselling author of *Predator One* and *Deadlands: Ghostwalkers.*

"A brisk science fiction novel full of rich characters and settings, it embodies 'sense of wonder' in the best traditions of classic science fiction. Well worth your time!"
– Robin Wayne Bailey, New York Times Bestselling author of *Dragonkin* and *Frost.*

"I found myself thinking of stories that I read during my (misspent) youth, including Heinlein juveniles and the Jason January tales, as well as Star Trek and Star Wars."
— Redstone SF.

"Bryan Thomas Schmidt's THE WORKER PRINCE will appeal to readers of all ages. Bryan deftly explores a world where those who believe in one God labor against oppressors, and a single man may have the power to change their situation for the better. But will he be able to rise above all that his powerful uncle has taught him?"
— Brenda Cooper, Author of *Edge of Dark, The Silver Ship and the Sea* and *Mayan December.*

"In THE WORKER PRINCE, Bryan Thomas Schmidt combines elements from the Biblical story of Moses with exciting outer space action to create a satisfying hero's journey that is well worth taking."
— David Lee Summers, Author of *The Solar Sea,* Editor of *Tales of the Talisman.*

"Bryan Thomas Schmidt's love for Science Fiction comes through on every page. THE WORKER PRINCE is fun for any age."
— Maurice Broaddus, Author of *The Knights of Breton Court* and *King's Justice.*

"Bryan Thomas Schmidt's debut novel is a fast-paced and deftly-told space opera adventure set in a well-envisioned political and social environment. It is classic space adventure in all the right ways, with plenty of action, twists, and characters with emotional depth."

— Gary W. Olson, author of *Brutal Light*.

"A very well written book, and a story very well told. It's nice to read a book where the heroes are heroes and the villains are villains. I thoroughly enjoyed the combination of the Moses story with the Sci-Fi themes...I would highly recommend it even if you are new to Sci-Fi."

— Ben Love, First Million Words Podcast.

"...Not a simple story, but a complex piece of work...the intricate plot alone is enough to carry the reader along....Bryan Thomas Schmidt depicts this absorbing world. Drawing on strong literary elements which are key to this type of fiction, the potential for the series is boundless."

— Ricky Brown, Howell Book Examiner.

"The Returning has romance, assassins, tension, both modern and classic science fiction notions, and very smooth writing. What more could you want? Bryan Thomas Schmidt keeps improving. As good as The Worker Prince WAS, The Returning is better."

— Mike Resnick, Author, *Starship* and *Ivory*

"The Returning blends themes of faith with classic space opera tropes and the result is a page-turning story that takes off like a rocket."

— Paul S. Kemp, Author,
Star Wars: Riptide, Star Wars: Deceived

"A fun space opera romp, complete with intrigues, treachery, dastardly villains, and flawed but moral heroes."

— Howard Andrew Jones, Author, *The Desert Of Souls*

Honorable Mention,
Barnes & Noble's Year's Best SF Releases

BRYAN THOMAS
SCHMIDT

Hugo Nominee

THE
RETURNING

The Saga Of Davi Rhii Book 2

Ottawa, KS

BORALIS BOOKS
Ottawa, KS 66067

ISBN-13: 978-1-62225-7925 paperback
ISBN-13: 978-1-62225-7935 ebook

First Boralis Books Paperback Edition: September 2021
Printed in the United States of America

10 9 8 7 6 5 4 3 2 1

Interior Design and Layout by Guy Anthony De Marcco at
PublicationEngineering.com
Cover Design: Audra Redington
Solar System Map: Jeana Clark
Borali Crest: Mitchell Davidson Bentley
Author Photo: Bryan Thomas Schmidt

Dedication

To Griffin, Noah and Kyle
With encouragement to shoot for the stars
you can do anything if you believe in yourself
and work for it
I'll never doubt you
May all your dreams come true

BORALIS
SOLAR
SYSTEM

CHARLIS (SUN)

REGALIS

PLUTONIS

KRONIS

ITALIS

XANTHIS

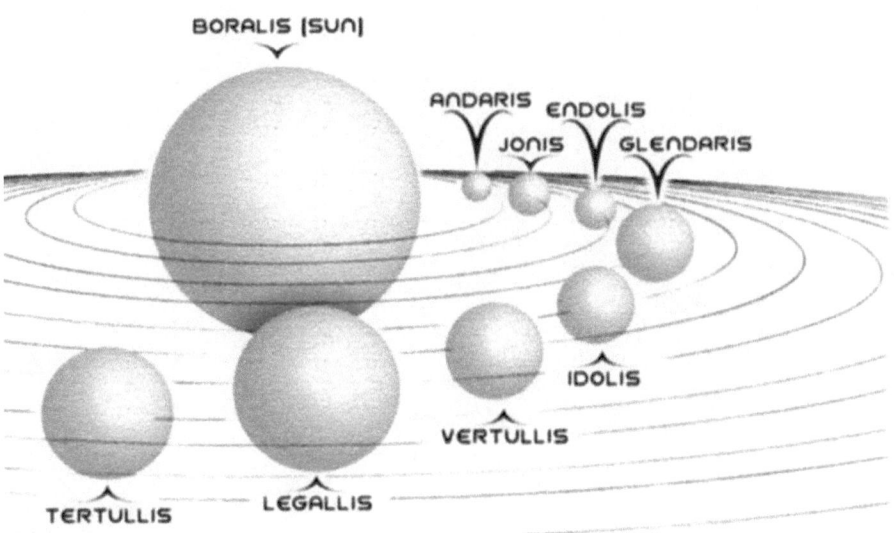

Chapter One

Either his eyes were failing or the shadows were alive. Dru blinked as he listened to his fellow cadets breathing and snoring around him. He lay at the center of a row of seven bunks with seven more lining the opposite wall. All twenty-eight were occupied and no one else seemed to be stirring.

As he lifted his head, he saw a dark shape like a shadow, slinking down the center aisle. The figure moved quickly, sliding between the bunks on the opposite wall and leaning over one of them. He saw a sharp movement. Did the shadow have four arms? Who could it be? His mind raced for answers. His clothes stuck to his body, an odd feeling. He never sweated at night. There was a gargling, then he watched as the shadow shot upright and ran back the way it had come.

Dru heard wheezing coming from the bunk and sat up, planting his feet on the floor. What was happening with Cadet Kowl? He jumped up. "Kowl, are you ok?"

No sign of the shadow. A metallic smell filled his nostrils. Others stirred around him. He heard a click as reflector pads flicked on overhead.

Dru gasped and stepped back as he stared down at Cadet Kowl's slashed throat as blood drained from it into two pools on either side of his bunk on the floor. He shivered, a sudden chill coming over him.

"Gods! He's dead!" The cadet behind him sounded as shocked as Dru felt. Cadet Walz was it? Dru couldn't remember. Then chaos erupted as someone pulled the alarm and he was shoved aside by arriving instructors.

"Wonder what Dru's doing right now?" Davi's cousin Nila's voice crackled over the comm as his squadron flew in formation around him.

"Whatever he's doing, it's a lot better than sitting out here babysitting transports and going through the motions," Virun groused as the other VS28 fighters slid back into formation and continued along the course of their routine patrol.

"Keep the chatter down so Farien and Brie can give their report." Captain Davi Rhii fought back a laugh. He'd long ago grown used to the boredom of patrol. So what if Nila and her friends were always chattering during patrols? It lightened the mood and kept them alert. Besides, Dru's reassignment couldn't help but be a fascination for his friends. Especially since their current patrol route passed Eleni 1, the Legallian moon which Presimion Academy called home.

Dru and the others had trained together then fought for freedom against their enslavers with the Worker's Freedom Resistance. They beamed with pride when they mentioned his name. It was a huge honor having one of their own be one of the first ex-workers admitted to the most prestigious military school in the system.

"A junked freighter." Brie interrupted his thoughts as she began her report.

"Class Seven, Tertullian made," Farien added. "A ghost."

"What? They just leave them out here abandoned?" Jorek's voice dripped with disgust.

"Kinda big to just park somewhere on the ground," Farien answered. "Especially when there are plenty of pirates and scavengers around to do the work for them."

"And plenty of empty space." Davi glanced across the formation toward his old friend and grinned. As liaison, Farien functioned as a member of the squad, working alongside Davi to ensure the pilots were treated like every other Borali pilot, from training to uniforms to schedules. Having his old friend around to compare notes with lightened Davi's load, and Farien, for his part, seemed pleased to be working with Davi again. The promotion hadn't hurt his self-esteem either. Farien acted more confident and positive than Davi had ever seen him.

"What if it floats off into a planet or someone crashes into it?" Jorek was a fount of never-ending questions.

Farien snorted. "Then the legal people and politicians get to do what they love and argue and someone else gets to have a funeral."

Davi winced. Farien still needed to learn some tact.

"Exactly," Jorek said, as if he'd proved his point.

"There have been very few incidents of ghost ships colliding with other ships," Davi interjected. "And none of collisions with planets."

"Just a matter of time," Virun said, taking his best friend's side. "Somebody's nav system could malfunction." Jorek and Virun were two of the smartest pilots Davi knew, right up there with Tela. They reminded him of his own academy days with Yao and Farien: rarely seen apart; inseparable to all who knew them; top of the class in training, despite a propensity to let passion rule over reason.

"Well, back at base, you two can write up a nice report requesting an official salvage ship, ok?" Farien sent the images he and Brie had captured to the entire squadron via his ship's computer. "It will be one of many."

"Ech. Paperwork. No thanks." Davi could almost hear Virun's frown.

Sensors beeped in alarm, sending a familiar tingle up Davi's arms. Davi looked down and typed a command into his computer, sliding forward in his seat to force blood flow into his drowsy limbs and keep him alert.

"Incoming ship of unknown origin." Brie's speed impressed him. On the surface, she was the antithesis of a pilot: a short, cute blonde with girl-next-door looks, prone to using her wiles to get what she wanted by playing the weak female in need. She'd once been considered most likely to fail among his student pilots, along with Nila and Dru. But somehow they'd struggled through and become real pilots, equal to everyone else on the squad.

Almost even equal to Tela. He closed his eyes recalling the sparkle in her eyes when she smiled, the soft warmth of her hand holding his. Command had been giving her fewer rotations for reasons unknown. Davi hadn't had a chance to inquire about it, but he really needed to. Tela became agitated whenever they discussed it.

"Wish you could fly as fast as you type," Jorek teased, the banter breaking Davi out of his thoughts and back to the tension of the moment.

"Funny how you're usually the one chasing me," Brie teased. Nila and Brie's laughter filled the comm channel.

"Save the flirting for your dates," Davi instructed. "What are we looking at?" His eyes darted back and forth between the computer screen and the view out his blastshield as his scanners evaluated the target's course and position, firepower, shield strength and other factors.

"What the—?" Jorek's fighter suddenly dove and Brie darted right. A black shape raced through the space where they'd just been. Davi leaned forward, eyes straining to identify it.

"Shields!" Farien ordered.

"The computer says its components may be Lhamorian," Nila reported as Davi's own computer returned the same results.

"Offensive formation," Davi ordered, hand tightening on his joystick. "Let's go give her a look."

The fighter's engines vibrated his cockpit as Davi accelerated. Circling back together, the pilots remained in tight formation. Davi took a moment to shift in his formfitting seat and stretch his legs. The one thing he did appreciate about long, quiet patrols was unsweaty cockpits. Being confined in a vacuum with his own body odor was something he'd never get used to, even with the distraction of combat.

"Heads up," Farien called. "There he is."

Davi sighed. The mystery ship accelerated away from Eleni 1 far too fast for a casual visitor, and so dark it was almost hidden by the starfield until the fighters moved in to surround it. Sleek and black starfighters with snub noses and three wings—two longer wings out of each side, and a third shorter wing extending vertically above the fighter's four engines—VS28s were dark black, but spotting each other was simple enough despite the gray, transparent blastshield. The squadron insignia on their sides helped, of course. This mystery ship, however, was tricky to see. It appeared designed that way. Line-of-sight stealth made little sense in space where sensory radar were relied upon to identify and track other craft, which meant the stealth was intended for something else. Plus the craft was unusually small, almost fighter-sized, yet appeared to have a passenger compartment behind the cockpit built to carry multiple passengers. Add to that the computer's dearth of information on its origins and that brought only two uses to mind: spying and smuggling. But spying on Eleni 1 made little sense.

Davi punched commands into the computer and the reports came up on his screen. "Sensors read one occupant. No weapons."

"The sensors didn't even find her until she was right up on us," Brie answered, her voice rising in pitch with the tension.

"We didn't see him either," Jorek barked, still clearly angry from the near miss.

"Whoever he is, he's not expecting trouble from us," Farien responded. *At least there's one voice of calm here.*

"Unless that's what he wants us to think," Nila added.

Davi smiled, pleased with his cousin. Her perceptiveness had developed with her flight skills. Davi had the same suspicion, and he knew Farien and others would, too, after hearing her voice it. Davi initiated another scan of the target. "Defensive formation." He switched his comm to a hailing channel. "This is Captain Davi Rhii of the Borali Alliance, identify yourself immediately."

The radio remained silent for what seemed like forever.

"Weapons range, Captain," Virun reported as Davi watched his sensors flash the alert.

"I repeat. Identify yourself. This is Captain Davi Rhii of the Borali Alliance." So much for unsweaty cockpits.

"'ello, Capt'in, my ship's transpond'r 's malfuncti'ning." It was the same accent Davi had heard in the market on Vertullis many times. The accent of Itolis, a Lhamor. A Lhamor on Eleni 1? It had to be a merchant but why the stealth ship?

"Slow down immediately and maintain course," Davi ordered the stranger. "Identify. Who are you running from?"

The mystery ship slowed onto a steady course as the fighters slid in to surround her.

"Not runn'ng. 'erchant, Capt'in. Negotiat'r f'r Minist'y of Trade. I mean no h'rm. I he'd for X'nthis Depot for rep'irs."

Davi muted the channel and keyed the private squadron channel. "Ministry of Trade, right? He's a smuggler for sure." Nothing else made sense.

"Legallis Depot is closer," Farien responded.

"It's also expensive. He's probably trying to save some bucks, if his story's even true."

"You don't think it's a spy ship?" Jorek asked.

"What's there to spy on at Eleni 1?" Nila sounded amused.

"The Academy. Military tactics, weaponry..."

"There are easier ways to gather that data," Nila responded.

"What about the big agro firms?" Virun asked.

"They send spies for agriculture?" Brie sounded surprised.

"It's a competitive field," Virun responded. "Some firms have secrets."

Once one of them got going, the others followed. The questions rained like a storm. Davi winced. *Let's get some answers.* He keyed the hailing channel again. "Why Xanthis? The Depot on Legallis is closer."

"My boss h's a contr'ct with X'nthis. Leg'llis 's very expensive."

"By protocols, we should detain him," Brie said over the squadron channel.

"I say we do it for almost killing us," Jorek answered.

"If his employer is the trade minister, he'll raise hell." Farien wasn't arguing but his tone made it clear he wanted to let the ship go.

"He could be a spy!" Jorek and Virun clearly wanted to take this to the next level.

"You heard his accent. Why would Lhamors want to spy on the Academy?"

"Who knows why Lhamors do anything?" Virun answered. "They're not like humans. Not even very smart in my experience."

"It's a small transport, probably an interplanetary shuttle. He's unarmed. He's made no aggression toward us. Is it worth risking bad blood toward Vertullian pilots if it becomes an incident?"

Farien had a point. Davi keyed the hailing channel and ran a deep scan of the ship's holds and passenger compartment. "Do you carry any cargo?"

"Jus' mys'lf, Capt'in. C'me to negoti'te."

There wasn't enough to hold him without risk of elevating something minor into a major incident, and that was the last thing Davi and his squadron needed to get involved with. The scanner beeped—nothing beyond basic provisions and supplies. The VS28s matched the mystery ship's speed and heading, forming a reverse cone around it.

Davi chose caution. "My squadron will escort you to the next sector. Our companions there can see you safely to Xanthis."

"Th'nk you, Capt'in, for your kindn'ss."

"We're gonna let him go?" Brie sounded as frustrated as Jorek and Virun.

"We're going to see he's escorted the whole way to Xanthis," Davi answered. "If he behaves, he won't be bothered. Virun, radio ahead to the patrol in Sector Omega and fill them in on our friend here. We'll meet them at the border in a direct line to Xanthis."

"Yes, sir," Virun replied, followed by a click on the channel as he switched to another frequency.

Davi sighed and slid back in his seat again, his tension evaporating. "Maintain formation, squad. Let's see our friend here to the border."

The Council leadership convened in a small conference room in the High Lord Councilor's Palace over breakfast. Serve-bots took care of the serving as the Councilors focused on the agenda handed to them by High Lord Councilor Tarkanius. Although Aron wasn't on the Council leadership, he'd been included because he had a presentation to make on an important issue affecting Council decisions, and Tarkanius wanted the leadership to consider it first before he took it to the full Council. Aron felt as at home as a child at the opera. He was still adjusting to the idea of being an official member of the Council, let alone carrying the title 'Lord' before his name. Still, they'd issued him the official robe of a Council member and an apartment near the government complex where other Lords lived.

The chattering Councilors quieted and took their seats as their leader, Simeon, stood next to Tarkanius at the head of the table and motioned for attention. Taller and thinner than Tarkanius, Simeon had earned the gray hair that topped his head. Older, more experienced and harder working than the rest, everyone respected him. "This meeting was called at the request of Lord Aron to discuss a matter which has begun to draw notice throughout the Alliance: a Vertullian holiday called 'The Returning.'"

The room broke into chatter again. Aron had hoped including the topic on the agenda would quell some of the emotions of the announcement, but the ploy had failed.

"What is this 'Returning'?" Lord Niger shifted in his chair along the middle right side of the table. "Several of our security men requested time off, saying it was religious." The dark-skinned, dark-haired, overweight Lord had taken over responsibility for the Lord's Special Police and Security Forces after the resignation and disappearance of the disgraced Lord Obed.

"I've gotten reports from several sectors of similar requests," the Council's sole female member, Lord Kray, smiled at Aron, her face showing not a trace of wrinkles. Skinny, tall, with warm, yet determined eyes, she'd played a major role in overturning Xalivar's coup and freeing Aron's people. Yet with all she'd fought for, the absence of gray in her hair surprised him. "The agricultural sectors are particularly hard hit. The entire planet Vertullis will be shut down."

Seated next to her, Lord Hachim scowled. Olive-skinned, bearded, short and round, he and Niger were close friends. "If we shut down every time one of our gods had a holiday, nothing would get done." Others mumbled in agreement and nodded as all eyes turned to Aron.

Aron smiled, his white robe whooshing as he stood and typed into his datapad. "The information I'm sending you explains the historical and religious significance of the holiday." He continued as the others pulled up the information on their datapads and began scanning it. "It celebrates the day our Savior returned to heaven after his death and resurrection. It's our most important holiday. This will be our first chance to honor it fully since winning our freedom. As you can imagine, that's very important to us after generations spent celebrating in private."

"Your Savior isn't ours." Lord Niger's face crinkled as he scanned the data Aron had sent. "Old Testament God of Israel? This is Boralis, not Old Earth!"

"No one else takes religious holidays which affect work," Lord Hachim snapped. "First, you want to be accepted as our equals, now you want special treatment. It's a double standard!" Several others mumbled in agreement and nodded.

Tarkanius raised a hand to silence them. "Part of learning to accept others as full citizens is learning to accept their culture, their traditions, and their beliefs. Compromise is a necessity."

"I see no issue with it, as long as adequate warning can be given and proper arrangements made," Kray added.

"And what of those whose regular schedules must be adjusted to accommodate those requesting a holiday? Regular days off will need to be cancelled, schedules adjusted." Lord Niger exchanged a furious look with Lord Hachim. "It may engender hard feelings."

"Hard feelings can be overcome in time," Lord Simeon offered.

"They often are." Lord Kray smiled at him. "Do those required to work essential services resent it when we celebrate each New Year and Thanks Day?" Aron knew both as carryovers from Old Earth tradition.

"Those holidays are not associated with a particular people group nor religion." Hachim shot her a disappointed look.

"This could create renewed animosity between our peoples," Niger said. "Many are still adjusting to the idea of Vertullians being Boralian citizens as it is. Some of our own have lost jobs to former workers whose years of experience as slave labor made them more qualified for those positions. There's been an outcry about lost jobs. Cries of unfairness."

"All such integrations force changes in industry and labor markets," Tarkanius said. "It will even out in time and be forgotten."

"Then perhaps we should hold this proposal until the tensions die down a bit," Niger continued. "Right now, there's still a lot of resentment. Do you really want to risk inflaming old biases?"

"Old biases which have never died, lest we forget the news reports—graffiti campaigns, a few instances of bullying." Hachim stared at Aron. The news had been reporting anti-worker slurs written on the sides of buildings and on sidewalks for months. And there had been incidents of violence with workers being attacked in dark streets and schoolyards.

Aron's heart broke when he recalled it, yet he knew his people were better off now than they had been. He spotted it in their eyes when they met his; their stride as they passed him on the street. He paused as all eyes returned to him. "I think the Council declaring it an official holiday would send the right message. We are one people now. Some are always slow to accept change, but others will recognize this change is here to stay."

"I'm sure our people would love to join you in celebrating your private god." Hachim said. Was that a smile or a grimace? Sarcasm dripped off him like sweat.

"Some may," Niger added. "I personally resent it."

"No one's asking you to celebrate our God. Celebrate life, your families. Celebrate freedom. Anything and everything that matters to you. We won't hold it against you if you define the holiday in your own way." Aron smiled, feeling a tinge of hope that the suggestion would calm their fears, but Hachim and Niger frowned, as if they hadn't heard a word. And others refused to meet his eyes.

"It could give the impression your religion is the most

important," Lord Qai said from the other end of the table. Young, yellow-skinned, descendent of colonists from the Eastern continents of the Earth, he had joined the leadership when Tarkanius became High Lord Councilor and Simeon became head of the Council.

"Only if you call it a religious holiday," Aron said. "If everyone has the holiday off, few will be concerned with how others use it." Explaining the significance of the day to people whose religion consisted of a series of rites rather than a deep personal relationship with their god had proved exhausting. But Aron kept trying.

"Word will spread of the special significance given the day by your people," Qai countered. "And certainly word of the Council's role will not be secret. People will draw the conclusion the two are related."

"Some people, perhaps, but not everyone." Lord Kray's eyes met Aron's with a look of reassurance. "The Lhamors have their Birthing Day Celebration. And don't the Xanthians have a holiday as well?"

"I believe it's a celebration of ancestors," Qai said with a nod.

"It only takes a loud few." Lord Niger crossed his arms over his chest.

"Lord Qai does have a point we must consider carefully," Lord Simeon said with a waved finger as Aron returned to his seat at the table. "If we recognize the holiday of one group, we have many others who will also want their holidays to be official."

"I can just see it now, an entire month with nothing happening because of holidays!" Hachim sat back in his chair and scowled as the others chuckled.

"Not all holidays occur in the same week, Lord Hachim," Kray said, her eyes bright with amusement.

"None of the other people groups have such a centralized religion," Tarkanius added. "We don't have to make a decision today. The holiday is not imminent."

"A free society cannot force people to work on days where they feel such a moral conflict," Simeon said with a nod. "If people do have religious reasons for objecting to working on a particular day, we must consider that carefully." Relief swept over Aron. At least a few of them understood.

"It's a privilege to have work; a privilege requiring sacrifices." Hachim remained firm in his resolve.

"Some research is suggested." Simeon panned the room, allowing his eyes to meet each of the others. "The High Lord Councillor and Lord Aron have done us a service by bringing this matter to our attention. Let us consider it carefully and not make a decision in haste. Lord Aron's suggestion about not emphasizing the Vertullians' connection is valid, and other cultures do celebrate official holidays. There were many on Old Earth, as I recall."

Aron read acknowledgement on the others' faces.

"Lord Kray, please send inquiries to the various planetary leadership inquiring about their cultural and religious holidays. We need to know what kind of resistance we might expect and who might campaign for their own holiday's recognition." Kray nodded and smiled as Simeon continued. "Niger and Hachim, research the potential economic impact of an official holiday. What real impact might there be on the economy." Hachim and Niger nodded, but their eyes never met Simeon's. "We'll all meet again and discuss this further later."

"I appreciate the leadership's willingness to consider my proposal," Aron said, resigned to whatever happened.

"Will your people refuse to work if we decide not to honor this holiday?" Lord Qai asked.

Aron couldn't answer for sure. Reestablishing this holiday had been an important topic among his people since their freedom was re-established and people longed for the day they could celebrate it openly again. Aron shared their joy. "I don't know, but many would be saddened and disheartened," he finally said.

"Perhaps some research of your own on that topic would be helpful," Simeon said. Aron nodded in agreement. "For now, this meeting is adjourned. Thank you for coming."

As the Lords scooted back from the table and resumed their chatter, Aron stayed seated, flickering like old reflector pads. This meant so much to his people, yet the Council couldn't afford to play favorites. How could he honor both his people's wishes and the needs of the larger citizenry?

A hand gently squeezed his shoulder. "Weighty decisions are the bane of a Lord's existence, Aron," Kray said, her eyes sympathetic. "Your suggestion was worthy. And the others will give it consideration and careful thought. Centuries of enmity don't disappear overnight."

Kray had been on the Council for a long time before Aron joined. She'd been one of his firmest supporters, helping him understand procedures and learn his way around the government complex, introducing him to contacts. And she also knew the others well. It reassured him having her as an advocate.

"Thank you, Kray. You've been a great support from the start." He remembered the look on Lord Obed's face when Kray and Simeon had burst into the Library Auditorium at Presimion Academy and overcome Lord Obed and the men holding the Vertullian peace envoys hostage there. "A good friend."

Kray laughed. "It's a pleasure to know you, Aron. You've taught us so much already about how wrong we were to let old rivalries turn our hearts and minds against your people." She squeezed his shoulder again and they both smiled.

By the time Yao arrived at the dorm, the Academy's poor semblance of an investigation was well underway. Presimion had no past experience with such investigations. In the school's storied history, no one had ever been murdered, or even assaulted, on the campus. He bristled as he took in the scene of the crime he'd only learned about after checking his messages. Cadet Kowl's skin was purpling and his body looked stiff. Yao should have been the first faculty member notified.

"Professor Brahma, I'm sorry we hadn't notified you yet." The Student Life Director looked dismayed as he approached, offering Yao a steaming cup of Talis.

Yao accepted it, sipping slowly. "I'm in charge of their assimilation, Alek. I should have been awoken immediately." For the premiere military institution in the system, Presimion was very behind the times in some important ways.

"We were a bit overwhelmed, as you can imagine."

You're always overwhelmed, Yao thought. His opinion of Alek Brak's capabilities would not have helped the man's curriculum vitae. "Where's the student who witnessed the murder?"

Alek motioned and Yao spotted the lanky, red-haired cadet sitting alone in the Dorm Attendant's small office, looking exhausted. "You okay?" he asked as he joined him.

Dru shook his head. "We switched beds."

"Switched? Cadet Kowl was in your bed?"

Dru nodded as his eyes dodged Yao's. "It used to be mine. We traded two weeks into the semester. Kowl had issues with the moonlight keeping him awake. Doesn't bother me." Dru's body shook as he spoke. He was a mass of fear.

Yao put a hand gently on his shoulder and knelt in front of him, trying to imagine how he'd have felt as a cadet if one his friends had been murdered across a dark room. "That doesn't have anything to do with this. Coincidence. I'm sorry about your friend."

Dru chuckled. "That's just it. We weren't really friends. I barely knew him. I just helped him out because someone had to. He was struggling a lot in classes. Why would anyone want him dead?"

Yao shook his head. "Things like this never make sense to sane people."

Dru shrugged. "Then I saw it." The cadet read the question on his instructor's face. "The message the killer left."

"The killer left a message?"

Dru pointed. "On the wall in the corridor. He was after me."

"Wait a minute. I'll be right back." Yao slid back out into the main room and hurried toward the corridor. The message jumped out at him right away. It was burned in the wall with a laser just outside the entrance to the students' sleep hall. The corridor still stank of smoke and charred paint.

YOU DON'T BELONG HERE

He knew immediately why Dru related it to himself. It was the most obvious motive for the attack. When ex-workers had arrived as students, Yao expected hazing; planned his response. But for the most part, it had been very minor and quelched quickly. Nothing like the schoolyard beatings in other parts of the system and none of the anti-worker graffiti seen in the cities. His memory flashed back to the controversy over his friend Davi's admission. He wondered how those who'd complained felt now that Davi's birth status as a Vertullian had been revealed. He'd suffered with his friend as Davi fought for acceptance.

"He's the Prince," the complaints said. "It's pure favoritism." There'd also been controversy when aliens like himself were first admitted and much of that vitriol had never really faded.

Still, Kowl wasn't Vertullian. It could be about something else—an old rivalry, Kowl's family's activities—they just didn't know. Vertullians weren't the only admissions people questioned. He stepped back into the office with Dru and leaned against the wall. "You don't know for sure what that means. It could mean a lot of things."

"Kowl was a nice guy. Who would want him dead?"

"Someone who hates his family. An old rival. It's hard to say. Davi's a nice guy, too, and he's got his share of enemies."

"Davi was once Prince. And he's no ordinary guy. Kowl was just ordinary." Dru reached up with his thumb to wipe tears from his right cheek. For a guy who'd slept over five hours, a lot at the academy, the cadet looked exhausted.

"There are still far too many unanswered questions to assume, okay? Have you eaten yet?"

Dru shook his head. "I'll make arrangements for you to stay with me for a while, okay? And I'm taking you to breakfast now, even if all you do is watch me eat. I'll order something strange only we Tertullians eat so you can stare."

Dru didn't even smile. He just nodded and stood, allowing Yao to lead him out the door.

Yao motioned to Alek as they entered the sleep hall. "I'm taking Cadet Dru with me. Have someone pack his things and send them to my apartment. He'll be staying with me for a while."

Alek nodded. "I can send the reports to your datapad as they develop, if you'd like."

"Do that. I'll be back soon to look into this more myself. Has anyone contacted Cadet Kowl's family?"

"Not yet."

"Don't, until I have time to investigate. We need to be sure we get this right. I take full responsibility for all notifications."

Alek shrugged. "That's fine with me."

Yao nodded, placing his hand on Dru's neck and leading him out. He deliberately turned so they wouldn't pass by the message as they walked through the corridor. It meant taking a longer route but that hardly mattered. He made a mental note to message Davi and Farien as soon as they'd ordered breakfast. Right now, he needed to help Dru get situated enough to function.

Tela flushed with warmth as she watched Davi's mothers, Miri and Lura, straightening furniture and artwork, discussing lighting and linens. She hadn't seen Miri so happy in months. The apartment was one formerly restricted for rental by government dignitaries, but Davi had been able to arrange with the government to open it for Miri. Sizable with a great view, it sat a block from the government center at Legon, the capital city of Legallis, not far from the Palace which had been Miri's life-long home. Across the street, amidst the high-rises, a preschool playground caught Tela's eye whenever she looked out the window.

The light blue-gray walls and lush navy carpet reflected light from the reflector pads overhead, lending a homey glow to the middle of each room. The central gathering, entertainment area sat like a hub amidst the spokes of the corridors leading to the kitchen, bedrooms, and sanitary facilities. The apartment also included an office which Miri used for a library. Altogether, the space wasn't really much smaller than Miri's suite at the Palace, even if it was less glamorous. Davi had often confided in Tela his worries about Miri's adjustment to civilian life, but from the vibe at her place, Tela thought Miri was doing fine.

She heard women's chattering coming from the kitchen as

Davi's birth father, Sol, sat on a sofa, reading the news on a datapad. A hard worker who'd spent twenty years imprisoned away from his wife and son, Sol's skin was dark tan and his hands worn from years of manual labor. Still, he knew how to relax when he wasn't at the plant, and Tela found herself relieved that Sol and Tela's father, Telanus, had been given lighter duties these days.

"Tela, dear, come here, we'd like your opinion on this," Miri called in her singsong alto.

"Don't let them drag you into this, Tela," Sol teased, "Run for your life."

Tela chuckled and patted him on the shoulder as she moved past and climbed the stairs toward the kitchen. Lura and Miri stood huddled together beside the balcony, watching the twin suns paint the sky with their setting. Shades of orange and blue mixed with pinks, yellows and reds in a stunning display. It took Tela's breath away.

The women themselves were a contrast. Davi's birth mother, Lura, was shorter with tanned skin and long, brown hair the color of her son's, whereas Miri, his adoptive mother, stood taller, her light skin accented by her light-blue eyes and short-cut brown hair. Both women's hair had streaks of gray, though it was clear Miri made more effort to cover it up. She stood with the regalness one might expect from a former Royal, while Lura's demeanor remained humble, a legacy of so many years spent in slavery. Lura wore a round and silver-colored necklace with a blue-green crest at its center. The four sections of the crest bore distinct images: laborers, soldiers, farmers and priests. Tela had seen the family crest many times now. Davi and Nila each wore identical necklaces. She'd never seen any of the three without them. Despite their differences, Davi's birth and adoptive mothers had made a concerted effort toward befriending each other. It showed in the way they smiled at each other and Tela.

"You wanted my opinion on a sunset?"

Lura and Miri laughed. "No dear. Lura was just commenting how nice it would be if this balcony were bigger. It would be a beautiful location for a joining, don't you think?" Many adoptive mothers would have been devastated to have their son's birth parents come back into his life, especially mothers as close to their sons as Miri was to Davi. But Miri had remained supportive and dignified despite any inner turmoil she must have felt. Miri's strength was an inspiration, except for those times when it made her pushy, like now.

Tela smiled at their eager grins. They'd been hinting at the idea for months, hoping Davi and Tela would set a date. "We haven't really discussed it. We're enjoying just being together right now. Working out the rough edges, I guess."

"Working out a man's rough edges is a lifetime's endeavor, dear," Miri counseled. "He'll be much easier to mold once he's officially yours, as they say."

Lura grasped Tela's upper arm gently. "We're not trying to pressure you. You're just so good together and it makes us happy to see you both so in love."

Tela nodded, locking the smile onto her face. "We are in love. But love's never perfect. I'm waiting for Davi to get over some of his archaic ideas before I even think about taking that step."

"Archaic ideas?"

Tela continued before Miri could start lecturing on women's place in society. "It's a different age, Miri. Women may have once enjoyed sitting at home waiting for their man. That's just not who I am. I fell in love with your son as we fought together for freedom, side by side with the WFR. He showed me respect and appreciation. But I still think he'd prefer me safe at home in the kitchen."

Miri looked as if she couldn't understand the objection. Lura smiled. "Davi's not like that. You mean the world to him. It's just that he worries about you. Can you blame him? You worry too."

"I worry sometimes, but we both love what we do, and I support him. I deserve the same consideration."

"Of course you do."

"I thought you were still flying patrol rotations?" Miri seemed confused.

"I am. But not as often as Davi is." That had been a decision by command, she realized, but Davi hadn't exactly jumped in to advocate on her behalf.

"Well, he's a Squadron commander. Their rotations are more frequent, naturally." Miri turned back to the sunset. "I worry about you both."

"Not much to worry about, Miri. We're at peace. The workers have their full citizenship. Patrols are pretty routine." So why did she miss them so much?

"Mothers can't breathe without worrying," Sol said as he came up behind them.

Tela and Lura chuckled as he wrapped his arms around Lura. "It gives us a purpose," Lura said as she caressed his arm.

"I'd be happy if you focused some of that attention on me." Sol leaned in and kissed her neck.

Lura blushed and pushed him away. "You're hardly neglected." Tela wondered if she and Davi would still be so affectionate if they made it twenty years together.

"You'd think after twenty years in prison, a man could get expect a warmer homecoming." Sol frowned, but the ends of his mouth jiggled, giving him away. When the women laughed, he gave up and joined them heartily.

"See what you have to look forward to in forty years, dear?" Lura said as she turned and kissed Sol's waiting lips.

Miri smiled and turned back toward the sunset. Another reason they weren't rushed was a shared concern about how Davi's adoptive mother would adjust to life alone. Eternally single, Miri had devoted her life to her son and her brother. Now, with her brother outcast and on the run and her son grown, Miri must be experiencing a loneliness she hadn't known in years. Both Davi and Tela wanted to be sure Miri never felt abandoned.

As Lura and Sol snuggled behind them, Tela put her arm around Miri. "It's really lucky you were able to get this apartment." After Sol's release, his lifelong friend Aron had arranged a new condo, courtesy of the government, for Sol and Lura on Vertullis, explaining it was the least the government could offer for the wrong it had done them.

Miri smiled, patting Tela's hand on her shoulder. "Yes. Davi's taking good care of me. All of you are. Sometimes I feel guilty for all the attention."

"After all you've done for him, you deserve it." She squeezed Miri's hand as it reached up and clasped hers.

"For all of us!" Lura echoed.

"I have a spare room available any time any of you want to visit."

"We'll be taking you up on it often," Sol said as he and Lura joined them beside the window.

"We're so close, we don't need a room at the moment, but you just try and keep us away," Tela said. She and Davi each had apartments in the pilot complex near the starport. It was ten minutes away by air taxi.

Miri glanced at the chrono on the wall and turned back toward the food preparation counter. "We'd better get supper started. Davi's patrol should be back any time now."

Lura and Tela hurried to help Miri as Sol watched them from his place at the window. "I'd love to know how a princess learned to cook so well."

"Royal secret," Miri teased as she handed Tela a plate of vegetables and reached back into the cooling unit for more ingredients. They all laughed once more as Sol escaped again to the other room, leaving the women to their task.

Bordox skimmed the Assassin's report as the man paced the opposite wall of the office. *Man? Funny to think of a four-armed freak that way.* He'd never liked Lhamors or any other aliens, but his present assignment required him to use whatever resources he could find and that included personnel.

"You got lucky with that patrol. I would have never let you go."

The Lhamor's accent was almost a hiss, yet it penetrated the room like a loudspeaker was attached to his face. "T'ey'r' not as susp'cious as when you serv'd the Alli'nce. H'ving no enemies encour'ges relax'tion."

Bordox's fist pounded the desk as he dropped the datapad. "What do you mean 'when I served?' I'm still serving the Alliance!

I'm a true servant, unlike those imposters!"

"It w's not meant as critic'sm."

"You'd be wise to consider your words more carefully." The Lhamor just stared at him in silence. "You're sure you got the right student?"

"He w's sleep'ng in the bunk you indic'ted."

"Did you use the photo image or not?"

"Hum'ns 'll l'k alike to us. Smell alike, too." The Lhamor's olfactory organ crinkled with distaste.

Bordox crinkled his nose. *As if you're one to talk.* "I don't need a four-armed freak criticizing how I smell. You'd best learn some respect."

"I don' work f'r you. You're just th' cont'ct."

"I'm empowered with authority to instruct you. That makes me your boss." Bordox frowned. He could swear the Lhamor was laughing. Nothing angered him like being mocked. He'd had enough of that in his life already. He'd suffered the greatest humiliation any man could at the hands of that idiot Xander "Davi" Rhii. The fullness of his rage rained over him. Revenge was coming. This was just the start.

He tossed a datacard across the desk toward the Lhamor. "Your next target's in Iraja. Go there immediately. I'll be out of contact for a few days. I have my own mission somewhere else."

"I won' need you until I'm finish'd." The Lhamor's top right hand reached down and clasped the datacard in its white-gloved fingers. The Assassins always insisted on wearing gloves, despite the fact they wore hardly any clothing over the rest of their insectoid-reptilian appearance. Disproportionally large, orange eyes glowed out of green-scaled skin which was stretched tight over a roundish frame. A rounded, capacious stomach lay between four arms, below the bottom set of which a brown belt held the translator which enabled their communication. Even the translator itself struggled to make sense of the gibberish the Lhamors called language, resulting in heavily accented translations. But without it, the Lhamor's native clicks and clacks would have been indecipherable for Bordox.

"Overconfidence can be a great weakness." The words

brought to mind Rhii again. Oh, how it would feel to finally put the bastard in his place.

"Onl' where it's not merit'd." The Lhamor whirled and headed out the door into the corridor which led to the converted hangar the warehouse exterior concealed.

Bordox groaned and leaned back in his chair. Was success worth tolerating insolence and insults from an alien freak? He'd tolerated worse for sure, while hating every moment. He laughed. When it was over, he'd even get his revenge on the alien freaks. They'd all suffer. In time.

Chapter Two

Davi's nose delighted in the cornucopia awaiting him at Miri's apartment—the hearty smell of boiled Gungor mixed with Gixi and a tart berry whose name he couldn't remember off the top of his head. Miri was becoming quite the cook these days, and, although the presence of both Tela and Lura hinted that she might have had help, he determined not to let on. Of the three, she needed the most encouragement at present.

"Mmmmm. Whatever that is, I can hardly wait!" He kissed Miri's forehead as he pulled her to him, wrapping her in his arms. The warmth of her embrace evoked memories of all the times she'd looked after him. She was the one doing the holding then. Now it was his turn to return the favor. "No time for chatter though. Let's eat!" He winked at Tela and the others as they laughed.

Miri pulled back and her eyes met his. "Don't tell me all that time in the cockpit has erased your memory of manners, Davi Rhii." Her scolding tone barely disguised her obvious delight at his compliment.

Davi released her and bent to kiss Lura on her cheek as his other mother hugged him.

"Welcome back, dear," Lura said with a wink. "Isn't it coming together nicely?"

Davi nodded as he pulled away to shake Sol's outstretched

hand. "The condo's starting to feel like home as well," his father said, grip firm, the calluses starting to fade from lack of hard labor.

"Did they at least let you cut the Gungor?"

Sol smirked. "I picked angberries for hours, all by myself."

Davi and the women laughed as Sol winked and Davi turned to Tela. Her form-fitting, black one-piece highlighted all her best places. Davi stopped to catch his breath before leaning in to embrace her.

"For a moment I thought you hadn't noticed me," she said as their lips met. Davi couldn't tell if she was teasing, until she tensed at his touch.

He relished her flowery scent, and soft, round lips on his. "Just obeying the scriptures and honoring my parents, Love," he answered, hoping to lighten her mood. Instead, she rolled her eyes and punched his arm with more force than he expected. "What? It's a commandment."

She forced a smile. "How was patrol?"

He knew it was serious when she failed to laugh at his teasing. They followed the others into a short corridor toward the dining area. Her hand grasped his and he winced as his fingers shifted under the firmness of her grip. "About as exciting as normal, until we got an emergency call from command."

She dropped his hand like it was poisoned and whirled to face him as the others turned to stare. "What happened?"

"A murder. One of the students at Presimion." He wished immediately he'd couched the information more gently.

Lura and Miri gasped. Tela looked as if he'd sucked the wind from her lungs. "Who? What happened?" she choked out.

Davi clasped Tela's hand in his. "Not a lot of details yet. Yao said it was no one we'd know. Farien was sent to assist in the investigation."

"Thanks be to God!" Lura said.

Everyone looked relieved except Miri. "So he won't be joining us then?" Since Farien's kindness during Miri's brief incarceration at the hands of her brother Xalivar, she'd treated him like a second son. Davi hated to disappoint her but shook his head.

"Let's not dwell on difficult things," Lura said in an obvious attempt to restore their former levity. "We can't let Miri and Sol's hard work go to waste." She winked at Sol, who shrugged guiltily as if he had her fooled. "Those are matters for others to be concerned with. You must be tired, Son."

Davi smiled as she put her hand on his arm and motioned toward the table. "I am, Mother. But it's good to be with all of you."

After they'd arranged themselves around the table, Sol said grace. Then the conversation turned to other matters and the food was passed. Hearty Gungor and angberry stew with fresh potatoes, carrots and beans mixed in, a rice casserole, and Gixi salad. Clearly they'd made an effort to prepare some of Davi's favorites.

"You know what would make things perfect now that I have so much free time?" Miri asked as she watched Davi savoring his first bite of her Gungor stew. "Grandchildren."

Davi coughed, struggling to keep from spitting out the food as Lura and Sol nodded. "That would be fantastic," Lura agreed.

"We're very much looking forward to it," Sol added.

Tela shook her head and chuckled as she patted Davi on the back as he coughed. Why did his throat feel so tight all of a sudden? "You three are relentless."

"This is what parents with grown children do." Miri smiled warmly as she took a bite of the Gixi.

Davi got control of the coughing and took a deep breath. "Sometimes I think patrol's less stressful," he said with a glare, but he couldn't hold it long and broke into laughter as they all joined in.

Gods, Xalivar hated Xanthis! Such a worthless lump of floating rock! It did have its advantages though. Only slightly more populated than its neighbor Italis, it was ice cold at night but pleasant during daylight hours. And its rocky plains were filled with hundreds of places to hide—cavern after cavern—making

Xanthis the perfect place to keep a low profile while he put his plan into place.

After the humiliation on Eleni 1, Xalivar hadn't looked back. He'd stopped at the starport on Legallis and swapped from the Imperial shuttle to a private transport. The as-yet-uninformed Royal staff had met him there with the belongings and supplies he'd requested already loaded. He'd bid them adieu and headed off on his "Royal retreat." He could only imagine the confusion they later experienced upon learning he wouldn't be coming back. As stupid as Gungors. He wondered if they'd welcome him back if he just showed up at the Palace doors one day. He wished all the citizens treated him so warmly.

To be an outcast! Like some criminal in his own empire! His fists clenched at his sides as he pondered it. He would redeem his family's honor and name. His power and position would be restored. They hadn't seen the last of Xalivar!

As he made his way into the hollowed out chamber he now used as a conference room, the rest of his core allies sat waiting around an old wooden table they'd procured from the abandoned settlement nearby. Who knew how long the place had been abandoned? Xalivar was just pleased the settlers had left so many valuable resources behind. If they ever came back, they'd discover someone had raided them with flourish. Not much remained to come back to.

The others watched him as he made his way past toward the head of the chamber and the table itself. The walking space was lumpy rock, making passage challenging and causing him to slow his pace whenever his feet found questionable footing. He did his best to nonetheless look confident. This was no time to be seen as weak. Any one of these so-called "allies" would jump at the chance to usurp his role and leave him forgotten in their wake.

His majordomo, Manaen, waited for him beside the chair at the head of the table, smiling and handing Xalivar a datapad as he moved past. An Andorian from Idolis, Manaen's yellow teeth stood out against his blue skin and red eyes. He stepped back as Xalivar accepted the datapad and slid into his seat, facing the others. The chair's wooden arms sent a cold tingle up his arm. He deliberately kept the temperature in his chambers set at a level which made the others uncomfortable—first, because he liked keeping them on edge, and second, because whatever energy and air escaped was then less likely to draw attention from passing air or ground security patrols. An unexpected heat source in this barren region would draw attention Xalivar didn't need. So far, he'd had no interactions with the local authorities and he much preferred it stay that way.

"You have word from Bordox?" he asked as he panned the table, meeting the others' eyes each in turn.

Lord Obed nodded from a chair to his right. "The Academy leadership is baffled as to why anyone would murder one of their own. The mission's expanding to Iraja and Legon now. It'll be a matter of time before the press takes notice."

Xalivar smiled. "They are all too easy to manipulate, as expected."

"Perhaps not if they knew who was pulling their strings," Obed replied with a somber expression and tone.

Xalivar fought to contain his annoyance. Obed was the former chief of the Lord's Special Police under Xalivar, the most elite security forces of the Borali Alliance, yet he made no effort to conceal his identity in public, going about in his old Council robes as if he had not a care in the world. Everyone else had resigned themselves to new, less-noticeable wardrobes so as to maintain as much anonymity as possible. Obed refused. Xalivar had only allowed him to join the allies out of necessity and a desire to have a scapegoat for certain treacherous activities which might be required. He couldn't wait to be done with him.

Swallowing the bile which had arisen in his throat, he kept his voice even. "When done well, they always believe they are the ones doing the manipulating, my dear Obed."

"And no doubt they will again, my Lord," Admiral Dek said, shifting in his chair opposite Obed. It was only the second time since they'd launched their plans that Dek had been able to meet with them. As the new head of Borali Alliance military forces, he couldn't slip away easily without undue attention so he primarily communicated with them via coded transmissions. Despite his years of military experience, the Admiral became noticeably uncomfortable whenever tension flared between the two ex-Council members. Their history of rivalry was well known, and Xalivar had no doubt Obed's current alliance with him was by necessity, not loyalty. It's why he'd asked General Lucius, his chief of security, to keep a special eye on Lord Obed. And also why he'd made sure Obed was in charge of the field operations. It would make it all too easy later on to let the right information slip out and watch Obed take full blame for a series of actions which would disrupt both the harmony and the integrity of the Borali Alliance. Xalivar, of course, would move in to restore order and save the day. He chuckled as he imagined it. "Make sure the proper messages get left at each location," Xalivar reminded his rival and enjoyed watching his reaction.

"He's doing everything exactly as planned." Obed stiffened, leaning back in his chair with a look of annoyance. Obed's son was a known embarrassment, yet the father still bristled when anyone criticized him in public. Except, of course, Obed himself. Bordox was yet another reminder to Xalivar why he'd never wasted time having children.

Xalivar couldn't resist needling him a bit more. "Good. We don't want the same incompetence he evidenced the last time."

"He more than redeemed himself on Eleni 1. It's hardly his fault the Council chose to interfere."

Xalivar forced a smile and nodded. "Are we making any inroads with the government on Italis?"

General Lucius sighed. "We are increasing the pressure, but so far they remain noncommittal toward our request."

"They fail to see the advantages for them in the arrangement?"

"They remain determined to play a neutral role and avoid any commitments." Lucius slid a datacard down the table toward Xalivar, who inserted it into his datapad and began scanning the report.

"The time has come to widen our circle. We can only proceed in strength."

"Perhaps our strength is what they question." Obed's eyes cut into Xalivar like a sword.

"Your choice can be unchosen at any time, Lord Obed. Should you desire another arrangement, you need only give the word." Their eyes met in a cold, staring contest.

Finally, Obed looked away. "Of course not. I have chosen properly."

Xalivar smiled, his eyes narrowing into a warning. "You have so far."

"They will commence construction of the ships as planned at the end of the month," Dek continued. "We have secured investors to cover the initial phase, but the rest remain resistant until they see results from our campaign."

"Are they unconvinced of our sincerity?"

"They remain determined to move slowly."

"The time for action is upon us." Xalivar slammed his fist on the table for emphasis, watching Dek flinch, while the others remained undisturbed.

"Some would rather speak to you personally."

"You explained why that isn't possible?"

Lucius nodded. "They question whether you're even alive, my Lord."

Xalivar sighed. That meant part of his plan might be working a little too well. He'd been forced to reveal his involvement to entice the types of investors he would need, but at the same time refused to meet with them in person. If proof of his activities leaked out to the rest of the system, it would destroy the mystique surrounding his disappearance. He may have been mistaken in assuming the assurance of his known close associates, like Lucius and Lord Obed, would be enough to engage their sympathies. Some of these men hated uncertainty and the changes occurring in the Borali Alliance since Xalivar's departure had increased their nervousness and left them on edge.

"Perhaps when the first prototypes are ready, a meeting will be necessary. For now, General, let them wonder if we've lost interest. If they don't meet our needs, there are other options." Xalivar never trusted anyone. He always had backup plans.

Lucius leaned back in his chair. "As you wish, my Lord."

"But keep them under watch to be sure they don't reveal anything in the meantime."

"The sincerity of our desire to maintain anonymity did not escape their notice, my Lord."

Yes, these men knew all about secrets; they were used to living out much of their lives in secrecy. It's why he'd dared to trust them, yet still, Xalivar never trusted anyone much. Not even men he knew had sworn their lives to his service. "And what of Phase I of the recruitment, Admiral?" He turned back to Dek. "We must maintain our schedule regardless of the status of any equipment."

"Indeed. The recruiters have found eager volunteers for the private militia, my Lord."

Xalivar laughed. Farm boys and poor laborers were as easy to manipulate as the media. Some things never changed. He leaned back in his own chair now, glancing around the table again. It pleased him to see that none of his allies looked as relaxed as he felt. That was the way he'd always liked it and he rued the day it might cease to be the case. Things were coming together just the way he'd envisioned it. The investors' hesitation was hardly a hiccup. Even they would become convinced in a matter of time.

He found he couldn't sit still. Such was his excitement at the thoughts of success racing through his mind. Adrenaline pumped through him as he spun around and reached for the remote to the broadcast channels. It was time they entertained themselves with news reports on the success of their activities. Nothing motivated men like watching their plans unfold perfectly. For the first time in his life, Xalivar reveled in creating chaos. It was the polar opposite of his previous drive for order in all things. But he knew this was only a phase. Soon this diversion would pass and order would be restored with Xalivar in the Palace again, right where he belonged.

Tela and Telanus crossed the street to the park opposite Miri's building, holding hands. With every word her father said to her, Tela fought the urge to giggle like a little girl. She was just so happy to have him back in her life after all those long years of not knowing if he was alive or dead while he was in prison. Now he was there with her to talk to, give her advice, hug her and cheer her on. He was so proud of her that it was almost embarrassing. But she, in turn, was just as proud of him. She couldn't believe she'd almost forgotten how great a man he was. She'd idealized him in his absence, of course, but now that he was here, she found the real thing surpassed her expectations. When he'd asked for a quick walk under the stars before racing back to Vertullis for his night shift with Sol, she'd been thrilled to oblige.

"What's bothering you?" he said as she shivered involuntarily.

She shrugged as their eyes met. "Nothing."

"Don't lie to me. You've been down all night." She looked away. "You've tried that on me since you could talk and I always see right through it." He looped his arm in hers as they strolled together along the sidewalk dividing the park from the street. The strength of his muscular arms brushing against hers made her feel so safe. She had her daddy back. She was a little girl all over again.

Tela giggled. "It's nothing. Just stuff."

"Stuff what? With you and Davi?"

How did he know that? Sometimes it scared her—like he could read her mind. She wasn't sure she wanted a father who could do that. "Yeah."

"He really loves you. It makes me so happy to see."

She sighed. "I know, Daddy. I love him, too."

Telanus laughed. "Then what's the problem, dear?"

"He treats me like some kind of glass doll or something. Like he has to protect me all the time."

"It's male instinct for us to protect our women. He doesn't mean any harm."

She stopped walking and frowned. They were standing near the preschool Tela could see from Miri's window. Miri had commented how much she loved watching the kids play in the playground. "I'm a soldier, too. Not some housewife." Pulling her arm from her father's, she gestured. "I'm strong, talented, well trained. I can outfly him."

Telanus grinned. "How many times have you proved that?"

Tela smiled. "A couple."

"Well, take me up sometime, okay?" He whispered like they were co-conspirators. "I'd really like to see that."

"I'm sure he'd love that." They both laughed and Telanus looped her arm in hers again as they resumed walking. Even his scent took her back. He smelled like Daddy, the way she remembered him. She'd thought she'd forgotten that smell.

"Look. He cares for you. So, of course, he wants to protect you. I want to protect you. Don't you want to protect him?"

She nodded. "Yes. And you, too." Their eyes met and she giggled again. Why was she acting like such a boob?

"I've missed this, you know? I wish we could do it every night."

"Me, too, Daddy!"

Telanus stopped again, pulling her around to face him and putting his hands firmly on her hips. "But you're all grown up, Tela. From now on, our moments are limited. You're an adult and you have to make your own life. And Davi's a big part of that."

Tela's eyes misted. "There's time. You can see me whenever you want. I'll come to Vertullis more often."

His fingers pressed to her lips to silence her. "Shh. You're not listening. I couldn't be happier for you two. He's a wonderful son and he'll make a terrific son-in-law someday. Now I know you'll be well taken care of no matter what happens. That's all any father could ever want for his little girl, Tela."

Tela hugged him, feeling the tears drip down her cheeks and onto his shirt at the shoulders. "I love you."

"I love you, too, Little Girl. And so does he. A whole lot. Don't let him get away."

His use of her childhood nickname gave her butterflies. For years, she'd never expected anyone to call her that again. Tela blinked then reached up with the back of her hand to clear away the tears. "It's just hard sometimes."

Telanus chortled. "Relationships are the hardest thing you'll ever do. But it's so worth it when you find the right one. And I know you, if I don't help him out a little, you'll keep pushing him away. You've always been so independent!" He pulled back and stared into her eyes. She giggled again. "Am I right?" Tela just smiled and nodded as their eyes met. He shook her gently as if knocking sense into her. "Okay then. Don't mess this up."

Tela stiffened and raised her hand to her forehead in a military salute. "Yes, sir!" They both laughed as he looped his arm in hers again and led her back the way they'd come.

Yao hurried through his kitchen to get the door, hoping the buzz of the bell hadn't disturbed Dru's sleep. The cadet was sprawled out on the couch, where he'd finally fallen asleep after hours spent fighting insomnia. The struggle had only added to his stress and Yao wanted to give him every opportunity to recharge after the events of the past twenty-four hours.

The door slid into its wall alcove to reveal a blonde Borali Military Captain in full dress, neatly groomed, waiting in the corridor. Yao smiled as he stepped forward and they embraced. Farien smelled as if he'd just showered and his appearance was textbook military formal. But his uniform bulged in a few spots, making him look healthier than he'd looked the last few times Yao had seen him. He seemed happier too, something in his eyes. Yao hoped that was the case "What are you doing here, Farien?"

Farien smiled with a new confidence. "Here to save your butt as usual."

"It's rare I'm the one who needs saving." Yao stepped aside and motioned for Farien to enter. Farien did and the door slid shut behind him as he followed Yao into the kitchen.

"Who's the kid?"

"Dru, one of Davi's pilots."

"The first Vertullian student? How's that going?"

Yao pulled two glass bottles from the cooling unit and popped the caps with an opener, offering one to Farien. "The students handle it pretty well. A little more hazing than usual, but the younger generation seems okay with it mostly, so those caught hazing get hazed themselves."

Farien finished a sip of his beer and broke into laughter.

"Listen to you! The younger generation? We were there not so long ago ourselves."

Yao chuckled. "Yeah, but it seems like ages, doesn't it?"

Farien shrugged. "The whole world's changed."

Yao nodded and sipped his own beer. It was a cheaper brand he'd settled for when his favorite Tertullian brew hadn't arrived with the last supply shipment. It tasted dry and bitter but slid smoothly down his throat to warm his stomach. "So why are you really here?" One look from his friend and Yao knew. "The investigation?"

Farien straightened and offered a salute. "Captain Farien Noa at your service."

"Has command lost their minds?" Yao kept a straight face and sipped his beer.

Farien growled and punched him in the arm. "They like me now, since I helped save the Alliance and all."

"You helped send one message. I was on the ground keeping the Peace Conference from being destroyed." Yao laughed as Farien scowled. It felt good to be with his friend again.

"You got reinforced because of me, pal!"

Yao laughed. "Okay, okay, so your e-post helped a bit."

"They asked me to help coordinate resources. Presimion doesn't have much experience with this kind of thing."

Yao crinkled his face as he guffawed. "No experience is more like it. You and I may be the only ones who have any idea how to run this show."

"I ran a prison for a year. What's your experience with investigations?"

Yao chuckled to himself. Farien loved to inflate things when it made him look more important. Centauri Two had definitely been an important assignment. It was one of the most secure and formerly secret prisons in the Alliance. "It was seven months, and I've done a lot of reading." Seeing Farien like this after all his guilt over actions he'd taken during the WFR rebellion, Yao hoped his friend had finally turned a corner and gotten back on track.

Farien rolled his eyes. "Book learning'll only take you so far there, Professor."

"I thank the gods every day we have you fighter jocks to straighten us out."

Farien clinked his bottle to Yao's outstretched beer. "And cover your butt." He smirked.

Both sipped their beer in silence for a moment while Yao gathered his thoughts. He knew all he had were suspicions. Still, he'd spent the last fifteen hours doing nothing but working on the investigation and his suspicions were the only thing that made sense from what he'd learned. His shoulders sank under the weight of it all. It exhausted him just thinking about it. "We don't have a lot to go on." Yao leaned back against the counter with a sigh. "I *suspect* it may be worker-related. Dru's convinced it is. But the student killed wasn't an ex-worker."

"I thought you said the hazing wasn't extreme?"

"That's when I thought you were an outsider paying a social call. There's been a few more serious incidents. Not as many as I'd feared when the program was announced. But enough to stand out as abnormal."

"So you think a fellow Cadet murdered one of his own?"

Yao shook his head. "No, I doubt it." Farien stared at him in confusion, sipping his beer and waiting for more. Yao tipped back his beer and took a long swallow, allowing it to warm his insides for a bit before continuing. "A Cadet would have known the student involved had no association with workers. So, no, I think there may have been a mistake involved. But that bed was originally assigned to an ex-worker."

"Let me guess—our friend Dru there?" Farien tilted his head toward the corridor.

Yao nodded. "I dug into Cadet Kowl's past, his family history. He's clean. No enemies. No rivals. It doesn't make sense for him to be the target." Kowl's father was a former religious leader turned therapist who had a successful practice. Everyone who knew him had nothing but praise. And Cadet Kowl hadn't been exceptional, but hadn't been a problem either. He'd blended in to the middle ranks and gone unnoticed by all except his friends and a few classmates.

"Did you look into the past and families of all of your ex-workers?"

Yao grabbed a datapad off the counter and tossed it to Farien. All the relevant data had been downloaded to it. "There are only four so far. They're all pretty clean as well. But the hatred of workers doesn't need the extra incentive." *Some people hate just to hate.* He recalled Farien's past biases and wondered if his friend would understand. Given his close contact with workers since they won their freedom, Yao didn't see how Farien could still be harboring his old stereotyped views.

Farien shrugged as he skimmed the screen. "Sure, it's possible. We can start there. Maybe up the security for the ex-workers. Try to prevent a repeat of this. But we can't rule anything out yet."

"Of course not, but I don't think this is going to be the last."

"Cadet murdered?"

"Ex-worker murdered."

Farien sighed and set the datapad on the table, pulling a chair out and sitting with the back between his legs as he drained his beer in one last swallow. "Conspiracy already? The old school people fled with Xalivar, Yao. Workers are equal now, full citizens. It's a new Alliance. We can't just start raising accusations like that."

"No. We keep it quiet for now. But what other theory makes sense?"

Farien set his chin on the chair back and thought a moment. "I don't have one, no. But one step at a time, okay? By the book."

Yao smiled. "Of course. I'm so glad you're here to help. I need the support."

Farien laughed. "Just so long as you remember I'm in charge." Farien's face became serious, frozen into a pose he might use for an official military meeting or ceremony. For a moment, Yao wondered if he might be serious, but then he caught a gleam in his friend's eyes.

Yao nodded. "Okay, but I'm not saluting you."

Farien cracked, grinning ear-to-ear and snorting. "You will if I order you to. I outrank you at the moment."

"I'm up for Captain next month."

"I'll take whatever time I can get."

They stared at each other a moment then broke into laughter

until Yao remembered Dru and waved his hand to shush Farien. "It's so good to see you again."

Farien whispered. "You, too."

Bordox fought his every instinct as he stepped off the shuttle into the starport landing bay on Legon. His mission required stealth, yet he stiffened at having to sneak around a place he'd once walked freely—admired and respected. Here he was, less than a year later, hiding in shadows like a wanted man. And there was only one person to blame: *Xander Rhii!*

He made his way through the pedestrian corridors and deliberately avoided areas frequented by pilots and maintenance crews with the hopes he'd be less likely to be recognized. The datacard in his pocket pressed against his leg with every step. He just needed to get to the flight data booths and insert it. The program it contained would do the rest, drawing out the desired intel from the systems, and he'd be on his way again.

"What's keeping you so quiet?"

He knew that voice, stopping to listen as it came from around the corner ahead of him.

"Nothing. I'm fine." A woman's voice answered. One he didn't recognize. He heard footsteps approaching and shrunk back into a shadowed doorway. "Just let me check the shuttle maintenance records for Aron and we'll be on our way."

"I know you, Tela. Something's upsetting you."

Rhii! Bordox gritted his teeth. His old enemy, the idiot who'd ruined his life, was coming toward him. What was he doing here this time of night? Last he'd heard Xander was a squadron commander. Military pilots didn't casually walk around this side of the starport.

Xander and the woman appeared around the corner and stopped as Xander jumped into her path so they were face to face. The woman was medium height, shorter than Xander, with long, brown hair and sparkling, blue eyes. Her pleasing curves stiffened in anger as Xander blocked her way. Both wore Borali Alliance flight uniforms with rank insignia on their shoulders and blasters holstered at their sides. Seeing Xander in uniform just launched him into a rage. Rhii had the career Bordox deserved.

"I know you, Tela," Xander said. "Why won't you talk to me about it?"

"Because it won't make any difference. We've tried before."

She stepped around him and continued down the corridor as he hurried after her.

"So it's about me then? What did I do?"

The woman, Tela, sighed. "I am not some delicate damsel in distress, Davi Rhii. I'm a fully qualified Borali officer, just like you." Davi! Such a stupid nickname! A slave name. The idiot's preference for that alone was evidence of his incompetence.

Xander looked confused. "Of course you are. What are you talking about?"

She stopped and whirled to face him, hands on her hips. Her eyes narrowed with annoyance. "Are you the reason I keep finding myself left out of any risky missions? Did you have me reassigned?"

"There haven't exactly been a lot of risky missions lately, and I don't know why you were reassigned but there's a rule about couples not serving together when one's in command."

Tela growled. "A convenient excuse. I am not going to be the girl who sits at home and pines after you. I want to do my duty like anyone else. I don't want to be protected."

"I'm not protecting you."

"Yes, you are!"

She whirled and started up the corridor toward Bordox again. He slipped further back into the shadows, sliding his hood up over his head as he enjoyed the show. They were so distracted with each other he doubted they'd even notice him. Bordox began to relax from his rage a bit as he watched Xander Rhii get put in his place by a woman. The only thing better would be the day he finally did it himself. Like instinct, his hand felt for the blaster at his hip, closing around the handle, he squeezed it. All he had to do was draw and shoot and Rhii would be dead. They would never see it coming, totally taken by surprise. His fist clenched and unclenched around the handle as he fought the urge. He'd blow his mission. But he might never get a chance like this. The feel of the cold steel of the blaster against his palm got his adrenaline pumping.

"Okay, maybe I didn't rush to argue." Xander smiled as if that alone would charm her. Bordox wanted to step out and wipe that smarmy grin off his face with a fist, but he swallowed, silent and hard, and stayed frozen in place. "Look, I love you, okay? Guilty! It's my instinct to want to protect you."

"We fought side by side in the Resistance. Why can't we do that now?"

"Well, there aren't really any enemies at the moment for one. And we were just getting into things then. Now we're together."

"So I'm supposed to sit at home and worry about you while you get to relax and know I'm safe? That's *fair.*"

Xander grinned and shrugged. "I'd feel good about it."

Tela groaned and punched him hard in the arm. "Well, I don't." She turned and marched on down and through the door into the landing bay as Xander raced after her, calling, "I was kidding!"

Bordox paused a moment, tempted to follow, but shook it off, remembering his mission and slid on down the corridor the way they'd come. There was more at stake. He had to remember that. Rhii's day would come. Just not today. In less than two minutes, he'd stepped into the data center and selected a private booth. He slipped the datacard from his pocket and inserted it into the terminal then watched as the screen exploded in thousands of numbers moving and changing at a pace so fast his eyes could barely recognize them. After another minute, the terminal beeped and the datacard ejected. He returned it to his pocket then slipped out and headed back the way he'd come.

Sol had arrived back at the Vertullis starport from Legallis just in time to make his night shift as a supervisor at the FTL components factory in Iraja. Both Lura and Davi had urged him to reconsider his desire to work after his release from prison, but for Sol the right to earn his way honestly was the greatest freedom of all.

"Aron's seen to it we have everything we need," Lura always said when the subject came up, caressing his arm with tenderness even as her eyes filled with worry.

"Everything except something to do with my hands," Sol would respond. "I've been a laborer all my life, and twenty-one years in prison didn't end my usefulness."

"It's not about being useful," Davi always argued when he took his mother's side. "No one would blame you for enjoying your life and freedom." But Davi had never done much manual labor and, without that common experience, didn't know the power a man felt when his sweat and brawn produced something useful to others. It made Sol's motives hard to explain.

"I want to contribute something. Our people fought for the right to full citizenship and a society can't thrive without the work of its citizens to make it better." For Sol, there was nothing left to say. He loved everything about working again—the uniform, the companionship, and the satisfaction of a task well done.

Telanus, Tela's father, felt the same way, and they'd gotten to know each other well serving side by side as supervisors on the night shift. "I may have been in prison, but I've got good years left" was Telanus' answer to Tela and Davi's questioning.

The warning came with a flashing light on their console and a beeping of the terminals in unison.

"What is it now?" Sol wondered aloud as he searched the terminal screen for answers. Probably some maintenance issue or routine malfunction. Nothing unusual ever happened there.

"Stoppage on the Third Line," Telanus responded as both typed codes on the keyboards and examined the data their terminals returned in response.

Sol sighed and nodded. "Doesn't look mechanical." The line had shut down two weeks prior due to sensor failures, but the bad sensors had been replaced and the rest reviewed and the system had worked fine since.

Telanus shrugged, picking up the comm. "We'd better call down and see what Reyna knows." His first call went unanswered and a second five minutes later also brought no response.

"Let's go," Sol said as they exchanged a look. Both men stood and hurried toward the door. Sol didn't panic. Reyna was reliable and her not checking in for the first time probably meant a quick bathroom run or that she'd already discovered the problem and gone out to fix it. It was just another routine night. What could go wrong?

The route to the Third Line operator's booth took them along catwalks and up and down ladders high above the factory floor. The supervisors used the routes to get a good look over the workers and machinery and avoid the obstacles which slowed anyone's movement when crossing the main floor. Their feet clattering on the metal catwalks combined with the humming and clacking of machinery, the chattering of workers, and the smell of smoke from lasers in the tubes below. Even at night the humid air up there was oppressive. The factory's ventilation system hadn't been replaced in decades. Sol remembered now why he avoided the catwalks as much as possible.

As they reached the final ladder and started down, Sol looked around for Reyna. The young worker was one of the newer employees, with an abundance of energy and positive attitude Sol admired. She had long, brown hair and light skin which reminded him of the way Lura had looked when they'd first met.

Reaching the bottom of the ladder, Sol hopped off and waited for Telanus to join him, before they moved off together toward the nearby booth. The air cooled immediately and Sol breathed it in deeply, relieved to be on the ground again.

Sol glanced around, still seeing no sign of the operator. "Reyna?" She'd never hear him over the noise of the floor.

Entering the booth, Telanus began checking the controls. "She must have gone out to check the vents for the source. Everything's normal here."

Sol nodded as both exited the booth again, then they moved along the tubes of the Third Line. The usual humming and vibrations were noticeably absent as they walked, finding no sign of opened vents and none of their coworker. The further they walked, the more concerned Sol became. Then as they drew near the end of the line, he spied strands of brown hair dangling through the bottom of the propulsion belt under the tube. Could Reyna have climbed inside to examine it? The vent wasn't open. Why would she have closed the hatch?

Sol and Telanus hurried to the vent and found the bolts fastened tight. "Reyna?" Sol called again as Telanus worked one side and he undid the other.

"Why would she have gone inside?" Telanus wondered aloud.

It took both of them, working together, to lift the vent cover. As it clattered to the floor beside them, the irony smell of blood struck their noses and glassy blue eyes and a bruised and bloodied face stared out at them. Reyna appeared to have been beaten, her right cheek and lower jaw smashed in.

Telanus gasped and turned away.

"Dear God, no!" Sol gritted his teeth to fight back tears. Written above the body in blood were two words:

YOU'RE NEXT

Tela and Davi rounded the corner of a corridor close to Aron's home. Why didn't Davi just let it go? She hated when he got like this: stubbornly focused on an issue until he got the answers he sought. It wasn't so bad when the issue didn't involve her, but this was all about her feelings and she didn't feel like talking about it yet. But he just wouldn't shut up.

"Come on, babe. What do I have to say? You know I never meant to make you feel like that."

"But you do—a lot."

Davi started to protest as they turned the corner and heard a scuffle ahead—a loud thump, boots on the floor, then heard voices.

"What do you want from me?"

It sounded like Aron. Tela's heart quickened as she and Davi exchanged a look then hurried around the corner.

Aron was backed against a wall as two figures in hoods confronted him. Each of them had four arms.

Lhamors!

"Please. I'm a friend to the Lhamors and all people of the Alliance."

On the wall nearby, a message had been begun in paint on the wall. So far, it was one word in all capital letters: LEARN.

Then the creatures' arms were in motion with one of the hooded Lhamors swinging two blades held evenly apart straight toward Aron while the other used two hands to swing a club at him from overhead. Aron shook as he lost his footing and sunk to his knees.

"Leave him alone!" The Lhamors whirled at the sound of Davi's voice as both he and Tela drew blasters from their holsters.

"Don' wan' you. Just th' t'rg't." The Lhamors voice was raspy, almost a whisper.

"If you hurt him, you'll answer to us," David said, his voice unwavering.

"We c'n kill 'll o' you," the other Lhamor said, whirling to face them, his blades at the ready.

"Why do you want to kill any of us? What have we done to you?" Aron stumbled back onto his feet, backing away from his attackers, attempting to slide past and join Davi and Tela.

"You 're en'mies o' the 'lli'nce." The larger Lharmor swung his club at Aron, who ducked then cringed as the club slammed noisily into the wall.

"The only ones here who will be dying are you," Tela aimed her blaster and fired it at the club. It disintegrated in the Lhamor assassin's hand as the laser struck, leaving a cloud of smoke and the smell of burning wood. She grasped the blaster tighter and aimed again.

The Lhamor dropped the remnants and drew sidearms of his own, four, one in each hand. "I 'm pr'p'red to die. 're you?" He jumped clear as Tela fired again, the recoil throwing her hand back and up as she did.

In unison, the Lhamors spun, the one with blades slicing backwards toward Aron with one hand and throwing the other blade in an arc toward Davi. Aron groaned as the blade sliced into his forearm, sending blood streaming toward his elbow. Davi ducked the other and fired as Tela took aim again and fired at the taller Lhamor. Laser bolts crisscrossed the hallway as the Lhamor returned fire.

Both blades clattered to the ground as their former bearer fell to his knees, struck by Davi's blaster. Davi rolled as he fired, narrowly missing being struck by bolts from the other Lhamor's blasters.

"Run, Aron!" Tela yelled as she dove and rolled the opposite direction, avoiding more lasers from the taller Lhamor, then screaming as one singed her upper shoulder. The laser stung as it burned into her flesh, but her arm was still functional and she aimed her blaster again as she landed, firing it at the Lhamor again. Davi fired seconds after and the Lhamor fell, just as Aron fell to his knees between them.

"Thank God you came!"

"Are you okay, Aron?" Tela quickly examined him. His arm was bleeding, but the cut didn't appear to have gone deep.

"I'm fine."

She heard Davi fire again and turned, ignoring the flare of pain in her arm as she aimed her own blaster and fired again. The remaining Lhamor's blasters clattered to the floor and he fell on his face, dead.

She and Davi quickly spun, backs touching, looking for other assailants. "Do you think there were only two?"

"They wouldn't expect to need more."

They turned at a thump to see Aron had fainted on the floor nearby. "Call for medics," Davi said as he hurried up the corridor to check the fallen Lhamors.

Tela nodded and knelt to examine Aron again. Her heart pounded as she set her blaster within reach on the floor and felt for a pulse. Then she keyed the comm on her shoulder. "We need emergency response. There's been an assassination attempt on Lord Aron. Outside his quarters on Level Seven, Corridor Six."

Davi kicked the weapons away from the Lhamors, sending them sliding down the hall toward her with scraping sounds as he bent to examine the bodies. Neither moved. His eyes met hers and he shook his head, sliding his blaster back in the holster at its side. Noticing something, he reached out and took a crumpled paper from one of the bladed Lhamor's fists. Unfolding it carefully, he read it over.

"What's it say?"

"I think it's the message he never finished." Davi's eyes met Tela's again as alarms sounded around them and footsteps and shouting voices drew toward them from nearby corridors. Davi held the note out so they both could see the words:

LEARN YOUR PLACE

Chapter Three

Once the doctor informed them Aron was resting and would recover in a few weeks from his wounds, Davi finally relaxed and breathed normally again. He left Aron's wife, Calla, to tend to him and returned to Miri's study where Lura, Miri and Tela were waiting anxiously.

"He'll be fine," he assured them as Tela flipped a switch on a wall terminal and stepped back.

"I've got them on the line." It took Davi a moment to realize who she meant.

Three older men with graying hair appeared in the monitor. Two wore military uniforms but only one the uniform of the Borali military. The other's uniform was blue rather than gray and bore medals and other markings from the Workers' Freedom Resistance Army. The third man wore a green robe in a style common to planetary leaders or Council members like Aron.

"How is he?" The man in the robe asked. All three men's faces showed their concern.

Davi made eye contact with the men. "He's resting. Calla's with him. The doctor said the wounds would heal in a few weeks."

"Do you have any idea who the assassins were?" General Matheu's voice had a natural growl which made him all the more imposing in his blue uniform.

"Other than Lhamors? No." Tela kept standing and pacing

around then sitting back down again.

"Well, there've been three deaths now and the attempt on Aron," the gray uniformed man said. "Coincidence seems unlikely."

"Three? We only knew about the one at Presimion." Davi and Tela exchanged a look.

"There was a housewife killed on Xanthis," Joram, the man in the green robe, explained. "Her husband was stationed there for an agricultural firm."

"And a technician was killed two hours ago at the FTL components factory," the gray uniformed officer said.

Davi's body tensed as his eyes met Tela's and she gasped.

"The factory where Sol and Telanus work?" Lura was on her feet in a minute with Miri rising beside her, grasping her arm with concern. For a moment, Davi considered pulling away from Tela to comfort Lura, but her legs remained steady and she continued staring at the screen with hopeful determination.

The man nodded. "Sol and Telanus found her."

"My God!" Tela pushed against Davi, allowing his arm to wrap around her as she buried her face in his shoulder.

"It's time for Aron to make the Council aware. Someone is orchestrating this." Matheu's face returned to his usual stern, emotionless stare, a look which annoyed Davi greatly when he'd dealt with Matheu during the Resistance. Matheu and Uzah had remained suspicious of Davi, forcing him to prove himself over time. But in the end, he knew he'd gained their admiration and full support.

"Why would the Lhamors start assassinating Vertullians? They've faced persecution themselves." Miri paced behind the couch where she'd been seated.

"We suspect they are mercenaries, not the orchestrators," Joram replied.

"The victims aren't connected in any way other than being Vertullians," Uzah added. "It would seem entirely random outside of that one fact."

"I'll contact Yao and Farien and see what their investigation has turned up." Davi took a deep breath and fought the urge to patch them in immediately. The Vertullian leaders didn't know his friends as well as he did and might not be comfortable sharing this conversation with outsiders at the moment.

"Are Sol and Telanus okay?" Lura's face had paled, her forehead creased with lines. Davi reached over and caressed her arm. He could find no words to say. She'd already been through so much.

"They're fine. The factory has been sealed and guards posted while we investigate." Lura looked relieved at Joram's response but still ready to rush out the door at any moment.

"I'll have my shuttle prepared to take you there immediately," Miri said, squeezing Lura's arm and hurrying toward a nearby corridor.

"You two may be safer right here." Davi didn't relish the idea of his mothers heading off alone into danger.

"I'm going too." Tela's tone muted any thought he had of arguing. Her eyes met Davi's with an intensity that caused him to nod and look away.

Miri disappeared into the corridor as he surrendered. "Just be careful, okay?"

"I know how to take care of myself." Her tone was terse, evoking memories of their earlier conversation. He sighed as his shoulders lowered in surrender.

"We need to handle this with great care," Joram had been elected President when the planet won its freedom. "Our status as citizens is still new. Old resentments remain. We must allow the authorities to do their jobs and not be seen as distrustful or accusing."

"At the same time, we have a duty to protect our own." As usual, General Matheu showed no concern for politics.

"We can do both for now." Joram's tone matched the General's in intensity.

"We will do what must be done. Together." Uzah was used to mediating between his strong-willed companions.

"Of course." Joram smiled and nodded to Uzah.

"You'll be on your way in an hour," Miri said as she returned.

"Check in with us please upon arrival," Uzah smiled, despite the worry in his eyes.

"You have enough to worry about without worrying about us," Tela answered.

"Save us the trouble of sending men to check on you," Joram said. The concern in his voice pleased Davi.

Tela looked ready to scold when Lura jumped in. "Of course. We appreciate your concern."

"I'll be in touch soon," Davi said as the three men nodded and the terminal went dark. He concealed his own internal panic until Tela and his mothers hurried off to prepare their things for the trip. Then Davi dialed into the military channels to see what information on the investigations had been made available.

Yao yawned as he poured another cup of Talis for Farien. The natural stimulants the drink was known for didn't seem to be doing their job. His body pleaded with him to lie down and sleep. The long hours they'd spent investigating Cadet Kowl's murder were catching up with them faster than either had hoped, and they were clearly losing the battle to stay awake.

"If you want me to go with you, I will," Farien said as he accepted the mug.

Yao shook his head. "It's my responsibility as the faculty member in charge of new student assimilation. Having an official from the military there might make it even more dramatic."

Farien nodded, sipping his Talis. "Either way. It won't be easy. Sorry you have to deal with that."

Yao closed his eyes as the warm liquid flowed down his throat to warm his stomach. "Thanks. I met the Kowls once at orientation. I'm actually glad it'll be someone they know."

"If word hasn't reached them already."

"That's why we've kept it quiet. It's only been three days. We wanted time to figure out what had happened and who might be involved." Only they hadn't learned anything yet. Yao had no idea what to tell them. He'd already dodged their calls twice, which was unfair, but so was giving them half-truths and guesses. He wanted more.

"What're you gonna tell them if they ask?"

"That the investigation is receiving all available resources. It won't be much comfort, but what else can I say?" He looked away, staring out the window as he wondered how he'd react to a professor showing up to tell him of his own child's death. The lack of information would just make it worse. All the Kowls knew at this point was that their son had been murdered, his throat cut. Who and why were still questions, and those were the kinds of things a parent would demand to know. Yao's head ached from a desire to have answers for them.

The comm beeped on the wall nearby and Yao turned and hurried to answer it. He pressed the brown button below the speaker. "Professor Brahma."

"Yao! Is Captain Noa with you?" Davi's smiling face appeared on the screen.

Yao felt some of the tension leave his body at the sight of his old friend. "Yeah, he's here causing all the trouble he can."

Farien walked over to stand beside him. "The trouble started long before I got here."

"This time." All three said it together and laughed.

Then Yao's thoughts went back to Kowl's waiting parents. "I hope you have good news for us. We could really use some."

"No progress on the investigation?"

"Not really."

"Well, I don't have good news, no, but I do have some information which may help." A seriousness filled Davi's face which Yao hadn't seen there since the Resistance.

"What's going on?" Farien's eyes met Yao's.

"We're up to three murders now and an attempt on Lord Aron's life." Davi leaned back in his chair, looking as tired as Yao and Farien. Yao leaned against the wall. He hadn't realized until now it was the middle of the night. Just realizing it brought an involuntary yawn.

"Who are the others?" Farien had his datapad out, prepared to take notes.

"A technician at the FTL factory on Vertullis."

Yao's eyes widened with concern. "The one your father works at?"

Davi nodded. "My father and Tela's father found the victim. Beaten and chewed up by the propulsion system of the line."

Yao cringed. "Poor thing."

"The other was a housewife stationed on Xanthis with her husband, who handles shipping for VerAgro."

Farien cursed as he typed into his datapad. "It's a conspiracy. Has to be!"

Davi nodded. "And the assassins are Lhamors—at least some of them."

Yao frowned. "Why would the Lhamors be after ex-workers? Surely they can understand what it's like to be persecuted."

"That's what Miri asked. We think they're mercenaries."

Yao turned away from the terminal, taking a deep sip from his glass again. *Come on, Talis! I need energy here.*

"You two look exhausted. You should get more rest." Davi didn't look much better. His eyes were hollow, his face haggard. Yao wanted to laugh but was too overcome with worry to manage it.

"Sol and Telanus are okay?" Yao felt Farien's stare at his back as his friend asked the question.

"They're fine. Just deeply worried."

Yao turned back to face the terminal and his friends. "So am I. This could be just the beginning. We have to get a fix on it fast."

Davi nodded. "I know. I wish I knew where to start."

"Bordox, Obed, Xalivar—I can give you a list of suspects." Farien counted them off on his fingers as he spoke.

"Xalivar's never liked aliens, we know that. But no one's seen or heard from him since the Peace Conference there. I can't imagine Obed getting involved in a murder plot. He used to head the Lord's Special Police."

"That doesn't make him honest," Yao countered. They all knew government police used lying and manipulation daily. They were skilled at it. "We can't just work on assumptions. We need real evidence."

"So we'll get some. Let me get on the Alliance database and call up those other investigation files." Farien moved toward the keyboard on a pull-out shelf in the wall beneath the terminal.

"I've already sent copies to you through e-post," Davi said with a smile. "I'll be back in touch tomorrow. Several high level meetings happening which may have impact on the information and resources available for the investigation."

"If command doesn't notify me first." Yao saw Farien stiffen, his eyes avoiding the screen.

Davi chuckled. "Relax, Captain. I'm just trying to help, not step on your toes."

Farien smiled. "Yeah, sorry. Just tired and stressed."

"Get some rest then. You'll need the energy."

Yao nodded. "We definitely will. Thanks for filling us in."

"You bet. How's Dru doing?"

"Better. Still recovering from the shock. But he went back to classes today."

Davi looked relieved. "Good. Tell him all his friends here are praying for him."

Yao smiled. "Of course."

"Hope we can talk in person soon about something a lot more pleasant." Davi smiled, but his slouched shoulders indicated he'd be headed for bed himself. "Rhii out."

The screen went blank as Farien hit a button and logged into e-post to retrieve the files Davi had sent. "Just let me look these over and I'll call it a night."

Yao yawned again. "I'll wait until morning. I wouldn't remember anything in them anyway as tired as I am. Don't stay up all night, ok?"

Farien rolled his eyes, attention still focused on the terminal as he typed in his login and password. When Farien got focused like this, he became oblivious to everything else. Best to leave him to do as he wanted. He'd fill Yao in the next morning.

Yao patted his friend on the shoulder then turned and headed for his bedroom. He wondered if he'd be able to shut his mind down enough to get actual rest. Lately it had been working overtime, and he'd only slept fitfully. Combined with the Talis, he assumed he'd face the same this night. He looked in on Dru, who was snoring on the couch in the study. When had Yao and his friends lost their ability to sleep like that? Most cadets excelled at it. They'd only been out two years. It seemed like centuries. Who could have imagined how much they'd go through in that time? He sighed and continued down the hall.

From the outside, the rocky opening looked like any other mine shaft—an arced entrance laser-carved from rock which became quickly dark black within and required everyone who entered to wear special mining hats with lights. Everything appeared exactly the way it had been designed to. Xalivar was tempted to skip the lighted hat but dared not tip off any onlookers that the whole thing was just a ruse.

The entrance tunnel descended slowly to a dark metal door. So dark you couldn't see it until you were almost upon it, even wearing a lighted hat. It opened with a special cardkey General Lucius carried in a pouch on his belt. He slipped the cardkey into the slot then stepped back as the door opened before their eyes. Xalivar smiled. Lucius had always been one of his finest officers. He felt relief knowing at least one of his co-conspirators might be trustworthy or even up to the task.

They stepped inside and walked into the chamber. Within a minute the door beeped and swung shut on its own. No accidental discoveries. And no chance anyone who did manage to find their way here by accident would ever get out. Even if they managed to fake the cardkey to get in, you needed a separate device to get out, a microscopic chip injected by the medical team. So far only Lucius and Xalivar had it and Xalivar's had only been implanted that morning upon his arrival.

Despite its primitive state, Xalivar could picture it as it soon would be—a huge cavern for training and assemblies, surrounded by smaller cabins with barracks, dining and recreation. Above, his own quarters with a dais and balcony overlooking it all. Other chambers would be storage, weapons, and quarters for Xalivar's allies and the officers. He laughed, feeling good to be alive as Lucius watched him. Soon all those who'd written him off would find out how foolish they'd been.

As Xalivar spun slowly back toward him from surveying the room, Lucius extended a hand offering him a similar looking cardkey to the one he'd used to open the door. "Only two in existence. Some of the engineers have already complained, but I told them they'd be handed out when their need had been determined."

Xalivar accepted the card and looked it over. "Good, very good, Lucius. I can always count on you."

He could see the pleasure in the General's eyes as he saluted. "The tunnels are forty-percent complete. So far we've dug out only this cavern and one other, but we are increasing our workforce."

"Any trouble from the authorities?"

"Xanthis has seven moons and this one was long ago deemed worthless. It's far out and just a cold rock. They hardly took notice when we told them a TriLithium spur had been detected. I'm not even sure they believed it. They'll be delighted if it generates revenue. But they hardly care much until it does."

"They've left you alone then?"

"So far. An inspector or two might wander out here before we're finished, but I have some TriLithium samples on their way which should distract them from wasting time probing these chambers."

"Once training starts they won't survive their landing, of course," Xalivar had a plan to deal with the questions such deaths might bring, but that didn't need to be revealed yet. He intended to keep as many secrets for as long as he could. No matter how faithful Lucius was, the only person Xalivar trusted completely was himself. "And the recruitment?"

"Quiet inquiries are being made in the right places." Lucius waved a hand to indicate the far reaches of the system. "Your request to focus on human pilots does make things challenging."

"We can recruit alien pilots once the human leaders have been trained and integrated. The aliens will be disposable. The humans will not." Lucius nodded. "Any word from Pres on recruitment within the Alliance?"

Lucius turned slowly until their eyes met. He hesitated as if choosing his words, but Xalivar saw in his eyes he had displeasing news to relay. "Pres' loyalty is not easy to turn. I told you she might waiver."

Xalivar frowned, controlling the surging anger rising inside. "She's betrayed us already?"

Lucius shook his head. "No, my Lord. She's expressed some concerns. So far I have allayed them, but she's not made the amount of progress desired."

"Perhaps we should request a meeting then." Xalivar inwardly cursed the weakness of women. He should never trust another one! He'd trusted his own sister, Miri, and look where that got him.

Lucius sighed. "You know how difficult the last one was to arrange."

Xalivar smiled. "Great plans require great challenges, Lucius. If your fellow General needs reassurance, I should meet with her myself. You know well my powers of persuasion."

Lucius smiled. "I'm sure it would be most reassuring."

Xalivar began walking toward the tunnel at the far end of the chamber. "Good. Arrange it. Now I want to see the beginnings of our flight hangar."

Xalivar's bootsteps echoed off the rock walls as the General hurried to catch up with him. "The Xanthians will be quite humiliated at what we've pulled off right under their noses," Lucius said.

Xalivar laughed as Lucius led him into the darkness of another tunnel. *The whole Alliance will be shocked.* Ahhh to be making history again! It was so close, he could feel the power already.

The restaurant smelled of seafood and exotic potpourri, one emanating from the kitchen through the vents, the other pumped in deliberately for atmosphere. Together they just created an olfactory mess. Miri's midweek luncheon always met at the restaurant just east of the Palace in Legon's ritziest shopping district. It started fashionably late as usual with various women trying to assert their importance by arriving more fashionably late than their rivals. Miri arrived early compared to most and was well into her third Tertullian Hammer by the time the food was ordered. She hated all the presumptions and political maneuvering. She'd gotten more than enough to last a lifetime at the Palace. Now that she was a civilian, she just wanted to relax. The Hammer did its job, warming her blood and lessening her tension, and had her feeling pretty good by the time the serve-bots circled around them, some taking orders and others filling drinks, appetizer trays, etc.

Then the gossip began in earnest.

"Have you heard the rumors about the Council making that Worker holiday official?" Hachim's wife Irais had a voice that was almost like a squeal.

Abena's dark skin was a sharp contrast to her puffy white dress. She shook her head with disgust. "My Niger believes the public will never accept it. They're just not like us. Besides, they have such crazy beliefs!"

Selina Noa's hand came to rest gently on Miri's forearm. "Some of them are quite nice, when you get to know them. And they're not as different as we've been taught to believe." Farien's mother had always been close with Miri, the families united by their son's friendship.

Abena and Irais guffawed as they shot her disgusted looks. "Your bias toward them is well known, as is Miri's."

"We are biased, based on a great deal of experience, Abena," Selina responded calmly. "Experience few amongst us have."

Irais scowled, her double chin wrinkling in the process. "I have all the experience I need. History speaks volumes."

"A history written with bias and the intent to maintain the status quo," Miri finally said. "History is filled with lies."

"We'd expect that from you," Abena answered, "a woman who couldn't even adopt a quality child but instead stole one from workers!"

Tarkanius' wife Danae stood, raising her open palms to signal for calm. "Please. We've all been friends a long time here. There's no need for such talk." Older, with gray hair atop a gaunt face but with a warm smile and eyes, Danae was a respected friend to everyone.

Selina raised her Talis in salute. "Here! Here! Surely there are much more pleasant things to talk about." Her blue eyes sparkled to match her smile as her long, blonde curls framed her face.

"Those people want to shove their ludicrous ideas off on our children," Irais said. "That's the issue! And it's no laughing matter!"

Miri slammed her empty glass down hard on the table. "They want no such thing. They want to live in peace if only we'll let them. They have shown respect for our ways and our views. Why can't we have the maturity to do the same for them?" It was the first time any of her circle had treated her like less than an equal, and she didn't like it at all.

Irais coughed. "Maturity? This from a woman who never got serious enough to marry? Who tried her best to undermine our entire government and way of life?"

"I said 'enough!'" Now Danae sounded annoyed. "This is not the place for such discussions. Stop it at once!"

"We're just agreeing with our husbands that citizenship is one thing but full acceptance of their cultural views is a different matter." Abena looked to Irais who nodded vigorously.

Your husbands side with whoever can give them the most power. They have no loyalty and no integrity, picking on the weak. Miri despised them and their wives too. *Go on, Miri, tell her.* "Your husbands joined with me in fighting to change the old system," Miri said instead, not even meeting their eyes. "They seem to have forgotten the values they once stood for."

"Miri!" Danae looked at her with exasperation. "You know that all members of the Council have a track record of serving the public interest with honor and integrity. I'm sure any objections they may have are based on very real concerns for the safety of all citizens."

"Besides," Selina patted Miri on the arm, her eyes urging Denae to sit back down, "these matters are not ours to decide anyway. I, for one, want to hear about Irais' new granddaughter."

Several other ladies mumbled in excited accord at this.

Irais smiled, reaching for her datapad. "I brought plenty of photos."

"Send them around then! What are you waiting for?" Selina's smile was contagious.

Miri sighed and lowered herself back into her chair as a serve-bot retrieved her glass and began to refill it. She'd never before felt out of place amongst these women, even as their princess. Now most of them looked like strangers.

"When are Davi and Tela going to give you grandchildren?" Selina's voice was almost a whisper.

Miri saw in her eyes that her friend wanted to distract her. *Bless Selina for her gentle kindness.* "We have to convince them to marry first," Miri responded.

Selina laughed. "All things in time, dear."

Miri nodded as she took a sip of her refilled drink.

The military briefing took place in the officers' conference room at Alliance Command just off the starport on Legallis. Uzah and Davi hadn't even had time for lunch after his arrival, because a delay put his shuttle's arrival time too close to the meeting. They made their way to adjacent seats at the large, circular conference table and waited while other officers filed in, noisily chattering around them. The Borali military's emblem, a blue crest with images of crossed blaster bolts, fighters, and the twin suns, was lasered onto the ceiling under crystals which lent it a special sparkle when combined with light from the reflector pads lining each side wall. The table itself bore a smaller version of the logo as did the uniforms of all attendees. Everyone had worn their dress uniforms, crisp and clean. Uzah sat up straight and Davi did the same as they waited. Generals Pres and Grif were listed as running the meeting, and both were known for expecting their personnel to be shipshape and spotless, as per protocols.

The two generals arrived together and walked straight past Davi and Uzah toward the head of the table. Grif was tall and thin with graying hair at his temples and fuller, darker hair between. He looked like a kindly grandfather to Davi, but previous encounters had shown him to be serious and intense, not unlike General Matheu. Pres was medium height with a softer demeanor, her shoulder-length dark locks braided on each side. Both wore decorations earned from many years of distinguished service. Everyone who spoke of them did so with well-deserved respect.

The officers stood and saluted as the two Generals arrived at the head of the table. They nodded and saluted back. "At ease," Pres said and the officers lowered their hands and sat back down.

"A murder took place four nights ago at the Presimion Academy on Eleni 1," Grif began without preamble. He looked around making eye contact with the attendees as several muttered and others gasped with surprise. "A young cadet's throat was cut; a message left on the wall reading: YOU DON'T BELONG HERE. Since then, two other murders have occurred with similar messages and an attempt was made on Lord Aron's life."

"By the same criminals?" A female captain inquired from a seat near Davi, her voice dripping with rage.

Grif's eyes met hers. "We don't know yet." The captain looked away in disgust.

"It does appear that the murders are connected," Pres said. "Separate investigations are being coordinated and combined efforts employed to find out."

Grif nodded. "From this moment, I'm putting all Vertullian military personnel under special security."

"Special security?" the blonde colonel's voice crackled as he tried to hide a laugh. "Since when do military personnel need security? They are armed, aren't they?" Davi struggled to remember his name. The Colonel was Jansen, if he recalled right.

"Sure they are," said a red-faced major whose uniform barely fit his rotund frame. "They're just not very good shots." He and the Colonel cackled in unison, a few others joining.

"What about when they're off duty?" The same female captain asked the colonel, clearly annoyed by his crassness. "It'll take a large detail..."

"I carry my blaster everywhere," Colonel Jansen said, smirking at her. "So should they."

"Nevertheless, we're providing extra security—guards for their barracks and quarters and modified assignments when necessary. Is that okay with you, Colonel? Major?" General Grif's face was stern; his tone firm.

The two officers shifted uncomfortably in their chairs as the smile faded from their faces. "Yes, sir, General." Colonel Jansen nodded, not meeting the General's eyes. The Major glanced toward Davi, his face startlingly familiar for reasons Davi couldn't remember. Where had they met before? And why did he look at Davi with such anger?

"Have any of the murders been military?" the female captain asked.

"Just the cadet so far." Pres' look suggested she feared there would be more.

The Major turned to Davi and Uzah. "If you need special treatment, perhaps we should get you special armor, special starcraft, special uniforms..." Laughter came from other attendees as Colonel Jansen smiled and chuckled.

"We didn't request it, but since the assailants are unknown—"

The colonel cackled, cutting Davi off. "You Vertullians are the Council's new pet project, didn't you know? You don't have to ask for anything. They just give and give and give."

Davi opened his mouth to protest, but Uzah put a hand on his shoulder. "Do you feel you're being treated unfairly, Colonel?" Uzah asked, his brow furrowed as his voice shook with anger.

"No, you earned everything you've got, Lieutenant General." Colonel Jansen rolled his eyes and turned to glance around the table for sympathy.

"Far more than you did, Colonel Jansen," Grif barked as he stood stiffly and glared.

Several officers chuckled as the Colonel stiffened and straightened his uniform. "My family has a distinguished history of service to the Alliance."

"Their history of service has earned them their places, too," Grif replied. "If you have a problem with it, feel free to set up a meeting in my office to discuss a cut in rank."

"Or mine," Pres said, frowning as her eyes also focused on the Colonel. The Colonel's face reddened as he ignored the smirks of those around him and held his tongue.

Shifting in his chair, the major shrugged. "All military personnel should be prepared for danger at any moment. What makes this special?"

"The High Lord Councilor's orders for one. Three murders in four days for another." Grif relaxed his shoulders and turned back to take in the other attendees. "We all know there are some of our people, perhaps even in this room, who bear old grudges against the Vertullians, but those feelings must be put aside. They are full citizens now and deserve the same rights and protections as everyone else. Part of our job is to ensure they get them."

"Does this mean we won't be allowed to do our duty like anyone else?" Davi turned slightly, so he could see the Generals' eyes as he asked.

"For now, no. We just want to be sure extra security is around to help avoid unpleasant incidents." Pres smiled reassuringly.

"What kind of incidents? Anything besides murders?" the major kept a straight face, but his tone dripped of sarcasm.

"Hazing of any sort will not be tolerated," Pres answered. Both Generals stared at Colonel Jansen and the major, their eyes clearly implying they included the men's actions in that category.

"No one will bother them if they do their jobs." The major glowered at Davi and Uzah, but his anger had changed to raw hatred.

The annoyed female captain rolled her eyes. "Women have served for two decades and you still haze us."

"Friendly teasing." The Colonel waved in dismissal.

"Criminal charges will be brought against any and all violators. Would further explanation be required?" Pres and Grif looked directly at the Colonel as she finished.

His smile faded and he took a deep breath. "No, of course."

"Good." Pres smiled and turned away.

"I want immediate reports of any unusual incidents—of any kind. We have no idea who's responsible and we need to keep our people safe." Grif looked around for any questions or objections. All the attendees just stared at the Colonel.

"They'll be safe," Colonel Jansen said as if he answered for it personally.

Grif nodded and turned back to Pres. "Any resources you need can be asked for. Contact General Pres. In the meantime, I'm putting all units on alert. We may need to act quickly once the guilty parties have been identified to bring them to justice."

"Isn't that under the purview of the LSP?" the Major straightened in his chair as all eyes turned to him.

"We'll be available as needed, Major. Is that a problem?"

The Major shook his head. "No, sir."

Grif smiled. "Good. Ex-workers are to be treated the same as any other citizen. Violations will be punished to the full extent of military code."

"And what about the civilians, sir?" the female Captain met the General's gaze with no hesitation.

"Plans are in the works to protect them as well, Captain."

"Meaning you don't know, sir?" Davi watched her with curiosity, admiring her nerve.

"No one knows, Captain. But we intend to find out."

They were dismissed moments later and Davi and Uzah headed for the commissary at a casual pace. As they turned a corner, someone pushed between them roughly, in a hurry to pass. Davi recognized the Major from the meeting. Davi exchanged a look with Uzah as the major spun around.

"Sorry, sir," he nodded to Uzah, but his sneer was anything but apologetic. His eyes turned toward Davi's glare. "Did you want something, Captain?" He pronounced Davi's rank as if it were poison.

"No, sir," Davi answered, continuing to walk as their eyes met.

"Let me inspect your weapon, Captain."

Davi stopped, Uzah beside him. They exchanged a look. Davi didn't know whether to comply. What was the Major after? He couldn't shake the feeling they'd met in the past. Uzah motioned for him to hand over his weapon.

Davi pulled his blaster from the holster and grabbed it by the firing tube, offering it handle-first to the major. Officers were allowed to make flash inspections of their inferiors at any time. The major tore it from Davi's hand and looked it over carefully. "Are you fully trained in its use, Captain?"

"A crack shot, sir," Davi answered with a smile.

"You'd better be." The Major frowned. "If one of my men dies because you can't pull your weight, I'll have you up on charges."

Davi frowned, fighting the urge to snap back. "If you make one more such comment, Major, I'll have you up on charges," Uzah said, his voice rising in anger.

The Major merely glared as he offered Davi back the blaster, ignoring safety protocols and holding it out firing tube-first. Davi grabbed it angrily, and the Major turned without a word and started back down the corridor.

Davi pulled the trigger and a laser beam charred the floor between the Major's boot heels. The Major spun angrily around, raising a hand in accusation.

"Ooops. You handed it to me the wrong way, sir. It accidentally went off as I tried to holster it."

The Major looked at Uzah, who kept a straight face despite the sparkle in his eyes. Davi holstered the weapon and stood at attention. The Major's eyes met Davi in a warning before he turned again and headed back up the corridor at an even quicker pace.

Davi waited until he'd turned the corner then laughed as Uzah shook his head. "He could charge you with insubordination."

"You could charge him with harassment."

"Officers can inspect weapons of anyone they outrank with a moment's notice. Be careful, Davi. We have enough against us already. We don't need to make enemies."

Davi bristled. Why was Uzah taking the idiot's side? "Sorry, General."

Uzah smiled. "At least he knows you're a damn good shot." They both laughed as Uzah clapped him on the back and they started down the corridor again toward the commissary.

After several days spent bedridden at home under Calla's mothering eye, Aron escaped via an emergency Council session where he detailed the various facts of the attack. He found the other Councilor's reactions disappointing.

"Did you really expect no resistance to the idea of full citizenship for our former enemies?" Lord Hachim asked from a table in middle of the room as Aron finished.

"A few murders with the only connection between them being ties to Vertullis doesn't convince me of a conspiracy," Lord Niger added from a table across the aisle from Hachim. Others around them offered mumbled agreement.

"It's certainly cause for concern," Lord Kray said. Aron could see on her face she was furious at their indifference.

Simeon and Tarkanius officiated the session from atop a large dais facing rows of tables at which the other Council members were seated. All wore the embossed white robes customary for Council meetings. Aron stood at a podium before the dais, where he'd made his presentation and now faced the others' questions.

"Murders happen throughout the system. What you're asking is to divert resources which might prevent them from occurring in one area to another, to offer special treatment to a segment of the population who not too long ago forced us to war demanding their freedom." Hachim shook his head. "They have what they wanted. Now, they want more."

Kray's clenched fist slammed against the top of the desk where she was seated. "Are you suggesting we just let them die?"

"I'm suggesting we treat them like any other citizens."

"We will not stand by and allow our citizens to be murdered, if there's any chance we can prevent it," Tarkanius said sternly, frowning at Hachim.

"Of course not! But what makes you think you can prevent it?" Hachim looked at him as if the question were obvious.

Aron sighed. How could anyone aspiring so much to be a leader lack such basic compassion? "We don't know that we can, but there have been three attacks in a matter of days. Something must be done."

"And it will be," Niger answered. "What we're here to determine is what action is appropriate."

"Obviously more effort must be made to investigate," Lord Qui said from his seat beside Kray at a table near the front. "If there is a conspiracy, evidence will reveal it." Kray and several others mumbled in agreement.

"Investigate! Of course! But we shouldn't go jumping to conclusions about conspiracies and increasing security until we know something." Niger's voice remained calm but rose in pitch along with his passion as he spoke.

"No one wants any more deaths," Hachim said. "But as we discussed in our previous meeting, offering these Vertullians special treatment will only inflame the passions of those who resent the freedoms they've already been given."

"Like who, Lord Hachim?" Kray sounded exasperated. "Yourself and Lord Niger?"

Aron coughed into his hand to cover a laugh and several of those present looked at him with sympathy as Hachim and Niger chafed at the accusation, shaking their heads in offense. "We are honorable men."

Lord Niger nodded. "We both supported suing for peace. We have been supportive of the Vertullian's citizenship."

"Until their own enterprise competed with yours," Lord Kray hissed.

Simeon raised a hand from the dais. "Enough! Fighting amongst ourselves is not providing answers. I will coordinate with security forces to provide increased resources for the investigation while also ensuring extra security for our Vertullian neighbors. I have the authority as Head of the Council to do that, so if anyone wants to argue, you can come argue with me!"

He panned the room angrily as he finished, as if waiting for someone to raise a challenge. Aron wanted to call for them to stay, to try again to convince more of them, but he had no idea what he'd say. When the Lords remained silent, Simeon dismissed them with a wave and they hurried out, chattering amongst themselves.

As the others had left, Simeon, Tarkanius and Kray pulled Aron aside.

"We're putting you under increased security, too, Aron," Tarkanius said.

Aron shook his head, grateful Calla wasn't around as a witness. "I'm just fine. The doctor said I'll be full recovered in a few days."

"If they tried once, they'll try again," Simeon said, shaking his head. "You need to be protected. We can't have our Lords coming under attack."

Kray kept angrily shifting positions as she stood with them. "I cannot believe the attitude of those two! The deaths must be connected."

"They are only asking questions of us which the media and our citizens will, Kray," Simeon said, placing a hand on her arm. "We must follow proper steps and avoid any risk of making things worse."

Aron smiled at Kray. "What the people would appreciate most are a few Council members making an appearance in the capital to offer reassurance. Perhaps Lord Kray would like to accompany me?"

Kray nodded. "Of course."

"I'll come as well." Simon smiled. "I'm sure others will join us."

"We must be careful not to put the Councilors at risk as well," Tarkanius warned.

Aron chuckled. "We must take the same risk we ask of our citizens, my Lord." The others nodded in agreement. The support of the leadership was such an encouragement. When they'd agreed on a time for their appearance in Iraja, each returned to his or her office to concern themselves with other responsibilities.

Despite his insistence that he was well, Aron felt his energy waning after just two hours with the Council. The injury had been harder on him than he'd imagined, and although he did his best to hide the effects from others, including Calla, he knew he had to keep up on his rest if he hoped to heal quickly and put it behind him. He made a note to stay in regular touch with Davi and Uzah so he could stay abreast of any new discoveries. He had nothing else pressing at the moment, and he knew too many inquiries from him would just interfere with their focused efforts. Leaving the Council Chamber, he headed back to Miri's apartment, knowing Calla would be there waiting and worrying about him.

It was kind of Miri to let them remain there while she visited Vertullis with Tela and Lura, but he hoped the Council's decision to provide security meant they'd allow them to return to their own apartment soon. He always rested better in a familiar environment.

The Garden was so peaceful and beautiful. Davi had spent a lot of time there since being stationed at the Legallis starport. He couldn't believe he'd never visited as a child—such awesome natural wonder and beauty available for his enjoyment and he never took advantage. It was too public, he supposed. Still, the sweet scent of the Cherelia blossoms, with their poofy red petals and long, thick, green stems, the musty scent of the local blue moss at his feet, and the chirping of baby Taffitas amidst the branches filled him with delight. It was his favorite place to come and think.

I wish Tela were here. It was their weekly date night, yet she was on Vertullis with his family. He needed to go back and call them to see how things were going; to find out more about the worker killed at the factory where their fathers worked. It was hard to focus enough to choose a path home, however. His thoughts were so muddled in their rushed search to find answers. Was this truly his uncle's plot? Who else was involved? How many more would die? Why would God allow this to happen?

He hated that he and Tela had been fighting when she left. They'd been arguing a lot more the past few months and he had no idea why. The arguments always started over things they used to just talk about and resolve. Why had talking about them become so much harder now?

Feeling overwhelmed, he knelt in the soft, cool moss and offered a prayer. *God, please protect my loved ones—Tela, Lura, Miri, Sol. Please show us how to stop these killings. Help us to protect our people.*

Lead us well. The thoughts came out in a jumble. He hoped somehow God could make sense of them. He felt like a child praying, so uncertain what to say, like he'd never done it before. *Help me talk to her, Lord. Give me the words to say. Help me to communicate well with all of them. And thank you for the many blessings you've showered on my life.*

As he finished, he felt a tingle on his spine. Was someone watching him? He glanced around the Gardens and saw no one. Then his eyes went to the observation booth high above. If someone was up there, he couldn't see them.

Relax, Davi! You're being paranoid! Trust God! Have faith!

He felt like a fool for having such doubt, but then who wouldn't, given the uncertainties? He wasn't alone in worrying about it. He hoped the combined efforts of his friends and coworkers would lead to answers soon.

Climbing back to his feet, he glanced once more at the observation booth then wound his way along the path again through the vegetation, taking note of whatever caught his eye. The curators had done an amazing job of collecting samples of native flora and fauna from each planet in the system, except a few outer ones where no such life was known. The combined colors, scents, shapes and sizes were a delight for the senses, and he took a moment to savor the divergent smells and sounds again as he reached the door.

Thank you, God, for the beauty of your nature. Such sights reminded him of God's ever-present spirit wherever he went. That presence was a great comfort to him right now. He glanced at his chrono and realized he had to call Tela before everyone went to bed. He pushed the button and waited as the door slid open before him, then stepped out into the steamy, noisy Legon night and headed for home.

Bordox slipped into the observation box above the Legon Botanical Garden quietly and found himself alone. He smiled. No one to recognize him. The lengths he'd gone to disguising himself might well be unnecessary. He'd retrieved and transmitted the information to his contacts on Xanthis without difficulty using a secure channel on his small transport. Then he'd landed again at the starport, claiming engine trouble and put his plan into motion. He could coordinate his assassins fine from anywhere. So far, except for the failed attempt on the slave Lord, they'd done their job well. A worker on the Council? He shuddered just thinking about it.

The time had come for him to take care of his own goals, not just those of his father and Xalivar. They'd isolated him away from them anyway, so they didn't need to know where he was or what he was doing. They'd both blow a vapor seal, of course. But Bordox was his own man. Sending the data instead of delivering it in person sent a strong message.

He watched Xander Rhii through the dark windows and smiled. His nemesis seemed deeply troubled. *Perhaps you're feeling a bit as you've made me feel, Rhii!* He chuckled at the thought. The hatred inside sent waves of warmth through his body. Rhii deserved to suffer as much as possible, and Bordox would make that happen, following his enemy wherever he went until the right opportunity to dispose of him presented itself. He wouldn't let the opportunity slip away like it had on Vertullis and Eleni 1. This time Xander Rhii would pay for what he'd done. Rhii paced amongst the foliage on a narrow path, looking lost in thought.

Worried about your friends Yao and Farien? The woman? Your family? The slaves you call your people? Bordox wouldn't stop at Rhii. He'd kill the woman and as many of Xander Rhii's loved ones as he could. If he got lucky, some would die before Rhii did, so Bordox could make him suffer. Others would be dealt with after. Perhaps even at the funeral. It hardly mattered as long as they all died.

He watched as Xander knelt on soft mossy soil beside the path and placed his hands together, his lips moving as he said a prayer.

"Gods, Rhii! A convert of their fool religion, too?!" Bordox laughed. "You will all see very soon that your God has no power to protect you!"

Bordox continued watching as Rhii finished his prayer then slowly turned and looked up at the observation booth. Bordox shrunk back from the window in panic, then remembered the booths can see out, but no one outside can see in. He was tired of hiding. Tired of Xander Rhii. He cursed Xalivar's orders. *Soon, Rhii, soon.*

Remaining in the shadows but still close enough to see, he continued watching his old rival until he left, slipping out quietly and unnoticed to follow him home.

Chapter Four

A cool breeze had swept over Xalivar in the courtyard as he exercised under the rising twin suns. Tickling his skin like Daken down, it made him feel more alive than ever. Smiling as he finished, he strode inside, greeting Manaen and the minor staff as he passed them in the corridors. He chuckled at their surprise. Keeping people on edge delighted him. He was having a great morning...until Manaen brought the report. Bordox had decided to remain on Legallis, even though it was expressly against Xalivar's orders. The assassination attempt on Aron had been foiled by Xalivar's former nephew, Xander, and a female companion. Xalivar needed better people. Their standards for themselves weren't high enough.

His teeth ground together as he growled, tired of being disappointed. "What kind of incompetents can't dispose of an old man, a woman and a boy?" He whirled to face Obed and Lucius who sat quietly waiting. "Your maladroit son has decided he doesn't need to follow orders, Obed. I should have known not to give him any important duties."

Despite Obed's obvious attempt to hide his reaction, he wouldn't make eye contact with Xalivar. "I'm sure he has his reasons, Xalivar." No objection this time? So even Obed knew his idiot son had blown his mission.

Xalivar's fists clenched at his side. "I want him back here, and I mean now!" He spun back to reading the message. "He's gone after my derelict former nephew."

"The report says that?"

Xalivar scowled as his eyes met Obed's again. "He's let his desire for personal revenge cloud his judgment. I'm holding you responsible for assuring he gets his focus back."

"I don't control him, Xalivar, any more than you can control your nephew."

Xalivar's clenched right fist flew out against a nearby pillar. "You know nothing about that, Obed! My own sister let that slave in my house and hid his identity from me. When I discovered it, I made sure he was treated appropriately."

"Only when it was discovered by others." Obed's eyes filled with accusations.

"I personally asked the Council to order him apprehended," Xalivar reminded him. "I did my duty to protect the Alliance." Fury rose inside him when the doubt in Obed's eyes never wavered. He pointed an index finger. "Be careful, Obed."

Obed smiled, amused by the warning. "I know my duty, Xalivar. Do you know yours?"

How dare the insolent cretin question him like this! Xalivar wasn't the problem. Obed's son was!

Lucius spoke quietly from a chair in the corner. "Perhaps I can send someone to bring him back. Our plan is succeeding. The information he provided is exactly what we needed. The list of ex-workers in the Borali military gives us plenty of targets. And we can confirm the status and defensive capabilities of all military posts. Information we sorely needed to plan our attacks."

Xalivar looked down, remembering the morning breeze and relaxing his fists as he nodded at the General. "Everything will continue as planned. Obed will coordinate the assassins himself from now on." It was brilliant. Obed wanted to set Xalivar up, so now Xalivar would turn it around and put it all on him.

"He can continue to execute the plan from anywhere, Xalivar," Obed said, his voice still dripping with irritation. "You've given me other responsibilities."

"You will see to it that your son doesn't fail. Your other tasks can still be managed." Xalivar glared at him, his eyes allowing for no argument. "In the meantime, training and recruitment can be increased. With the base construction well on its way, it's time we begin the second phase."

Lucius nodded. "Admiral Dek has the recruiters out and some

have already been successful. We've recruited several Borali officers and a number of foot soldiers as well."

"The disappearance of Alliance military personnel will not go unnoticed," Obed said. "Alliance Command will investigate."

"And find nothing. Their people will simply disappear." Xalivar smiled at the thought of their bafflement.

"They will no doubt be suspicious."

Xalivar brushed Obed's concerns aside with a wave of his arm. "And by the time they discover the cause, it will be too late." He nodded to the two men as his eyes met theirs. "You have your orders. I want regular reports."

Lucius nodded. "As always, my Lord."

Xalivar reread the report again in silence. After a moment, the others assumed he was done and quietly slipped out. Xalivar cursed his former nephew. *Miri will pay for all she's done. Miri and her bastard son!* Xalivar chuckled at the thought. Perhaps he'd even get to watch their faces as they died. Their father would be so disappointed in his daughter. She had thrown away everything their family had worked generations to achieve. *Sister dearest, how I wish I could see you now.* With Tarkanius now the High Lord Councilor, he wondered how she was enjoying life as an ordinary civilian. Miri had always prided herself in her royal status, always been special. Laughter rose from his belly like a wave, echoing off the walls until it filled the chamber around him.

The call to the High Lord Councilor's Palace took Davi by surprise. Atop a rise at the center of Legon, the Palace grounds held an imposing complex of white buildings of various shapes and sizes which offered an unobstructed view of the entire city. The meeting took place in the throne room. Davi hadn't been there since he joined the Worker's Resistance, and although the Palace had been his childhood home, he felt out of place being there again. Every corner he turned brought flooding memories. He'd known every inch of the place, even its secret passages. He'd explored them all in fantasy adventures of his childhood, fighting dragons and other fabled creatures to save the world time and again. Such foolishness it seemed now, yet how many times had he been called on to fight for his people? He'd imagined it as glorious then, but it hardly seemed so now.

Lord Tarkanius stood from the throne and greeted him as he entered, looking older than Davi had ever seen him. His slight paunch hung as if he hadn't the will to hold it in, and his kind eyes were filled with darkness that matched the worry creasing his brow. Davi was surprised to find Aron, Uzah, and Lords Kray and Simeon also in attendance. He'd had no idea why he'd been called there, but now he knew it was important. As he shook the High Lord Councilor's outstretched hand, then placed his right fist atop his left, crossing his right index and second, ring and fifth fingers to form the traditional salute, the others nodded in greeting, somber looks on their faces. Davi stood at attention, waiting expectantly.

"There's been another assassination," Aron said, in a breach of protocol. Usually the High Lord Councilor spoke first at such meetings. Yet Tarkanius didn't even react.

Davi turned to him. "Where?"

"Some sort of sabotage at the mechanic's depot in Alpha Base," Tarkanius answered. "Five mechanics were killed and seven others injured."

Davi couldn't believe it. He'd been stationed at Alpha Base briefly, by his Uncle Xalivar, to protect him when he was wanted for the accidental death of a Borali Sergeant. Located on Plutonis, an ice planet in the outer solar system, it was a remote and barely habitable region, and Davi couldn't imagine an assassin sneaking onto the base undetected.

"We've decided to ask you to represent the workers on the investigation," Tarkanius continued.

Davi looked at Tarkanius, surprised. "I thought Farien had been placed in charge."

"You will work with him and Yao Brahma as partners. Both have been temporarily reassigned to the investigation."

"We need a Vertullian on the team to assure our people it's handled properly," Aron said.

"We can't afford the possibility of any doubt," Lord Kray added.

Aron nodded. "You're one of the heroes of our people now. I'm afraid we must call on you again for service and whatever sacrifice it entails." Davi winced at the thought of being a hero. Certainly the idea would be far from the minds of his mothers and Tela when they heard of this mission. They'd gotten used to Davi being home a lot, in between quiet patrols, and wouldn't react well to Davi taking off on a dangerous assignment.

"It's my honor and privilege to serve my people and the Alliance," Davi responded, offering another salute. But he still worried about how Farien might react. He and Farien had come to loggerheads during Davi's time with the WFR and had just gotten back to a normal relationship. He didn't want to do anything to jeopardize that.

"You seem troubled? What's the matter?" Lord Kray's expression reminded him of Miri and Lura. He hadn't meant to wear his feelings so blatantly on his face.

"It's just Farien. He may see this as a lack of confidence in his abilities. We've managed to put past tensions behind us. I'd hoped to avoid any in the future." Farien had always had insecurities about his superior's confidence in him. This would just stir those up all over again. He didn't relish the thought of reigniting that old conflict with his friend.

"You three will be serving as equals on this assignment," Tarkanius said. "We're hoping your friendship will allow you to cooperate well in the investigation."

"We'll do our best, I can promise you." Davi forced a smile, despite his ongoing inner tension. Whatever his feelings, they weren't asking. The decision had been made. He took a deep breath and met their gazes.

Tarkanius smiled back. "We knew we could count on you."

Aron nodded. "We'll expect regular reports to the High Lord Councilor and me."

"Any resources you may need are at your disposal," Uzah said. "You have only to ask."

Despite any concerns about Farien, Davi felt a sense of relief. Having such support behind them could only make their challenging mission easier. And he wanted to know as much as anyone if his suspicions about Xalivar's responsibility for the attacks were correct. "I won't let you down."

One by one, they each stepped forward to shake his hand and utter words of encouragement. Then, seeing the meeting was over, Davi snapped to attention once more and saluted the High Lord Councilor before turning and marching out the door.

The lectures began from the moment he told them. The ladies followed him around as he packed, pecking at him like Daken hens at seed.

"Why you? There are other competent people," Miri said, hovering over him. "People with a lot more experience at investigations."

"They want to avoid the appearance of any impropriety." Davi folded his spare uniform just in case. "The Vertullian people are demanding answers."

"Of course we are!" Lura said, moving up beside Miri so close Davi almost couldn't move around as he packed. "Our people are being slaughtered."

Davi's eyes met hers. "And it's my job to find out who's responsible."

"How long will you be gone?" Tela asked from her position leaning against his bedroom doorway. Of the three, she was the most subdued, which really had him worried.

"As long as it takes."

All three ladies frowned. "You have no idea then?" Tela refused to make eye contact.

Davi finished neatly folding his uniform and placed it into his bag, then gently pushed between his mothers and crossed to her, putting his hands on her waist. "I'll be fine. I promise."

She brushed his hands away and straightened as she faced him. "You don't know that! These people have been committing murders. They won't be afraid of killing you."

"I have a duty to the Alliance."

"What about your duty to me?" She turned away, arms

crossed over her chest.

"You know I love you. And I really need your support."

Tela's lips pursed and her brows knit as she turned back to face him. "And I love you, too, but I'm scared, Davi. We have our whole lives ahead of us. What about all our plans? Our dreams?"

"Those things will all happen, Tela. I want to spend the rest of my life with you. But I'm a soldier and these are orders from the High Lord Councilor."

"Maybe I should stop by the Palace and let the High Lord Councilor know how I feel about his orders then." She put her hands on her hips, her blue eyes darkening and lips puffing out as she said it. Her face was determined, but he saw in her eyes she was only bluffing.

"I'd certainly go with you," Miri said, her determination not wavering at all.

"For heaven's sake, leave the boy alone," Sol said from his position in the hallway. The women scowled as Sol and Telanus poked their heads through the doorway. "He's an excellent soldier. He knows what he's doing."

"Of course you men are behind this. You love nothing more than proving your manhood by fighting and killing." Miri glowered.

"I'd hope we don't have to fight or kill anyone," Davi said.

Miri looked at him and shook her head. "You know this won't end without a fight. Don't lie to your mother, Davi."

Lura rushed toward Davi and wrapped her arms around him. "You be careful."

She held on so tight he had trouble breathing for a moment, then he pushed her gently away as he hugged her back, nodding. "Of course I will." He let her head rest on his shoulders a moment before dropping his hands.

Miri embraced him next. "We expect regular reports of your welfare. Don't disappoint us."

"I'll communicate when I can."

"That's all anyone can ask," Telanus said as he put a comforting arm around Tela.

Davi extended his right hand first to Sol and then Telanus.

Both shook it firmly. "We're very proud of you, son," Sol said with a warm smile.

Davi choked back tears as he turned to Tela. Moving towards her as Telanus lowered his arm, Davi embraced her, then reached up to wipe away the tears which rolled down her cheeks. "I've already requested that you lead the squadron while I'm away. Make me proud, okay?"

She sniffled and smiled. "You know I will."

He leaned forward and she leaned in to meet him. The kiss was passionate, almost as if all their emotions were channeled into it. They stayed with their foreheads touching after they finished, staring into each other's eyes. "You are my future."

Tela nodded, sniffling again. "Mine, too." It came out as a croak, barely audible.

Davi smiled. He kissed her again then gathered himself as he moved back toward his suitcase. "I have to finish packing. I'm to be on my way as soon as possible."

Tela hugged him again, then let go and moved toward the bed and began folding the rest of the clothes he'd laid out there in silence. They worked side by side for the next few minutes as their parents quietly slipped from the room. When they'd finished, Davi closed the suitcase. Tela reached over and grabbed his hand, squeezing it tightly. Then they embraced and kissed again, and Davi wished he'd never have to leave her.

Bordox watched from inside his shuttle across the landing bay as Xander went through pre-launch preparations in his fighter. From the quantity and type of cargo being loaded in the VS28s small hold, he could tell Xander was leaving on more than just a routine patrol.

"Where are we going, Rhii?" He said to himself, knowing wherever his nemesis went, he would follow. He was just awaiting the right opportunity to enact revenge.

He heard the hum of the fighter's engines as Xander initialized the pre-launch sequence. Bordox started his own shuttle and did the same. When Xander launched a few minutes later, Bordox launched through the civilian launch tube and sped around until he spotted the VS28 and slid into position to follow. Xander was following the standard military flight path, so Bordox just blended into a civilian route that paralleled it and kept his sensor locked on the fighters' vapor trail. In their Academy days, Xander had proved the better pilot but no more. Bordox had been practicing, even getting coaching from a few mercenaries. He'd fly circles around him now. Maybe this trip would give him the chance.

As they passed through the atmosphere, Xander turned the fighter toward nearby Eleni 1. "Going to see your old friends, are you?" Bordox chortled at the possibility of enacting revenge on all three of the troublemakers. It would ensure Xander's friends never bothered him after Xander's death, leaving Bordox free to work his way back to prominence in the new Borali military under Xalivar's new government. There'd be no one to prevent him from taking his rightful place this time. He whistled as he matched the shuttle's speed to that of the VS28, then settled back to decide the safest place to land.

Voices echoed off the chamber walls as the assembled Lords chattered while awaiting the High Lord Councilor. Aron did his best to make small talk with Simeon and Kray, but he was too nervous to remember much of what they said. It was quarter past the hour when Tarkanius strode into the chamber. His mood was somber, and before he'd reached the podium, the conversations trailed off. Aron, Simeon and Kray rose from chairs atop the dais to stand behind Tarkanius. The announcement he was about to make was important and Aron hoped the Lords' reactions would not echo those the leaders expressed in regard to the Returning.

"I have just appointed a commission to oversee the investigation into the assassination of Vertullians throughout the system," Tarkanius said as he stood before the mic. "So far there have been four successful attacks, the last of which killed five mechanics at Alpha Base."

The Lords broke into chatter again, some expressing their shock, others proposing theories as to whom was responsible for the violent incidents. Tarkanius raised a hand to silence them.

"The commission will be overseen by Lords Kray and Aron. I have also appointed Lieutenant General Uzah from the Vertullian forces, General Grif from Alliance Command and, to investigate, Captains Davi Rhii and Farien Noa and Lieutenant Yao Brahma, a professor at Presimion." This time the Lords held their chatter, waiting for him to continue. "The attacks seem to be systematic. At this point all that we know is that all of the victims, except one, were Vertullians. And we believe that was an accident and a Vertullian was the target. Attacks have occurred on Legallis, Vertullis, Plutonis, and Xanthis. The assassins in the attempt on Lord Aron were Lhamors. We have yet to confirm the identity of the attackers in the other incidents. I believe the time has come for the Boralians to pull together. The Vertullians are one with us now, our brothers and sisters. We must set an example and show unity and respect as a Council." Aron closed his eyes, offering a quick prayer. The moment had come. "Therefore, I am asking you to vote in favor of Lord Aron's proposal declaring The Returning an official holiday."

To Aron's surprise, the Lords' faces brimmed with support. Some even shouted it out or waved at him. Only a few, including Lords Hachim and Niger expressed their displeasure. The two Lords frowned and shouted in protest. Hachim crossed his arms over his chest while Niger stood and glared at the dais.

"Lord Kray's inquiries to the planetary leadership on all planets showed no serious resistance. And although in the short term some may object, I believe if we pull together in unity, they will come to accept it as we have." Tarkanius looked around the room, making eye contact with the Lords to see if any would object. Aron watched closely but no one stepped forward or voiced an objection. Niger and Hachim just stayed where they were, and Aron glimpsed in their eyes, they knew they'd lost.

Aron stepped forward and Tarkanius motioned him to the podium. He smiled, proud in this moment to be one of them, as he faced his fellow Lords. "I want to assure you all that I share your concerns about tension between our peoples. But we will do our best on Vertullis to earn your trust and respect and be good citizens of the Alliance. I hope you'll give us every opportunity to do so. Your support to this point has been admirable and a blessing, and, on behalf of my people, I thank you." Kray and Simeon began to applaud and soon the chamber filled with its echoes.

Aron nodded to Tarkanius as relief swept over him and took a step back as the High Lord Councilor reclaimed the podium. "I want any reports you receive about attacks on Vertullians given to me and Lords Aron and Kray immediately. And I expect each of you to cooperate fully in anything they may ask of you during your investigation."

Lord Simeon stepped forward to join Tarkanius. "The High Lord Councilor has my full support in this. Please make no public statements without running them by myself and the High Lord Councilor. This situation needs to be handled with great care so that no one says or does anything to jeopardize the investigation." He stepped back again to join Kray and Aron.

"All in favor of declaring The Returning an official holiday say 'aye.'" Tarkanius waited as the responses sounded from around the room. It was clear the Lords were overwhelmingly in favor of it. "Any opposed say 'nay.'"

Although he'd watched Lords Niger and Hachim stay silent while the others approved, both held their tongues, saying nothing now. The mood in the room was one of overwhelming support. Aron quelched an urge to smile. The last thing he needed was to rub his victory in the opposition's faces. But internally, tension rolled off him in waves.

"Congratulations, Lord Aron. Your proposal has been accepted." Tarkanius extended his hand to shake Aron's. Aron beamed. It was one of the proudest moments he could remember.

"Council dismissed," Lord Simeon said again from his seat atop the dais.

The Lords broke into chatter as they scattered. Several came forward to shake Aron's hand.

After bidding Davi goodbye, Miri returned to her chamber in sadness. He had a duty to obey his commanders. The High Lord Councilor himself had ordered this. But that meant seeing him go off toward danger again. She'd already lost him once when he joined the Resistance and fought for the Vertullian's freedom. He'd told her later of his many near misses. And she'd been relieved when his recent duties involved quiet patrols with little action. Now, still reeling from the animosity she'd encountered amongst her friends at the brunch, her son was being sent off to risk his life. All she'd tried to do was the right thing. Why was it costing her so much?

As the door slid shut and sealed behind her, the lights automatically came on and she moved to her terminal to search for the latest news. A flashing e-post alert filled the screen. She clicked the e-post but it was from an unknown sender. For a moment she was tempted to ignore it, then curiosity got the better of her and she opened it. Her heart raced as she read:

To: MRhii@Federal.emp
From: Unknown

My dearest sister,

It's been too long since we spoke. I'm sure you miss my delightful presence. Don't you? How's my precious nephew? I'd hate it if something happened to him before we meet again. Oh how I miss your voice, the lies, the betrayal. I imagine you hoped you were done with me. But I'm afraid your wishes won't be granted in this case. Soon, my beloved sister, we will be reunited. I hope you're as anxious for that day as I am.
Your loving brother,
Xalivar

Miri couldn't believe it. She'd known Xalivar was alive when he'd disappeared, escaping the wrath of the Council after his betrayal. But no one had seen or heard from him. Until now. Where was he? She reread the message and felt a chill, her skin tingling. The threat was implicit. Xalivar was bent on revenge. She'd hoped she'd never see him again. She suspected the assassinations of the Vertullians were his handiwork. Maybe it was time to notify the Council. Many of them thought Xalivar was gone with the past, but they didn't know her brother like she did. Xalivar was capable of anything. They had to stop him no matter what.

Davi brought his VS28 in for a landing on the small landing pad near Presimion Academy and made his way across the campus toward the Library. The campus looked much the same as it had almost a year before when the Peace Conference between the Vertullians and Borali Alliance took place. His prior visit had been during the rainy season, but now the Ambrose lilies were abloom, their intoxicating perfume filling the air, and Astreu Vermelho trees wore vibrant leaves of many colors. It was here that his Uncle had tried to arrest him and here that Bordox, his old rival, tried to kill him. It was here that his people won their freedom and the whole world changed.

As he reflected back on all that had happened, he spotted a familiar figure waiting for him outside the Library—a tall, humanoid with dark, orangish-tinted skin and purple eyes. Davi smiled as their eyes met. His old friend offered a wave and a grin.

"They notified me you'd landed. Word of your assignment just came over the military channel." Yao patted Davi on the back. "It's good to see you."

"It's good to see you, too. How'd Farien take the news?"

Yao shrugged. "You know Farien. He'll get over it once we're all together."

Davi shook his head. "We used to be a team, the three of us, helping each other through. When did it become a competition?"

"It's not unless you make it one." Yao was right. Farien would get over it if Davi just focused on what he'd been sent here to do. Yao stepped toward the Library and the large doors slid open, allowing them to walk inside. As they walked side by side through rows of video terminals and data card storage shelves, Davi ignored the activity on the lifts and staircases which connected the seven-story shelves housing a collection of old Earth paper books.

"How's the investigation going?"

"We've reached a dead end locally," Yao said. "Farien took a trip to Vertullis to interview your father and Tela's about the worker killed at their factory. The next step is a trip out to Xanthis and then Alpha Base."

Davi nodded and followed Yao as he zigzagged through study cubes and long tables drowning in stacks of books and papers deposited by the cadets and research assistants who came and went from them like butterflies. "We'll all go together."

Yao shook his head. "I have duties here, classes to teach."

"You've been temporarily reassigned. Someone else will fill in for you."

Yao frowned. "I haven't received any orders."

"Don't they send them through the Provost? They come from the High Lord Councilor himself, so the Provost won't have a choice."

Yao smiled. "The Three Musketeers together again?" Yao loved references to the Old Earth classics he'd read so many of in his spare time.

"You know I keep meaning to read that..."

"You and Farien have no appreciation for the history of the arts."

Davi laughed as they left the Library's main collection and moved into a series of white corridors toward the rear of the building. He squinted at the bright reflector pad glow bouncing off the walls and floor as they passed through. "Since when did they move your office here?"

"It's the only place they had space for Farien. I'm working here temporarily so we can stay easily in touch as things develop."

"How's Dru?"

"Improving. He's back to classes now, but he's not the same positive, carefree kid he used to be. He feels a lot of guilt over Cadet Kowl's death. He thinks it was meant to be him."

"What do you think?"

Yao stopped outside a door, his finger poised on the button. "It's probably not coincidence that Dru's original bunk assignment was the one where Cadet Kowl was killed." He pushed the button and the door slid open.

Davi saw Farien bearing a frustrated scowl as he scanned data on a monitor. "Look who I found." Yao's voice was cheerful in an obvious effort to diffuse any tension.

Davi strode forward and extended his hand. "They tell me you've done a great job here, Farien. I promise I'll do my best to be an asset and stay out of your way."

"We're all listed as equal by command. I'm told the High Lord Councilor himself ordered it."

Davi nodded. "The Council wants a Vertullian representative on the investigation to assure the people it's been handled fairly."

Farien glared. "I've served the Alliance with integrity. They have no reason to doubt me." The reaction Davi had expected. Yao sighed as he and Davi exchanged a look.

"No one's doubting you, Farien," Davi said. "But you served as an overseer of worker labor on Vertullis."

Farien spun toward him in rage. "I was always fair in my treatment of them!" For a moment, Davi half expected him to leap from his chair but Farien stayed there, seated, staring up at them.

"No one's saying you weren't, but there are political implications to this."

"What about all I did to help the workers and you since then? Does that count for anything?"

"Of course it does. This isn't about you."

Farien ignored him. "I have everything under control."

"I'm sure you do. And I'm counting on you to bring me up to speed."

"Come on, Farien," Yao said with a smile. "It's just like old times, right?"

Farien frowned at him. "Oh yeah, Xalivar threatening us, Bordox causing trouble, trying to kill us—"

"Actually, it was usually me he wanted to kill," Davi said with a grin.

"Bordox torturing me...oh yeah, good times." Farien's face remained stern, but Davi detected a glint in his eyes.

"Bordox and Obed arrested by the Council," Yao inserted.

Farien raised a hand to stop them. "Please, you're making me tear up." He broke into a grin. "That last part was well deserved." Davi and Yao laughed.

"Agreed," Yao said. "We don't get many excuses to pal around these days. It'll be just like old times."

Farien brushed it off with a wave. "We have no choice. We're under orders from the Palace."

He was starting to sound like the old Farien. Davi grinned.

Farien motioned to a datacard file box on the desk beside his monitor. "All the information we've gathered so far is on these cards. It would be easiest if you spent some time reviewing them. Yao and I can answer any questions you have."

"Can't one of you brief me a bit—"

Farien frowned. "Stop wasting time and get to reading, Captain."

Davi laughed. "What about all that stuff you said about the three of us being equals?"

"I'll treat you like an equal when you start pulling your weight. You can't do that until you're up to speed, so get busy."

Davi offered a mock salute. "Yes, sir." Yao laughed as Farien held out the data card file to Davi.

"There's another terminal next door you can use," Yao said as Davi accepted the file from Farien. "I'll get you set up in there."

It was heavier than he'd expected, forcing Davi to balance it against an arm as he carried it. Davi followed Yao back out into the corridor.

After some quick talking to get through military patrols, Bordox landed his shuttle in a clearing outside Eleni 1's capital city, Joia, in an agricultural district far enough out not to draw ground security forces' attention. He'd been allowed to land by blending in with farm traffic, and the last thing he needed was further attention, even if it meant he'd have to find a transport into the city to locate Xander and his friends.

His lungs felt heavier as he stepped off the shuttle. Although the atmosphere on the moon was comparable to that of Legallis, where he'd grown up, Bordox had spent so much time lately in the thin atmosphere of Xanthis and other planets that it would take a bit for his body to adjust. If he got lucky, he'd be inside the domed city long before it mattered. Joia kept the atmosphere inside its dome much closer to that of Legallis than the outer areas. He wondered if natives had difficulty with the changes every time they stepped outside the dome.

Making his way through the dense foliage and tall Dalee trees surrounding the clearing, he heard the calls of Eleni falcons as they circled hunting their prey somewhere overhead. The grunts and whines of Eleni bovines sounded around him in call and response patterns almost resembling echoes as the animals talked to each other. The bovines were called Krikatrus officially but nicknamed Krikees by locals if he recalled—a stupid nickname appropriate to a planet full of stupid people. He heard rustling in nearby Mrobi bushes and saw shadows skittering between branches. One of the falcons' intended victims was on the run.

"Run, little ones," he mumbled with a grin. *Real hunters will chase you to moon's end.* Bordox was a real hunter. No matter how far or fast Xander Rhii fled, he knew he would eventually find and defeat him. Moving on, he kept his eyes peeled for a road busy enough for him to flag down an air taxi into the city.

Davi spotted a tuft of red hair before they found Dru studying in a cube on the third level of the Library. His face was a mix of surprise and delight at seeing Davi. "What are you doing here?!"

Davi shrugged. "I hear you've been nothing but trouble. Someone had to come and straighten you out." He laughed as

Dru embraced him like a long-lost brother. The young cadet looked haggard and his energy was lower than usual.

"You know me, trouble seems to find me. I don't even have to look for it."

Davi rolled his eyes. "That sounds so familiar." He turned serious even as Dru laughed. "I'm sorry about your friend."

Dru nodded and looked away. "It shouldn't have been him."

"It shouldn't have been any of you, and we're going to find who's responsible. I promise."

Dru nodded, his eyes avoiding Davi's as he sat back down at a desk and fiddled with the buttons on the keyboard.

"The professors said you've been doing better in your classes." Yao shot Davi a sympathetic look.

Dru dismissed it with a wave. "I can focus better, for what that's worth."

"I'm sure I can get everything I need from the reports Yao and Farien have already written, but if you need anything, I'll be working with them on the investigation, okay?"

Dru looked up and smiled. "It's good to see you, Captain."

"The whole squadron misses you," Davi said with a grin. "They keep complaining about how much more fun your life here must be compared to our patrols."

Dru guffawed. "They have no idea, do they?"

Davi shook his head. Dru turned back to his studies, chuckling to himself as Yao and Davi slipped quietly away.

"We have a lead on Xanthis," Yao said. "We're planning to head out there in a couple of days."

Davi nodded. "Good. I've never been there. Should be interesting." He kept staring back at Dru, wondering if the boy he'd once trained would ever be the same. Dru was focused at the terminal now but stood out from the students around him with the face of a kid with a whole world weighing him down.

"He'll be fine. Trust me. It's just the shock and fear. He's taken it harder than most of the others, but he'll recover in time." It was Yao's turn to pat Davi reassuringly on the back.

"So it's either depressed Dru or angry Farien. Not many good options for us, huh?"

Yao chuckled. "We could stop for a draft in the faculty lounge. I mean, if I left that off the tour, it would be sheer neglect."

"And horrible manners." Davi led the way.

Finding a place to connect the data interceptor Xalivar had provided proved easy. Bordox simply walked into the data center at Joia's small starport, signed in under his fake name for an available private cube, and plugged it into the terminal's port. The data center had ten private cubes lining the walls around two long counters containing rows of open terminals. Only four of the private and six of the open terminals were occupied, so Bordox was just another traveler checking in with the office back home or making arrangements he didn't want to be public. He couldn't have blended in better if he'd tried.

Despite its status as the home of a premiere preparation school for future Borali military officers, Eleni 1 was hardly a major destination and Joia's starport was its major point of entry. It took only a few simple commands before Bordox had the interceptor feeding him data from all sorts of sources, and, within five minutes, he'd isolated it down to the Academy itself and begun searching for Xander, Farien, and Yao's signatures. *Amateurs.*

So far their investigation seemed to be going nowhere. Bordox amused himself imagining their rising frustration. He saw the orders assigning Xander to join the investigation team. No doubt Farien would view that as a sign of distrust by his superiors. *He always was paranoid. Idiot.* But then Bordox didn't trust anyone either. Only his father and two loyal friends. He'd been betrayed enough to know that only a foolish man put his faith in his fellow humankind. He couldn't blame Farien for being wary, but Farien didn't even trust those who'd shown him loyalty and dedication his entire life. Farien had many more people like that than Bordox. It showed Farien was weak and lacked the timber of a true officer.

His mind filled with images of their frustrated faces. Bordox settled in and sent an e-post for an order of food to be delivered. He hoped his wait wouldn't be a long one, but he had no intention of wandering anywhere he might be noticed or, gods forbid, recognized. Better to just settle in here and make like any other traveling businessman using Joia's blip-on-the-map port to take care of important business dispatches and other activities on his way to somewhere far more important.

Farien's e-post arrived even before his food did—a notification to command of his plan to travel with Yao and Xander to Xanthis to investigate the Lhamori assassins. The mention of Xanthis raised his blood pressure. Could Xalivar's operation have been given away somehow? No, it was too well hidden. Farien's report mentioned only the attack on a worker couple there and suspicions about the assassins for which Xanthis had a known underground market. His old rivals were going to the heart of the matter and they didn't even know? Bordox laughed. He couldn't wait for his assassins to give them a surprise. If he were lucky, none of the three would make it to Xanthis.

Bordox relaxed as he finished reading. They had nothing to go on. The trip was routine and predictable. Since the assassins had been hired through an off-planet contact from Xanthis and neither Bordox, Obed, nor Xalivar had been involved, they would be impossible to trace. Bordox's first contact with them had been through comm-links, and, at the starport on Legallis, he hadn't even told them his name. *Alien freaks!* Who cared if they got caught? Lhamori assassins were notorious for killing themselves before interrogators' techniques ever extracted anything useful. His old classmates' trip to Xanthis would prove to be another disappointing dead end. They were total incompetents. Farien even outlined their travel plans in his e-post, a security breach only an amateur would make, but then Farien never had been the smartest, and neither the investigators nor their superiors would ever suspect spies intercepting such routine communications. None of it would matter anyway.

He typed a command and the interceptor sent the travel data to its memory card. Bordox would send all three assassins. Only two of the three were traveling by VS28 fighters. Yao would be in a military transport, so he could be easily dispatched first, leaving the three assassins to deal with two distraught friends who'd be taken totally by surprise. It would all be over too quickly. Bordox's only disappointment was that he himself couldn't take part in it. *Just to see the look on your face, Rhii, that would be worth it.* He'd have the assassins record all audio channels on the off chance they'd intercept something he could replay and enjoy later as he celebrated the end of his troublemaking rival.

The last thing he did before ejecting the data card was initiate the script Xalivar had installed there. Bordox had no idea what the script would do, but he'd deliberately put it off for last to avoid the risk of detection. The script only took seconds to run; the terminal beeped as it finished. Bordox hit the eject button and grabbed the datacard, sliding it back into place in his bag as he hurried out the door.

"I want to go with you."

Davi turned his head and looked down from the cockpit of his VS28 to see Dru faced off with Yao beside the transport, looking tense and confrontational. Yao wore a blue flight suit similar to Davi's while Dru wore his old red WFR flight suit.

"It's an official Alliance investigation. You're not a military officer. Besides, you have school work that's important."

Dru shook his head, his eyes never leaving Yao's. "I need to go with you. I need to find who did this."

Yao lifted a hand and placed it on Dru's shoulder in an attempt to calm him. "I understand how you feel, but you'll just be in the way. We can't worry about protecting you and find the killer at the same time."

"I fought in the Resistance. I have the training. You don't need to protect me."

"You can't come. That's the end of it!" Farien's voice came from Davi's right, filled with irritation.

Dru whirled around, looking for Farien, who was in the

cockpit of his own VS28. "You can't order me like some soldier."

"You're training to be a soldier. If you can't follow orders, might as well quit." Farien didn't even look up as he said it, his face stern. "Cadets aren't allowed on official missions."

Davi stood in his cockpit and made his way down the ladder, drawing Dru's attention. "We know how you feel, Dru, but we'd need permission from command, and that's really unlikely. On top of that, you're in no condition to help."

Dru's hands went to his hips, his chin lifting as his legs spread in defiance. "I worked hard to get where I am! To not be cut out of important missions!"

Davi nodded. "I know. You're on an important mission. The first of our people to be admitted. A role model for everyone who follows. We need you here, doing well, focused."

Dru shook his head. "I can't focus on anything right now but getting the bastards who are killing our people."

Davi closed his eyes, taking a deep breath. It was so hard to refuse. He knew he'd feel the same way if their roles were reversed. "You can't, Dru. I'm sorry."

Dru's eyes filled with fury as he spun and marched back the way he'd come.

The look still haunted Davi as he flew in formation with Farien's VS28 and Yao's transport. Designed for as many as two pilots and four passengers, military transports were similar to shuttles except for armament and FTL capabilities, and the restraints attached to each passenger seat in case prisoners were along. They were also dark with only small official seals on the hatches indicating their official nature.

"You didn't have to be so hard on him." Davi keyed his comm and glanced over at Farien.

"If he wants to be an officer, he has to learn the chain of command." Farien showed not even the slightest sympathy. Why was he so wound up? Still angry about Davi being assigned to his team?

"Look, I know you're upset about the decision to send me here, but don't punish him."

Farien glanced over, his eyes squinting at Davi. "I'm not mad.

I have a mission. And that's my sole focus."

"He'll get over it, Davi," Yao said from the transport. "Dru does need to learn how to accept orders, even when he doesn't like them. And you're right, he belongs at school. It'll take all of his focus to catch up as it is."

A beep on his console distracted Davi before he could respond. Three incoming contacts of unknown origin. "You guys seeing this?" He punched a button and put his computer to work with its usual scans: speed, shields, firepower, etc. The sparse results looked all too familiar.

"Yeah. Type unknown. Who are they?" Yao's voice shook with tension as Davi reached down and flipped on his shields. His friend had never flown in real combat before, just simulations at the Academy, and to be alone in a transport with only manual turrets now wouldn't help things. Davi would have to keep a close eye on him.

"Better find out." Farien didn't wait for an answer, sending his fighter into an arc and looping back toward the targets. "You stay with, Yao. I'll be right back."

"Three against one? Better to stay together," Davi warned, but Farien was already gone. He closed in with Yao, tightening formation. Moments later, they heard an explosion over the comm.

"Farien? What's going on?" Yao sounded alarmed.

Davi wished Yao still had a fighter. A military transport needed a gunner to be effective in a dogfight. It was up to Farien and him. "Get ahead of us, while we head them off. You can't do much good alone."

"Do I have a choice? Why can't professors have fighters?" The transport's engines flared as Yao accelerated, speeding on ahead. "You two be careful."

"Farien, what are we up against?" An explosion to portside rocked the fighter. Davi had been so distracted he hadn't seen the target approach. His scanner showed an enemy ship locked onto his tail. He accelerated and began evasive maneuvers. "Damn it, Farien! Where are you?"

"I'm a little busy right now with some old friends!" Farien's ship came into view on the scanner with two targets tailing him. He went into a dive, then arced around on top of the contacts and fired at them, hitting one in the wing.

Davi watched through his blastshield as one of the targets locked back onto his friend's tail. The ship looked familiar, so dark it was almost hidden against the starfield—a stealth ship like they'd encountered on patrol!

"Just like the one we questioned with the squadron."

"Yep. Only this one brought buddies along." Davi saw Farien's fighter go into a dive again. "They're fast, too."

"Hang on while I give you a hand," Davi answered, turning his ship toward the others, as his cockpit shook from another blast exploding off his right wing. The targets were moving so fast, his computer couldn't provide useful tactical alternatives.

"You've got troubles of your own," Farien said, turning his fighter toward Davi.

For the next few minutes, the five ships shifted position like checkers on a board, explosions beating them back and forth, but no one managing to score any direct hits or damage beyond singed fuselages and frayed nerves. The ships zigzagged in and out, switching places with the enemy on Davi and Farien's tails and then Davi and Farien on theirs. Davi banked right, then hard left, the move jostling him so hard against the cockpit wall, he feared his whole left side would be black and blue. He felt a sharp pain as the family necklace he always wore under his flight suit jabbed his flesh. Ignoring the sweat sliding down his forehead, he blinked, trying to regain focus as it stung his eyes. The target was coming straight at him. They both fired within seconds of each other. The target banked at the last moment, sending the blast from Davi's fighter's triple canons wide to explode in empty space, but the target's own blast raked a line down Davi's fighter's right wing.

Davi slammed his joystick forward and went into a dive to avoid further shots, glancing over at his damaged wing. The VS28 still handled well, but it wouldn't stay that way with a few more hits like that. Growling, he rolled the fighter and dove back up to reengage, attempting to lock onto his attacker's tail. The pilot dodged his every attempt, staying just out of range.

"They're fast. You're right. Who are these guys?" he mumbled into the comm as he saw Farien land a hit. The enemy scurried away as smoke peeled from a charred hole just below his blastshield, but the damage didn't affect his ship's ability to maneuver.

"You okay?" Farien turned back to inspect the damage to Davi's fighter.

"For now, yeah, but that one hurt."

Then one of the targets whizzed between them and both fired. Farien's shots hit the blastshield and ricocheted off and away. Davi's missed and exploded near Farien's engines. "Shoot them, not me!"

Davi chuckled, mumbling, "You make it so tempting though." Davi lined up on the ship chasing Farien and saw the targeting screens flash as his weapons locked on. "Got him!"

He fired again, using both his nose and twin wing cannons again, and watched his lasers travel straight for the target's engines. Farien lined up on the ship following Davi and fired, but his shots missed as the target behind him exploded.

"Nice shot," Farien said. "Give me a moment and I'll try again." But he was too late.

The enemy tailing Davi had already fired again. Davi tried to evade but was jolted back in his seat when the laser bolts exploded inside one of his engines. Davi heard Farien curse over the comm as he ran a diagnostic to check the damage. "That oughta slow me down."

"Good thing there are only two of them left."

Davi checked the scanner and saw only one blip. "Only one on the scanner. Where's the third one?"

Both he and Farien spun their heads, scanning through their blast-shields. Davi reset his scanner with the same results. The lone enemy stayed locked on Davi's tail as Davi swung his ship in wide arcs and jerky turns in an attempt to stay out of target range. "Would you take him out before he hits my other engine?" The scanner beeped and Davi looked around, spotting Yao's transport circling back with the third ship on its tail.

"I need a little help here, guys!" Yao called. With his ship's minimal systems, Davi guessed Yao must be having to do all targeting and evasives manually. He couldn't keep it up long against this enemy's speed.

"I'm coming." Farien switched direction, turning his fighter toward Yao. Davi's fighter rocked as the ship tailing him landed a hit on his left wing.

"You okay, Davi?" Yao sounded worried.

Davi's eyes scanned his instruments. "Yeah, just a scratch. But the next one will hurt me."

He dove, evading the tailing ship's next shots, but the enemy stayed with him, diving back into position at his rear. Suddenly a panel atop the transport opened and a laser turret appeared, firing at the ship chasing Davi.

"You can control the turrets like that?" Davi's voice shook as an enemy shot exploded outside his blastshield. Beads of sweat started dripping on his brow.

Yao sounded confused. "No. Not sure what's happening."

The turret fired again and the ship chasing Davi exploded.

"That was a hell of a shot!" Farien sounded as impressed as Davi was.

"What shot? It wasn't me. I'm a little busy flying."

Farien's fighter dove in and fired at the ship tailing Yao, but it abruptly changed direction and accelerated, fleeing for safety as Farien maneuvered and gave chase.

"Who's there?" Yao's question was drowned out by cursing from Farien.

"You missed?"

"I'm a better shot than that!" Farien cursed again.

Davi watched, relieved as his friend's fighter turned and circled back toward them.

"Forget it for now. Let's find a place to land and inspect the damage." And find out who's on board Yao's transport. Davi had a pretty good idea, and Farien was going to be furious. He only hoped he could get there first and mediate. Tension left his body, as slid down to relax again in his cockpit seat, stretching his limbs.

Farien rejoined them and they headed toward the outer moon,

Zeeri, which was vacant except for a storage facility. The dock had just enough room to land their three ships and take off again. He hoped they'd be ready. Especially Dru.

Chapter Five

You had no business sneaking aboard that transport!"
Davi thought Farien might actually pace himself right
into the wall. Unless his head exploded first. He wouldn't
make eye contact with any of them and Davi expected to
see steam rising off of him any moment.

"I told you, I need to do this!" Dru stood defiantly, staring
him down in the landing bay of the supply depot on Zeeri. The
techs there had been quite surprised to receive an emergency
landing request from three military vessels. The bay barely had
room for them to land and take off, but after examining it closely,
Davi knew his VS28 wasn't going anywhere without repairs.
Three of the techs were pouring over the fighter doing all they
could but parts would have to be brought from the nearest depot.

"You were given a direct order!" Farien whirled and tapped
his index finger hard against the cadet's chest.

"I don't take orders from you yet!" Dru pushed the finger
away, defiantly.

Farien lifted his arm, causing Davi and Yao to jump between
them for fear Farien might strike the young cadet. "Calm down,
Farien. He saved our butts out there!"

Farien's eyes stung Davi's face like a sunray as his friend
whirled to glare at him. "We would have been fine!"

"You said: 'That was a hell of a shot!' I heard it on the
comm!" At Dru's comment, Farien froze, anger boiling again,
refusing to look at him.

"It was a great shot," Yao agreed with a smile, then turned
somber as he saw Dru's glowing reaction. "But you're in the
Academy preparing to enter the military. If you can't learn to obey

orders, whether you like them or not, you might as well quit."

Dru groaned. "You're all three welcome, ok? I'm not going back!" The cadet had no understanding of why they were so concerned.

"Yes, you are! I'm calling in another transport to pick you up!" Farien nodded for emphasis, looking at Davi and Yao for backup. But Dru's excited gaze never faltered.

"I can just steal a ship and follow, you know? I know how to fly."

"Not many ships around here to steal, so good luck finding one!" Farien turned toward his VS28. Davi's hand on his arm stopped him.

Davi turned back to Dru, forcing back his own frustration to speak with a calm tone. "It's not so easy stealing military ships. Get caught and your career's over. Plus you just announced that plan to everyone here." Mechanics around the hangar gaped at them. Davi's eyes met Dru's as he assessed his former trainee. "Don't you want to catch whoever did this? We can't have an emotional victim interfering while we investigate." Dru's persistence was a character trait which served him well during their flight training. But Davi wasn't so sure it was a good thing in this situation.

"You're emotional, too. Your friend was attacked." Dru's eyes darted away from Davi's stare. Davi could see his mind racing.

Davi smiled, acquiescing. "Yes. And our people are being killed. None of us like that. But this is far more personal for you. The last thing we need is you going off half-cocked on a witness or suspect and threatening our investigation."

"I can help you, Davi! If you'd just think about it." Dru's eyes flitted between Davi and Yao, trying to win them over. "You're military men, officers. You stand out in a crowd. I'm just a kid. No one takes me seriously. I can lurk around unobserved in places you can't; talk with people who'd be uncomfortable talking with you."

Davi and Yao exchanged a look—he was right.

"What about your classes?" Yao frowned at Dru, playing the concerned professor.

"Field experience is more important than classroom learning. You told us that during orientation." Dru's tone changed, his expression turning thoughtful.

Yao grimaced, looking at Davi. "How did I know I'd come to regret that?"

Dru smiled, all enthusiasm again. "See? We listen to you. Come on! I want to help catch whoever killed Cadet Kowl." He looked first at Yao, then Davi, then back to Yao, hopeful as a baby Qiwi.

Yao shrugged at Davi and both turned to Farien, who was pacing along a nearby wall.

"I can get you excused from classes for the week, but if you miss much more than that, you'll never catch—" Yao stopped, drowned out by Dru's whoop.

Farien turned and shook his head vehemently. "Uh-uh. No way. I'm running this investigation."

"I'll take all responsibility," Yao said.

"He and I both," Davi echoed.

"You're damn right you will!" Farien growled. "If that kid screws up, they're not hanging this one on me!" Farien slammed his fist against a nearby beam then cringed with the pain.

Dru practically bounced as he headed for the transport, his body language showing he knew he'd won.

"If we're partners, how come you two aren't backing me up?" Farien looked at the others, cutting them with cold eyes as he rubbed his sore hand.

Davi shrugged, amused. "We could wait days for another transport, Farien. Besides, Yao's the one who actually said he could come." Farien winced again.

Yao coughed, stifling a laugh and waved a finger at Davi. "You didn't object to it!"

"Can you two sort this out later?" Farien frowned. "Let's get the parts ordered for the VS28 and get back in the air, ok?" Exchanging amused looks, Davi and Yao saluted Farien. "Don't make me write a report asking command to put me officially in charge of you."

Farien motioned toward Davi's damaged fighter. Davi

yawned, covering a laugh and hurried over to get back to cataloging the damage. His fighter's right engine was a charred, melted mass. It would need to be replaced and the scorching to the surrounding fuselage would require replacement panels and a new paint job. On closer inspection, his wing was also worse than he'd thought. The dark streaks he'd seen from the cockpit concealed tears in the fuselage which had to be repaired. He was lucky he'd been able to land where he did, instead of winding up stranded in deep space.

An hour later, a request had been sent to command for a maintenance shuttle to drop in on the supply depot and assist with the repairs, and Davi joined Yao at the controls of the transport as Farien started launch preparations nearby in his VS28. The supply techs didn't seem sorry to see them go. They left Dru to himself in the passenger compartment and followed Farien out of the atmosphere and back on course for Xanthis.

Xalivar's fists clenched as he finished the report and then started reading it all over again. Once or twice his datapad almost popped out from between his tightening fingers but he caught himself, relaxing his grip so it slid back down into place as he continued. Xalivar hated whiners.

Assassins of unknown origin had attacked Xander Rhii and two companions as they left Eleni 1 to fly to Xanthis. So Xander Rhii was coming to him? Xalivar smiled at the thought of an encounter. But that pleasure would have to wait. First, he would have to calm Pres who was convinced the attack had been ordered by Xalivar and feared that the peak in official interest it brought would lead to the discovery of her communication with Xalivar and the entire plot. Xalivar cursed her for being so weak minded. Why couldn't she trust that he had many safeguards in place? Borali officialdom would only discover what he wanted them to discover, when he wanted them to discover it.

"You sent for us, my Lord?" Lucius entered with Obed, interrupting his thoughts at just the right moment. The last thing he needed was to lose focus in anger.

He whirled to face them as they came to a stop a few feet away. "Your son's revenge scheme could jeopardize everything we've worked for," he said, pointing an accusing finger at Obed.

"My son will soon be back with us," Obed said with confidence.

"You've made contact?"

Obed shook his head, still smug. "No, but I sent an inquiry through personal channels. And when he responds, he won't dare disobey me."

"Disobey you how? By launching personal attacks on Borali military pilots in flight perhaps?" Xalivar watched Obed carefully. The wavering appeared first in the former Councilor's eyes. "Three assassins attacked two VS28s and a transport en route to Xanthis from Eleni 1, only hours ago. Do you suppose the identity of those pilots might make me suspect your son?"

"Who were they?" Obed frowned.

Xalivar locked his eyes on Obed as he responded, "Captains Farien Noa, Xander...Davi Rhii, and Professor Yao Brahma."

Obed's eyes avoided Xalivar's. "He knows them, yes, but they've all three made many enemies betraying our people."

"Your son goes rogue and his lead rivals from the Academy are attacked, and you want me to believe it is coincidence? You take me for a fool, Obed!" Obed simply stood where he was, stiff as if at attention. "Worry not, though. I'll deal with it. If you can't control your own son, I have men who can fulfill that responsibility." He glared at Obed, who finally met his eyes. Both knew the meaning of the threat.

"I will leave at once to bring him back," Obed said, his determination weakening.

"If you even know where to find him." Xalivar waved dismissively as Obed hurried out. "General, see to it our people not only stop Bordox, but bring me Davi Rhii alive. What happens to Bordox and Rhii's friends is immaterial to me. It's Rhii I want."

Lucius nodded. "Of course, my Lord."

"The training?"

"We have the first platoon assembled, my Lord. They shall begin exercises tomorrow. More will be arriving in the next few days."

Xalivar smiled. "Be sure the transports are handled properly. We cannot risk discovery until the time is right. What of the funds for our fleet?" Xalivar clasped his hands behind his back as he paced and thought.

"Our contacts have not come through with further funding," Lucius replied, looking frustrated. "Perhaps it's time to motivate them in other ways."

Xalivar growled. "They'll be plenty motivated when I'm back in power and they've lost my favor. I think instead it's time to implement the other option we discussed."

Lucius nodded. Only the two of them knew of the secondary plan. Xalivar had entrusted Lucius to make the inquiries and prepare the plan for implementation at a moment's notice. It had risks, but the time had come.

Lucius snapped to attention and saluted. "I won't fail you, my Lord."

Xalivar nodded, pleased, then turned back toward the General. "You never have. You're my best man, Lucius, and very soon you shall be rewarded for it."

Lucius remained rigid, his military training engrained, but his eyes gleamed with pleasure. "Thank you, my Lord."

"And set a meeting with Pres. Her lack of confidence is starting to disturb me. It's time we talked face to face and put her fears to rest."

Lucius' face showed understanding. "It will be difficult for her to get away, my Lord."

Xalivar jerked his head and gave a choppy wave. "Convince her then." Their eyes locked and Lucius nodded, acknowledging the message. "Give her a story about inspecting some facility in a neutral location. I can meet her half way."

"Shall I plan to come along, Lord?"

"No. I'll go personally." If Xalivar couldn't get results, she'd never return from their meeting. Lucius saluted again.

Xalivar took a deep breath and turned away, and Lucius took

it as his cue to leave quietly. Miri's face popped into his mind. She hadn't responded to his earlier missive, but he smiled at the thought of her reaction. Alas, he couldn't give his location away. But he could taunt her. He laughed as the idea came into focus in his head. His most cutting betrayer, his own sister, would soon find out how alive and powerful her departed brother still was.

One woman would have been enough to drive Sol crazy, but Lura and Tela had both been treating him and Telanus like children for the past week. Both men had made excuses about overtime at work and other errands just to get away, and one or another of the women always insisted on going with them on the errands or calling to check on them at work. The only time they'd truly gotten away from them was during questioning by Farien, when they'd been taken inside the command center at the star-port. After a week, Sol was on edge.

"Stop treating us like we were victims! You're driving us nuts!" He sipped a beer to help him relax.

"The assassin could have killed the both of you if you'd been in the wrong place," Lura said, shaking her head.

"We've got enough pressure already with Boralians accusing us of lax security at the plant," Telanus added as the women attempted to stare them down. "They're trying to maneuver back into positions once held only by Boralians and get many of us demoted." He watched the foam settle on his own mug, then tipped it back for a long swallow.

"Well, that's not going to happen," Tela said, her voice sharp with irritation, "because it wasn't your fault. Professional assassins like these could have gotten past security at any plant in the system."

"They don't care about the facts, Tela," Telanus answered. "Just the appearance of incompetence is enough."

Sol nodded. "And this is just one case. I hear they're making similar moves at all locations where workers dominate the workforce. We've heard complaints of unfairness for months, but no one's tried to force change until now."

"It's despicable to use the deaths of workers to make such power plays," Tela said as her face reddened. "They ought to be ashamed!""People will use every opportunity, dear," Lura said with sadness. The effect all the stress was having on her was what worried Sol the most. She'd been through so much already between his time in prison and Davi's disappearance. He never wanted to be the cause of any more heart-ache for her. "...with little regard for circumstances. It's human nature to compete. And since we stood up and fought against unfair treatment, why shouldn't they?" Sometimes Sol wondered how his gentle, sweet wife survived all the trouble they'd faced over their lifetimes.

"This is different and you know it," Tela frowned. "I hope the Council can make some headway quickly. They need to nip this animosity in the bud."

"It will take more than Council edicts for that," Sol said. "You cannot legislate people's fears and emotions." If you could, he had no doubt they'd have already done it. Politicians loved control, but more than that, they hated chaos and the world was roiling with it at the moment.

"Thank God the military's been spared most of that drama," Tela said with a sigh, as she relaxed back onto a chair beside the comm panel and sipped a cold glass of Talis.

"Let's hope it stays that way," Lura said with a smile and slid her arm around Sol's waist. Sol and Telanus mumbled in agreement, sipping again as the comm panel beeped.

Tela turned and typed commands into the terminal. "Incoming message from Uzah. It's marked urgent."

"What now?" Lura shot a worried glance at Sol, who stepped forward to wrap his arms around her as if he could shield her from any concerns.

Tela typed on the keyboard, pulling up the message. Her brow creased with worry as she read.

"What is it, dear?"

Tela turned to meet Lura's gaze. "Davi and his friends were attacked on their way to Xanthis."

Sol winced as Lura gasped and rushed toward Tela. "Oh no! Are they okay?"

"Attacked by whom?" Sol asked as he and Telanus moved closer, reading the missive over her shoulder. As he came alongside her, Lura reached over and put her arm around his waist. He pulled her closer.

"Lhamorian assassins, it says." Tela scanned the message again quickly. Sol could see she was close to exploding.

"Thanks be to God, they're okay." Telanus said with relief. He and Sol clinked their mugs in a toast.

Tela stood again with a loud sigh and began pacing along the wall. "How could they know? His mission wasn't public knowledge. Someone's intercepting communications." Sol's gladness faded quickly.

"Someone inside command?" Telanus' words made Sol's heart pound faster in his chest. Lura's hand slipped from Sol's waist as her shoulders sank with worry.

"Will we ever be free of this? Davi's in danger again? Who now? Why do so many resent him?" Tela's words matched the choppiness of her paced steps as she zigzagged back and forth in front of the wall.

Lura drew near and put a gentle hand on Tela's arm. "It takes time to erase years of enmity, dear. It won't happen overnight."

Tela stopped pacing and turned to face her. "Private resentment, a few public complaints, okay, but people are getting murdered now! The Council has to put a stop to it!"

"No doubt they're trying to do that very thing," Telanus said, moving over to wrap his arm around Tela. "That too will take time."

"Well, I hope we have time. I'm not ready to lose Davi yet!" Tela slipped from his grasp and started pacing again.

"Neither are we," Sol said as his eyes met Lura's. Lura winced at the thought and Sol moved to her again to offer what comfort he could. He wondered if the warmth of his closeness relaxed her as much as having her close relaxed him. Just holding her clarified his thoughts. He was torn between wishing the military were less informative and feeling thankful they had the connections to stay abreast of such events. He didn't know which was easier: knowing or not knowing? Either way, the worry he felt lay across his heart like a storm cloud blocking the suns. Concerns about his job suddenly became less important.

🏰

Uzah and Matheu entered the command center just in time for the morning briefing and found it in chaos. Technicians checked equipment as controllers reviewed data on their screens, everyone chattering loudly. Louder voices coming from the Conference Room quickly drew their attention. As they dodged scurrying techs and hurried toward it, a worried Joram appeared in the doorway.

"What's going on here?" Matheu demanded.

Joram shook his head. "Some kind of computer glitch with the assignments."

"What kind of glitch?" It made no sense to Uzah. The system had been generating assignments with a well-worn algorithm for ages and no one had ever complained. "What happened?" He turned to Joram who'd followed him inside with Matheu. Officers, of both Vertullian and Boralian birth, were arguing and pointing at the various terminals, their faces heated.

"What happened is favoritism!" a Borali Colonel said, turning from a nearby confrontation. Uzah recognized Jansen from the briefing a few days past with Grif and Pres. "All the best assignments given to your people, with total disregard for seniority!"

"Forget seniority! Simple protocol!" a Borali Captain from the same group said, nodding in agreement as many in the room turned toward the new arrivals.

"Officers of all seniorities rotate through the various positions over time," Uzah said, still puzzled as he pushed forward toward the wall terminal around which they'd all gathered.

"Not like this!" Jansen said. "Now all our people get the all night shifts, the crappy locations all at once, for an entire month?"

"The rotation cycle is two weeks as always," Matheu said.

The Captain slammed his fist hard against the wall, narrowly missing a terminal. "Check the list yourself! It's a whole month and it's every assignment!"

"Our people have faced a similar situation in the past," a Vertullian Major said from Uzah's right.

"Not for an entire month!" The Captain said, angrily, his red face whitening with the cresting of his anger. "Some of us already served the past two weeks on nights. Aren't we allowed to see our families, too, or do just you 'chosen people' deserve that?"

"Look! Enough of this talk of their people and our people!" Joram said, his face whitening as his temper flared. "We are one people now. All equals and serving in a united military."

"Easy to say when the favoritism's on your side!" Colonel Jansen's sarcasm assaulted Uzah like a series of shells. "We should have seen it coming. More and more of our best men relegated to irrelevant roles as your own people got priority. Why is it you always assume the worst where we're concerned?"

Uzah put a hand on Joram's shoulder to calm him. As he checked and double checked the assignments, their complaints matched the data on the list, but he could detect no errors in the program. "It's done by an algorithm in the computer as always!" he insisted. "I'm sure it won't happen again."

"Or maybe it'll be a regular thing! I'm not waiting to find out!" Jansen turned and marched angrily from the room as the officers exploded back into loud arguing.

Matheu's voice cut through the room like a blaster bolt. "Are you men officers or not?! Enough of this bickering! We have a chain of command and you will follow it or be brought up on charges! Am I clear?!" Despite his rank, Matheu's uniform stood out all the more for its lack of medals comparable to those of the Borali officers surrounding them. The same was true for all of the Vertullians, whose time in service hadn't been long enough to earn them such accolades. Matheu glowered at them, his eyes as commanding as his glare.

The arguments died in moments as the other officers watched Matheu, their anger only in check, not faded.

"You'll be expected to discharge your duties as always or I will hear about it!" Matheu didn't even blink as he panned the room, staring them down.

Gradually, the officers lost their nerve—some sighing, others shoulder's slumping—a few offered weak salutes and mumbled acquiescence. Uzah was once again thankful Matheu found the thought of retiring insulting.

Matheu turned to Uzah. "We'll send the briefing report to your datapads. I want everyone to their stations right now!"

It only took a moment for the room to clear, but Uzah and Matheu were already reviewing the assignments again on the terminal.

"It is highly irregular," Joram noted as he read the lists on the terminal next to Uzah.

Uzah nodded. "Unfortunately, yes, it does seem odd. I'll get command on the frequency. We should at least request that they check the algorithm." Joram nodded and followed Uzah and Matheu into the command center.

"Soldiers do not question orders!" Matheu groused.

"I think it has less to do with orders and more to do with other recent tensions," Uzah answered, shaking his head. "Either way, command needs to be made aware of it."

Matheu nodded, his frown showing his distaste. "I will write up any officer who fails to obey orders under my command." He turned and hurried toward a corridor as Uzah sighed and headed for the communications station. He couldn't remember a day of service without some sort of crisis arising.

Pres felt grateful she'd been assigned to work with Admiral Dek after the debacle of the loss against the Workers. She and her fellow leaders could have easily been brought up on charges by the Council, but General Lucius' disappearance, combined with the new High Lord Councilor's desire to integrate the military and return things to normal as quickly as possible, conspired to make experienced leadership invaluable. Thus, Dek and Pres had been given a second chance. All soldier, Dek's hair was close cropped and his muscular frame highlighted by the fit of his gray uniform.

It was times like the present when Pres counted on Dek's

experience to see them through a crisis. The computers responsible for duty assignments had been in place for decades, running an algorithm developed long ago; one which had never drawn complaints until now. She and Dek had arrived that morning to face a near mutiny of angry officers and men complaining that worker counterparts had been given favored assignments over them, and not just for the usual two week duty cycle but an entire month. In all her years, Pres had never experienced such hostility from other personnel, most especially command personnel she'd served with much of her career. Dek handled it with precision and calm she could only admire. It didn't bother him in the slightest. She was surprised later, when he actually confessed in private his frustration at having to deal with such a situation.

"We got a call from General Uzah on Vertullis, while you were talking with them," Pres answered. "They arrived to a similar crisis this morning."

Dek shook his head. "Call the techs and have the computers checked. It may just be an odd coincidence, the rare probabilities come to pass, but I'd rather be sure. And see if they can work on reprogramming the algorithm to avoid it in the future. We cannot have such routine matters threatening our morale."

Pres nodded as she headed for her terminal. "You handled that situation with such calm. I didn't know where to begin when we arrived."

"To maintain command, you must always give the appearance of being in control, even amidst chaos," Dek said with a chuckle. "I could have thrown up my hands in frustration, but that would have solved nothing. It would have only encouraged even more lax discipline from the personnel, and that's the last thing we need."

Pres nodded, her fingers bouncing off the keys in a barrage of clicks as she typed commands instructing the terminal to search for the contact information required. "I'm thankful we're still working together after all that's happened. Your experience is invaluable, especially at times like these."

Dek sighed and leaned against a nearby pillar, looking sullen. "We're both lucky to be working at all after that fool Xalivar's personal vendetta overtook his common sense."

"I thought we all agreed with him at the time?"

Dek sighed. "Well, my sentiments have never been favorable toward the Vertullians. But it was foolish to defy the Council on such an important matter, especially when the Council was in line with the will of the populace. It should have cost us our careers."

"Thank the gods it didn't." Dek nodded in agreement then turned away as Pres went back to her terminal. An alert flashed at the corner of her screen. An incoming message on her private secure channel. Forgetting the search, she clicked a button to open the comm, patching it to the earpiece she and all officers wore as part of their uniforms.

"Link 78A6," the message said in a droning computer voice, then repeated again.

Pres froze. It was a code few but she knew. It meant she had a private message even Dek couldn't be allowed to see. She pressed a button to delete the alert, then hurried back to her search. Finding the name of the Head Technician, she sent him and his senior officer the instructions, marking them as urgent and top priority. She struggled throughout to maintain a relaxed routine. Inside, her heartbeat soared and she found her eyes wandering, darting around with her thoughts. As soon as she'd finished, she stood and turned to where Dek was already conferring with a newly arrived junior officer on other matters.

"I missed my morning Talis. Can I get you any?"

He shrugged her off with a wave, not even noticing as she disappeared into the corridor. Hurrying to a private terminal at the nearest comm station, she logged onto the secret database and then clicked the secure link. After entering a few more code combinations, the message resolved onto her screen. She felt relief as she began to read:

Meeting. 1100 hrs. Starport. Talekyn.

In two days? Italis' moon was a long distance for her to go on such short notice. Xalivar and Lucius were threatening her credibility. What excuse could she use for an emergency?

She erased the message quickly and weighed it over in her mind all the way back to the command center. Dek was waiting for her. "What happened to the Talis?"

She suddenly realized her hands were empty. She struggled to stay relaxed, not give any reaction. "I got distracted by some more officers arguing about their assignments."

Dek smiled sympathetically. "It's happening everywhere. I need you to go out to Italis. They've had a particularly bad incident there with an officer threatening to shoot Vertullian soldiers if his assignment wasn't revised. He's to be court martialed. I want you to address the men personally. Go among them, make a personal connection, remind them the chain of command is doing its job, etc."

"Why not go yourself?"

"A cold hearted old warmonger stands far less chance of success than a beautiful female officer, Pres."

She fought a smile as blood rushed to her face. Had the environmental systems failed? The room felt hotter. "I hardly think they'll look at me like that."

"Regardless, you have a gentler manner and spirit than I." Dek said, the glint in his eye revealing his enjoyment of her discomfort. "The Alliance needs you to use it. We cannot have our ranks falling apart. Appear commanding, in control, but concerned."

"I'll do my best, of course, Admiral." Pres couldn't believe her luck. Could Xalivar have arranged it?

Dek nodded. "Your shuttle's being prepared. I'll expect you back in four days."

She nodded and turned toward the door. "I'll be in my quarters if needed."

The Admiral had turned back to other business before she'd finished spinning back toward the door. She couldn't stop his words from repeating over and over in her mind: "a beautiful female officer, Pres." And each time it repeated, her heart fluttered and she smiled.

The ninth planet from the sun Boralis, Xanthis was even drearier than Davi had expected. Known for its cold nights, Xanthis had few habitation centers and few natural mineral deposits. Spaces which appeared to have once held vast oceans were now filled with scattered lakes of craters filled during the scattered rainfall, a spelunker's paradise. Skimming the surface side by side, shuttle and fighter, on their way into the capital city, Nasyru, Davi and his companions chattered about the landscape.

"Like nothing I've seen," Farien commented.

"I've read about other desolate planets but it's hard to imagine people live here," Yao responded.

Dru just stared silently out the window even as the towering buildings of the city appeared on the horizon. Nasyru's buildings were of all shapes and sizes and the city itself looked fairly modern except for the barren, reddish-brown soil surrounding everything.

"Not even an attempt at artificial landscaping," Farien noted. "Must not be too proud of their city then." The few sections of open land they saw were scattered rocks and clay with occasional patches of sand. Davi found it surprising no effort had been made to add foliage or flowers, or wouldn't they grow here?

"Maybe some species take value in different aesthetics, Farien," Yao said. It made sense. It was hard to imagine anyone who didn't take pride in their capital city.

Davi and Farien made arrangements with the starport for a private military landing bay and led the way in.

A hurried city official met them there. His long dark-red robe ran from neck to toe, fitting his body like a second skin. Other than his blue-green skin, he appeared human, with dark-grayish hair and a slurred accent, and a bone structure reminding Davi of lightning-thin models in commercials he'd seen on the networks. "If we'd known you were coming, the Planetary Governor himself would have come..."

"We're on a classified mission," Farien said. "We don't want that kind of attention."

The official nodded. "It's rare we have military officers in the city itself. Most of them stay to the bases and landing strips on the other side of the planet." He looked to them as if he expected some sort of reaction then waved his arms, palms up as if shrugging it off.

"They say Xanthis is a rough place," Farien said.

Davi watched the official's blue-green skin darken, the Xanthian version of a blush perhaps. "Rumors exaggerate. Please allow us to give you a proper impression." Davi and his friends nodded politely as the official led them toward a large sliding door, presumably leading out of the bay. "A military attaché has been requested and will meet you at your hotel."

"We don't need him!"

Farien's words struck the official like missiles, causing him to grimace and shrink back. "Just someone to see to any needs which may arise; show you around and such."

"I'm sure any assistance would be very helpful, thank you," Davi said. The last thing they needed was Farien's lack of tact causing any drama with local officials.

"Our mission is not very important, I'm afraid," Yao added. "We're here about recruitment for Presimion Academy. Now that Vertullians are successfully entering service, we've had discussion about admitting other groups as well."

The official brightened, looking at Yao and Davi rather than Farien this time. "How wonderful. A grand opportunity for our people to contribute to the Alliance's defense. We will be most proud to serve."

The door slid open, almost silently, with only a slight hum to be heard. Davi and his team followed the official into a well-lit corridor with patterned walls resembling a large three-dimensional relief map—squares, rectangles, circles of various lengths and sizes scattered across the surface of the walls like buildings on a planet's surface. Davi wondered if the pattern had any significance but wasn't sure this would be the time to ask. The official kept walking and they followed.

"We've heard of an unsettling incident in one of your residential districts," Farien said.

The official nodded. "The incident with the Vertullian woman, I presume?"

Davi met the official's look with a nod of his own. "There's been many other incidents throughout the system. Very sad."

The official looked down. "A most unfortunate situation. Our condolences go out to all citizens. We can assure you all efforts will be made to prevent further incidents."

"Given Xanthis' reputation as a recruiting point for assassins, I'd imagine that'll be a hard promise to keep." Yao and Davi both shot Farien a look.

"All planets in the system share similar concerns for our Vertullian brothers and sisters," Yao jumped in. "The Alliance is prepared to offer you any support you need."

"Thank you. A most kind gesture." The official's expression returned from shock at Farien's boldness to a welcoming smile. "We've arranged quarters for you at the city center."

"We have our own arrangements—"

Davi cut Farien off with a chuckle "But yours sound so much nicer. We are forever in your debt."

The official's palms came together as he smiled and offered a slight bow of pleasure. They walked on in silence, passing various other Xanthian workers, administrators, and other visitors as they wound their way through the corridors of the starport. To Davi's surprise, he saw only two humans, mercenary types if he had to guess. Both glared at them as they passed, showing an aversion to their military uniforms. A portent of the challenges awaiting them. Davi knew they would need to use extra caution here. He'd be sure to speak with Farien about it as soon as they were alone.

The official escorted them out onto a dusty street and into an air taxi which rose above the city and took them on a scenic ride to the city center as Davi and his companions assessed the city around them. It looked like most big cities, constant motion on the main avenues, quieter residential streets to the side, culminating in the center city. But this city had a dark underbelly which mostly showed at night. Davi knew he and his friends would see more of it than they wanted before their time in Nasyru was done.

The invitation had been Danae's idea, an attempt by the new lady of the Palace to ease the growing uselessness her predecessor felt in her new lesser role, Miri assumed. The gesture was appreciated, but coming so close after the incident at her brunch, Miri couldn't help feeling restless, even a little trepidation about what might occur.

"You'll do fine," Danae said with a reassuring smile and a gentle nudge to Miri's right shoulder. "To them, you're still a princess."

Miri's smile never wavered as she sat next to Danae on the dais awaiting introductions. "I hope their reaction isn't like those of our circle." She fidgeted in the hard-backed chair, trying to get comfortable.

Danae's eyes darkened. "Of course not. These people don't have bias acquired from years of special privilege. These are the everyday citizens, the kind who can most relate to the Vertullians' plight."

As his peer finished the announcements and vacated the podium, their host stepped to the mic, smiling as he panned the room with delight. "So many good people here today—people who are the heart and soul of this Alliance. The work you do keeps the Alliance strong; keeps it moving. Gods know you don't get recognized for it enough, but today, this Commission celebrates you for it. Just as we celebrate all the little people who matter a lot everywhere in this Alliance. Our next guest knows the value of those people as much as anyone. Her own adopted son is a fine example of a person rising above his station to great heights, disproving the assumptions that genetics determine one's fate, perhaps."

With that, he glanced over to Miri and Danae and smiled. Miri held her smile firm, nodding, as he gave a slight bow before continuing. She knew he'd meant it as a compliment but still felt, as any mother might, that he'd stated it in a way that cut Davi down. She hoped her own words could rectify that.

"The daughter of a once mighty dynasty of great leaders, High Lord Councilors, Lords all, Miri Rhii has lived a life of service to others, making many sacrifices. Every time we needed her strength, she never failed us, including during our most recent difficulties, a time of great change. Miri Rhii has always been there for us, loving us as her people, her extended family perhaps. And she's here today to tell us more about some who are new among us but have now joined the family. Let's welcome Princess Miri!" He turned, applauding as the attendees joined him from tables placed around the room. It was a modest-sized ballroom and modestly appointed, appropriate to the status of those present, except perhaps Danae and Miri herself.

With a nod from Danae, who joined the applause, Miri stood, smoothing her dress and stepping forward to take her place at the podium. Those present seemed delighted to see her, their faces filled with anticipation. Most even offered warm smiles. As the applause faded, she surveyed the room, smiling at the mostly adoring faces. A few toward the back looked bored, as expected, but the warmth of the reception thrilled her after her experience the previous week. She closed her eyes, took a breath and began.

"Good afternoon, my friends. It's so good to be here with you today and share with you about some new friends who are now part of us. We all know the history, the years of animosity and fighting between our peoples. I think I speak for generations of mothers when I express my joy and relief that those days are finally behind us for good."

She paused as new applause broke out around her from most of the tables. The bored onlookers toward the back remained indifferent.

"You're no strangers to hard work, like our new friends. They too have worked hard for generations."

Then it happened. A deep voice from the shadows in a back corner rose: "Not hard enough, and not long enough, I'd say."

Pain stabbed at her insides like a knife and Miri struggled to maintain her composure as her eyes sought the source of the voice. "Why do you say that, my friend? Are not all humans worthy of appreciating benefits from their labor, including times of rest?"

"All they do is rest these days," the taunter said, stepping forward, "while we do all the work!" His hair was graying at his temples, but his body had a muscular form. He was obviously a man used to hard work, not far from Miri's own age. His eyes and wrinkles added depth to his countenance. And he spoke with an authority and confidence, as if no one could dare disagree.

"We are all doing our part, my friend," Miri answered, averting her eyes from his hateful glare.

"Since when are we friends?" he snapped.

She ignored him and continued: "They share our labor, work alongside us as equals, with the same demanded of them."

"In appearance it would seem," the man said, "but how long 'til it changes? We've seen the beginnings of it now." Grumbles of agreement came from the tables around him.

Miri breathed deeply and glanced to Danae for reassurance but saw her friend was at a loss.

"They're already starting to get priority, the best assignments, favoritism clearly!"

This time some of the grumbles were decipherable: "That's right!" "You tell her!" "Send them back where they belong!" Miri stepped back from the podium as her host and Danae rushed to her side.

"Please, we are not here for negativity," the host said, leaning to the microphone. "This is a time to recognize our common achievements."

"Achievements like betraying our people? Let our speaker speak to that. She's an expert!" The taunter raised a fist in triumph as several others jumped to their feet around him, applauding.

"I did no such thing. I only wanted the best for us all," Miri mumbled, her voice cracking, the microphone barely picking it up. She felt small all of a sudden, a tightness in her chest making it harder to breathe.

"They are not like us," a woman near the front shouted. "You are kind hearted, because of your son, Princess. But it can be exploited. And those tricksters are masters of exploiting us!"

"Yes!" Several shouted at various points around the room.

Miri stepped back in a daze as the host looked panicked. Clearly the room was out of control, and he had no idea how to respond to it.

"The people supported this," Danae shouted over them, stepping to the podium. "Your Council acceded to your demand to end the slavery, to make peace."

"There can be no peace with their kind!" A well-dressed young man raised his fist in solidarity with the taunter at a table in the middle of the room. Fists rose into the air around him.

"My gods," Danae whispered as she lost her resolve and stepped back to stand beside Miri. Miri didn't look at her, focusing instead on fighting back tears. She refused to let these people see her cry.

"We cannot change hundreds of years of hate overnight," Miri reminded her.

"But the public outcry during the fighting was in favor of freedom. Now they demand the opposite. What would they have us do?"

Then their host was before them, his eyes pleading forgiveness as he gently waved them toward the back of the dais. "I'm so sorry, my Ladies. Perhaps it's best if you go to a safer location. We must address their fears, open a dialogue, but I fear their animosity may be a threat to you."

Several of his companions joined him, circling Miri and Danae and leading them toward the stairs at the back as the host turned back toward the podium. Both women walked in silence, but, for the first time, Miri felt truly afraid. Drops formed at the edge of her eyes, and she quickly dispatched them with her finger. Would she never again know the respect and endearment in which she was so long held? Had she thrown it all away? How could the people's hearts be so different from her own? She ached to go back, to speak with them, win them over, but then doors slid open and they were ushered through and the noise and commotion were but a memory.

Later, as they passed through the Lobby, many people who had attended apologized, warming Miri's heart. It was a relief to realize that not everyone shared the sentiments of those vocalizing it. Could she dare to hope it was a minority? Regardless, the fact that such strong, anti-worker sentiments existed left Miri feeling cold and concerned.

"Steps must be taken to change the stereotypes, the misconceptions," she whispered as she and Danae settled onto the Royal Shuttle which had brought them there. "We have no hope of really being one people, unless we can accept each other and put the past to rest."

Danae nodded. "Tarkanius and I and many others share your concerns. Conversations and plans are being made. Staying strong and holding firm in your message is invaluable, Miri. I intend to ask you to speak again, if you're willing."

"As always, I live to serve the Alliance." Miri forced out the answer, but inside she wondered if she had the strength.

Tela had found Uzah in the command center, during the quiet of mid-afternoon, pouring over reports on a datapad. He'd always been supportive of her and Davi but, this time, it didn't take long for them to wind up on opposite sides.

"You can't let personal feelings dictate assignments," Uzah responded to her request. "If anything, this is all the more reason why you shouldn't get involved."

Tela fought to control the anger she felt swelling inside. "He's my future husband. And he could be in danger!"

"We're all in danger. It goes with the job. Gallivanting off to protect your lover is not one of your duties, I'm sorry."

"This is not a normal situation. Assassins are attacking our people—"

"And our job is to protect them. That goes for Davi and everyone else! We have to put our personal feelings aside and do that duty, Lieutenant. I'm sorry." With that, he coldly turned back to his datapad, making it clear the conversation was over. She was tempted to punch him. No understanding or respect for women or their needs!

For a moment, Tela had toyed with approaching Joram about it, but planetary Governors never overruled their military commanders on assignments. She even briefly entertained the idea of General Matheu, but he was so hard-nosed about such things, she feared a bad reaction could harm her career. In the end, she went back to meet her friends for dinner, depressed and worried and feeling worse for the effort put forth.

"What's wrong, Tela?"

The voice jolted Tela back to the restaurant and she looked up to find them all staring at her—Nila and Virun, Jorek and Brie, the two couples. If command knew, they wouldn't be allowed to serve together. Tela wished she and Davi had kept their relationship secret now. It just hadn't been anything to worry about at the time. She shook off her thoughts and smiled at Nila. "Nothing. I'm fine."

"Fine for someone who looks like a Gungor just tore apart her pet." Nila shook her head. "We know you too well. What is it?"

Tela sighed, moving the food around on her plate with a fork. Couples and groups chatted and laughed at nearby tables, enjoying their food and camaraderie. She felt even more alone. "Davi. There was another attempt on them on their way to Xanthis."

Her friends perked up. "Assassins?" Even Brie's jovial tone softened, deeper with worry.

"Probably. Lhamorians."

"They're out there alone? Just the three of them?" Virun pulled his arm away as Nila reached across the table and put her hand atop Tela's.

"It's supposed to be a low profile secret."

"So we have a leak?" Jorek's temper was already flaring, she could see.

"I just want them safe. And there are people hunting them."

Virun finished his Zizi, a fruity beer made on Tertullis, and slammed the glass down on the table. "Let's go."

"I'm in!" The others all spoke in unison.

Tela shook her head, hiding the joy she felt knowing they were always there for her. "We can't."

"We have ships. We'll just file a flight plan—"

Tela's eyes met Virun's. "We've been ordered not to." She had responsibility for the safety of her people. She was a military officer. Davi could take care of himself. Her head knew this. But her heart...

"You asked already?" Brie sounded surprised.

Tela sighed. She didn't want to rehash it by repeating the whole story.

"And they ordered you not to go?" Blood rose to Jorek's face.

"Not specifically, but it was clear they don't support the idea."

"They misunderstood." Virun and Brie mumbled agreement with Nila.

"They understood. 'Danger goes with the job. Gallivanting off to protect your lover is not one of your duties.'" She cut to the chase. Davi was important, not just as her fiancé, but as a hero to his people. There was a reason command picked him for so many choice assignments; a reason he'd risen so quickly to a position of trust. But what if he needed her? Would she ever forgive herself for not being there?

"Uzah forbade you?" Jorek's mind was clearly racing to formulate a plan.

Virun smiled. "Not forbade, discouraged."

Jorek nodded, as if their minds were one. "And he's second in command to Matheu over the Army. But technically, we're still under Air Defenses, which is—"

Tela saw it coming and raised a hand in protest. "He acts as our commander and coordinates with Air Defenses on Legallis. He has the authority—"

"But he never issued the order," Virun said with a grin.

Jorek grinned back and nodded. "We also have standing orders to defend our fellow pilots when one of them gets in trouble."

Virun nodded as they all looked at Tela.

"That refers to pilots in our immediate airspace, not three planets away." Tela felt a headache coming on. They were saying all the things she wanted to hear. Still, mutiny was the last thing they needed to involve themselves in right now.

"We have a long patrol tomorrow night. No one defines how long." Virun chuckled, raising a hand to high five Jorek.

"We can't do it!" She was their superior. It was her job to set an example and enforce discipline despite her personal feelings.

"Nav computers make errors. It's happened." Brie smiled,

clearly enjoying being a part of the men's scheme.

Nila nodded. "It happened on that long range patrol last month, remember?"

Tela tried to hide it, but they laughed when they saw her grin.

"We're just going to check it out while we're in the vicinity," Jorek said. "You know, once we realize where we are."

"We'll be short on fuel and provisions—"

"When we get lost, we'll stop and refuel." Nila shot Tela an urging look.

"They could court martial all of us."

"Better to go out together than alone. Davi needs us." Virun raised his glass. The others quickly followed suit, looking to Tela.

Nila pointed an accusing finger at Tela's glass.

Tela laughed, shaking her head again. Who could resist friends like these? They were right. She had to go. If Davi were in trouble, no one else was going to back him up. The assignment was dangerous. If they found he was okay, they'd just be out a little longer on patrol because of it. They'd come right back. She had to know. She raised her glass and they all clinked theirs together. "So much for our short-lived military careers."

Chapter Six

The Council Chambers were abuzz as Aron entered for the second time since the attempt on his life. A few Lords took notice and nodded in greeting, but mostly his arrival went unacknowledged as he made his way to his usual spot at a table in the center section along the right aisle. Assigned seating for the Lords had not been intentional, but came about through a combination of personal preference, political rivalries and friendships. Tarkanius had chosen Aron's spot himself, negotiating for the previous occupant to relocate. Since Aron was the first Vertullian to serve on the Council, the High Lord Councilor wanted him to see and be seen, a reminder for others of the Vertullian's new status as full citizens of the Alliance and an opportunity for Aron to observe well and learn the Council's proceedings.

"This decision smacks of favoritism and a total disregard for the tensions dividing our citizens," Hachim was yelling, his finger pointed at Tarkanius and Kray, who stood on the floor before the dais, facing him. "The vote was rushed. Not enough consideration was given to the issues and repercussions. The price is being paid for that!" Since the vote, those opposed to the holiday had become even more vocal in their protests, to Aron's discouragement.

"I will not allow this Council nor my Palace to be held hostage by terrorists and bullies, Hachim. I won this seat on a platform of unifying the populace, and I intend to do it. No matter what's required!"

Hachim shook his head as Niger joined him. "You cannot force a unified opinion. Too many people have objections, and those are more often than not leading to violent outcries or actions against others. We must squelch this resistance first before we make decisions which will only serve to raise tensions further."

Niger nodded. "This Council's always been about serving the people, not just ourselves."

"It is in the people's best interests that I push these decisions forward," Tarkanius said, his brow furrowed with frustration.

"Xalivar said the same thing, and we impeached him for treason because of it!" Hachim's eyes bore into Tarkanius as Niger grunted his agreement. Tarkanius cringed from the comparison, which Aron thought was quite unfair.

"Xalivar's decisions were self-serving and against the wishes of the majority," Kray said. "The majority of our people want slavery to end." Her voice seemed to rise above the pitch around them until Aron realized many of the other conversations had stopped as people tuned in to this one.

"Well, you wouldn't know it from the broadcasts of protests and attacks airing constantly," Niger said.

"We warned you when this idea first came up," Hachim looked around him, meeting the eyes of other Lords as he gauged their support, "and the issues have escalated daily since then. Anti-worker sentiment is on the rise. That cannot be ignored." Several Lords around them grunted in agreement.

"If we allow them to bully us, to control our actions, we encourage them," Kray argued, shooting challenging looks at some of the grunters. "Do we want to be known as the pet Council of such men?"

"Don't oversimplify, Lord Kray." Lord Qai stepped forward shaking his head. "If we base our actions on only one set of voices, we ignore our duty to represent the entire citizenry, not just the ones whose hearts match our own."

"But what if they're wrong?" Kray looked around, dismayed at the lack of support.

"It seems clear we cannot take any action without first addressing the realities of violence and protest," Lord Simeon said. "But it is difficult to know how to do that."

"There are many precedents from the history of forefathers

on Old Earth," Aron said as all eyes turned to him. "Slavery in the nineteenth century there almost divided an entire nation and caused much strife on several continents. We so often look back on them as primitive and unenlightened because of our knowledge and technology, but what have we really learned, when we ourselves allowed slavery to exist in our midst?"

"Perhaps yours is not the voice to provide such commentary," Qai said. For a moment, Aron thought he was being scolded, but their eyes met and he saw a sparkle in the other Lord's eyes. "So let me add my own. This abomination we have tolerated for generations must be abolished. We can no longer call ourselves higher society, or even civilized, if we allow it to exist. But changing the hearts and minds of our people is not a simple matter. It cannot be accomplished merely by the power of a High Lord Councilor's will or that of the Council. It requires a long-term plan to reeducate our people. It will involve not just relearning history with new perspectives but the kind of one on one experience which can only come through personal exposure of our peoples to one another." The words impacted Aron and he saw he was not alone.

"And if our people refuse to be taught such things?" Hachim raised his hands to emphasize the question.

"There will always be some who will, which is why such a program will take years to succeed." Qai looked Hachim and Niger in the eyes one at a time, challenging them to resist, but neither held his gaze for long. "It begins with us, the members of this Council. We must demonstrate with our own actions and attitudes our unity and common belief. If we cannot do that, we cannot hope to lead the people to a similar conclusion."

Hachim sighed. "I will not be intimidated into following a program. I'll continue to stand against any policy which favors old enemies over our own people, which is unjust to our own in favor of welcoming another."

"Perhaps your definition of justice should be on trial then, Lord Hachim," Kray said bitterly.

Hachim's cheeks flushed as Tarkanius stepped forward. "Our brother Lord Qai is most wise. And it shall begin with us. We will continue to discuss our differences and educate ourselves first, before we impart these lessons to our people. And we will stand together, unified always in this matter. Beginning this week."

He stopped a moment, glancing around to meet as many eyes as he could. "I will go personally to Vertullis to announce that 'the Returning' is to become a people's holiday. A committee will be formed led by Lords Qai and Aron to make recommendations how this can best be implemented. I invite all of you to travel with me to make this announcement, but to those who refuse, I say, I will tolerate no dissention. Any questions or complaints shall not leave this room. We will settle this matter amongst ourselves, not through public debate. Is that clear?"

"The High Lord Councilor does not control this Council!" One of the senior members, Lord Kretzu, shouted.

"Hear, hear!" his tablemate, Lord Elul, echoed.

Tarkanius remained undeterred. "Part of serving the people is leading by example. How can we expect them to unite, when we ourselves are divided?"

"Then let us settle our differences first, before we address them," Kretzu said.

"My responsibility to the people includes the responsibility to insert order into chaos," Tarkanius said. "With the violence, rumors, and divisions center stage, they need a reminder that we are all one people and our future is a common cause."

"It will take more than words this time," Elul responded. Several Lords, including Kretzu, Hachim and Niger, grunted in agreement. Aron feared they were right.

"Which is why we must take action and stand together," Tarkanius answered. He looked around again for any who might disagree but Hachim, Niger, and those known to support them refused to meet his eyes. He nodded. "Very well then. I'll have my aides make travel arrangements with your offices. I look forward to seeing you then."

"Let us postpone our official meeting then until after our return," Simeon said, stepping up beside Tarkanius to show his support.

The Council immediately dispersed, with Lords resuming

private conversations with friends and adversaries as they cleared the room.

"It's a dangerous game to force their hand, Tarkanius," Simeon said, when only Kray, Aron and Tarkanius remained with him.

"I lead them the way I expect them to lead the people. We are not leaders if we are not firm in our course and confident in our wisdom."

Simeon nodded. "Nonetheless, we must be prepared to meet any resistance with equal determination as that we have toward our own success."

"I am prepared for any necessary course," Tarkanius said.

"Even if that course takes you down paths similar to those your predecessor trod?"

Tarkanius turned, his eyes meeting Simeon. Simeon didn't flinch. And Aron realized then he was not alone in his fears of what might be required to make unity work. "I hope it never comes to that."

Simeon nodded. "You must be prepared lest it does."

Kray put her hand gently on Tarkanius' arm. "We have much to consider and much work to do. Together. You won't be alone in it."

Aron smiled. "Indeed. I will support you in whatever must be done." He extended his hands, forming the traditional salute with his fingers crossed atop his fist. It was ordinarily a custom only military officers followed when entering and leaving the High Lord Councilor's presence.

To Aron's pleasure, Simeon joined him in it. "As will I."

Kray's hands echoed theirs as she too offered the salute.

Tarkanius' eyes closed as he took a deep breath in gratitude then started slowly up the aisle, the others following close behind him. Aron hoped the line would be far longer at the gathering on Vertullis.

Tela yawned then flinched. Telanus looked much too awake for this hour as he smiled at her from the terminal beside her bed.

His smile almost sparkled. "Morning, Little Girl."

"You should not be this cheerful this early in the morning." Tela rubbed her eyes. What time was it anyway? Why was he waking her up? She sighed.

"You know I'm always cheery when I get to see my girl's beautiful face," Telanus winked then beamed at her. "Besides, it's midday. Check your chrono."

She frowned. Midday? Rolling over, she checked the chrono on the wall. He was right. Crazy pilot hours. It felt like the middle of the night, as if she'd just gotten to sleep. She yawned again. "You know if anyone's making it hard for Davi, it's you. Spoiling me with such sweet talk. I wish he talked like that."

Telanus laughed. "I'll have a word with him. We can fix that."

"Don't you dare!" She had patrol call in two hours and briefing in ninety minutes. She had to wake up. She searched his eyes and saw he was teasing then stretched her arms and planted her feet on the floor, willing her body to get up. Instead, every cell shouted at her: "More sleep!"

"Hey! What else can a father-in-law worry about but making sure his daughter's spoiled properly?"

"We're not married, Daddy."

He brushed it off with a wave. "You will be."

"You're relentless."

"Your mother said that, too." He laughed.

She forced herself to sit up. "Look, I have patrol soon. So I'd better get busy preparing. Thanks for calling, Daddy." She ignored the voices of protest inside and took a deep breath.

"You be careful out there."

She nodded. "I always am."

"I love you, Little Girl."

"I love you, too." The terminal went blank as she stretched again with another yawn and grabbed her uniform, heading for the cleansing room. Today was the last day of her short-lived military career.

The meeting took place in the back room of a warehouse beside the starport on Talekyn, Italis' largest moon. After taking her command shuttle to the starport on Italis herself and then insisting her crew remain with the shuttle, Pres had slipped out under the pretense of contacting command, gone to the civilian areas and changed clothes, then hired a private shuttle to take her to the rendezvous. The whole thing wasted a lot of time and she knew her command crew would be searching for her by now, but secrecy had to be maintained and it seemed the only way to prevent discovery. Even the private shuttle had been instructed to leave her at Talekyn's starport and disappear. She'd walked the rest of the way on foot. Talekyn's starport hardly qualified for the name. It was basically a one-room arrival hall with one corridor dedicated to ticketing kiosks, a fact that made further precautions unnecessary once she'd stepped off the shuttle.

Using her datapad to hone in on the coordinates given her, she found the nondescript, gray building. The warehouse appeared to be rarely used, and its insides smelled of dust with scattered bits of crates and cardboard decorating the floor. Entering via the northeast door, as she'd been instructed, she made her way to the center of the storage space and waited. At the top of the hour, a cloaked figure appeared out of the shadows.

The figure approached until they were almost face to face before removing his hood. Xalivar stared at her, his expression unreadable. She knew better than to speak first, so she waited for him to finish assessing or intimidating her, whichever this was.

"I'm told you have...questions?"

Pres nodded, hesitating to ensure he really expected an answer before speaking. "The High Lord Councilor has put security on high alert due to recent attacks on ex-workers—"

"They won't be for long."

"Pardon me?"

"Ex-workers. Soon they will be returned to their former duties, as will we all." Xalivar smiled, the embodiment of confidence as usual.

"While they remain citizens, recruiting has become a highly risky endeavor," Pres continued. "It cannot be done by normal means for risk of detection."

"I left the means up to you and others," Xalivar answered. "It's the results I care about."

"We all face great risks while we remain there—"

"You shant remain there long, either. Get me my men and you'll have no more to worry about."

"You intend to call them to training immediately?"

Xalivar shrugged. "The time is ripe to escalate and commence with our plan. Everything is in place except personnel. I am depending on you to provide them." Pres nodded, surprised at how quickly Xalivar's other efforts must have succeeded. "Can I count on you, General?"

Pres stiffened, her fists balling as her fingers crossed in salute. "Of course, my Lord. I have always been your servant." Xalivar's confidence had always been inspiring to those who followed him, and it was no different now. Her fears and doubts just faded away in the face of his passion.

Xalivar nodded. "Good. I have need of loyal officers. I'd hate to be forced to make other arrangements so late into our plan. Don't worry, in a few weeks, you will be back safe on the right side again."

"Of course, my Lord."

Xalivar laughed. "The High Lord Councilor looks like a baby Gungor who's lost his way. He's beside himself with confusion. Everything is going exactly as I foresaw. Enjoy this, Pres. It will be a great triumph for us all."

Pres nodded. "I won't let you down, my Lord."

Xalivar turned his back to her, his hands crossed behind him. "How are General Grif and Admiral Dek responding to this new crisis?"

"They do the best they can. We've had mutiny in our ranks of late to deal with as well."

Xalivar smiled, turning back toward her. "All according to plan, General. And it's working wonderfully so far, I'd say, wouldn't you?"

Pres had no idea how Xalivar could have interfered with the computer algorithms for duty assignments, but she'd suspected he was behind it. He seemed quite pleased with himself as always. She nodded and smiled. "Indeed, sir. We're investigating the cause now."

"By the time anything is discovered, you'll be safely elsewhere, fear not. In the meantime, you must prepare to leave. Two weeks from now at this very hour, your recruits will depart with you for their new training base. I expect everything to be ready."

"Sneaking soldiers out under the Alliance's nose is going to pose a great challenge—"

"You will not have to sneak. You will merely correct the course once you depart. Just make sure the ship is loaded with men loyal to you and me."

Pres nodded, stiffening to attention again. "Of course, my Lord."

Xalivar stopped a moment, his eyes cutting into her again, like a medical scanner. He seemed to be looking past or even through her as his eyes moved up and down. "We can tolerate no more delays. Bear that in mind." With that he spun on his heels, the hood sliding back over his head again, and walked away, disappearing into the shadows from which he'd come.

Despite the veiled threat in them, Xalivar's words reassured her. He was firmly in control, and when Xalivar was in control, he made things happen. Nothing less than success. She'd chosen the right side, and she felt more confident than ever. She wished she could be open with Dek. She hated the idea of facing him as enemies when the time came.

Pres waited a few moments before turning and making her way back to the civilian shuttles, her eyes searching the departure lists for Italis.

Tela and her friends arrived at the launch bay fifteen minutes before their scheduled departure time to find the mechanics finishing final pre-flight checks.

"That's not regulation," one of them noted as Tela added extra provisions to the pocket behind the seat of her VS28.

Tela smiled at him as she slid the seat back into place and climbed into the cockpit. "You never know these days what might happen on these patrols. With all the attacks on workers, we might be at risk too. Being pilots isn't exactly low profile."

The mechanic shrugged, thinking it over. "I sure hope it doesn't come to that, but I guess it doesn't hurt to be prepared."

Tela nodded. "I ordered everyone to carry extra just in case. Long patrols cut through a lot of isolated areas. You never know who you might run into."

The mechanic accepted it with a look that assured Tela she'd planted a seed to sway any doubts from others who might have made similar observations. She strapped on the belts securing her in place as the mechanic checked each one, adjusting them to fit smugly around her. "Good luck. Come back bored and ready for excitement, okay?"

Tela laughed. "Not too much excitement, ok?"

The mechanic joined her laughter as she glanced over to see Nila and the others settling into their own cockpits. The mechanic disappeared down the ladder as Tela initiated preflight checks, reviewing the fuel tank indicators and long range scanners first just to be sure.

Then she switched on the private squadron channel. "We ready?"

"For what? The last act of our official military careers?" Tela could hear the grin in Virun's voice.

"Let's cut that kind of chatter, ok? You never know who might be listening," Brie's voice sounded far fiercer than the timid young girl had ever appeared.

"Yes, ma'am," Virun said, his and Jorek's chuckles blending on the comm channel.

"Let's get rolling," Nila said, shifting nervously in her seat as Tela glanced over.

Tela smiled. She'd always admired their constant enthusiasm, sometimes wishing her own could match it. As much as she loved flying, these days she found herself more and more longing for legs on the ground, a side effect, she supposed, of being relegated to less exciting duties. Still, she wasn't about to admit it to anyone.

"Squadron, start your engines."

Just then alarms blared overhead as an alert flashed on her cockpit screen.

"What's going on?" Jorek sounded as confused as Tela felt.

"I have no idea. Squadron Alpha Six Leader to flight control." Tela muted the alarm klaxon on her control panel as she waited for a response.

"Alpha Six Leader, this is flight control, launch cancelled."

"Launch cancelled?" Jorek's voice rose as it always did when he was irritated.

"Hold on." Tela tensed in her seat and switched comm channels, keying the mic. "Squadron Alpha Six Leader to command. Is General Uzah there?"

Uzah's voice came back immediately, almost as if he'd been expecting her call. "Alpha Six Leader, we have a situation. Report to flight control for further instructions."

"What's going on, General?" For a moment, she panicked. Had command overheard Jorek's comment? Or perhaps someone at the restaurant?

"We need every available hand for protection duty. The High Lord Councilor's making a speech this afternoon."

"The High Lord Councilor's coming to Vertullis?"

"He's supposed to announce 'The Returning' as a new official holiday."

Tela frowned, despite her relief. "Just what we need—more inspiration for those who already hate us."

"Lord Aron proposed it. They want to make a show of unified support. I need your team to lead the protection detail. Another squadron's covering the patrol."

Tela muted her comm so he wouldn't hear her fist slam into the arm of her chair.

He continued, unaware of the rising temperature inside her head. "We didn't get any notice, Tela. You're one of my most experienced officers. I need you to report as soon as possible."

Tela sighed, switching the mic back on. "Yes, sir. We'll be there in moments." Her fingers flew across the control panel as she hit switches to shut down the fighter. The servos whined overhead as the cockpit blastshield slid back up. Tearing off her straps, she began climbing out of the cockpit, glancing up as her feet hit the floor to see the rest of her team emulating her. Once they'd joined her, she led them out toward the elevator.

"What's going on?" Nila asked.

"We're security for Tarkanius' visit. 'The Returning' is about to become an official holiday."

"That oughta rile the nutjobs up," Virun mumbled.

"You're always saying you want more action," Jorek teased. Nila cut him off with an elbow to the ribs as she nodded toward Tela, who punch-ed the elevator button and paced in front of the doors as they waited.

"We'll find him as soon as we can, don't worry." Brie's eyes were full of worry.

"If this announcement has the effect we're all imagining, we might not be slipping away for anything in the near future." She rushed aboard the elevator as the doors open.

"Well, I hope you're wrong about that," Nila said as the others followed her onto the elevator and Jorek punched the button for Flight Control.

"Me, too," Tela mumbled, her head racing with thoughts of Davi and his friends. She said a silent prayer for safety as the doors shut and the elevator rumbled into motion. Uzah had been right. It was personal. She couldn't shake the feeling Davi was in danger, and just like him, her instincts were to protect her mate. Problems aside, she cared about him and if anything happened to him, she'd never forgive herself for not taking action. Still, she was under orders to protect the High Lord Councilor. There was no way to slip away. She just had to pray and focus on her duty. Why did that thought feel so impossible at the moment?

Xalivar relaxed in his cabin aboard the small freighter as it crossed deep space from Talekyn back to Xanthis. To pass the time, he turned on the broadcast nets and watched with delight as Orson Sterling and the other talking heads replayed over and over Miri's disastrous speech and the riotous aftermath. He chuckled at her dismay and at Danae and their host's uncertainty at how to respond.

"It couldn't have gone any better if we'd planned it ourselves," Lucius said from the seat beside him.

Xalivar nodded. "Perhaps we did plan it." He glanced over as Lucius shot him a startled expression. Xalivar laughed. "Don't think just because you've earned my trust that I'm going to enlighten you with every detail of my plan. It's got many facets, and many teams will be involved in its success. Including some who have only to disrupt life whenever they can."

Lucius smiled. "Forgive me, my Lord. I should have remembered your facility for thoroughness."

Xalivar nodded, his grin widening. "Many wish they could forget all about it. Some may even think they have. The time is upon us for them to be disavowed of such treacherous notions. And the first amongst them shall be my beloved sister, Miri."

"Her life is not what it once was," Lucius said, almost looking sympathetic. "I imagine she has many regrets."

"She destroyed our family's legacy." Xalivar frowned. "She hasn't begun to know the amount of regret due her."

Xalivar stood and left Lucius to watch the broadcasts as he took a seat at a terminal on the cabin wall.

Time for another missive from your dear brother, Miri. He winced as an image of their childhood flashed into his mind. They'd always been so close, and it had broken his heart when he'd discovered Miri's deceit and betrayal. Still, Xalivar had long ago learned to control his emotions, and he'd quickly brushed it aside to focus on doing what he must. Still, Miri and her bastard son managed to ruin everything the family had worked generations for, but Xalivar would restore it. He would bring the Rhii name back to glory and set the Alliance back on its proper course. Even if it meant total destruction of every worker, young and old, he would do it. And nothing—no one—would stand in his way this time.

His fingers clacked on the keys as he began to compose the e-post. Taunting her might be seen by some as childish, but Xalivar enjoyed the clever wordplay, especially knowing how it upset her and threw her off balance. Unlike him, Miri had not trained in controlling her emotions. They ran rampant, and, as a result, they dominated and controlled her in ways that made her weak and easily preyed upon. For the first time, Xalivar found himself pleased at the thought of it.

You're no longer my liability, dear sister. Your relationship with this family is in name only. You'll have no part in our new glory.

As he typed, he chuckled at the thought of Miri whiling away her last days in seclusion and poverty while he returned to the Palace. Oh, how that would eat away at her.

A well-deserved ending for a turncoat, father would agree.

He smiled again as he considered the perfect ending for his post, then typed it in and punched send. His only regret was that he wouldn't be able to be there to watch her open it.

Soon, my dear sister. Our day will be soon.

Farien pushed the joystick forward, racing to catch Davi. Hot air pounded his skin as the g-forces threatened to pull his hands free of the controls. Clearly the time spent training worker pilots in the forests of Vertullis was paying off, as Davi had taken the previous corner so sharply Farien couldn't believe he'd stayed aboard his Skitter.

As Farien slowed and pulled alongside, Davi glanced back at Yao who was trailing them. "Well, we haven't lost him yet."

Farien grinned, shaking his head. "It wouldn't be hard." He keyed the comm. "Come on, Brahma, you fly like your grandmother!"

"My grandmother's survived this long for a reason—no one in our family's insane." Yao's tone was one of patient calm. By now, his friends' antics didn't cause him any stress.

"Well, try to keep up, okay?" Davi said. "The streets are getting narrower and none of us know the city."

"Plus, the blackmarket could be dangerous," Farien added. "Wouldn't want you left alone."

"Don't worry, I'll find the impact crater or crashed-in wall easily enough," Yao said, unaffected.

Davi and Farien laughed as both slowed down for their friend to catch them. The streets were getting more crowded anyway, and they needed to work together to make sense of the Skitters' cheap nav system's directions. Sleek and fast one-man ground craft operating on a system allowed them to float above the planet's surface, Skitters' controls and handling resembled those of a VS28, but their nav systems didn't come close.

"You don't really expect anyone to tell us anything?" Yao pulled between them, his pace constant as if it were up to them to stay with him, not the other way around.

"Just stick to the cover story and we'll see what happens," Farien said.

Farien wondered how long it would take for Dru to get himself into trouble back at their lodgings. He'd only agreed to stay behind, after Farien threatened to send him back to Eleni 1 on the next shuttle. The black market would be rough enough for the three officers without them having to worry about a cadet, especially when it seemed Dru couldn't keep himself out of trouble for very long.

Davi pulled to a stop at the next intersection, checking his nav computer. "It looks like it should be on the next block west of here."

Fairen and Yao halted their Skitters beside his. All three glanced around. Yao looked particularly alarmed. "I really hope this cover story works. This doesn't look like a place we want to be identified as military officers."

Farien didn't remember them being this soft at the Academy. He rolled his eyes at Davi, then frowned at Yao. "Just let us do the talking, okay? Chances are you'll blend in with the other non-humans around here just fine."

Davi nodded. "Yao's right, though. We need to be really careful. If this place is half as dangerous as the rumors say—"

"I can't believe we went to the same Academy. You two sound like scared kids. Just watch my back and I'll handle it." Farien accelerated the Skitter, turning left and heading for the next intersection as his friends hurried to follow him.

"Be cool, Farien. The last thing we need is to set anyone off."

Farien sighed into the comm, cutting Davi off. "I'm leading this team, remember? Trust me."

"That's what worries us," Yao replied.

Ignoring them, Farien turned onto the next street which dead ended at a large open field covered with ramshackle buildings and scattered canopies. A potpourri of scents struck his nose—fruits, raw meat, smoke, sweat, oils, perfumes. A handmade sign read "Xanthis Independent Market." Farien parked and climbed off his Skitter as Davi and Yao stopped nearby. Already shady-looking characters gawked at them from the aisles between the market's buildings. Farien saw Xanthians mixed with rough looking humans, a couple Tertullians like Yao, an Idolian and two Lhamors. He nodded his head toward the Lhamors, looking at Davi and Yao.

Farien strode past the sign and up the aisle, passing right past the Lhamors as if they weren't there. Davi and Yao hurried after him.

The signage was scarce and buildings not well marked. Finding anything here would be an accident. He debated the risks of splitting them up until a solution presented itself. A young Xanthian appeared, offering himself as guide. "Just a small fee for my services is all," he responded to Farien's inquiry about what he charged. The Xanthian wore ragged, mis-matched clothes and clearly was overdue for a cleansing. Not to be trusted.

"We'll figure it out on our own," Farien replied as Davi hurriedly handed the youth some credits.

"It's been a while since we visited the market," Davi said, shooting Farien a look. "Your help will be most beneficial."

Farien sighed and motioned for the guide to lead the way. He shot Davi a look that said: *Your responsibility!* The youth pocketed the newly counted credits and smiled, walking as if he owned the place. "My name's Qajuan. Whatever you need, I can find it for you, just ask."

"Right now, we're looking for something special," Farien said, his memory racing to recall terms he'd heard used in stories of the market. You couldn't just outright ask for assassins. There was a proper slang here, and one had to use it or be seen as an outsider who couldn't be trusted.

"Lots of special things here," Qajuan replied. "Anything you can imagine. A little more specific and we'll find it for you."

"Specialists," Davi whispered, using the term Farien had been searching for.

Qajuan whirled and stared at him, his face indifferent. "Ah, many we have. Depends on your needs."

"The three-armed kind," Farien said.

Qajuan frowned. "Those kind are very rare, very expensive. Haven't seen many here lately, but we have many others. Perhaps one of them can solve your problem."

"Take us to someone who can arrange for any type we want," Farien suggested.

Qajuan smiled, satisfied, then whirled around and started up an aisle to the right.

They wound through rows and rows of tables offering everything from Qiwi and Gungor meat to fruits like Feruca and Gixi, various dried beans and leaves and powders both medicinal and for brewing. The scents mixed together, a kind of pungent sweet, dusty smell filling Farien's nose.

They passed into another section and here were various items of clothing and household goods—furniture handmade from high quality Vertullian wood, Idolian sand weavings with their intricate patterns of colored sand speaking messages from some mysterious religion long forgotten, Tertullian cloth of all shapes, sizes and colors. Farien had seen similar items in museums as a student and spent little time examining them, hurrying after their guide who seemed confident of the path he'd chosen.

They passed under a narrow archway between two canopied booths and Farien stopped dead. Stretching before him were endless tables of every weapon and armament imaginable, from the blasters he and his fellow cadets trained on to the more sophisticated blasters he and his friends carried as officers to the laser rifles sharpshooters carried into battle and the tiny weapons those with ill intentions hid in various nooks and crevices of their bodies. Yao and Davi shot him a look of warning as they passed him nonchalantly, following Qajuan. Farien stepped forward, moving slower but keeping pace. Then they rounded a corner and he saw military-issue laser targeting systems, the most sophisticated, restricted type. Troops trained for months just to learn how to operate them. No one outside the military was supposed to have access to them. He couldn't believe his eyes. He knew stolen military weapons made it to the blackmarkets, but to so openly sell them?

Noting his interest, the dealer stepped forward. He was dressed in khaki from head to foot—pants and a shirt, even his shoes a light tan. His face was long, odd shaped, and at first Farien wasn't sure if the man was human or some other species. Then he smiled and his teeth were a cornucopia of colors—Idolian. The teeth always gave them away. Their skin and hair colors often quite matched humans but with the long faces and arms and colored teeth, you could always tell. "How can I help you, my friend?"

The accent was sharp but the words understandable. "Just passing through."

"These are very special," he said, reaching his elongated arm out to stroke one of the targeting units. He leaned forward as if sharing a secret, his grin widening. "No one outside the military has them, except for me."

Farien took a deep breath, tensing with the urge to arrest the man on the spot. "You must be very well connected."

The man laughed, nodding. "Yes, I am. It's very fortunate you've made my acquaintance."

"How much?"

The man rubbed his hands together, stroking the target system while keeping his eyes locked on Farien. "How many?"

Farien glanced up to see Yao and Davi waving impatiently as Qajuan waited behind them.

"How many do you have?"

The vendor raised his hands in a questioning gesture. "I can get you more than you can afford."

Davi cleared his throat. "Other matters await us."

"Please," the vendor frowned and waved dismissively without even glancing away from his new customer, "we don't rush here.

There's always time."

Then, amidst the shadows, Farien thought he saw a familiar blue face, red eyes staring at him. He blinked, looking more intensely and saw a tall, thin figure hurrying away. Hurrying to follow, he pushed the vendor roughly aside, sending him back into a table as two targeting units fell to the ground. Farien heard a cracking sound but didn't look back.

"That's no way to do business here!"

But Farien was off and winding through narrow alleys between buildings and canopies. He barely noticed Yao and Davi following, with Qajuan bringing up the rear. "Where are you going? The man you need is not this way!"

Farien increased his pace, seeing the tall, thin figure bobbing in and out ahead of him in the dense crowd. For mid-afternoon, the market was hopping.

"Where are we going?" Davi's breaths were heavy as he hurried to catch up with Farien.

"Does that guy look familiar?"

"Which one?"

"The tall, thin one. Andorian maybe?"

"Andorian?" Davi stretched up to get a better look as he struggled to keep up.

"It's Manaen."

"You saw his face?"

Farien shook his head. "No, blue skin, red eyes."

"That describes every Andorian. Why are we chasing him?"

The Andorian slowed ahead, trapped by a shoulder-to-shoulder crowd watching a demonstration. He turned slightly and Farien caught a glimpse of his face. He motioned to Davi. "Look! Manaen!"

The Andorian shrunk into the shadows as Farien called, then suddenly disappeared into a building.

"Cover the back. Let's find out for sure!" Farien hurried toward the front of the building as Davi and Yao hurried to cover the sides and back, Qajuan shooting them a puzzled look as he hung back.

Farien burst into a dark room, tables covering every available space, with only narrow aisles between. He slowed as his eyes adjusted—the Andorian nowhere in sight. A startled Xanthian vendor turned from negotiating with a Tertullian couple over some Gungor carcasses. His nose caught a slight hint of rot mixed with dust and curing solutions. Their purple eyes lit up the darkness, reminding Farien of Yao outside. Farien ignored them, winding around and past tables. He heard a shuffling from behind a curtain and pushed through.

"You cannot go there!"

The vendor's voice faded as Farien entered a narrow corridor lined with stacked goods, hurrying onward. And then he burst through the back door and into shadows between buildings. Davi whirled, his blaster drawn as Farien waved. "Where'd he go?"

Yao appeared, shaking his head. "We never saw him."

Davi relaxed and started sliding his blaster back inside his shirt when the Xanthian vendor rushed through the back door with his Tertullian clients.

The Idolian vendor appeared around the corner behind Davi, pointing and motioning. "There they are!"

Two burly Lhamors followed close behind with another Xanthian, who carried himself like some sort of official.

"He has a blaster!" The Xanthian vendor pointed at the bulge in Davi's shirt.

The Lhamors slowed, fumbling with all four hands for weapons of their own.

Farien hurried to Yao and Davi, forming a defensive circle as they backed toward the opposite corner.

"No weapons! A misunderstanding." Yao smiled, his voice its usual calm. But the new arrivals continued staring at Davi with menace.

"We were negotiating, then he shoved me aside and ran off!" The Idolian's teeth flared with rage.

"I was only looking." Farien raised his hands to proclaim his innocence.

"You're making a lot of trouble for men we've never seen here before," the Xanthian official said. "Identify yourselves!" The Lhamor guards waved their weapons menacingly behind him.

Then Qajuan appeared between them. "They're with me. Here to see Beauran."

"Beauran?" The official and the vendors exchanged worried looks as the Lhamors' weapons lowered slightly.

"They damaged two expensive items," the Idolian said. "Who will pay for that?"

"It was an accident," Yao said with an apologetic look.

"They're not easy to replace!"

"They thought they saw an old friend." Qajuan offered a wave of dismissal. "They just wanted to catch up with him."

"At what cost to me?"

"Send the bill to Beauran," Qajuan said. "He'll see that you're compensated." Who or what was Beauran? A person? A place? All the locals reacted to it each time with recognition and fear.

The Idolian shrunk back, his face changing, as if it suddenly wasn't so important. "Just tell them to be careful. We don't need trouble here!"

Qajuan smiled. "Of course."

The Idolian turned and disappeared back the way he'd come as the Lhamors holstered their weapons and the Xanthian and Tertullian customers disappeared back inside his shop.

Qajuan nodded to the Xanthian official and moved past them, motion-ing for Farien and his friends to follow.

Within moments, he'd led them out a gate to the street and hurried around a bend where Farien could see the parked Skitters. "What about this Beauran?"

Qajuan laughed and continued on toward where they'd first met. "You can't go anywhere near him after what happened. Word spreads quickly. No one will trust you, least of all Beauran."

"We came here for information," Farien frowned, his voice rising with his irritation.

"I can tell you what you want to know." Qajuan stopped a few feet from the Skitters and turned back to face them. "An Andorian hired the Lhamors. The one you saw."

"How do you know it's the same one?" Davi asked, before Farien had the chance. Despite recent tensions, it felt good to be back working with people who knew him so well.

"The Andorian represents powerful interests. He's seen here often."

"Who are these powerful interests?" Farien asked.

"I don't know. But all treat him with respect." His look told Farien he meant fear.

"What's the Andorian's name?" Davi jumped in again before Qajuan could answer. "Have you ever heard the name Manaen?"

Qajuan shook his head, then glanced around to make sure no one would overhear. "I only know he buys what he wants and no one cheats him."

"If Manaen's here..." Yao's eyes met Davi and he didn't even finish the thought.

Davi turned back to Qajuan. "Can you get his name?"

Qajuan shrugged. "I don't know. Take me with you."

"We're on an official mission," Farien protested.

Qajuan shook his head. "I can't be here when Beauran hears of this. I'll explain when we're far from here." His eyes darted around them and back toward the market.

Davi nodded, helping Qajuan onto the back of his Skitter, then climbing on and firing the turbos as Farien and Yao did the same. The Xanthian youth held on to Davi's waist, looking grateful, but his eyes remained peeled for trouble.

"How do we know we can trust him?" Farien looked at Yao and Davi, ignoring the boy.

"He saved our lives," Yao said with a shrug.

"Let's discuss this later," Davi pushed the joystick and his Skitter begin moving as Farien followed his glance. The Xanthian official and Lhamor guards had arrived and headed toward them again. Yao accelerated after Davi and Farien followed, aiming straight at a crowd of Xanthians walking along the side of the street. They scattered, chattering angrily and blocking the official and his thugs from view.

Chapter Seven

Tela and her team finalized security arrangements for the High Lord Councilor's visit to Vertullis the day before the Royal Shuttle arrived. It felt different being on her home planet on official military duty. Since joining the Alliance pilot corps, Tela hadn't been home much and now here she was in charge of security for an important historical visit. She'd never seen Telanus so proud, walking around beaming from ear-to-ear, treating her like she was the princess herself. No matter how many times she scolded him for making such a fuss about her, he kept it up, unable to help himself. The one good thing about her present assignment was it distracted her from worrying about Davi. He was still out there somewhere. She checked in daily with friends on the command crew, but no new reports had come in of any altercations. She prayed he was fine and all her worrying was for nothing.

They'd had only a few days to prepare for the High Lord Councilor's visit and the entire Borali leadership, including Joram and Uzah on Vertullis, remained determined to ensure no protests would occur. This was to be a day of great historical significance. They'd given her a big responsibility but one she'd thrown herself into entirely. She'd asked Uzah why more senior people from Legallis hadn't been put in charge. He told her it was a chance for the Vertullians to prove themselves worthy, and, with Davi gone, she was the best person for the job. As flattered as she felt, she also resented the pressure.

Fortunately, most of the pressure was manufactured by politicians. The actual preparations went smoothly with few hitches. A few angry citizens maneuvered for better seats and special passes, but that was normal politics. Overall, when the day came for Tarkanius' speech, Tela felt confident there would be no problems.

The morning of the event, she had breakfast with Telanus, who frowned at her silence and worried expression. "Is it Davi or the speech you're so worried about?"

Tela sighed, continuing to run her fork aimlessly through her food. "A little of both?"

Telanus smiled. "You worry too much, Little Girl. You are such an amazing officer. I couldn't be more proud."

"They picked me because Davi is off God knows where, in God knows what danger—forgetting all about anyone here who might give a damn about him." She flicked some eggs to the side at a nearby bush.

Telanus reached out and put a hand atop hers, in an attempt to calm her. "Stop it. They picked you because you're good at what you do. And because they trust you. And I'm sure Davi is fine but just too busy to communicate. Trust God to care for him, Tela."

Tela's eyes met his, but she quickly looked away. He loved her so much. Yet as good as it felt after growing up mostly without her father, it also scared her a little. So much of her life he'd missed. So much of his, she'd missed. She sometimes wished they could drop everything and just spend their time getting to know each other.

"You always were high strung, even as a child," her father continued, his brow creased with concern. "That's something your mother and I always wished we could have changed about you."

She took a deep breath and reminded herself there was still plenty of time. "I'm trying, Daddy. Really."

Telanus chuckled, relaxing his hand and resting it beside his plate on the table again. "I love when you call me that."

Tela blushed as she saw his grin, turning away again. "Stop it."

Telanus shrugged. "Sorry. It's just now that you're all grown up, I didn't expect you'd still call me that."

"It's what you are to me. What you'll always be." Turning

back, she reached across the table and squeezed his hand.

"For what it's worth, I'm sure Davi's as worried about you as you are about him."

Tela sighed. "I hope so." If Davi knew the responsibility she'd been given, perhaps he would be worried, more than he might be at the moment. Her father was right. Davi cared about her. And he could truly be out of communications range. She glanced at her chrono. "But I'm late. I have to be there early to make sure everything's done right."

Telanus squeezed her hand back and smiled. "I'm proud of you. Go show them how amazing you are."

Tela felt herself blushing again. "Stop embarrassing me."

"Can't a father be proud?"

Tela stood, hesitating, then walked around the table and leaned in to kiss his forehead. "I love you, Daddy."

"I love you, too, Little Girl. See you soon."

She felt a shiver up her spine as he said those words. Every time. So many years she'd given up hope of ever seeing him again. The warmth of his smile stayed with her as she turned and hurried off.

One of the largest crowds ever assembled on the planet gathered for the event. It was the first time Vertullians would have the chance to see a High Lord Councilor in the flesh in decades, and as full-fledged citizens, that had special meaning for her people. She scanned their multi-colored faces, filled with excitement and awe—Vertullians of all Old Earth races and backgrounds united in anticipation of what the High Lord Councilor would say. The dais was packed with dignitaries. A majority of the Council accompanied their leader with Simeon seated immediately to Tarkanius' right and the others arranged in order of seniority around them. Military leaders were present as well, including Uzah, Matheu, and various leaders from Legallis. Representing senior command was General Grif, whom Tela met for the first time. She'd seen him on broadcasts and in passing but had never actually spoken to him until now. She was surprised to find he knew a lot about her. He was tall and thin, hair graying at his temples and initially came across almost like a grandpa in the way he spoke to her. But Tela had heard from Davi and others that he was quite serious and intense about military matters, much like Matheu.

Joram and Matheu made brief speeches, followed by Simeon, before Joram introduced Tarkanius. She'd never seen Joram looking so proud. It reminded her of the way Telanus had been looking at her since she got the security assignment. She chuckled a bit as he shifted nervously before the mic, then backed away, as if afraid to dishonor Tarkanius with his back, as the High Lord Councilor took center stage.

"My dear people," Tarkanius began, scanning the crowd with a broad smile that let them know he considered them his own. Tela felt a chill run up her spine as he said it. Hearing him say it on the nets was one thing, but in person it was electrifying. It had the same effect on the crowd. He won them over immediately, the rest of his speech interrupted with cheers and spontaneous applause throughout. He spoke for around thirty minutes, assuring them that the extension of citizenship had come because they'd earned respect, that it was long overdue and that it was permanent. He spoke of the significance of unity and service and then addressed 'The Returning.'

"In a way, you, joint citizens with us of a former age on Old Earth, are now returning to your proper place at our sides." Cheers and applause broke out all around him. Tarkanius smiled warmly, waiting for it to subside before continuing. "And it with this thought in mind that we are honored to declare 'The Returning' an official holiday for all of us."

The explosions came as the cheering and applause commenced again. Flashes of oranges and yellows from the corners of the podium and back in the crowd. Loud explosive reports blended with people's screams as the crowd began to scatter. Smoke rose from beneath the podium. The dignitaries on the platform looked like frightened Gungors caught in spotlights of a night hunt. Some stood and looked around, unsure what to do. Others cowered in their seats. A few fled the shaking dais.

Tela's breath caught in her throat as Tarkanius fell to his knees. A piece of the dais had split apart beneath his feet. For a moment, she thought his leg was trapped. The podium wobbled as if it might fall back on him. Then the personal security detail she'd assigned swept in, lifted him to his feet and raced him to safety. The comm channel remained a constant stream of agitated voices in her ear. Reports flew in so fast her mind hardly registered the details: sightings of possible suspects; suspicious packages; locations of possible explosives; endless questions. Just as her team reached the stairs with Tarkanius, the entire dais collapsed, sinking to the ground. The dignitaries all joined the chaos, scrambling for safety, mixing with the scattering crowd. Tela and her people quickly lost control, concentrating their efforts on the Council members and leader-ship. The comm channels continued with endless streams of reports. Virun and Jorek claimed to have found someone with detonators running away amidst the crowd. A couple of other security personnel found others with suspicious residue on their clothes. She ordered them all rounded up and taken for interrogation, waiting until Brie and Nila finished the count and assured her all the dignitaries and leaders were safe with only a few minor scrapes, bruises and burns amongst those closest to the edge of the platform.

Tela saw Joram, Uzah, Tarkanius and Simeon looking at her and wished she could crawl back into the shadows. She had no idea what to say to them. She'd failed in her most important assignment ever. How could this have happened? Everyone had been checked so carefully, the whole area swept. She knew she'd be busy for a while sorting all that out. She grimaced as Tarkanius led the others toward her. His ceremonial robe was singed at the bottom, his hair disheveled a bit, but he appeared otherwise fine.

He stopped, facing her, and smiled. "Don't worry, Tela. I'm okay. We're all okay."

She struggled to fight back the tears welling at the corners of her eyes. "I don't know how this could have happened. We were so careful."

"Those who want to harm us are always more determined than we are to protect ourselves," Tarkanius said, putting a hand on her shoulder.

Uzah's face was a mixture of anger and embarrassment. "We

will get to the bottom of it, my Lord. It's unacceptable!" He turned to Tela. "I hear rumors workers were involved?"

"We don't know yet. There were some people with residue on their clothing and others with detonators. They're being rounded up."

"I want answers right away!"

Tarkanius winked at Tela then turned to Uzah. "General, answers in such cases can take a while to become clear. We all want them, but let's not ask the impossible of our dedicated men and women, all right? I'm sure they'll all do their best."

Uzah looked as if he'd been called into court martial. Joram forced a smile and nodded. "Of course, my Lord. We all will. All we want is to ensure your safety."

Tarkanius sighed. "Right now, I have fear for the safety of all of us, not just me."

"It was a good speech, my Lord," Tela finally said.

Tarkanius smiled. "With an explosive ending." He laughed and soon the others joined him, nervously. Tela relaxed a bit, grateful for his generosity, then excused herself and hurried off to question the suspects her people had taken to the command base.

Xalivar closed his eyes and took a deep breath after hearing Manaen report seeing Xander and his friends at the black market on Xanthis. Xander and his friends were getting too close. They knew where to go and who to talk to. How was that possible unless someone had left too many clues? When he'd heard they were coming, he'd expected them to be chasing rumors, but this... He knew their encounter with Manaen had been pure coincidence but it exposed his operations to risks he couldn't afford. Xalivar whirled back around as his fists unclenched at his sides. "Get Obed now!"

Manaen nodded and hurried off, looking relieved to have an excuse to be away from his master. Lucius remained silent in a nearby chair, waiting.

"That idiot son of his should have never been allowed into

this! He seems intent on doing everything he can to thwart our plans!"

Lucius nodded. "He's incompetent and careless, but I doubt it's intentional. He doesn't have the brains, from everything I've read in his file."

Xalivar paced, fists continuing to clench. "I want them eliminated, Lucius. All except my former nephew. I want him alive! Now!"

Lucius stood, hands closing to form the salute. "Yes, my Lord, I'll see to it."

Lucius hurried out as Manaen appeared in the doorway, waving Obed past him. Obed's face remained casual, but Xalivar saw a glint of irritation in his eyes. "Oh, I'm disturbing you?"

"Nothing that can't be resumed later."

Xalivar stopped pacing and turned to face his old rival, noting Manaen had disappeared with Lucius. "My former nephew and his friends are here."

"Davi Rhii? On Xanthis?" Obed seemed genuinely surprised.

Xalivar nodded. "Yes. And asking questions of the wrong people. The result, no doubt, of the foolish carelessness of your son."

"Bordox would never jeopardize this operation. He's as invested in this as the rest of us."

"You've wanted for years to ruin me, Obed. Don't take me for a fool."

"I want my family restored to its rightful place, yes," Obed said, straightening with pride instead of shrinking back as most would when facing Xalivar's wrath. "But I joined you in this plan because we share a common goal."

"I'd better not find out otherwise."

"Are you threatening me?"

"You and your son, yes!"

Obed coughed. "Don't be a fool. You have few allies in this. You need me."

"I trust no one but myself."

They stood a moment staring into each other's eyes, neither blinking nor looking away. Then Obed motioned, the wave of a hand. "I'll have someone deal with your former protégée, don't worry. He won't get off Xanthis alive."

"Lucius is seeing to it. You'll do nothing except find your son and bring him here. I want him now!"

"Fine. I will find him. But we did not betray you."

"You've waited for an opportunity for decades!"

"Serving you! I led your Special Police! How dare you question my honor. I won't stand for it!" Obed pointed a finger at Xalivar in warning.

"Then sit down where you can remember your place." Xalivar's fist clenched as he glared coldly at Obed, daring him to respond. After a moment, Obed turned and walked out the door.

Your day will come, my old enemy! When all this is finished, I will deal with you. But first, my young Xander, you will answer to me!

Imagining Xander's reaction to the death of his friends lit Xalivar's heart like laser lights and he chuckled to himself. There were few things Xalivar enjoyed more than enacting revenge.

When news of the bombing flooded the comm channels, Pres knew it was time to move. Xalivar had promised a distraction—an incident requiring military mobilization in response. The pretense was a call to respond, but while they'd depart under the same orders and headings as responders, she and her team would slip off course and disappear. She went quickly about her duties as required, sending out various orders via comm and e-post. Mixed among them, she sent the code ordering her recruits to meet at the transport in half an hour. By the time they were discovered, they'd have safely disappeared on FTL routes. The chaos surrounding the attack on the High Lord Councilor took some of the pressure off. Although they'd be missed, no one would have time to really search for them right away, allowing them time to put distance between the transport and anyone who might give chase.

Confirmation codes flooded her inbox, as she continued coordinating troops sent to escort the Royal Shuttle, seeing to the wounded, and investigating the assassination attempt. She glanced across the command cnter to where Dek was also busily coordinating the flood of calls. He stayed so cool under pressure. She thought back to when things fell apart over Vertullis. Even then he'd been calm, while she'd struggled just to stay on her feet. She glanced away before he noticed her stare. He could read her well after all the hours spent working together. She couldn't let him read the message in her eyes now. She was about to leave him, probably forever. If they did see each other again, she wondered if they'd ever do so as friends. Dek was an honorable man. He didn't tolerate betrayal or dereliction of duty. She hated to disappoint him and hoped someday she'd get the chance to explain.

As the last confirmation code came in, she ran the calculations. Three hundred officers and troops, including a tech she could see across from her in command. The last challenge was to slip away herself. Dek had already announced plans to leave for the surface within the hour, leaving her in charge. So her betrayal of him began with an unavoidable lie. She waited a moment, taking a few calming breaths, then stood and approached Dek.

"I've got a crisis to handle down at the launch bays. A few angry pilots wanting to take off and wreak revenge on the entire planet for attacking the High Lord Councilor."

Dek sighed. "I've had a few of those myself. Take names. We need to keep track of these people."

She nodded. "I'll be back as soon as I can."

"Of course, Pres. I have every confidence in you."

It took all her strength not to cringe at his last remark. Instead, she forced a smile, turned on her heels and hurried out, motioning for the tech to follow. "Come with me and bring your datapad."

The tech nodded, looking relieved that her quick thinking saved him from making his own excuse. He followed on her heels out the door.

The café looked abandoned as Hachim entered and made his way toward the back room. A waitress and a cook barely looked up from their conversation as he slipped past, saying nothing before returning to their gossip. Niger had arranged the location the day before, based on information from a friend serving in the military here. The spaceport was not its usual bustle today due to the speech. Even the assassination attempt didn't have people rushing for transports. Hachim looked around a moment before pushing the door and disappearing inside.

"Tell me you didn't rent this room under your name," he said to Niger as he entered.

Niger sat at a round table. Seated beside him was a Borali major, whose bright red hair stood out despite the low lighting, his uniform appearing stretched to the max over his rotund frame. Lords Elul and Kretzu occupied the other seats with one left for Hachim. He slid into it quickly as he sighed, noting the others were already savoring cups of wine.

"It's under the name of our lead employee, Ner Zebah," Niger answered.

Hachim searched his mind. "A man captured by the authorities?"

Niger smiled. "It's perfect, Hachim. His co-conspirators met without him. Only by the time they discover this reservation, there'll be no one who can identify them."

"Employees saw us enter," Hachim reminded him.

"They'll soon be hiring new staff," the major said.

Hachim scowled. The implication was clear. "My gods, you plan to murder them?"

"The major will make sure they don't talk," Niger said. "I leave the details to him."

"Our plan worked perfectly," Lord Kretzu interjected. "The dignitaries were traumatized. The people terrorized. The blame on Vertullians."

"We don't know that for sure yet." Hachim shot him a look. Kretzu didn't waiver. Older, tall, and thin with a narrow mustache, he'd been on the Council almost as long as Simeon. So long that he'd seen many crises and it wasn't easy to rattle him.

"Stay calm, Hachim. This was your idea after all." Lord Elul was almost as large as the Major but from fat instead of muscle.

His robe bulged in all the wrong places and his puffy face reddened with annoyance. The looks the others gave Hachim were warnings to stop protesting and play along. Any one of them would gladly reveal his involvement and pin him with public blame if he dared rebel. The Major sneered and slid a cup over toward him.

Niger nodded, chuckling at Hachim. He reached across the table with a pitcher to fill Hachim's cup with wine. "It will happen, Hachim. The blame will be placed on those who clearly perpetrated the crime. We have nothing to fear."

"We must be very careful," Hachim answered. "Our goal is to increase the divide between Boralians and Workers. Protestors at speeches for a former princess, carefully planned bombings intended to injure and alarm. We cannot let ourselves lose focus."

"We also cannot allow ourselves to risk detection," Niger said. "We'll do what must be done for the glory of our people and the Alliance." He raised his cup and the others joined him in toast, sipping wine and laughing. Hachim raised his last, forcing a smile.

"Tarkanius wasn't even wounded. Your employees failed their task."

Niger shook his head. "Wounding Tarkanius would have been a bonus. Showing him incompetent and not in control was the goal, and that we accomplished quite well."

Kretzu nodded. "Indeed. We have only to await another such opportunity and strike again."

"We have an opportunity here to ruin their leadership," the Major said. "Men like Lord Aron, General Matheu, Governor Joram, and Davi Rhii should be implicated, their reputations clouded."

"Aron and Rhii are particularly known for their integrity. They fought hard to create this union, why would they destroy it?" Hachim stared at the Major, who would neither meet his eyes nor offer an explanation.

"We don't have to actually prove their involvement, just hint at ties," Elul said. "The confusion would be enough to cause damage, question their trustworthiness."

"Only those who don't personally know them would ever

believe it," Hachim said, shaking his head.

Niger frowned, irritatedly, and glared at Hachim. "You've been against every idea Lord Aron has presented since he joined the Council. Why are you defending him?"

"I am commenting on his character. He won't be easily slandered. His reputation for loyalty and integrity is widely known."

"What about Rhii?" the Major asked.

"The Vertullian people's hero? Oh, yes, he'll be easily discredited." Hachim rolled his eyes.

"Discrediting them is not of any importance to the plan. As long as we sway public opinion in our favor, our mission will succeed." Niger looked at them one by one for agreement. None objected, although the Major never met his eyes. "Your doubts, Hachim, only discredit *you*. I suggest you reconsider your attitude immediately." His eyes met Hachim's.

Hachim and Niger had known each other since childhood. Was it a threat or an advisement? Either way, Niger's face made it clear he wouldn't tolerate argument. Hachim sighed and stood. "Let's get out of here before we're seen together." He quickly downed the rest of his wine, needing to calm his nerves.

"I can handle any witnesses," the major said.

Hachim looked sadly at Niger and hurried out the door. It had been his idea, but he'd wanted mild diversions—enough to increase the tensions and throw doubt on the integrity of the workers. He hadn't really intended to get anyone killed. He should have known things would get out of hand with the co-conspirators they'd chosen.

He kept to the shadows and took the nearest exit, not spotting anyone taking notice of him, then hurried back out toward the city.

The bar was a dive. There was no better way to describe it. Bordox supposed he should be used to it given his new life, but this place was a new low. His father sat there as if it was completely normal for men of their status to be in such a place.

"Can you at least try to look relaxed? We don't want to draw attention to ourselves."

Bordox fought the urge to scowl as he carefully set his glass down on top of a stack of paper napkins, checking it for balance before releasing it. "Not my kind of place."

"It is if you don't want anyone to know about this meeting. So act like this is perfectly normal for us." Obed's eyes darkened in disappointment.

Bordox's anger rose with every disapproving word. He was tired of being treated like a total failure, his accomplishments going unrecognized. No wonder his military superiors never acknowledged his genius when his own father couldn't.

"Xalivar was quite angry to discover Rhii and his friends here on Xanthis," Obed continued with a smile. "Your leaks were most effective."

Was that a compliment? He couldn't remember the last time he'd heard one from his father. "Steps are already being taken to deal with them."

"Xalivar's sending his own people as well."

Bordox bristled, fumbling for his cup as he glanced away in an attempt to hide it. He had this situation handled. Why couldn't they just let him deal with it?

"Rhii and his friends saw the majordomo at the market. Xalivar blames you for revealing his location."

"They caught Manaen? Spoke with him?"

"No. He got away. They may not even be sure it was Manaen."

Bordox gulped his beer, almost choking. He coughed. "I hope we did reveal his location as planned. I hope the whole Alliance comes down on him!"

Obed frowned, glancing around. "Keep your voice down. This isn't a place Alliance talk would be welcomed." Bordox shrunk back in his seat, sipping slower this time. Obed's eyes scanned the room. But the few other patrons paid them no notice, chattering and eating as before. After a moment, when no one seemed to have taken notice of them, he relaxed again. "Xalivar will get what's coming to him, don't worry. Just stick to the plan."

"I want Rhii!" Bordox whispered it, but his voice sounded much louder because of the intensity.

"Rhii will get what's coming to him, too. He and all his kind will soon be back where they belong—as slaves. It's the only reason we're here with Xalivar."

"He blames us for everything that goes wrong. Treats us like idiots, like we're worthless."

"Our perceived alliance with him is a means to end, Son. That's all. You need to learn to better control your emotions. They've brought you much trouble."

Bordox wanted to shout at him but managed to restrain himself. "How can you tolerate being brushed aside as irrelevant? After all your hard work?"

"It is a passing phase, Bordox. Soon, they will be the irrelevant ones."

Both whirled at the sound of Orson Sterling giving a broadcast. The bartender had raised the volume and it now filled screens scattered around the room.

"—the attack today on the High Lord Councilor, while he was giving a speech in the Vertullian capital of Iraja. This unprovoked attempt to assassinate our leader appears to have been perpetrated by disgruntled Vertullians. Authorities made several arrests in the incident and the suspects are being interrogated now. Fortunately, the injuries for those present were relatively minor."

The chatter in the restaurant had died as everyone gaped transfixed at the broadcasts. Bordox couldn't believe his ears. "Workers tried to assassinate Tarkanius?"

Obed smiled, eyes locked on a monitor with delight. "Xalivar's lust for power knows no bounds."

"Why would workers help Xalivar?" He took a long draw from his beer and waited.

Obed finally turned back to face him. "His powers of manipulation are legendary. Don't underestimate him. This attack will help us."

"It will certainly inflame anti-worker sentiment—"

"It will do more than that. As I already told you, there are many on the Council who share our sentiments. This will mobilize them; make them good potential Allies for us. They have no love for Xalivar either." Obed sat back on the bench, looking excited. "Soon, my Son, we will restore our family's greatness. Just control your emotions and stick with the plan."

Bordox nodded, as he continued nursing his beer. He'd do what he had been doing and prove himself to his father and everyone else. Even Xander Rhii.

Xalivar reran the recording of Orson Sterling's report—an assassination attempt on the High Lord Councilor. He cringed at hearing someone else's name given that title. Soon enough it would be his again. Someone else was working to undo the tragedy that had befallen their people at Tarkanius' hands. Just before the broadcast, his own people had reported back. The protestors at Miri's speech were not his. Someone else had been responsible. And now the attack on Tarkanius, in which he had no hand. Lucius hadn't even needed to initiate their backup plan. This attack had provided all the cover they needed. *I have allies I didn't know about.* He chuckled at the thought: people who would hail him as a returning hero—likely members of the Council themselves. As long as they continued to aid his cause, he would be sure to reward them when the time came.

Too bad you weren't even injured, Tarkanius.

Still, it would be all too easy to overthrow the imposter. He was weak and weak leadership never survived long. The Boralian people deserved the strength the Rhiis had always provided them. Miri and Xander aside, the Rhiis were a strong people, unfaltering in their determination and drive. Not easily shoved aside no matter what people thought.

"Manaen!"

His majordomo appeared quickly, datapad in hand. "Yes, my Lord."

"I want all the information on the investigation of the attempt on the High Lord Councilor's life. As soon as it's available."

"Of course, my Lord." Manaen turned away, already typing into his datapad.

Xalivar watched him. *Good old faithful, Manaen. Thank the gods Andorians are as lazy as they are stupid.* At least they were trainable. Xalivar had spent years cultivating Manaen's usefulness. "Use every resource, Manaen. If Orson Sterling gets it first, I'll hold you responsible."

Manaen nodded. "Yes, my Lord."

Xalivar rewound the broadcast again as his aide hurried out. It had been a while since the networks had provided him with such quality entertainment. The looks on the Council members' faces as they fled for their lives made him laugh. They were all weak. *Your shepherd is returning, my sheep.*

"Turn that off. It's depressing." Davi turned back to watch the cityscape out the window as he paced. The images flashed through his mind again: explosions, Tarkanius falling, the platform collapsing, panicked people running, and, somewhere in the midst of it, he could swear he'd seen Tela. Farien's running the broadcast over and over again for the past hour hadn't helped either. Davi's chest tightened with urgency. He had to get home now. "Where could that kid be?"

"We'd better go find him." Yao sat hunched down on a sofa as Farien turned off the broadcast and leaned against the wall.

"Where do we look, Yao? He could be anywhere." Farien rubbed his hand along the plush, upholstered wall. "I told you it was a bad idea to bring him along."

The accommodations the government had arranged must be amongst the finest in the city, Davi thought. Everything was finery, almost on a scale with the Palace where he'd grown up— gold-encased fittings on reflector pads, doors, window frames, and the cleansing room; Andorian tapestries, Tertullian tile. Even the view itself was the finest, showing the skyline in all its glory. The twin suns' light shone down from high overhead, sending shadows dancing across the faces of the buildings and the street surfaces in between. They'd arrived back at the hotel to find Dru missing. So much for promising to wait for them. Davi wished he was surprised. Dru's impulsiveness had always been his greatest liability.

"I can help," Qajuan said. Davi had almost forgotten the boy was with them. They all turned to look at him. "I know the city. I can ask questions of people who wouldn't talk to you."

"Let's call down to the front desk and ask if the concierge saw him leave," Yao suggested. "He could be somewhere in the hotel."

"If we split up, we can find him faster," Farien said, already moving toward the door with Qajuan.

"Fine. I'll start in the hotel and we can stay in touch by comm." Davi nodded as Yao stood and followed Farien, then picked up the wall comm to call the front desk.

Thirty minutes later, Davi exited for the street. None of the staff had any recollection of Dru leaving the hotel, so Davi went to find Yao, Farien and Qajuan. It took a moment to raise them on the comm. They rendezvoused in a central square near the city market, a cornucopia of chattering voices, bustling bodies and scents. No one paid them any attention as they stood in a circle facing each other.

"This is just a waste of time." Farien sighed, checking his chrono. "It could go on for hours. What if he took an air taxi or something?"

"He knows better than to wander off too far alone," Yao said. He and Davi exchanged a look. In Yao's eyes, Davi saw the same doubts about it that he had.

"I'll find him," Qajuan said. "Let me go alone."

"You don't even know what he looks like." Farien could hardly stand still from irritation.

Yao started punching buttons on his datapad, then held it up for Qajuan to see. A picture of Dru's face filled the screen. "That's him."

Qajuan nodded. "Okay. I'll find him."

"Bring him back to the hotel," Davi said. "We'll be packed and waiting."

Qajuan disappeared around a corner with a nod as Farien frowned. "How do we know we can trust that kid? He's a hustler, probably an orphan, homeless, totally unreliable."

"Who happens to be right," Yao said. "He knows this city and can talk with people we can't. Give him a chance."

"Yao's right," Davi nodded as they started together back toward the hotel. "Besides, he saved our lives at that Black Market and he's made no move against us since. We need to get our things together and get back to the ship. We'll be needed at home now."

"I'm surprised we haven't been recalled already," Yao said as they rounded a bend into the alley Qajuan had shown them as a shortcut between two larger streets.

A Skitter appeared, darting into the alley and parking sideways, blocking their path. The rider grinned, staring right at the three of them.

"This doesn't look good," Yao mumbled.

"Let's just go back the other way," Davi agreed as they turned around.

Two more Skitters appeared at the end of the alley from which they'd just entered. These riders just glared menacingly.

"Any ideas?" Yao asked.

"I don't see any weapons," Farien said, reaching for his blaster.

Davi put a hand on his arm to stop him. "You want us to shoot them? We don't even know what they want."

"Look at their faces. Do you really think this is the time to chat?" Farien kept his hand near his weapon as Davi motioned to the men.

"What do you want?"

The three drivers drew weapons from beneath their jackets with one simultaneous motion, aiming them at Davi and his friends.

"Can we shoot now?" Farien drew his weapon and aimed back, searching for cover as Yao and Davi did the same.

Davi heard the men's laser rifles hum as they warmed up and bolts came flying toward them. He and Yao ducked left, Davi rolling and landing crouched beside a building wall lining the alley as Farien fell to his knees in the opposite direction. The alley floor smelled of urine and decaying trash. All three friends fired back immediately at the riders, who tried to dodge with their Skitters. The grinning man made it, Farien's blast exploding against the building behind him, but Davi's blast hit as the other two riders got in each other's way. Smoke rose from the blackened engine compartment, but the rider maneuvered clear of the alley and ducked around the corner for cover.

The riders fired again, their blasts forcing the three friends to dodge again. Yao ducked and rolled back further along the wall as Davi and Farien dove, ending up switching sides.

"We're dead if we stay here," Farien said as all three crouched again, aiming their weapons.

Other than trash scattered by winds, the alley was clear of anything suitable for providing cover.

"We have to run for it," Yao said with a shrug.

Farien scowled, motioning toward their assailants. "Which way do you want to die?" The three friends fired again, but missed.

"Set your blasters to rapid repeat," Davi said as an idea came into his head. "Three against one's the best odds."

"You're crazy!" Farien shook his head as all three adjusted their weapon's settings.

"We lay down a stream of fire, forcing him to dodge as we rush him. Only chance we have." He motioned to Farien. "You cover the rear to keep them occupied. On three, okay?"

Farien sighed, his eyes indicating resigned agreement as all three readied themselves.

God protect us. Davi prayed silently. "One...two...three!"

All three friends fired as they ran, Farien turned partially around to fire toward the two Skitters at the far end of the alley, the barrel of his blaster swinging back and forth to spread his blasts throughout the area behind them. Beams burst from Yao's and Davi's blasters, one after another, the noise deafening. The rider they rushed stopped grinning and fumbled with his controls as he dodged out of the way at the last second. The other two riders were too busy running to fire back. Too preoccupied with protecting themselves from Farien's chaotic fire.

Davi's group reached the end of the alley to find the Skitter waiting. They turned in unison and fired back, forcing the rider to dodge again as they headed away from him down a major street. Pedestrians screamed and scattered. All three simultaneously reset their blasters to normal. There were too many pedestrians to risk it here. Besides, blaster's power packs could only last so long under constant streaming and Davi hadn't brought an extra. He doubted his friends had either.

Rounding a corner into a plaza, they raced to the middle of the crowd before looking back. No Skitters in sight.

"We can't have lost them," Yao said, looking as puzzled as Davi felt.

"They didn't follow us? Why would they stop?" Pedestrians shied away as Farien panned the area with his blaster.

"Farien, lower it. You're scaring people." Davi reached out and pushed Farien's gun arm down.

"I found him!" It sounded like Qajuan. All three looked around for him. After a minute, they saw hands waving from a nearby alley where Dru was waiting with Qajuan.

Davi couldn't believe it. *This kid is good!* He heard the hum of the engines followed by the laser rifles. Blasts landed around them as pedestrians screamed and scattered.

"I knew we didn't lose them," Farien said, raising his gun to fire back as all three took off toward Qajuan.

"What's going on?" Dru asked as they drew near.

"Run! Back to the hotel! Now!" Davi waved his hands to impart urgency as Qajuan and Dru turned and raced up the alley with Davi and the others. As they hit the far end and started down another street, Davi heard the echoing of Skitter engines as the riders entered the alley.

"Who are these guys?" Dru asked, slowing down a bit and forcing Farien to dodge around him.

"Stop and ask if you want," Farien said, annoyed as he picked up his pace again.

Davi grabbed Dru's arm and dragged him along. Lasers exploded on the pavement around them sending chunks of rock and debris flying. Davi felt a sharp pain as one struck his cheek.

"We'll never make it on foot."

They were forced to dodge the Skitters, air taxis and air cars which filled the street. An air taxi exploded behind them, its yellow striped body flipping end over end on top of a nearby air car so fast their occupants had no time to react. Woman screamed as pedestrians scattered trying to outrun the flying debris.

"They don't care who gets hurt," Yao observed.

"Follow me!" Qajuan yelled and nodded urgently as he darted to a side toward a set of office buildings.

"There are too many people!"

Qajuan ignored Davi's warning. "Trust me!"

Three more Skitters appeared headed toward them from the opposite direction down the street. The riders were dressed similarly to the others, laser rifles held at the ready.

"Do we have a choice?" Farien asked.

All four of them switched direction to race after Qajuan into pedestrians who started to panic in confusion at what was happening. A few froze; others ran; and others pushed and shoved. Screaming and shouting broke out as a fight erupted.

"Where are we going?" Farien demanded as Qajuan led them twisting and winding through the frightened spectators until he came to a small stairwell and started down.

"We're going where they can't follow."

Shadows covered them as they descended almost into complete darkness, where Qajuan stopped and fumbled a bit in the dark. Then sudden-ly, a door swung wide and light from small reflector pads lining the ceiling of a tunnel pierced the darkness.

Qajuan immediately started running along the tunnel. "Hurry! And close the door before they see."

They followed quickly, Davi glancing up the stairs as he closed the door behind them. No one had followed them...yet. "What is this place?"

"Maintenance tunnels for the cables that power the city and its networks. Few people know about them, but the underground do. We use them more than city workers." Qajuan smiled back at him as he continued running.

"Where do they go?" Farien asked.

"All over the city. We'll be at your hotel in no time."

Davi smiled at Yao, glad their hopes for Qajuan's trustworthiness looked well founded.

"You can relax now. They can't find this easily, and they won't know their way around." Qajuan turned onto a side tunnel as they all followed. "Especially because they won't know which way we went."

Davi looked around as he entered the new tunnel. It was like a maze with tunnels leading off in various directions. He relaxed and holstered his weapon, seeing Yao and Farien do the same.

After meeting with his father, Bordox accompanied his assassins to the hotel in which Rhii and his friends had registered. It wasn't under their names but Alliance delegation, booked by the city government. Since no broadcasts had spoken of any official delegations, it hadn't been too hard to figure out who the delegation must be. Bordox fumed when he saw the hotel. Rhii and his friends were in luxury while Bordox was stuck in diner dives like some low class scum. He would end this today!

They'd waited what seemed like an hour with no sign of their targets. Then six men on Skitters rode up, and Bordox recognized right away from their level of interest and coordination meant that they were professional hit men. They circled the hotel then managed to secret themselves away in various hiding spots from alleys to shadowed doorways. Xalivar's people!

He tensed, cursing. Xalivar would not steal this moment from him! "We need a distraction," he said into his comm. "Those men are here for the same targets."

"L't th'm do th' job for us," an assassin answered.

"No! We're the ones who get to take down Xander Rhii!" Bordox answered through clenched teeth. *Hired assassins telling me to back off? What did I hire them for?* Still, he knew if they all shot at once it would draw local law enforcement and a lot of attention they didn't need. His mind raced for a way to distract the riders and lead them away.

Then it was too late. Rhii and his friends appeared on a corner across from the hotel, from a stairway Bordox never would have noticed which seemed to lead down into the ground. Where had they been?

Their guide, a young blue-skinned Xanthian, led the way across the street. The Skitter riders appeared from their hiding places and moved in, firing laser rifles. Rhii's group drew weapons and immediately scattered, shrinking back into the shadows for cover. Then the guide did something Bordox would have never expected. The Xanthian youth ran straight for a Skitter swinging some kind of primitive elastic band with a metal bar attached. The rider sneered and ignored him racing right toward him, but as he neared, the youth released the bar and it slammed end first into the rider's face, knocking him from the Skitter.

As the rider bounced across the ground and the Skitter slowed to a stop, the youth hopped aboard and gunned it, taking off down the street. Two other Skitters followed, giving chase as Rhii and Brahma fired on the remaining three.

"Th'y'r fight'ng each oth'r," an assassin noted over the comm.

"Ignore the riders and get the targets," Bordox ordered. He couldn't spot Farien and the cadet who'd been with them on the corner. Where were they? Brahma and Rhii continued firing at the Skitter riders as they dodged rifle blasts. Rock debris flew off buildings as walls were struck. A streetlight exploded from a hit. The two officers kept moving.

Xalivar's men are terrible shots.

Then he heard the humming of more Skitters and suddenly Farien and the young cadet appeared from behind the hotel, racing toward them. Both fired on the riders from behind, causing them to stop shooting and flee for safety. One rider flew right into Rhii's path and was shot down, flying backwards off his Skitter as a laser blast burned a hole through his chest.

Farien and the cadet pulled up alongside their companions who hopped on behind them, grabbing hold of their driver's waists. Then Farien and the cadet spun the Skitters in an arc and headed back for the hotel. Bordox's men opened fire on them, causing them to fly erratically to avoid being hit.

A yellow flash drew Bordox's attention as a bolt struck one of the Skitters, leaving burn marks on the back panel but not disabling it. *My own men are incompetent. No wonder they have to kill one at a time in close quarters.* Bordox drew his own blaster, prepared to ignore his father's orders to let the hired men do the dirty work. Just as he raised his blaster, the Skitters disappeared behind the hotel to safety.

"Get them!" he screamed into the comm.

As soon as they cleared the building, Farien and Dru took Davi and Yao to the third Skitter.

"How'd you guys make it undetected?" Yao asked as he climbed down and ran for the third Skitter.

"The tunnels," Dru said. "We used Farien's datapad nav system to find one leading under the hotel. Not hard when you know where it is."

Davi and Yao laughed. "Good thinking," Davi said as he motioned to Dru. "Get inside and stay hidden. We need to go help Qajuan."

"And leave me out of all the fun? Come on! I'm great with a Skitter!"

"I don't have time to argue with you."

"Good, then don't." Dru stayed put on the Skitter. The building overhead shook from explosions, rocking back and forth, as they heard the whistle of laser fire overhead.

"There were more firing after the riders fled for cover," Yao said. "More of their friends, I suppose."

"We have no idea how many there are," Farien added.

"What's the plan?" Davi asked.

"They'll be here any minute!" Dru reminded them.

"You two go find Qajuan," Yao said. "We'll do what we can about the people here."

"I have an idea," Davi said. "Don't go inside the hotel. We don't know how many might be in there."

"We can worry about that after we've dealt with these guys," Farien said.

"Here they come!" Dru shouted and accelerated the Skitter as Davi struggled to grab on. Farien and Yao quickly raced toward the oncoming riders as Dru raced into an alley away from the hotel.

♜

"Shoot them!" Bordox screamed.

"Th' rid'rs k'ep g'tting in th' way, boss!" an assassin replied.

"Then shoot them, too! I want Rhii's blood on our hands!" Bordox took aim at one of the riders and fired as streams from his assassin's guns rained down on the five dueling Skitters below.

♜

Farien cursed as the field of fire became thick around them. Were the assassins firing on each other?

He and Yao flew in circles, zipping in and out between the three riders attacking them, dodging fire while firing their own blasters when they could.

Then he heard a yelp as Qajuan appeared on a Skitter and raced toward them with two Skitters tailing. Yao took aim at one of those riders, who hadn't even noticed them yet and blasted him straight in the leg, causing him to veer straight toward Farien. Farien took aim and shot the man off his Skitter with a blast to his face.

"Two down, four to go," Yao said with a laugh.

"But we're badly outnumbered."

Then a blast hit another rider who had just aimed at Farien, knocking him forward over the front of his Skitter, smoke rising from a hole in his back.

Qajuan raced toward another as the rider looked distractedly for who had shot his fallen friend. The youth seemed determined to crash right into him, but the rider finally took notice and fumbled for his joystick. Qajuan jumped off his Skitter at the last minute as the two Skitters crashed and exploded, smashing the rider.

Then Davi and Dru appeared from another alley and raced toward them, both firing simultaneously at the confused riders who'd been chasing Qajuan. One of the Skitter's engines exploded, jostling the rider roughly in his seat. The other rider screamed as a bolt hit his arm, then another shot from overhead struck the back of his head, sending him leaning forward against the joystick. The Skitter took off like a shot, exploding against the side of a nearby building.

"Where'd you learn how to fly a Skitter?" Yao asked as Qajuan climbed on behind him.

"I can fly anything with a little practice. It looked easy and it was."

Yao laughed. "Our people spend months training for it."

"To the starport," Davi said with a wave of his hand.

All three took off down the street as laser blasts rained down from above. Davi aimed at a window above them, firing. Farien saw a shadowed face moving aside.

Bordox ducked as glass exploded, shards flying in all directions, inches from where his face had just been. Rhii had spotted him and fired. Could he have been recognized from so far below?

He watched with frustration as his men's shots failed again and again, striking the Skitters with minimal damage. The cadet swerved as a blast hit his arm, but Rhii reached forward to steady the Skitter and all three disappeared around a corner out of range.

"Follow them! Go! Go!" Bordox waved his fists in the air, feeling helpless. His men would never catch them. *Where would they go?* He cursed over and over. *I can't believe this is happening again!*

Chapter Eight

An hour after escaping the hotel, Yao landed the transport on a small government landing pad. The Xanthian official who'd greeted them upon first arrival met them with their belongings from the hotel and a doctor to look after Dru's arm. On the ground for only twenty minutes, Yao took off again and rendezvoused with Farien, who was circling above the city, and they set a course for the depot where they'd left Davi's VS28 fighter.

Davi sat in the cockpit beside Yao, while Dru rested in the back. Davi searched the bands for news reports from home. He'd never felt so anxious about anyone as he did after seeing Tela on the broadcasts. What had she been doing there? Security for the event, he guessed. But she was so close to the platform. He took deep breaths as he prayed for her safety and that of everyone else there. Losing Tarkanius would be a huge tragedy for the Alliance right now. It could set back all he and his friends had fought for. Who was trying to kill him? It had to be Xalivar. Tarkanius had always been widely respected. He had no real enemies, only political ones.

An hour after they'd left Xanthian airspace, a message from command came in ordering them to Legallis. All available resources were being called back to quash unrest and ensure the High Lord Councilor's safety. Davi was tempted to ignore the order and head straight for Vertullis, but Farien wouldn't go along with it, and he didn't need to make trouble. Maybe Tela was already back on Legallis as well.

Finally he found a broadcast confirming no deaths and only minor injuries in the attempt on the High Lord Councilor. No official suspects had been named, but some Vertullians were in custody. *Idiots! Why would anyone try to destroy all their people fought for after everything it cost them?* He knew many still held anger towards the Boralians for past treatment, but they'd won their freedom. They were full citizens. The time had come to let it go and move on, for everyone's good. They had a future to build. It was time to leave the past behind. Some people just had no idea how to do that.

Farien had scolded Dru loudly over the comm as they departed, but now the channel was silent with everyone keeping to themselves. Dru hadn't said a word since just after departure. Given the attack on Tarkanius and the expectation that assassins could find them again at any moment, conversations between the others remained brief and to the point. Davi imagined they were as lost in thought as he was. An attack on their leader was an attack on all of them. He and his friends had grown up with respect for the Palace and what it stood for. Being that close to power had both humanized the man and his office and garnered deep respect and love for all it stood for. Davi's heart ached thinking about the societal tensions which led to such an event.

"We have to go in, Davi." Farien broke the silence.

"I know."

"Just in case you were thinking about violating orders, I wanted to say that."

"She might be there waiting," Yao said.

Davi smiled, thankful for the comfort of friends. "I hope so. If not, I can get a message to her when we land."

"I'll drop Dru at the Academy, then I'm coming, too."

"To do what? You're assigned to Presimion," Farien asked.

"Whatever I can. I feel like I was attacked, too. I can't just sit there."

Davi smiled, glad he wasn't alone. "We all feel that way. I'm sure they'll be glad to have you."

"Great. And I just get to go sit in boring classes through all this." Dru yawned as he joined them in the transport cockpit.

"You can skip a day and get some rest first," Yao said. "You need to see to that arm."

Dru smiled, admiring his scar. "My first battle wound. The girls'll love it."

The others laughed and the comm channel fell silent again as they flew onward.

To her surprise, Miri found herself taking to some of the mundane activities of civilian life. In particular, she loved shopping. As a princess, it had always been done for her, but now, she often went with Lura or a friend. It was an opportunity for the women to bond in a unique way, and her favorite stores were supermarkets. She loved the colorful variety of the fruits and meats and other items, the varied smells—from fresh and sweet to sour and earthy, the warmth of spices mixed with the cool smell of raw meat—brought her senses to life.

Today, because of packed shuttles since the attempt on Tarkanius, Lura arrived mid-afternoon, so they had arrived at the market during a busy hour, not Miri's favorite time to go. But she needed items for dinner and Lura happily accompanied her.

They were working their way through the produce aisle when Miri first heard the whispering. She glanced behind them to see two women pointing at them and talking. As princess, she'd gotten used to being gawked at in public, so she blew it off and turned her attention back to Lura and their shopping.

But the whispering followed them. And it grew and grew.

At first, it was one or two people behind or to the side. Then it became several pairs or trios pointing and whispering. Then there were sneers and laughs with the whispers. Soon it seemed everyone in the store was talking about them. Were their food choices so fascinating?

"What's the matter?" Lura asked, her brow furrowed with concern.

"Did you notice the whispers?"

Lura chuckled. "Women gossip in groceries. It's part of the fun." Then she saw Miri's face and her grin faded. "What is it?"

"It's not just the whispers. Some are laughing, pointing. At you and me."

Lura glanced around again and Miri's eyes followed. A couple of women pointed and laughed from a nearby counter. Miri knew it couldn't be good from their expressions. She'd avoided going out much in public since her speeches. She'd been a frequent topic on broadcasts. While some pundits supported her because of the past and her commitment to the Boralian people, other pundits gave the past no regard, calling her a traitor, slave-lover, and more. It was a far cry from the positive press she'd received during the slave's battle for freedom, when she'd helped uncover the Delta V massacre footage and her brother's betrayal of the Council.

Lura frowned. "Do you want to go?"

Miri nodded. "What about dinner?"

"That's what restaurants are for. Come on." Lura took her by the arm, leading her back toward the front of the store. As they passed the cashier, Lura set the basket she carried down. "I'm sorry, we have to go."

The cashier shrugged, obviously unperturbed. They were almost at the door when they heard a voice.

"From princess to traitor—how far some fall."

Lura whirled around, eyes raging. "How dare you!"

Miri turned also, but it was impossible to identify the speaker.

"None of you know anything to say such a thing! This woman has sacrificed so much for you that you don't even know!"

Miri shushed her with a hand on her arm. "Let's go, Lura."

"I won't stand for it." Lura waved a menacing finger around the room at those watching. "Your ignorance disgusts me. You should all be ashamed."

Miri grabbed her arm and dragged Lura from the store. As the doors closed behind them, Lura relaxed and then her face fell. "I'm sorry, Miri. I didn't mean to embarrass you. It just made me so angry hearing that."

Miri smiled. "It's okay, Lura. I feel so lucky to have a friend like you. Truly."

Lura clasped Miri's hand and squeezed it. "That's right. And you just try to be rid of me now."

Lura's glare was so intense it made Miri laugh. Soon Lura

joined her as they walked away, hand in hand.

The call to Assembly came with orders for full dress uniforms. Pres arrived to find her soldiers waiting for her, but they weren't alone. Another, equal-sized, group was lining up opposite them in the chamber. Her mind raced to place some of the names, then her breath caught in her throat. Standing near the front was Admiral Dek. She fought the urge to run to him, instead only quickening her pace slightly. It took only a few moments to cross the distance, where she spun on her heels, positioning herself next to him looking back at the assembling troops.

"I didn't expect to see you here," he said, glancing over.

Words almost failed her. "For the good of the Alliance and our people," she managed.

"My respect for you has been well placed, General." He offered a warm smile.

Both turned their backs to the troops as Lucius appeared on a dais before them with Lord Obed.

Each stepped to opposite sides as Xalivar appeared and came forward to the edge of the platform. He stood, hands crossed behind his back, staring, panning them. And then he raised his arms and smiled. "Honorable friends, welcome to the future. You have made the right choice in joining us—the choice to honor our people and save our Alliance. Events have taken place which we all regret. Our Alliance has become but a shadow of what it once was. The leadership is weak. Values our people treasured for centuries have been compromised. The time has come to restore it to the glory it once held."

He paused as the troops broke into spontaneous applause and cheering. Xalivar savored it, smiling, then resumed as it died down. "You know my leadership. You know my reputation. Forget all the lies my enemies have spread to discredit me. These were said to elevate themselves and you've seen the results. You're here, as I am, and the General and Lord you see with me, because you want what we once had. And you cannot continue to watch your beloved people's history fall to ruin. Join with me and we will restore the Boralian people to greatness. The Vertullians will be enslaved or destroyed. We will tolerate no dissension. Join me, and pride in your work and service will be yours again."

The troops cheered and applauded again, then Admiral Dek stepped forward, joining his fists and raising them in the traditional salute to a High Lord Councilor. Pres followed, and, one by one, so did every other soldier in the room. An awesome display of unity, it was made all the more touching by Dek's presence at her side.

"May it be as you have foretold, my Lord," Lucius said, joining them, with Obed being the last to offer the salute.

Xalivar stood in silence a bit, reveling in the attention, then raised a hand. "You all have duties to attend to. Let there be no more delays." He spun and exited the way he'd entered with Lucius and Obed on his heels.

Their troops broke into excited chatter, shaking hands, joking with one another as Pres turned to Dek. "How long have you known?" Her heart pounded.

"Almost a year. And you?"

"The same."

"I could not risk telling you."

She nodded. "I understand. For me it was the same." She'd never experienced such a mixture of joy, pride and relief.

Dek nodded. "It will be good to continue serving alongside you." He stepped forward and raised his voice. "Officers to the conference room immediately. Enlisted to quarters. Rest while you can. Training begins in two hours. Dismissed."

The troops, who had quieted down to hear him, now began to disperse. Pres followed Dek into a corridor toward the conference room, excited and nervous about the future which awaited them. If they succeeded, they'd be hailed as heroes. If they failed, labeled traitors. Either way, both had already made the decision which would define the rest of their careers. Pres felt relief knowing they were in it together. She wondered if Dek felt the same.

Xalivar's heart raced as he led Obed and Lucius back to his chambers in the Xanthian caves. To be greeted like a hero by his own soldiers—men and women who'd served under him since their cadet days—after all that had happened, reassured him that victory would soon be his. *How sad it is that honor and loyalty are thicker than blood.* His own sister and the boy he'd raised as close as a son had betrayed him, leading to his downfall. Yet here were total strangers cheering him like he'd risen from the dead. For some, it would soon seem that way indeed. He laughed at the thought. *Oh to see the looks on your faces, Tarkanius, Miri, Kray, Xander.* The fact that his former nephew might have suspicions of his presence did nothing to lessen the glorious visions in his head. All the months of planning, the careful maneuvering, even his suffering would all be worth it soon.

As the door slid shut behind them, Xalivar whirled to face his companions. "Our moment is here, my friends."

"We've not yet won," Obed said. "There's still much to be done."

"Oh ye of little faith, Obed. Can you not already feel the triumph? Our own people recognize me for what I am—their salvation from ruin. These soldiers won't be alone in that sentiment. Haven't you seen the outcry all over the nets? Once we capture the hearts and minds of the people, victory will be swift."

"We'll need a far larger army than these if we hope to claim victory, Xalivar."

Xalivar frowned, shaking his head. He turned his eyes to Lucius who met his gaze. "This is the weakness of which I've warned you, Lucius. Weak leaders make weak Alliances and weak people. Purity is what we need; a cleansing to renew our strength."

"Insult me all you will, Xalivar." Obed stood firm, head held high. "You are far from perfect. You have been defeated before."

Xalivar whirled, fists clenching to face his old rival. "I was betrayed! Lies told. My own family conspired against me. That is not defeat!"

"And who lives in the Palace now, Xalivar?" Obed grunted, undeterred.

Xalivar bit his tongue, raising his fist in warning. "You push me, Obed. Overstep the lines. Choose your words with care."

"The workers mock you now. And so do many others."

"The workers will soon be back as slaves where they belong, and anyone else who cares to join them can do so freely." Xalivar's eyes bore into Obed, reminding him that he, too, could wind up there. Obed just stood quietly, staring back. Xalivar took two breaths before continuing. "And once we've dealt with them, we'll deal with all the others."

"What others, Xalivar? The workers and anyone disloyal—who's left?"

Xalivar smiled as Manaen brought a tray with a pitcher and three glasses. "Any foreign influences will be removed." Xalivar looked at Manaen as his aide sat the tray on a table and proceeded to fill the three glasses with Talis. "No more tolerance for alien influences. We will purify ourselves and be stronger for it."

"You would eliminate races with whom we've lived in peace for decades?"

"I would eliminate anyone who threatens the sanctity of our people." Xalivar stared at Obed again, the meaning clear.

Manaen finished pouring the glasses as they stood in silence and carefully handed one to each of the three men, then nodded and took his leave.

Xalivar fought the urge to smile as he saw the meaning sink in on Obed's face. Was his old rival actually horrified? Such weakness from a man who actually aspired to Xalivar's position. *You too would be ruin to our people, Obed. And I shall see to it you never have the chance.* Even those who'd served him during his triumphant reclamation of office would have to be purged for purity. No weak links could be allowed to remain—Obed, Manaen, all of them—gone.

Obed sipped his Talis in silence, waiting, as Xalivar turned to Lucius. "Begin the training immediately. I want units training around the clock."

"It shall be done, my Lord."

"And begin the second phase of the recruitment."

Lucius nodded. "At once, my Lord." He saluted then hurried

off, leaving his half-finished glass on the table next to the tray.

"We have more allies than you imagine, Obed. Men who are even now working to destabilize the government on our behalf."

"They know nothing of us or our plans. How can you be so confident they'll side with us when the time comes?"

"There will be only two choices. They will go the way of assured victory."

Obed sighed, shaking his head. "Your overconfidence is a true liability, Xalivar."

"As is yours, Obed."

Obed stared at him a moment, then stepped forward, set his glass next to Lucius', and disappeared through the door, leaving Xalivar alone.

Xalivar wondered who the unknown allies were, and more importantly, who was their leader? Could it be someone like Hachim or Niger? The two Lords had sided against him during the workers' rebellion, but perhaps their true sentiments had been against Xalivar, not toward the workers. If such was the case, they too would require elimination at the right time. But for now, they could be very useful to him. And Xalivar intended to use every resource available in achieving his ends.

He hurried to the terminal and sat, logging into his secure band and sending missives to his contacts. He needed an update on the investigation into the events. Surely more clues had been found which would confirm his suspicions about whom he could count on to support his cause. It would only be a matter of time. *Gods, I love the feel of victory.*

Within hours of their arrival back on Legallis, Davi, Yao and Farien reported to command for a debriefing. After taking Dru to the infirmary, Davi sent Qajuan to personnel with a note asking them to make use of his gifts. He'd check on the youth later, as clearly the last thing any of them needed was a bored Xanthian underfoot. There'd been no chance to send a message to Tela. Davi had barely had time to change uniforms.

General Grif, Aron, Uzah, and the High Lord Councilor sat at a large, round table, waiting as the three officers entered the conference room. They stood at attention as the door slid shut behind them.

"At ease, gentlemen," Tarkanius said immediately. "Join us please."

Davi and his friends found seats at the table, facing the leaders.

"The report you sent en route mentioned an incident at the Black Market on Xanthis," Uzah said. No time for pleasantries? Clearly recent events were taking their toll.

Davi nodded. "Yes, sir."

"You confirmed the identity of the Andorian?" Grif asked, his face emotionless as usual.

Farien shook his head. "We tried. He got away."

"But the locals said he's often at the market," Yao added.

"For what purpose?" Grif asked.

"We're told he hired mercenaries, buys supplies, etc. No one will cross him."

Farien jumped in as Yao finished. "He hired Lhamors."

"He has a powerful employer." Davi emphasized the last word, letting it hang as his eyes panned the leaders.

"Xalivar, you believe?" At the sound of his voice, all eyes turned to Tarkanius. "The situation has reached crisis here, gentlemen. The attempt on my life was but part of a larger conspiracy. At the very moment that attack was occurring, Admiral Dek, General Pres, and numerous officers and soldiers left their duty stations and disappeared. Communications sent on various channels were ignored. Several ships left the system, but controllers had no log of their destinations or flight plans. We're still trying to locate them."

Davi couldn't believe it. The conspiracy had reached heights he'd never expected. He knew Xalivar was bold and had his supporters, but to steal warships with full crews? Davi's mouth got dry as he struggled to wrap his mind around it. His throat tightened as waves of sadness poured over him. Yao and Farien looked as shocked as he was. Did so many really want another war? As memories of dead friends flashed through his head, he struggled for words. "Defections of senior staff?"

"The defections stretch throughout the ranks. A total of six hundred so far." Grif's face remained steady, but Davi thought he detected anger in his eyes.

"So it *is* Xalivar! It has to be! Who else would be able to command such loyalty?" Davi looked around, waiting for the leaders to agree.

Tarkanius nodded. "We suspect you're right."

"No one's seen nor heard from Xalivar since he disappeared from Eleni 1," Grif said.

"Disappeared, still alive," Tarkanius said.

Aron's eyes met Davi's with a sadness which matched Davi's own. "We believe Xalivar is alive and involved in efforts to destabilize the populace and government to regain his power," he said.

"Just after the attempt on the High Lord Councilor, a secret meeting of conspirators took place at a café in Iraja," Uzah said. "The entire staff was left dead as those in attendance departed."

"If no one's alive, how do you know of this meeting?" Farien asked.

"Security cameras captured a few images—several men entering, whom we believe to be those responsible."

Davi frowned. "I thought you had people in custody."

Aron nodded. "We don't believe they acted alone. They know too little and all of them claim to have been hired by a major in the Borali military."

"Do you have a name?"

Uzah shook his head. "Only a description. But security footage captured a face you may find familiar." He slid a datapad across the table to Davi.

Davi took it and looked at the image on the screen. A rotund face stared back at him, uniform collar and insignia showing at the bottom of the image. This time he remembered exactly where they'd met. "I know this man. From the corridor after the Generals briefed us." Uzah nodded.

"Who is he?" Farien asked.

Grif punched a button and a screen on the wall filled with the major's picture and accompanying data. "Valenti Broks, a Major in intelligence. Current whereabouts uncertain. Solid service record."

"In other words, your average officer who stayed off the radar?" Davi looked to Uzah for confirmation. The General nodded.

"Off the radar but suddenly gone missing from his duty post?" Farien's scowled. "Let's find him." Despite the troubles he'd faced from honoring orders, Farien's convictions about loyalty duty hadn't changed.

"We're working on leads now," Uzah said, typing into a datapad and pausing a moment to read the screen. "Men were already sent to his residence and current post."

"Hence the 'whereabouts unknown,'" Davi nodded. "He doesn't seem the type to act alone."

"We're sure he didn't," Tarkanius said. "However, he's the perfect type to organize the murder of civilians at a café."

"How many?"

"Five employees, two customers." Aron sighed, his face shadowed with grief.

"How many conspirators do you believe he has?" Yao turned from the screen to look at Tarkanius.

"Four to six from the meeting. Who knows how many could be involved." Tarkanius shook his head. "We believe more than one is on the Council." The High Lord Councilor looked gaunt, his shoulders sinking as he said it.

"But you don't know who?" The answer shone in the leaders' eyes as soon as Davi finished the question. "And you think they're in league with Xalivar?"

Aron shrugged. "We could be dealing with more than one conspiracy."

"My gods! If there's so many, how can we begin to stop them?" Farien leaned back in his chair with dismay.

"I'm prepared to declare a state of martial law, restrict interplanetary travel, whatever it takes," Tarkanius said. "We must restore order while there's still time."

"The outcries are increasing, anti-worker sentiment growing, ever since the attempt on Tarkanius," Aron added. "The Alliance is becoming quickly divided."

"So whatever they're doing, it's working." Farien shook his head.

"We need full reports of everything you encountered and discovered as soon as possible," Uzah said. "Farien and Davi, your investigation will be expanding."

Tarkanius turned and nodded at Yao. "You're still needed at the Academy."

Yao bowed his head. "I'm needed more here. This threatens all of us." Davi had never heard Yao object to an order before but his friend's red eyes almost glowed with determination.

"I'm due leave. I'd like to stay."

Tarkanius smiled. "I thought you might feel that way."

General Grif cleared his throat. "You'll need to escort the cadet first, then you'll be temporarily reassigned to continue assisting with the investigation."

Yao looked up and broke into a grin. "Thank you, sir."

"We must proceed with extra caution. Those responsible for these murderous acts will not allow anyone to deter them." Tarkanius suddenly looked weary and concerned.

"They've made several attempts against us and failed," Davi said, exchanging looks with his friends. "Just keep yourself safe, my Lord." He stood and offered the traditional salute. Yao and Farien joined him, soon followed by the others.

"The gods be with us all," Tarkanius said as they finished.

Niger's aide escorted Hachim into the fellow Lord's study and left him to wait. It seemed an interminable period before Niger appeared, smiling and relaxed in a way unexpected from someone who had the entire planet searching for him.

"Hachim!" Niger extended his hand, shaking Hachim's warmly. "Our plans are proceeding perfectly."

Hachim shook his head. "You've crossed a line, Niger."

"We crossed it together, Hachim."

"You gave me no choice. Those people did not need to die."
"They were in our way."

Hachim swallowed a gasp, stunned. Human life had value.
Elevating slaves at the expense of their own people was one thing.
But this was another. Murder was too far. When had he and Niger
grown to be so different? "A year ago, we supported Tarkanius
and Miri in removing Xalivar. We allowed the Vertullians to
become our equals."

"They can never be our equals!"

"They are human beings, Niger." Hachim turned away,
pacing, his chest tightening with worry. "This is not what I
wanted."

"What did you expect, Hachim? Their humanness does not
make them our equals. We enslaved them through our superiority.
And we freed them in weakness. We must be strong again.
Sacrifices will be necessary."

"I agreed with you that things went too far. I agreed that we
needed a change of leadership. Destabilizing leadership is one
thing. I never agreed to murder."

"We're overthrowing a government, Hachim. People often die
in such pursuits."

Hachim stopped pacing, spun and pointed his finger in
warning. "Not like this, Niger."

Niger stared at him, holding his gaze. "We agreed to do what
must be done for the good of our people. And that's what we've
done."

"I don't know you. You're not the man I thought."

"Neither are you."

Hachim held the stare a moment then turned away toward the
window, moving across the room to stare out at the cityscape
under the bright light of the twin suns. Shadows reflected off
windows, painting the streets and ground with varied patterns like
a puzzle. It reminded him of what his life had become. He'd been
a man of integrity once, determined to live honorably in
conducting his business and all of his affairs. What had happened
to him? He'd been angry. He'd shared reasonable doubts and

resentment about the direction of the government. Now he was a party to murder.

He had to stop it, change course somehow, before it was too late. "We've done what we set out to do. Now we can wait and let things unfurl."

Niger shook his head. "We have yet to achieve our goal. We cannot stop until we do."

"We've gone beyond our goal, Niger. We serve the people. With honor. We've done so for many years. Do not forget who you are." His eyes pleaded with his old friend but were met with an icy glaze in return.

Niger leaned forward over the desk so fast he almost flew, his hand waving threateningly. "Do not forget who *you* are, Hachim."

"I do not forget. But I have a choice. We made this plan together, recruited our allies. And now you act as if it yours alone." Hachim prepared to dodge, but Niger stopped just short of him.

"Someone must have the vision and see it through. If you are too weak, I am willing."

"It's a distorted vision, Niger!"

Niger slammed a fist into a pillar beside the door. "If you do not have the stomach for it, do not stand in my way. Or you will become like them."

Hachim gasped. "Are you threatening me?"

"I will do what must be done."

"You go too far. And yet nothing will stop you."

"Never forget it."

"I cannot." Hachim whirled and hurried out the door, rushing past Niger's aide, who came from a room down the hall to attend him, and letting himself out the front door. He hurried up the street as the blinding rays of the suns bore down on his neck and shoulders, adding external heat to match the internal one. He and Niger had been friends since joining the Council at almost the same time. But he no longer recognized his old friend, and he had decisions to make. *A threat on my own life?* The time had come to set aside loyalty and take care of himself.

Davi watched from the observation deck as Tela's Squadron landed. After the briefing, he'd finally tracked down her whereabouts—on a long security patrol around Vertullis. He'd gone to rest, setting an alarm on his datapad to awake him in plenty of time to shower and greet her. The VS28s set down one by one on parallel landing strips, rolling to a stop in a neat row, like the pilots had practiced it for hours, which they had.

Taking the lift to the hangar floor, Davi watched them climb from their fighters. Jorek and Virun were the first to see him and rushed over to shake his hand and ask about his adventures on Xanthis. Then Brie and Nila and a couple of others joined them. Davi kept an eye out for Tela, but she took her time filing a flight report before sidling up with the rest. Their eyes locked on each other as soon as she arrived, despite Davi continuing conversations with the others. It always amazed him how her blue flight suit highlighted her figure. Despite twelve hours in the cockpit, she looked ravishing. Finally the others said their "goodbyes" and started clearing out, leaving Davi and Tela alone.

As soon as the door slid shut behind the last of them, Tela rushed into his arms.

"I've been worried about you." They both said it at the same moment, then turned their heads to kiss, lips locked passionately for what seemed like forever.

"I saw the footage of the attack on Iraja—"

"All we had were rumors—" She stopped as she realized she was talking over him.

"You first," he said, hugging her again.

"Barely a word from you for ten days, Davi Rhii. Rumors of attempts on your life. All kinds of things. You've had us all worried."

"I'm sorry. Other than Dru getting shot, I'm fine, really."

Tela gasped, her hands tightening on his arms. "Dru? Shot?"

"Just in the arm. He'll live."

Tela relaxed and shook her head. "I need to know, Davi. I need to hear from you."

He nodded. "You'll understand better when I explain, but you're right, and I'm sorry."

Tela sighed as they stared into each other's eyes a moment, then kissed him again.

"I caught a glimpse of you in news broadcasts. I didn't know what to think."

"They put me in charge of security," she said. "I'm fine. And thankfully, so is everyone else."

Davi nodded. "I got the briefing while you were on patrol."

"They pulled in anyone they could. Things have really heated up since you left—politicians ranting, news media debating, people protesting. Any underlying tensions are now inflamed and on the surface."

Davi shrugged, not knowing where to begin. "I heard. But an attempt on the High Lord Councilor—"

Tela nodded. "Whoever's behind all this is using violence to incite the tensions, divide the people. It's working." As soon as their eyes met, she knew. "Xalivar's behind this?"

Davi sighed. "Some of it. We're fairly sure. We believe we spotted Manaen on Xanthis but couldn't catch up with him. An Andorian working for a rich, secretive boss has been hiring Lhamors and buying up weapons and resources."

Tela's face turned sad, her eyes telling him she'd reached conclusions similar to his own. "We knew he was alive somewhere."

Davi took her hands in his as their eyes met again. "Which is why I need you to be safe, Tela. No more dangerous security details and such. I need you to come home to."

Tela frowned, pulling her hands away. "Don't you think I feel the same about you?"

"I don't need distractions. I have to focus on my job."

"And I don't need them either." She pulled her hands free of his, frowning.

Davi dropped his hands his sides, wondering how he'd managed to upset her again. "I just want to protect you."

Tela turned away, cheeks reddening with anger. "But I'm not allowed to protect you?"

"I'm not saying that."

"Either we both take the risk or neither of us do. You can't expect me to sit at home and worry while you're out there in danger—"

Davi sighed. "I'll be safer knowing you're not in danger, too."

"Maybe you'd prefer not having to worry about me at all."

Davi reached over and put a hand on her shoulder. "Come on, Tela, I'm just trying to take care of you. I love you."

She shoved his hand away and spun. "Then stop being such a jerk!"

They turned at the whoosh of a door sliding open down the way. A bulky man strolled casually into the hangar. Davi's heartbeat pounded. It was the major! The man glanced over then, perhaps sensing their stares. As soon as he saw Davi, he turned around and bolted back toward the door.

"Wait! I need to talk with you, Major!" Davi started after him as Tela followed.

"Who is he?"

"A man we suspect in the attack on Tarkanius." Davi reached the door, but it didn't open automatically. He punched the button on the wall and got no reaction. "Go back to quarters. I'll catch up with you later." He punched the button on the door again, several times in rapid succession.

"I'm not letting you go after him alone."

"I can't face him if I have to protect you at the same time."

"I don't need protection. I'm an officer, just like you."

"There's no time to argue. Just stay here!" It came out as order. After another punch, the door slid open and Davi stepped through, turning back to motion. "Please. Just be safe, okay?" His hand went to his blaster and he hurried up the corridor, leaving Tela fuming. He hadn't meant to sound so harsh. How could he be so bad at communicating with the woman he loved?

He searched the hallway for a sign of the major. A few mechanics and techs passed but the man had disappeared. Davi hesitated a moment then went toward the next hangar. His pace increased with every step. The landing bays were always busy. There'd be plenty of witnesses. All Davi wanted to do was talk. He thought about radioing for Yao and Farien but by the time they got there, the major would probably be gone. Then it struck him how stupid it would be to call them, when he'd refused Tela's help and sent her away. Maybe he was being a jerk. He swore he'd make it up to her later.

He reached the next hangar and the door slid open immediately. Stepping inside, Davi nodded to the techs at the flight status station and moved on through, wading along rows of shuttles and passenger craft. If the major was already aboard a ship, he'd never find him. But then if he'd intended to leave by fighter, he might have to steal one. Pulling out his datapad, Davi began typing as he walked, calling up the departure sched-ules from the military channel. For pilots, both civilian and military schedules were interspersed in separate colors making the flight class easy to distinguish. It was a quiet day for schedule. He remembered flights had dropped since the violence.

Turning right at the end of a row of shuttles, he glanced ahead, looking for any sign of the major. Then he heard running footsteps and turned just as a bulky figure dove out of the shadows and threw him to the ground on his stomach. They wrestled on the floor of the bay as Davi's datapad slid away out of reach. The man's breath was hot and stunk of wine. Davi finally managed to turn on his side and catch a glimpse of his attacker. It was Major Valenti Broks.

"I just want to talk with you, Major."

"Talk? Like you did with my brother?"

"Who? I don't know your brother."

"Oh, yes you do!" The Major's fist slammed into Davi's stomach, knocking the wind from his lungs and forcing him to cough and gasp for breath. In the process, he released his hold on the major's arm, allowing his opponent to attempt flipping him onto his stomach again, but as the major rolled him, Davi pushed, rolling over and over out of reach and landing on his back. The Major hurried toward him, but Davi jumped to his feet, squaring off to face the man.

Both stood there a moment, sweat soaking their clothes as they gasped for breath. Then the Major drew a blaster, pointing it at Davi. "I've waited for this moment for too long, Rhii."

"You're Valenti Broks, right?" Davi hoped the mention of his name might prove a distraction.

Broks frowned. "How do you know that?"

"Put the blaster down and talk to me."

"There'll be no talking. This is vengeance, period."

"Vengeance for what?" Tela's voice came out of nowhere and Broks spun around. Tela stood nearby, blaster aimed at him.

The Major took aim but Davi dove, knocking him from his feet and sending his blaster spinning across the floor and under the shuttle. They wrestled and rolled again as Tela hurried over, trying to get a clear shot. Neither man could get a solid grip on the other's sweaty body, but they continued gasping for breath as they rolled and struck blows at each other.

"Stop right now!" Tela held the blaster steady, aimed at the man as he and Davi jostled for position on top of each other.

Davi heard footsteps pounding toward them on the hangar floor. "I told you to stay out of this," Davi said.

"You should be glad I didn't."

"Drop your weapon!" A voice called as armed security men appeared, weapons raised and pointed at Tela.

"We're on official business," she said.

"Three officers fighting? Have a little too much to drink?" the lead security man asked, looking her over. Tela lowered her gun slightly as she turned to argue.

Broks pushed with both legs, slamming his fists into Davi's stomach from below and sending him flying toward Tela. Tela tried to dodge and aim her blaster again, but Davi had no control and his feet spun and forced her to jump to avoid being knocked off her feet. As her aim faltered, and the security men dodged her fall, the Major jumped to his feet.

"You stop right there!" The security lead ordered.

The Major plowed right through, shoving them aside and disappearing behind the shuttle.

"That man's wanted for murder!" Davi called as he helped Tela up and started after Broks. The security men blocked his way.

"What are you talking about?"

They spent a few minutes explaining, then the security chief called to confirm. Afterwards, they searched for the Major together but found no sign of him. Finally, the security men went back to their posts, leaving Davi and Tela alone.

"Aren't you going to thank me?" Tela asked as she holstered her blaster.

"Thanks. Look, I didn't mean to be so harsh before. You didn't deserve that."

Tela shrugged it off, not meeting his eyes. "Forget it!"

"I can't help wanting to protect the woman I love. I hope you can see that."

She spun back to face him, forcing him to stop inches from her as their eyes met. "What I see is your lack of trust in my abilities as a soldier and pilot and a woman, Davi! You're treating me like I'm less than you are!"

"I'm treating you like my future wife."

"How do you know I'm your future wife? We've never talked about it."

"We've mentioned it."

"Not seriously!"

Davi sighed, his shoulders rising and falling as he caught his breath. "You're amazing. Everything to me."

Tela sighed, too, shaking her head. "I don't know if I want to be anymore."

"What does that mean?"

"I don't want to be treated like some fragile child. I want a man who respects me as an equal partner. You don't seem capable of doing that, no matter how many times I prove my skills."

"Would I have appointed you to lead the Squad in my absence if I felt that way about you?"

Tela shrugged. "I don't know, Davi. I don't know what you'd do. I'm beginning to wonder if I know you at all."

Before he could respond, she spun as the door opened to admit two mechanics, then she raced past them and disappeared around a corner. Davi started to chase her, then stopped, shocked, as he processed what she'd said. What had happened to them? When had things gotten so hard again? Had he lost her?

Did she really believe what she'd just said?

A mechanic appeared, waving his arms at Davi. "You dropped this, Captain." He held out Davi's datapad.

Davi sighed and nodded, retrieving it from the mechanic's hand. "Thanks." The mechanic nodded and hurried off, as Davi headed for the corridor. He had to figure out what to say before he found Tela. Why was he so bad with words?

Chapter Nine

Miri stood quietly at her apartment window watching the playground below. The preschool stood out as an oddity in her neighborhood of high rises and high prices, but for Miri it was a blessing. With all the changes she'd endured, watching children laugh and play, oblivious to the problems of the world around them, was a reminder of a future filled with possibilities. No one knew who those children might grow up to be, what impact they might make, the decisions they'd face. But maybe one or two of them would actually make a difference; change the world for the better. Imagining that gave Miri hope.

She needed it, too, because her hope for her son's future was clouded with insanity. How could two people once so in love make such a mess of things?

"Should we go to her?" Miri turned as Lura finished refilling her mug of Talis.

Lura shook her head. "Whatever's the matter, she'll tell us when she's ready."

Tela had arrived an hour earlier in tears. Miri and Lura did their best to comfort her but all she'd managed to choke out between sobs was "Davi wants to marry me." Miri was thrilled. Why was Tela in tears?

"It makes no sense. We know they love each other. Why isn't she dancing with joy?"

"Something else must have happened. They haven't seen each other in weeks. You know how touchy she can be and how careless Davi is with his words sometimes."

"But he proposed! My gods! I'm bouncing off the walls for them!"

Lura laughed. "I feel the same, Miri. We just need to give her time."

They heard feet shuffling in the corridor and turned as Tela appeared, sniffling and wiping her eyes on a sleeve. "I'm sorry." Her cheeks were red from constant rubbing and shadows clouded her eyes. The girl was way too stressed for someone with such good news.

Lura smiled. "It's okay, dear. We're just concerned about you." Her eyes glistened with sympathy.

Miri nodded. "Come, sit with us. Can we get you some Talis?"

Tela nodded and walked over, sitting on the sofa beside Lura. Lura tried to get up, but Miri waved her off and went to retrieve another mug herself from the cabinet where they'd left the pitcher on a warmer.

"I seem nuts, right?" Tela sniffled and offered a weak smile.

Lura laughed. "Well, we did expect a bit of a different reaction."

Tela sighed, sinking back on the couch. "It wasn't like he got on his knees. It's just that he referred to me as 'my future wife.'"

Lura nodded as Miri returned, handing Tela a mug of hot Talis and taking a seat on the other sofa across from them. "It's about time he got serious."

Tela sipped her Talis then shook her head. "He's not."

Miri laughed. "I know my son, Tela. If he's mentioning marriage, you can believe me—he's serious!"

Tela stiffened as if she'd been insulted and looked away. Gods, these younger generations were so dramatic! "He treats me like I'm incompetent. Like I'm not a good soldier. Like I need protecting."

"That's instinct. Men protect their women. It's been that way forever, dear; since Adam and Eve you might say. It's best to allow them their illusions. We know who the real strong ones are." Miri chuckled, looking at Lura for affirmation.

Lura smiled, lost in memories for a moment. "Miri's right. Sol still treats me that way. But I've grown to appreciate it. It's men's way of showing they care about us." Miri admired the glint in Lura's eyes as she spoke of it. What must it be like to know a love like that?

"But neither of you are military officers. I've been through training in weapons, flight. I saved his life today." Tela's eyes found Miri's again.

"What?" Miri demanded as she and Lura both stiffened and they leaned forward with alarm.

"He met me at the bay as my squadron landed. We ran into some major whom command suspects in the bombing. Davi tried to talk to him and the man attacked. Davi had told me to stay where I was when he chased the man, but it's a good thing I didn't listen."

Miri and Lura both nodded. Who could argue with that? Miri's biggest mistakes in life had come from listening to men. Especially Xalivar.

"But then, after, he acted so disappointed that I didn't respect his request to stay safe. I'd just saved his life and he was angry at me for being there."

Miri and Lura exchanged a knowing look. All of a sudden, Tela's emotional outburst made sense. When would Davi learn how to talk to this girl? She wasn't like his mothers. She was a different breed. He had to stop treating her like a delicate flower and treat her more like a peer or he'd lose her. Miri felt a sudden tension as anger rose within. She hadn't been mad at her son in ages. If only he were here! "You just let us handle him, okay? We'll set him straight, I promise."

Tela shook her head, relaxing as if their support had relieved her of her burden. She held out her hands and squeezed as theirs joined hers. "No. We have to sort this out ourselves. He'd probably be mad I even told you. I mean, he wants to marry me, right?" Then as if the realization had just hit her, she smiled. "He thinks of me as his future wife!" She looked at them as they nodded and grinned.

Lura hugged Tela as Miri stood and hurried over. "We're so happy for you both!"

Tela stood and Miri hugged her. "And for us, too!"

A low rumble rose from the street. Tela and Miri struggled to stay on their feet. The building started shaking and a huge flash lit the window; then she heard an explosion and saw rising smoke. All three women rushed to the window.

Miri's throat went dry as the breath rushed from her lungs. She couldn't believe her eyes. Debris layered the street outside, clouding the air. A smoking crater was all that remained where the playground and preschool had been moments before. *My gods, the children!* Miri's hand went to her mouth as Lura and Tela gasped beside her.

"Isn't that—" Miri nodded, cutting Tela off.

Miri pushed against a column to steady herself, suddenly feeling faint. Children, teachers, staff—the entire building had been wiped away by the explosion. Pedestrians stumbled out of buildings below, faces frozen in shock as they tried to make sense of the site before their eyes.

Tela hurried to the wall and turned on the flat screen, dialing up the news channels. Vooriflies fluttered in Miri's stomach. *Gods, please let it be some horrible accident.* They'd know as soon as the talking heads did. But even as she thought it, she knew it wouldn't be so.

Tarkanius' aide turned on the broadcasts as soon as the first reports came in. Tarkanius and Aron had been discussing recent events, but the footage of the crater left them in stunned silence. The talking heads were all speculating at this point. Although they made mention of the possibility of a terrible accident, all assumed the bombing was intentional. Just the thought of it had Tarkanius feeling weak in the knees. Boralian children murdered? Who would ever do such a thing? And these children came from elite homes, too. The outrage would be uncontrollable.

Catching his breath, Tarkanius motioned to his aide, who muted the broadcasts as Tarkanius punched in a code on the throne room comm station, motioning for Aron to join him. Soon Joram and Uzah's faces filled the screen. "Good afternoon, my Lord," both said simultaneously.

"Have you seen the broadcasts?"

Joram shook his head. "Something's coming up now."

"My God!" Uzah exclaimed as they stared at a screen off camera.

"I need to know as soon as anyone claims responsibility. Things are about to get a lot worse." Tarkanius winced as images of protestors carrying 'Vertullian babykillers' signs appeared on the broadcasts. Months of attacks had built up a certain numbness in him but this...the nature of this attack shredded that inner wall in an instant. Children's body parts were scattered for blocks.

"I assure you, my Lord, we will make every effort to find out if anyone here's responsible." Joram choked out the words, clearly overcome with emotion at the images he was seeing.

"To kill innocent children..." Aron's voice trailed off as his face darkened.

"It's possible it's an accident," Uzah said.

"Let's hope for all of our sakes that proves to be the case," Tarkanius said. "Gods help us if this crisis has reached such a level."

"You'll hear anything as soon as it comes in," Uzah said with a nod.

"Our prayers are with everyone there through this time," Joram added.

"Thank you," Tarkanius said before the screen went dark.

Aron sank onto a step, looking gaunt and pale, similar to how Tarkanius felt. "I can't believe this. Has the world gone insane? A year ago, we had such hope."

Tarkanius sighed. "Long simmering differences were ignored too long. We grew complacent as things went our way. We should have addressed them all along. Now we're paying a price." Tarkanius blamed himself. How could he have been so short-sighted? What kind of leadership had he shown in ignoring the issues? He'd been tired of the conflict and drama; caught up in the excitement of hope for change. As a result, he'd failed to lead well. Now even children were paying for it with their lives. He'd never forgive himself.

"You're not responsible, Tarkanius. No one could have predicted this." Aron looked up at Tarkanius, his sadness replaced by concern.

Tarkanius shook his head. He couldn't even meet Aron's eyes. "I should have. It's not like the tensions weren't there before. We just ignored them, as if they'd disappear. Instead they've blown up like a nuclear wave, radiation tainting everything it touches."

"The Council must unite to push through this crisis and be an example for the people."

"The Council members can't even agree amongst themselves,

Aron. Until we can, a united front is impossible." Tarkanius saw, as their eyes finally met, that he and Aron both shared the fear that unity might never be achieved. "If Council members are part of the conspiracies, we have no hope of coming together."

"All we can do is pray," Aron said sadly, his eyes lifting toward the ceiling.

"I'm afraid you'd be better with that than I would. I'm quite out of practice." Tarkanius' mind raced with possibilities. He had so much to consider, so many choices and decisions to face.

Aron smiled. "Would you like to pray together?"

Tarkanius hesitated. Two men of different religious views praying together? Would it even be possible when they didn't share the same gods? Aron was a good man and had become a close friend. *It can't hurt anything, Tarkanius. If you want to unite the people, the willingness must start with you.* Tarkanius nodded and moved toward Aron, who stood. "Please lead us."

"Of course." Tarkanius regretted it the moment he said it. He'd never been religious. His participation in rituals had come from honoring tradition, not belief. Internally, he'd never put much stock in faith or gods, but Aron really seemed to believe and somehow he couldn't refuse.

They bowed their heads together as Tarkanius closed his eyes, hoping that somehow the powers of the universe might hear and intercede. At that moment, he longed to be proven wrong.

The two freighters were already exchanging fire by the time Davi and his Squadron arrived. Splitting his pilots into two groups, one lined up on Farien, the other on him, Davi headed for the Boralian freighter and keyed the comm. "This is Captain Davi Rhii of the Boralian Alliance, Squadron One Alpha. Cease fire immediately and identify yourselves."

The Boralian freighter was almost twice the size of the Vertullian one. It reminded him of a bully picking on a runt, and Davi had always hated that scenario. The Vertullian ship's markings identified it as an agro supply ship, while the Boralian freighter was designated for deep-space shipping of larger cargo. Whereas both appeared clean and well maintained from the outside, the Boralian freighter had ten years on its Vert-ullian counterpart and the modern weapons to prove it. The Vertullian ship's hull already showed significant damage. Davi's Squadron had arrived just in time.

Neither freighter responded, the larger Boralian continuing to fire on its smaller counterpart.

"Okay, I want warning shots fired off the bridge of both freighters on my mark," Davi ordered. "No damage. Just a warning."

"Ah gees, Captain, sir, that's no fun," Brie said in a mock whine. Davi could picture her grinning ear-to-ear.

"Lined up and ready on your mark," Farien confirmed.

Davi looked around to confirm that his group was ready as well then keyed the comm. "Fire!"

Nine fighters simultaneously sent lasers to the same point just outside the bridge windows of each freighter—Davi's group the Vertullian and Farien's the Borallian. The lasers exploded harmlessly, vibrating the bridges. Suddenly, Davi heard other voices on the comm.

"Wait! Alpha One Leader, this is Captain Jel Cain of the Agro Freighter *Eden One*. We're delivering a shipment of grain to Xanthis when this guy comes out of nowhere and starts blasting us."

"Your people declared war on us today by murdering innocent children! This is Captain Vrel Dagan of the Freighter *Dragon Dancer*, Captain Rhii. We're just defending our citizens from further attacks by these terrorists. Doing our civic duty, you might say."

The attack on the preschool was two hours' old. *This is just what we need, overzealous mercenary captains taking the law into their own hands!* "Last I heard, Captain Dagan, no one had yet claimed responsibility for that attack nor had any suspects been named."

"We all know who did it, Captain! They're all animals, these people!"

"We weren't even aware of the incident ourselves until this madman attacked us!" Captain Cain responded.

"Regardless, civilian commercial vessels are not authorized to attack each other in official shipping lanes," Davi said. "Your vehicles are permitted weapons for defensive purposes only, per regulations."

He could almost hear the Boralian Captain frown. "Don't quote regulations to me! This is a time of war! Exceptions must be made!" The Boralian freighter fired two more cannon blasts at the *Eden One*.

"This guy has a hearing problem," Virun muttered into the comm.

"Another failed cadet wannabe living his fantasies at any excuse," Jorek agreed.

Davi laughed. The two men could have been describing themselves as new recruits a year before.

"We had nothing to do with those children's deaths! We regret it as much as anyone!"

"Captain Dagan, one more blast from your freighter and I'll shoot out your weapons myself." Davi allowed the irritation he felt to come through clearly over the comm.

Dagan's voice changed pitch as he stuttered for words. "We're on your side, Captain!"

"This is a Vertullian unit, Captain Dagan," Davi said, smiling as he imagined the man's reaction. "But my duty is to protect all civilian and commercial interests regardless of their origination."

"We don't take orders from slaves!"

"Then take them from me!" Farien yelled. "This is Captain Farien Noa of the Borali military. Cease fire as ordered or I'll personally make sure you're enjoying the comfortable vacuum of space in the next thirty seconds!"

The Borali freighter's cannons relaxed to their resting position as the ship's Captain cleared his throat. "A Borali officer serving with slaves?"

"These men and women are free citizens just like you, Captain! And I use the term loosely. You clearly lack the character deserving of such a title!" For once, Davi found Farien's temper useful on a mission. He watched as Farien fired a shot toward the Dragon Dancer. It exploded just off the wing outside the bridge window.

"Stop! Please. We'll comply with your instructions." Captain Dagan pleaded.

"Order all crew members away from weapons and prepare for boarding," Davi said, relaxing a bit as the confrontation ended. The last thing they needed was every civilian in the system taking up arms and choosing sides. "I'm sending someone aboard to supervise as we escort you back to Legallis."

"I have a deadline to meet!"

"You won't be meeting it," Farien said.

Davi debated for a moment whether it should be Farien who boarded then decided he'd rather send the Captain a message and keep Farien handy in case the man made trouble. "Nila, land in their bay and get to that bridge to await my orders."

"Me?" Nila sounded as confused as Davi expected the freighter captain was.

"We're sending a message, Nila. You're the perfect choice."

Brie chuckled. "Oh, he'll love taking orders from a woman."

"Trust me. She loves bossing men around." Virun's voice dripped with mock suffering as Jorek and the others' laughter filled the comm.

Davi saw Nila swing her ship around and head toward the Borali freighter. "Eden One, damage report."

"We've got some scratches and bruises, but we can still make Xanthis," Captain Cain replied.

"Do you want an escort?"

"Negative. We'll keep to distance shipping lanes and we should be okay."

"Affirmative. You're cleared to leave."

As Davi and his Squadron formed up around the Boralian freighter, the Vertullian ship began to turn and head off away from them.

"I wonder how many more heroes like this we'll be dealing with," Jorek muttered.

"They'll likely be hundreds. Tensions will spin out of control after today." Yao sounded sad. He'd been assigned to Davi's Squadron as part of his temporary reassignment.

"Jorek and Virun, you pair with Brie and Yao on those weapons, in case the Captain decides to be difficult. Farien and I will take the lead, the rest of you cover the engines." Davi formed with

Farien and headed for the front of the freighter as the rest peeled off to their various assignments. He hoped Yao's prediction was an exaggeration but feared it wouldn't be. The preschool incident would send things to the next level and that meant this incident was only the beginning.

Manaen should be meeting with the first of them by now, Xalivar thought. He'd sent his majordomo off with recorded messages to the leadership of various alien species in the system. It was time to implement phase two of his plan. If they joined his cause as expected, his army would triple in size in a few hours. With most of the alien species on his side—he had doubts about the Tertullians who were fiercely loyal to the government and the Idolians who were fiercely independent—victory would be his all the faster. He'd always treated the aliens with indifference, but they hadn't been persecuted, not any more than would be typical of systems where various species lived in close proximity. After all, his grandfather had stopped terraforming on planets like Xanthis when intelligent life was discovered there. They'd been allowed to maintain their lifestyles and home planets under his family's rule. Most of them still lived as they had for generations. The fact that Xalivar planned to destroy them once he regained power would go unmentioned, until they helped get him there. *Even an idiot like Manaen can't screw this up. Just play the recording and let me do the talking.*

He wished he could go himself. Undoubtedly his presence would be more convincing, but with the government suspicious of his involvement, he couldn't risk stumbling into a patrol or having video footage confirming his presence make its way onto the nets. No, he'd continue to maintain a low profile for now. The time for glory would be soon enough.

Watching Generals Lucius and Pres and Admiral Dek take their recruits through training was thrilling. Xalivar hadn't been on a battlefield since the Delta V incident thirty years before. He'd seen a few training exercises visiting his former nephew at the Academy, but now he felt like a real military leader—strategizing with his commanders, watching the troops train to implement those plans. He leaned his head back and laughed with delight at the images flooding his mind. Was there any sweeter sensation than that of victory?

A younger officer stumbled as he jumped from the Floater. Despite the wide opening behind the long benches where troops rode, he managed to get his boots caught as he leapt off the ledge to the ground and fell flat on his face. Why did he suddenly miss Xander? So many times as a child, he'd watched his nephew and designated heir keep at such exercises until he had them down perfectly. Xander had been awkward and clumsy until his mid-teens. To see him successful now as a pilot and officer ought to be a source of pride, but instead it stung with betrayal. Xalivar cursed his sister again for raising her son to be weak. He cursed her for adopting a slave behind his back, contaminating his household and manipulating Xalivar to care about him. *Damn you, Miri! I hope your new life is so much less than you want!*

He turned and motioned to an aide. The aide hurried forward with a pitcher and cup. Xalivar took the cup and held it as the aide poured cold Talis. Xalivar drank slowly, allowing the energy inherent in the brewed beverage to calm him as it flowed down his throat. Not only had Miri and Xander both betrayed him, they'd stolen his rightful power and left him with no heir. That was another issue Xalivar would have to resolve. He might even have to take a mistress to bear him an heir personally. He scowled at the thought. Women were such an encumbrance—so emotional, demanding, weak. He hoped another alternative would present itself, but knew he couldn't risk another embarrassment like Miri had caused. Perhaps adoption would be the best course. He'd have to run any cand-idate through rigorous genetic testing first, of course.

He thought of Manaen again. At least his Andorian servant was too stupid to betray him. No ambition whatsoever, these Andorians! He laughed. The perfect aide. He reached for his datapad to check for incoming messages. No word yet on alien leadership responses. He supposed he'd have to be patient, but patience had never been one of his strengths. He'd already wasted enough time waiting for what was his to be restored.

He heard footsteps on the stairs and turned as General Lucius joined him on the balcony, smiling. "They're doing quite well, wouldn't you say?"

Xalivar nodded. "Who is that young one?"

"The one who stumbled dismounting from the Floater?" Lucius read the answer on Xalivar's face and continued: "I don't know. Do you want him removed?"

"No. He reminds me of someone is all, Lucius. See that he gets some extra attention. It won't do to have our troop's entrance marred by such accidents."

"Of course, my Lord," Lucius said. They turned back to watch the troops continue their training.

Normally Xalivar had a very low tolerance for failure, but, for some reason, he felt charitable toward the young soldier. He supposed it wouldn't hurt to extend some leeway to his recruits. After all, he wanted and needed their loyalty. His reputation had been scarred enough. For now, they respected him. He wouldn't want to damage that over something so minor. At least for now.

"Our plans are succeeding, General. It's only a matter of time." Xalivar's eyes met the General's as Lucius beamed with pride. Xalivar finished his Talis then turned, handing the cup back to his aide, and marched back into the building toward his new office. It was time to turn on the networks and see if his latest surprise for Miri was having the expected impact. He hoped she was home to see the explosion. By now, he imagined the Boralians would be close to declaring war on the Vert-ullians over it. His head went back as he laughed and disappeared inside.

LSP Major Isak Zylo paced inches from the other side of the one way glass as Tarkanius and Aron watched with General Grif. Lord Kretzu sat calmly, erect in his usual dignified manner, so far unperturbed. Even when confronted with the camera images which revealed his presence at the café, he watched impassively, looking like he was fighting a yawn.

An experienced veteran, Zylo had aligned himself with Xalivar during the war with the WFR but survived because he had followed orders and had an outstanding record prior to that. Tarkanius had been in a bind. If he'd eliminated every officer who'd obeyed Xalivar, he'd have no officers left to lead the military. And since the WFR's victory, Zylo had served with distinction. Mid-forties, Zylo had short, blonde hair and a muscular frame for a man his age, although signs of his age appeared around his growing midriff and in the gray spotting his mustache.

"Come on, Kretzu, this is your chance to tell your side of it," Zylo said, his voice menacing. "You won't get another one. We know you were there."

Kretzu frowned as his head spun so their eyes met. "It's 'my Lord,' Major. No matter what you accuse me of, do not forget your place."

"My apologies, *my* Lord. Perhaps your title won't be an issue much longer."

Kretzu slammed a fist down on the metal table. "Do not threaten me, Major. Lord Elul is a personal friend of mine. He'll hear of any mistreatment or disrespect!"

Lord Elul won't know this yet, Tarkanius thought. *You two are too close. He's under suspicion as well.* The thought that his trusted security chief, head of the Lord's Special Police, might be involved in attempting to assassinate him had been giving Tarkanius nightmares. He'd handpicked the Major for his experience, hoping that once the circumstances had been explained, he could rely on the man's complete discretion.

"Ner Zebah, my Lord, have you heard the name?" Zylo's tone hadn't changed, despite his interrogation subject's anger.

At the very least, Tarkanius had hoped the images would shake the older man. Cameras had been secretly installed in the area surrounding the metro center prior to the High Lord Councilor's speech—added security measures. The conspirators wouldn't have expected them, but Kretzu held up well.

"Who else was with you? Who else shall I be charging with murder?!" Zylo slammed his palms down on the table, leaning across it to look Kretzu in the eye as he emphasized the last word. It came out almost like spit.

"Murder?! How dare you! I have served this Council and Alliance since before you were born!"

Tarkanius exchanged a look with Aron. "This isn't working."

Aron's shoulder sagged. "He doesn't believe we have enough to charge him."

General Grif cleared his throat and the two Lords turned toward him. "Perhaps an alternate tactic might be more effective." He continued staring through the one-way glass even as he spoke.

"Alternate tactic?" Tarkanius looked at Aron again, worried. "What are you suggesting, General?"

Grif smiled. "The battlefield here is Lord Kretzu's mind. He believes he has the upper hand, that he's in control. We need to remove that confidence."

"How?" Aron asked then watched the General as he stepped back from the window and turned to face them.

"Lord Aron, will you accompany me? And follow my lead?"

"Of course, General."

Grif turned and opened the door, stepping into the corridor. Aron followed, leaving Tarkanius alone in the observation room. Moments later, they entered the room with Major Zylo and Lord Kretzu.

"Ah, General," Kretzu sighed, "here to put an end to this spectacle, I hope. Please instruct the Lieutenant to release me at once."

Grif offered a forced smile. "Of course, my Lord. You're released."

Kretzu shot Zylo a look of hatred as he immediately stood.

"Into the custody of Lord Aron."

"Excuse me?!"

"Yes. You're to be temporarily assigned to help Lord Aron and the Vertullian leadership with the crisis," Grif continued. Tarkanius smiled, grasping the General's tactic. *It just might work.*

"I have business of my own to deal with. I have no time—"

"We must all make sacrifices at times like these," Grif continued, cutting him off. "Wouldn't you agree, Lord Aron?"

Aron smiled and nodded. "Of course, General. We're all in this together."

Kretzu frowned. "Custody? I am under arrest?"

"Not exactly," Grif said. "But, unfortunately, word of your detainment leaked. It's already been on the broadcasts. And we are worried for your safety."

Brilliant! Tarkanius chuckled to himself.

Kretzu's eyes widened and he stiffened. "So you're sending me to the planet of those who might harm me?"

"Your presence there shall be low profile," Aron said, "and the military will provide a protective detail."

Grif smiled. "Of course. Your generous dedication to helping the Vertullians through this can only serve to endear you to them and change the minds of any who might oppose you."

Kretzu shook his head, arms crossed over his chest. "I refuse. I want no part of this."

"You have no choice," Grif said.

"I most certainly do!"

Grif crossed his own arms over his chest and leaned back against a wall. He waited in silence as Kretzu's eyes continually darted toward the door, as if gauging whether it was unlocked, so he could bolt. "The High Lord Councilor has evoked the Emergency Powers Clause and, as such, has requested your compliance. As you know, in times of Emergency Powers, even Council members are expected to serve as needed by the High Lord Councilor. Your refusal gives the military power to take other necessary actions, which include detaining you further. Major, please check the status of open cells at Centauri Two."

Zylo pulled the datapad from his belt and began typing. "Of course, General."

Tarkanius noticed Kretzu's robe darkening with sweat at the mention of the Alliance's most secure prison. "I know nothing of a café. I am a loyal citizen!"

"The warden confirms availability," Zylo said, with a casual glance at Grif.

Kretzu's legs seemed to collapse from under him as he fell against the wall. Aron hurried over and took his arm, helping him to a chair. Grif sat in a chair across the table, the Major taking another beside him. Tarkanius almost felt sorry for the old man.

"Okay, Lord Kretzu. Tell us about Ner Zebah." Grif's stare was so intense, even Tarkanius felt a tinge of nerves on the other side of the glass. And then Kretzu leaned back and began to talk.

The group gathered in Simeon's apartment, the same one once occupied by Tarkanius when he headed the Council. Owned by the Alliance, it was one of the perks of office for the Council's elected leader. With a 360-degree view of the city center through its windows, the round, revolving penthouse sat atop a highrise near the Palace and government complex was the envy of all who visited and Simeon knew many of those present dreamed of a day they could call it "home."

Lords Kray and Qai sat together on a lush sofa made of Krikatru leather from Eleni 1. Dark, almost shiny, it had a tendency to mold to the skin such that anyone sitting on or wearing it almost didn't notice the separation between the leather and his or her own skin.

On an identical sofa across from them sat Pharah Brahma, Yao's father, and Lords Buj and Amie. Younger than Pharah, they had joined the Council together two years before but had quickly risen in influence due to their strong values and work ethic. As a Tertullian, Pharah could not serve on the Council, but his red eyes were famous for their warmth, and, with his smile, won him much admiration from all he knew. He'd long been a respected citizen and worked his way comfortably into the upper class elite, so many on the Council knew him socially. But Simeon had asked him there for other reasons.

Shiny, gold-encrusted lamps and handwoven Tertullian tapestries and carpets complemented the Idolian woodwork on the walls and furniture. Even most of the Lords' lifestyles were severely lacking compared to this. Usually it made Simeon embarrassed, but today it aided his cause.

"Thank you all for coming," he said as he sat in a plush, white lounge chair made from Gungor fur which sat at the head of the two sofas. "As you all know, the Alliance faces a great crisis, one which threatens to tear it apart. And plans are being put in place to protect it, but today I would ask your help."

"The entire Council must be willing to help," Lord Qai said.

Simeon's sleeve rustled as he raised a hand in agreement. "Of course, Qai. But this meeting is to be kept private until I grant permission for you to speak of it. We have matters to discuss of a very sensitive nature. And you're each here because I respect your judgment, covet your advice and need your support—unofficially for now."

Pharah looked around at the others, shifting on the sofa as if he felt out of place. "Of course, Lord Simeon. Whatever we can do."

Qai frowned. "Mister Brahma is not on the Council. Why is he here?"

"His presence is the most important of all." Simeon glanced reassuringly at Pharah. The Tertullian had smartly worn a robe to the gathering; despite its different coloring, it helped him blend in with the others, though he was the only nonhuman present. "He represents citizens for whom we cannot speak." Simeon made a wide arc with his outstretched arms. "Not just the Tertullians but all the alien races. They are citizens of our Alliance, too, and it is time we started treating them as such."

"You have always been most gracious to us," Pharah said, smiling as if embarrassed at being singled out.

"No, my friend, we have not. And that must change." He couldn't bring himself to match Pharah's smile. A generous man like his son, the Tertullian was far more forgiving than Simeon himself would be in his place.

"He has no official authority," Lord Amie noted, looking down from his towering height at Pharah with an apologetic look. Pharah waved it off.

"That's why this meeting is unofficial," Simeon said. "And must remain our secret for now. Our friend, Pharah, is needed to deliver a message to the alien citizens of this Alliance."

Pharah nodded, leaning forward with interest. "I will, of course, do what I can. I'm not an ambassador."

"But you are a diplomat," Kray said, "a very talented one." She smiled as Pharah's purple skin lightened with embarrassment.

"Thank you, my Lord. Your faith in me is most humbling."

"This message is from the High Lord Councilor," Simeon said, his discussion with Tarkanius flashing through his mind. "It is time for all our citizens to be equals and have equal voice in this government." Qai and the other Lords exchanged surprised looks. "If you nonhumans will help us fight off the threat that menaces us all, we will work with you to re-invent a government that's inclusive of all our peoples."

Pharah's purple eyes lightened as they widened, staring at Simeon and then panning the others, his lips opening and then closing again as he sought words. "It is a message which will surprise many, but one which some of us have been waiting generations to hear."

"Will the majority be receptive?" Kray's eyes met his with eagerness.

"Some will be fearful of a trap. Others encouraged. But I will do all I can to get the dialogue open."

Simeon smiled. "Good."

Lord Buj, shorter and stockier than his counterpart Amie, nodded but looked to Pharah as well. "Will they fight with us?"

"Many of us are not belligerent peoples. We have no history of warfare like you do. But there are many ways to support your needs, wouldn't you agree?" Pharah's eyes moved between them, seeking agreement.

"Of course," Kray was the first to say.

"Dialogue is the first step," Simeon said, encouraged as he took a moment to meet each of their eyes in turn. "Once that begins, many details will come into focus. All we ask at the moment is a commitment to work together. The rest will come in time."

The others exchanged looks then mumbled in agreement, smiling back at him.

He had them! It was in their posture and faces. He'd chosen his group wisely, it seemed. Now for the hard part. "But first, we must discuss some recent events and discoveries involving members of the Council. Sadly, not all of us appear to be on the same side."

"That explains why you're handling this outside the Council," Lord Amie said with a sigh.

"You have evidence of treason?" Lord Buj asked.

"Let me show you what we've uncovered so far," Simeon said and clicked a button on the arm of his chair and a black flat screen lowered from the ceiling at the opposite end of the couches. Everyone turned to watch as images began to appear. He observed them carefully, offering a prayer to the gods that their passion would soon match his own.

The Idolian landscape shifted from gold to gray as the twin suns slid further down the horizon under the encroachment of night. Manaen felt a small quake under foot, the result of orbital interference from Charlis, the system's smaller sun. With Idolis currently at its nearest orbit to Charlis, quakes were a daily occurrence, along with hotter days and shorter nights. He hadn't felt one in years. Legallis' orbital pattern brought different effects.

He sighed as he stood there, watching the suns, basking in the warmth of the humid air, the sweet scent of Andolian berries in the nearby trees. Their purple shells still glistened in the remaining light. How fortunate he was that Xalivar sent him here this time of year. It had been decades since he'd had the opportunity to experience these smells, and tonight he would taste fresh Andolian berry pie for the first time since he was a teenager. A smile forced its way to his lips despite worried thoughts.

He heard the shuffling of feet on the sandy path and turned as his younger sister, Vibryd, stopped beside him. "A smile, my brother? How long it's been since I've seen such on your face."

Manaen laughed. "It's good to be home."

"It's good to have you here." She smiled as she reached over to gently stroke his arm. "Why do you stay?"

"It is my sworn duty to serve."

"But you're unhappy."

"Andolian oaths are not modified by emotions. It's a sacred trust."

Vibryd sighed, rolling her red eyes. They stood out starkly from her dark-blue skin. The extra time she spent in the sun had given her a tone Manaen's body never matched. "You're still young enough to find a promisemate and build a life here."

"It's too late for me, Viby."

"He's not the High Lord Councilor anymore!"

"Perhaps he will be again."

Vibryd scowled, exhaling deeply. "I hope not for all of us. I could never serve such a man as you do."

"There is more to Xalivar than his reputation, my sister." But Manaen found her words echoing in his mind.

Why did he stay? Xalivar was not kind to him—insulting, condescending. Manaen was like a piece of furniture or a walking datapad to him. The purpose of his mission came back to his mind then. He'd chosen a course of action, almost immediately, when told the assignment. His whole life, Manaen had never made such a decision. The consequences could bring harm to him and his family. He was willing to bear whatever came to him, but he longed to protect Vibyrd and her children. The alien leadership deserved his honesty. He could have just delivered Xalivar's pretaped messages and let them speak for themselves. But then the leaders always had questions and would turn to him, and Manaen found himself wanting to be honest with them. It came easier to him than he'd imagined, a fact which made him question himself all the more. *What does the oath mean to you, Manaen?*

Vibryd yawned, reaching up with a delicate hand to cover her mouth. Manaen's nose crinkled at the smell wafting from the kitchen window of the domed, mud-brick house behind them. "Mmmmmmm. Andolian berry pie."

Vibryd laughed. "Mother's recipe. I made two, so you can have extra."

Manaen shook his head, shooting her a stern look. "Mother wouldn't approve."

She rolled her eyes as she punched his arm. "Mother's not here. I'm the only one left to spoil you now so prepare yourself. You might even need your extra stomach tonight!" Laughing, she turned and headed back toward the house, disappearing inside.

Manaen laughed as he thought of their childhood. Their father worked hard, long hours and was rarely home. It was he who had taught his children the meaning of honor and service. Their mother raised all four children with stern discipline, yet much love. In truth, she'd snuck him a few extra slices herself from time to time—when he'd had a bad dream or a bad day at school or for his birthday. Vibryd looked so much like her; laughed like her. And he knew in that moment he'd made the right choice. He just hoped he had the strength to see it through and protect his family and all who might share their fate.

The noise of the open air market crowded their senses—vendors of all species yelling in competition with bleating Qiwi, roaring Gungor, grunting Krikatrus and screeching birds of all shapes and sizes. The earthy smell of manure and dried feed mixed with sweat, the nectar of flowers, the sweet scent of fruits. The market was cleaner than any Sol had visited in a long while, catering to the Borali capital's elite. He and Telanus had jumped to comply when Lura asked them to go for some ingredients she'd need at dinner. Tela offered to accompany them, but they'd waved her off, allowing her only to drop them off while she ran another errand, so they could enjoy "man time for a bit."

Weaving their way through crowded aisles, the rush hour, Telanus read off items from the list as Sol kept his eye peeled. "Tertullian turnips."

Sol spotted the long, bulbous brown taproots to their right. "How many?"

"Three."

Sol forced his way to the table and picked up a very large, conical vegetable with the pointed brown taproot converging into a round, greenish, tomato-like top. "This one's big enough; it might suffice."

"Get three just in case. We don't want to run short."

Sol snickered. "We'd never hear the end of that!" Telanus laughed, too. Sol grabbed the roots and turned on his heels, bumping into another man and knocking a handful of Gixi to the ground. "I'm sorry—" The man shrugged as he bent to retrieve the purple fruit and Sol recognized him. "Joram?!!"

Joram looked up as he retrieved the last Gixi and smiled. "Hello, Sol."

Sol shook his hand vigorously as Joram juggled his left arm, trying to keep the Gixi from falling again.

"You do your own shopping?" Telanus smiled quizzically as Joram shook his hand more gently.

"My wife said just three things, and here I am."

The men laughed at the familiar scenario. "We're here escaping, too." Telanus sighed. "Tela's sad. Miri and Lura are bossy. We haven't gotten away in three days."

Joram laughed. "A trip to the market was sounding good, I'll bet." Sol and Telanus joined his laughter, nodding.

"Why are you shopping in Legon?" Sol asked.

"We're at a hotel around the block. A meeting with Aron and Telanus today." Joram shifted as he almost dropped his fruit again. His body twisted as he juggled them, trying to find his balance again.

"Can I help?" Telanus reached for the Gixi, but Joram waved him off.

"We just have a couple more things," Sol said.

"I'll walk with you."

Sol and Telanus smiled. "Great."

They pushed through a crowded intersection of aisles into a section with meat on the left and breads to the right. The smell of fresh, uncooked fish filled Sol's nostrils, mixing with the earthiness of the leaf vegetables across the aisle. Sol noticed a few people staring. They must have recognized Joram. The Governor ignored them and walked on, searching for the next item on the list.

"Why's Tela so down?" Joram asked.

Telanus rolled his eyes. "A fight with Davi. Something silly they'll get over soon."

Joram chuckled. "Sounds like my teenage daughter."

Telanus slapped him on the back as he guffawed. "Do they ever outgrow it?"

Sol stopped as three husky men blocked the path. Looking up, he found their eyes watching him—full of hate. He smiled. "Excuse me."

As soon as he moved to push through, a man growled and grabbed him. "Don't touch me, slave!"

Joram stepped forward, frowning as Sol shook free of the man's grasp. "There are no slaves in the Alliance now. All are free."

"A mistake!" Another of the men said—gray-haired but just as bulky, with muscles bulging from his shirt and every exposed piece of skin covered in thick hair.

"Not your decision." Joram didn't meet their stares, instead attempted to pass. The gray-haired man threw him to the ground, Gixi scattering, bruised, across the aisle. The first man caught one and smashed it with his foot.

Sol hurried to help Joram up. "Do you know who this is?"

"A slave who knows his place before us—on the ground, kneeling," the first man said and guffawed with his friends.

Sol grabbed Joram's arm and helped him up as Telanus went to retrieve the fruit. "Leave it. I'll get more."

All three turned to go back up the aisle the way they'd come and found three lanky men there, blocking the way. "Where you going?" one of them asked.

"We're just picking up items for dinner." Telanus stood relaxed, his shoulders slumped, not meeting their eyes.

"Not anymore, slave!" The lanky man's fist slammed into Telanus' jaw, knocking him back into Sol and Joram. Then the six men were upon them, fists punching, feet kicking, grunting, groaning as Sol, Telanus and Joram struggled to defend themselves.

"Why are you doing this?" Joram pleaded. He was silenced as one of their attackers smashed a Gixi against his face.

Sol heard others mocking laughter around them, as he lost his footing and fell to his knees. The pounding and hitting increased. He ducked his head down beneath his arms for protection. He heard a grunt. Then Telanus cried out. He turned and saw a man beating his friend with a wooden crate, which shattered and disintegrated a bit at each strike.

Joram was pleading next to him, but also was forced to his knees by the gray-haired hulk. A boot to his ribs knocked the wind from him and he gasped, tears rolling down his cheeks, as his eyes pleaded with Sol.

Two men smashed crates over their heads now. A splinter dug into Sol's shoulder, adding to the throbbing already coming from dozens of other places and causing him cry out.

"Stop! You're hurting them!" A woman's voice. *Tela?*

Sol couldn't see through the men, but then he heard a blaster bolt and the men started to scatter.

"Leave them be!" *It was Tela!*

The men ran past, kicking them again as they passed. Some dropped fists down for one last shot as well. Tela fired again, kicking up dust with her boots as she pounded up the dirt aisle toward her father and his friends. Laser bolts struck an attacker, who screamed and grabbed his shoulder as his buddies pulled him to safety around a corner, and they all scattered into the crowd.

Telanus was lying face down, blood pouring from his scalp.

"Daddy!" Tela ran to him, holstering her blaster, looking to Sol and then Joram.

"I'm fine," Sol said, but his ankle throbbed and his arm was numb.

"Someone call help, please!" Joram said.

People moved around them—shoppers fleeing the scene, vendors retrieving smashed or scattered merchandise, and others approaching with offers of help. Sol brushed them off, but sweat and tears clouded his vision. Then his head began to ache and he felt weak, his eyes hazing over as he fell to the ground.

"Sol!" Tela's concerned yell was the last thing he heard before the world went dark.

Chapter Ten

Obed denied he needed security, but Bordox insisted. He held anything and everyone suspect. His father was taking a great risk even going to Legallis, but the meeting had been arranged for a café in Estrela, a small city on the far side of the planet, away from the capital. Since Council members travelled frequently, Obed thought no one would question Niger and Elul's trip, even though Estrela was far from a popular destination. At least this café wasn't a dive. The booths were well lit and clean with sparkling, waxed tabletops and smooth Gungor leather benches. The waitress greeted them as they entered and took their drink orders as they settled in at a booth.

By the time she delivered their order, Niger and Elul had slipped into the booth to join them. Bordox glanced around. The café was almost empty at this early hour—a good thing. The last thing they wanted was for their conversation to be overheard.

"You look well, Obed," Elul said with a grin. "Life as an outcast agrees with you." The Lord's rotund belly jiggled as he laughed.

Bordox shot him a cold stare as Obed smiled back. "Exiled by choice, my friend. We are not fugitives."

"Indeed." Niger hadn't smiled once since arriving, even when shaking their hands in greeting. Bordox wondered what had him preoccupied. "You said you had information which might be of use to us?"

Obed nodded, looking pensive. "Perhaps. If I can trust you."

"How do we know we can trust you?"

Obed chuckled. "Touché, my friend. I understand not everyone shares Tarkanius' views on the success of the slaves' integration as citizens."

"Surely that comes as no surprise to you," Elul said.

Bordox wondered how long it would take for the constant grin to permanently warp his fat facial muscles. Bordox's fist balled involuntarily from his desire to wipe it off the man's smug face.

"Like many of us, your reservations are well known," Elul continued.

Obed looked at Niger. "Yet some were supportive of Tarkanius at first."

"I objected to Xalivar's attempts to control and deceive the Council. Plus the citizenry seemed in favor of the idea. But the citizenry's optimism has led to economic disaster for many. Tarkanius is an honorable man but utterly unprepared for the realities of leadership, I'm afraid." Niger's eyes met Obed's as each tried to read the other for several moments.

"What do you want in exchange for this...information?" Elul's grin finally went away as he sized up Obed.

"I want what we all want—the glory of our Alliance restored. The strength of our people assured."

All three men stared at each other a moment, as Bordox watched, his eyes darting back and forth. How could his father stomach working with men who so clearly held him in contempt? Politics was insane.

"I ask only for your support, when the time comes, and I wish to have a voice in affairs again," Obed said.

At last Niger smiled. "I believe the Council has greatly missed your voice, Obed. Although I fear restoration to your former status is unlikely."

Obed nodded. "I don't expect it to be easy. Although I will happily play whatever part I can. For now, it must be behind the scenes, as they say."

"What's the source of your information?" Elul's face dripped with suspicion. Bordox tensed and fought the urge to slap the man. His father had more honor in one finger than Elul had in his entire paunch.

"I cannot reveal my sources at this time, except to say, you will find the information proves quite reliable." Obed clearly saw the Lord's doubts but never faltered.

"You may count on our support, friend. I'm sure your information is as reliable as you say." Niger looked at Elul. "The former head of the LSP is a highly qualified source, I'd say."

Elul shrugged, relaxing a bit on the leather seat.

"Good. Shall we discuss this over provisions, then?" Obed leaned back and smiled at Bordox. The waitress appeared again, anxiously holding her datapad ready. Bordox could see his father remained determined to plunge ahead. He hoped the trust would not prove misplaced. He'd do whatever it took to protect Obed. Especially from men like these.

Pharah Brahma began his meetings with the leadership on his home world of Tertullis. It was where he had the most contacts and having an ally already on board would strengthen his case when meeting with alien leaders from other planets. Major Isak Zylo kept his opinions to himself. He'd been assigned as security for Brahma on the tour, not as a partici-pant. In fact, he wasn't even allowed in the room for the discussions so he had no idea, beyond hints Brahma himself let slip, what was actually being said. Zylo felt lucky to even have a career. After the debacle of the loss to the Vertullians in their rebellion, during which his ground troops on Vertullis had born huge casualties, he was grateful to have been allowed to remain in the military, let alone trusted with security detail on an important diplomatic quest. Despite being out of the official discussions, Zylo was listening carefully and the information he'd gathered would be of great interest to certain highly-placed friends. One, in particular, would be excited to learn of the discussions. He decided to wait until the journey was a few days in and gauge the leaders' reactions before sending his report.

To no one's surprise, the Tertullians jumped aboard almost before Pharah Brahma finished asking them. The Xanthians were more hesitant, although, given their planet's black market activities and their interest in maintaining a level of low interference from the government that was hardly surprising.

Now they were meeting with the leaders on Italis. A sparsely populated, terraformed planet, colonized by human outcasts from a variety of backgrounds, it had always been surprising Italis didn't draw more interest. From what Zylo could see, the terraforming was a complete success. The vegetation was lush, the landscapes beautiful, the land plentiful. There were plenty of natural resources from water to food to various minerals and gasses easily available for use by settlers. He'd have expected a lot more migration, but for unknown reasons it had stalled. Zylo's guess was the location. Except the great recreation hub of Regalis, another terraforming success, the planets further out were barely habitable and highly undesirable. That made Italis the edge of the universe as far as most people were concerned and populations seemed to gravitate toward the centers in solar systems.

Pharah Brahma emerged from the meeting with a broad smile on his face. "Well, that was easier than dealing with the Xanthians."

"The Italites are mostly human. Why are they being treated like an alien race?"

"Because the majority of them never bothered to apply for official citizenship. Strengthening our ties and unity is the goal of this mission, so we need to bring them on board."

"Bet they don't take too kindly to being lumped in as aliens."

Brahma smiled. "They refer to themselves that way. They claim they have more in common with the alien races than regular human Boralians. I believe I just convinced them they were wrong about that."

Was it the purple eyes or the orange skin I wonder?

"In any case, they've signed on tentatively. It's enough to mention them to the other leaders at least."

Zylo nodded. "Any change to the agenda?" Maintaining his casual tone and manner kept him on edge whenever the Tertullian was around.

Brahma shook his head. "No. We'll proceed on to Kronis as planned. The Italites offered to throw a reception this evening, but I declined on the basis of urgency. The High Lord Councilor really needs this alliance solidified as soon as possible."

Zylo sighed as the tension he'd felt dissipated. The sooner this was over, the better. "Whatever you say, sir. I'll alert the flight crew."

"Thank you. Let me just grab refreshment at the spaceport for an hour and I'll be ready to go."

Zylo finished adding to the notes in his datapad and pulled the comm from his belt. "We'll be waiting for you." Brahma was so old fashioned when it came to technology that he hadn't noticed Zylo never communicated with the pilots by datapad but always used the comm. Just a mention of the pilots and Zylo could freely take notes right in front of his subject. *So much for diplomats being smarter than the rest of us.*

Brahma smiled as he hurried off to find a restaurant while Zylo keyed the comm channel and hailed the pilots.

***

Davi gasped for breath when he reached the top of the stairs. The hospital was busy today, and he hadn't felt like fighting for an elevator. He raced down the slick, newly waxed floor, his boots slipping with each step, searching the walls for the room number. He rushed past startled nurses and burst inside. Tela was crying as she sat beside the bed, holding Telanus' hand. Telanus looked white as a cloud and thinner than ever, dark bruises circled his eyes and spotted his face. If his eyes had been closed, Davi would have thought he was dead. Davi saw Lura just past Miri, holding the hand he knew must be Sol's but he couldn't see his father yet. Miri stepped back when she spotted her son and turned to embrace him. As she did, Davi caught a glimpse of his father.

"My God! What happened to them?" Davi's eyes flickered from Miri to Lura and then Tela. Of the three, Tela was the most distraught.

He heard a moan and saw Sol's eyes open. A smile formed on his lips as he looked up at his son. A hand raised slowly, as if with great effort, reaching out. Davi hurried over and grasped it. "Don't move, father. I'm here."

Lura smiled. "He's okay. The surgery was successful." Davi nodded as her warm eyes met his, then frowned, nodding toward Tela. Lura gave a slight shake of her head. Davi squeezed his father's lukewarm hand before releasing it and hurrying to Tela.

"Don't touch me!" She shoved away his outstretched arm.

"It'll be okay, babe."

"Okay? My father's dying! Those bastards murdered my father!" She spoke loudly, almost a scream, her eyes biting into his as they met, like blades. Davi didn't know what to do or say.

"What happened?" His patrol had been tied up with incidents and run long. He'd gotten word of the attack but hadn't been able to break free for twenty-four hours—the longest day of his life.

"We just needed a few items for dinner," Miri said. "They went alone to get them. Tela dropped them off and ran an errand. When she came back..." Miri's voice faded as her face sunk into sadness.

"Who did this?"

"Animals!" Tela shrieked, her voice almost unrecognizable to Davi. "Boralian monsters!"

The hospital was a government facility. Nurses and an orderly glanced in through the doorway as they walked past. Miri hurried over and shut the door.

"This is not all Boralians, Tela. You know that."

Tela scowled at him. "Just the true ones. The ones who don't bother to hide who they are!"

"We've lived and worked among them, Tela," Davi said, shaking his head. "You know better." She'd never looked so lost and distant. The eyes that met his were like a stranger's, with a coldness that made him shiver.

"I know nothing! They're our enemies! Our persecutors! Killers!"

"Your father's still alive, dear," Lura said softly.

"Barely." Tela continued staring at Davi, even though her voice softened in response.

"They'll find who did this. Put them on trial."

"They'd better put them under *protection*!"

Davi forced himself to hold her glare, narrowing his eyes in sympathy, as he struggled against his own emotions. "Don't make threats, Tela. I know you're upset—"

"All those years, Davi! I missed him! Wondered if he was

alive! Longed for a father!"

Davi choked back tears, wanting to take her in his arms, but unable to move. Instead, he stayed still, feeling impotent. "I know, Baby."

Tela released her father's hand and stood, hurrying over to clasp his hands. "Names, Davi. Get me their names. Find out who did this."

"The authorities will handle it."

She shook her head. "If you ever loved me, you'll do this." Davi didn't know what to say, he squeezed her hands and pulled her to him in an embrace as she cried on his shoulder.

A brutal attack on the eve of The Returning—the first time the holiday would be shared by all citizens. Aron couldn't imagine a worse scenario. He'd ridden the shuttle back with Joram from the hospital. Of the three men, his injuries had been the least somehow. Joram barely spoke to him, then stayed secluded in his home the next two days. Aron was meeting with Uzah and Matheu when he appeared, taking them by surprise, joining them around the table in the conference room at Borali command near the starport in Iraja.

"How are you feeling?" Matheu asked.

Joram brushed it off with a wave. "Fine."

"We're so sorry about what happened," Uzah said as the others continued staring at Joram.

"Telanus may not live. There's a deep sickness in people these days." Joram's eyes were hollow and his skin paler than ever.

Aron nodded. "Hatred is a powerful motive to wrong thinking and bad decisions."

"Bad decisions? Is that all this is to you? They attacked us like wild animals, Aron. All we did was walk around. That's it!"

Aron closed his eyes and leaned back. "I know. It's horrible."

"They can't take it back, Aron. They can't do anything to change it. It's permanent. We'll carry it with us all our days, the three of us, if Telanus even survives." Joram's fist pounded the table in emphasis with his words.

"Take some time off, whatever you need," Uzah said, putting a hand atop Joram's wrist. "We all understand."

Joram shook his head, pulling free of Uzah's touch. "No. The Returning is in two days. I must be a part of it. It's important for our people."

"I've already discussed it with Tarkanius," Aron said. "He's making a speech this afternoon, but we agreed the ceremonies will be low key. We don't need to aggravate tensions at this point."

"Aggravate tensions? By what? Celebrating our religion? How dare us!" Fury filled Joram's eyes as his cheeks reddened with anger.

"We agreed to downplay the religious aspects publicly and promote unity." Aron had never seen his friend like this. He shifted in his chair, tense with worry.

"Maybe we were wrong? If anyone needs the power of salvation, the understanding of grace, it's the Boralians!"

"They can't get it being beat over the head with it," Aron said, his eyes locked on Joram's.

Joram refused to meet Aron's gaze. "Maybe they can't get it at all. Maybe they don't have the intellectual capacity. Have you asked yourself that? I used to hope, like you do. Now, after this, after so many failures, I have to ask a different question."

"If you're right, unity is doomed."

Joram laughed, turning side to side in his chair. "Unity is fiction, Aron. And I think we've all known that all along." He looked at Matheu, as if expecting agreement, but the old General kept a straight face, waiting. "So how are the plans coming?"

"We can handle it, Joram," Uzah said. "I think rest is a better idea for you."

Joram shook his head. "No. I want to be a part of this."

"We will make you a part, I promise." Uzah smiled, reaching over to pat Joram's shoulder, but Joram pulled away again.

"All we want is for you to recover quickly," Matheu said. "We'll get the plans in order and let you sign off later today. But you don't need to sit here for this part."

Joram scoffed, panning the three men. Their faces showed

agreement. "Fine. If I'm not wanted, I can leave." Joram shoved back in his chair, sending it across the carpet with a tearing sound as he stood. "But I am elected the leader of this planet. I will have my say, I promise you." Not waiting for a response, he turned and stormed out.

Uzah frowned, watching him go. "I hope his anger subsides quickly."

"Can you blame him for his feelings?" Matheu asked.

Uzah shook his head as Aron nodded. "Leaders have to lead with reason and forethought, not emotion at such times. Uzah's right. If Joram doesn't gather his senses, he could make things worse for all of us."

"Let's pray for God's peace then and hope it's enough." Uzah bowed his head. Matheu and Aron followed. Aron's mind raced for words of comfort he could offer his friend but none came. He himself had been attacked, his life in danger. But he'd never carried the anger Joram had just evidenced. His attackers had been Lhamors, however. And they had not beaten two others in front of his face. They did not have the history of enmity the Boralians and Vertullians did either. At such a moment, he supposed, those things mattered more than they might at other times.

As Uzah began the prayer, Aron added his own internal voice to the chorus, calling their God, the God of Israel and Jacob, to work a miracle in the hearts of the men and women of the Alliance. If He didn't, Aron feared, the Alliance's future history would be all too short.

"You'd think I'd be used to this by now," Tarkanius said as aides finished preparing his hair and makeup for the broadcast. Inside a tent, just off the edge of the very market where people he admired had been violently attacked three days before, Tarkanius found himself as nervous as a little boy. He'd botched everything as leader of his people. He already knew his reign would go down in history as a troubled one. All he could do now was to try and fix things so that his legacy spoke better of him than his term in office did.

Simeon and his allies on the Council had stepped up and become a great support to him. They'd already seen to spreading false data around the Council in an attempt to flush out leaks and betrayers. They'd chosen the time, date and location of Tarkanius' planned meeting with alien leaders. Even Simeon didn't know the real information, so when the press reports came in, those Councilors whose unique information had been leaked would be suspect. Some might, of course, discuss it amongst themselves first and discover the trap, but even then, many would arrogantly assume their own information must be correct, that they were trusted. Still, Tarkanius feared a scenario requiring him to incarcerate half the Council. He'd spent the prior afternoon making libations to the gods and meditating at the Temple. What could it hurt? Aron's faith inspired him to hope, and he needed all the help he could get.

Simeon appeared in the door of the tent, smiling. "It's almost time, my Lord."

Tarkanius nodded. "Tell me this is not a big mistake, Simeon."

Simeon's smile faded as both their thoughts turned serious. "The people need to hear from you, my Lord. It's vital during such a crisis."

"When I think on all that's happened, I can hardly speak. I have no words."

Simeon sighed. "Me too, Tarkanius. But we must try. The others and I will stand beside you, lend you our strength."

"Please forgive me for saying, I hope you are all very strong."

Simeon chuckled. "We share that hope, my Lord."

They walked outside together, their aides trailing behind, and found Kray, Qai and Aron waiting for them. Aron's report from his visit to Vertullis the day before was deeply disturbing. If the planetary Governor was no longer on their side, so much could result from it, none of it good. He vowed to go there himself soon and offer what comfort he could. If the man would even see him.

The crowd itself was small, less than expected. Security almost outnumbered them, with palace guards and military officers well in sight at each sidewalk and beside each tent or building. He saw snipers on rooftops, and Floaters of soldiers in nearby clearings waiting armed and ready. Their presence was a regret he'd not been allowed to reject. It would not add to the ambiance he wanted to project. Those present might even be more afraid instead of less, but it couldn't be helped. He knew his own death could be the catalyst for disaster. So protection was unavoidably necessary. He just wished his men knew how to be more discreet about it.

He stepped to the microphone, cameras and lights aiming in his direction, and felt like a first timer rather than a veteran politician of decades. The heat assaulted his body, causing him to sweat as the lights themselves blinded his eyes. The air was surprisingly clear of the ash which had grayed it since the explosion. He took a deep breath, savoring it as the cool rush relaxed his body. He looked down at the datascreen on the podium. The speech was there, waiting. He'd memorized most of it, but still, it was a comfort to have the prompt available. Licking his lips, he took several deep breaths then waited for the broadcast people to signal their readiness. The signal came, and with one final breath, he began:

"My dear fellow citizens, I stand today on the very spot where a great tragedy occurred. Three of our fine citizens, shopping quietly, were brutally attacked. Now two are in the hospital, and one's life hangs in the balance. The attackers were fellow citizens—Boralian men, every day people, with good jobs and families. What hatred drove them to such desperate measures? It's hard for most of us to understand why anyone would commit such violence. How could someone be so brutal and cold? It almost seems inhuman."

"But make no mistake, these attacks were perpetuated by men just like us. Men with emotions and five senses, capable of feeling pain and empathy. Yet men who shut such things off. How? It's a question asked for centuries, as long as there have been criminals. And these men are criminals, mind you. Despite declaring themselves heroes, they are the worst of us, not the best, and we must not allow their actions to go unpunished. My administration will do everything in our power to bring them to justice. We will not let this crime go without proper response. It's an incident I, for one, can never erase from my mind. And I truly believe many of you feel the same."

"For years our own government allowed violence against the Vertullians for ancient crimes by their ancestors against our own. The time has come to join together and stop blaming each other for the actions of our forefathers. In two days, we will celebrate together, a new holiday for many of us, The Returning—one our new allies have long celebrated as their own. Yes, it bears religious significance for them, but we don't ask you to worship. Instead, for Boralians, The Returning symbolizes a return to civility, to common recognition of our mutual value, to living and working in peace together, to no longer spreading blame and hatred to divide us over perceived wrongs of a dark past. It's a returning to the right way, not the wrong way symbolized by that disgusting attack. I humbly ask you: return with me to a new era of the Alliance we all love—an era of peaceful coexistence and mutual respect like we all desire. Do not allow the recent incidents to cloud your focus on what really matters, to stop you from pushing for the future we all desire for ourselves and our children."

"I urge you, my friends, my fellow citizens, to unite with determination to not allow such evil to win. We are better than that. We are stronger than that. We are wiser than that. And if we come together, such wisdom, strength and superiority will prevail. Will you join me?"

He stopped, eyes panning the multi-colored faces in the crowd before him. They stared back a moment, clearly moved by his words. Then he heard clapping from behind him—Simeon and the other Councilors. Gradually the crowd joined in and along with it a chant began, their voices uniting to cry out: "We will do it!" over and over again. Myriad emotions overwhelmed him like waves at the sight of his people, their faces spark-ling with determination and pride, tears gleaming in the corners of their eyes as their voices rose as one. Tarkanius stood there and listened and watched, hoping they truly meant it.

Xalivar laughed several times during Tarkanius' speech. Emotion had been rife on his old friend's face, a weakness leaders could ill afford. You led with wisdom, power, assurance that you knew best. Emotion could only encourage doubts, regrets, weakness. It just proved all the more Tarkanius' failure at leading their people. He was unfit, illogical, and totally incompetent. Xalivar's people needed him. The attacks on workers were a cry for help. Even the attack Xalivar himself had arranged on the preschool wasn't necessary. The people were taking charge of their own destiny and demanding change. Xalivar loved every minute of it.

"What they demand, Tarkanius, is a return to the old ways of recognition of our superiority, our strength, and our deserved place above the Vertullians and anyone else in the Universe. You have cost us much with your foolishness. Humiliated and embarrassed our people. But the time is upon us for change, Tarkanius. Your failures have only served to remind our people how great my leadership was; how successful they were with me showing the way." Xalivar giggled as he watched the pathetic applause and chanting from the ridiculously small crowd in attendance at the High Lord Councilor's speech. "I never made a speech in the presence of under a thousand people. You speak to hundreds. What does that tell you, Tarkanius?"

Xalivar reached forward and clicked off the monitor, whirling to where his military leaders were watching. All three stood in silence, waiting. For a moment, Xalivar wondered where Obed and his fool son had run off to. "Family business," they'd claimed. Xalivar had sent spies to discover the truth of it. But they'd been gone a week already. It was too long. Their focus needed to remain here until the right time. He would be ready to deal with them if they dared to return.

Manaen had yet to report in as well. But one of Xalivar's informants had sent word of Pharah Brahma travelling on a diplomatic mission to the alien leadership on Tarkanius' behalf. The informant was travelling with him in the security detail. He had limited access to discussions, but Xalivar already knew the purpose of the mission matched his own goals. Tarkanius wanted the alien leaders on his side as well. But Tarkanius offered them only weakness. Xalivar felt sure they'd recognize where the strength lay and align themselves appropriately. They all knew how he'd respond if they didn't, and fear would keep them in line.

"Do they really believe such drivel?" he asked as he faced Generals Lucius and Pres and Admiral Dek. The military leaders shook their heads in amazement. "How could our people have fallen so far from the greatness they once knew? I ask you? What reputation and future do you want for our people?"

"A superior one, my Lord," Lucius said. "The one the gods have called us to."

"Yes! Anointed by the gods we are! And who can restore that?"

All three military leaders spoke in unison this time: "Only you, my Lord!"

Xalivar laughed. "How can so many of our people be fooled? We must reexamine our sense of values, our educational system. We cannot raise our children in such weakness and disbelief. The ignorance of it disgusts me!"

"And us as well, my Lord," Dek responded.

Xalivar smiled at them. "Your valiant service and dedication will be rewarded, my friends. I promise you. You have stood by me through so much adversity. It will not be forgotten."

"Thank you, my Lord," all three said, their eyes lowering to the floor in humility Xalivar wondered if they really felt. Men and women of such discipline rarely let emotions rule them. What were they thinking? Not that it mattered as long as they continued to obey his orders. They were a means to an end. Xalivar trusted no one. He'd learned his lesson when his own family turned against him. Trust was for fools and weak men. Xalivar Rhii was not weak, and he would never be a fool!

The door slid open and Manaen appeared, hurrying toward him. "You're late!"

Manaen bowed his head, his red eyes fading to pink with embarrass-ment. "I'm sorry, my Lord. I worked as fast as I could in delivering your messages."

"And what was their response, Manaen? Did our new allies embrace their future?"

Manaen nodded. "The meeting is arranged. Some had doubts, of course, but I believe they recognized the importance of the decision and they will be there."

"Do none accept me at my word? They all insist on a meeting?"

"The Andorians and Lhamors are ready, my Lord. We join with you willingly to embrace the future you alone can provide. A few are less certain. They need reassurances."

"I can assure them their failure to align themselves will lead to their destruction."

Manaen sighed. "As did I, my Lord. I followed your instructions exactly."

Xalivar smiled. "Of course you did, Manaen. Why wouldn't you? You've served me most of your life. Haven't I always been kind to you? What reason would you have to do anything but accede to my wishes?"

"None, my Lord. Of course." Manaen bowed, eyes focused on the floor at his feet.

Xalivar watched his aide carefully. He detected nothing to alarm him. Manaen had done just as he reported. His loyalty remained intact. Xalivar took several breaths as he turned back toward the window to ponder what was coming. Andorians were weak. They had no backbone. But they would never betray him. Their years of service to his family had brought them many benefits no other species had. They couldn't afford to choose otherwise. It was a comforting thought. Xalivar rarely let kindnesses dictate his policies. Occasionally, it did serve his purposes to be merciful. The thought of it made his stomach roll. At the moment, he needed allies. Tossing them aside later would be all too easy. But for the moment, he needed them, and it appeared his preparedness throughout his reign would pay off, after all. A warm rush coursed through his veins. Loyalty had that effect on him. At least some people knew their place.

Ignoring Manaen, he turned back to the military leaders. "I'll call a meeting with the local leadership. We must find out if a delegation from Tarkanius was here."

"We've had no word of it, my Lord," Lucius said.

Xalivar brushed it off with a sweep of his arm. "You've been preoccupied with training, my dear General. But we will soon know the truth. I want armed soldiers in the meeting, standing close and ready. The leadership will know what to expect if they try to deceive me."

"I thought they didn't know we were here," Pres said.

"They don't, my dear. But the time to reveal ourselves has come. We have need of information they alone can provide. And my presence should be enough to extract it easily."

The Generals and Admiral nodded. "Fear is a great weapon, my Lord," Dek said.

Xalivar chuckled. "My favorite one, Admiral. The time is fast approaching. Increase your efforts. Train around the clock if necessary. Our soldiers will not have to wait much longer for their victory."

All three leaders quickly formed the salute with their hands. "Yes, my Lord." Then whirled on their heels in unison and marched out under Xalivar's silent scrutiny.

The Vertullian's official ceremonies for The Returning were well attended. A crowd of regular citizens joined the dignitaries at their new capital in the heart of the government center in central Iraja. Aron arrived early, hoping to catch Joram before the official activities started in order to gauge his frame of mind. Uzah had already arrived and was waiting along with the two religious leaders who would lead prayers and offer a brief message. Several low-level government people who'd been involved in the planning surrounded them.

It was fifteen minutes until the start of the ceremony when Joram finally arrived. Matheu had barely beat him and stood there chatting with Uzah and Aron as they all waited. Their wives were behind them chatting as well, and a large crowd was well in place, conversing, laughing, etc. The electricity in the air surpassed what Aron had experienced during Tarkanius' visit. Their people had never celebrated The Returning with such public fanfare since leaving Old Earth for the stars, and so, although the standard celebratory expectations were in place, everyone also anticipated something special for the occasion. Aron hoped he and the others wouldn't let them down.

As soon as Joram stepped from the air car, Aron moved to intercept him. Joram extended his hand as if he were on a campaign tour. "Aron! Good morning! Good to see you." His smile was as plastic as his enthusiasm.

"How are you feeling?" Joram's grip was firm and confident, but Aron searched his eyes trying to see if it was how he really felt.

"I'm fine, my friend. It's a special day for our people. Very exciting."

"Yes, it is. We're glad you're safe and able to celebrate with us."

The smile stayed frozen on Joram's face as he released Aron's hand, but Aron caught a flicker of sadness in his eyes. "I only wish Telanus could do the same."

With that Joram was gone, moving into the crowd of dignitaries to offer similar greetings and handshakes. Aron watched him go, sadly, as Calla joined him and they returned to their seats together. "He seems fine."

Aron sighed and nodded. "That's what worries me."

A few minutes later, the ceremonies opened with an Invocation by the pastor of the Cathedral of Iraja, a newly built, modern structure of sharp edges and spires which had quickly come to define the downtown skyline of the capital of free Vertullis. The pastor spoke of God's faithfulness, of the history of deliverance of His people from oppression—first from the Egyptians, now from the Boralians. He noted the significance of the fact that the Israelites fled and started over elsewhere, but their own people had instead befriended and worked alongside their captors to build a new, united nation and forge a new way. This was the way of love, the way of the Gospels, he said. "And it is a path which will carry us throughout our lifetimes and which requires diligence and con-stant dedication but of which course we can be very proud."

Although Aron agreed with the words, he kept glancing over and wondering what Joram might be thinking, especially after the part about the Israelites fleeing Egypt. Joram had been making statements about leading their people to the stars to make a fresh start. None of the leaders took it seriously. They all considered him to be blowing off steam, residual anger from the attack he'd suffered. But still, if the idea went public and caught fire, it could lead to disaster.

The Invocation was followed by remarks from Uzah about the security of their people and God Himself as their protector who deserved their trust even in times of uncertainty and opposition. It was quite moving considering it came from a military leader and not a pastor. This was followed by a sermon from the pastor of the planet's second Cathedral, newly built in the past three months in Vertullis' other major city, Pam-pulha. The pastor was young and nervous, but the sermon was concise and well written.

As the sermon drew to an end, Aron saw commotion near where Joram was sitting. An aide hurried up the aisle, a comm attached to his ear, and bent over from behind the row of chairs to whisper in Joram's ear. Joram frowned, looking concerned, then nodded as his eyes went to his feet. Bad news, it appeared. Aron tried to get the attention of the aide, but was ignored. He looked at Uzah, who had also seen the commotion, but the General shrugged. Then the pastor finished praying, and Joram headed for the podium to great applause.

"Good morning, fine people of God. It is good to be here among you. It is good to know my words will also be broadcast to our brethren throughout the system, for this is indeed a monumental day. The pastors and General spoke of the significance of our history—the returning of our Lord; the constant presence of God amongst us, His people. God is good!"

The people echoed back in unison: "He is good indeed!"

Joram smiled and nodded as they quieted back down. "But God's goodness is not always enough. Sometimes we have to rely on His Spirit to give us wisdom to make tough decisions in times of great difficulty. Unfortunately, this is one of those times. And the pastors' and General's goodwill is duly noted, but I believe their generosity is misplaced."

Aron glanced at Uzah, as both men tensed in their chairs, trying not to panic. *Please, God, guide His words,* Aron prayed.

Then Joram dropped the bombshell.

"I was just informed that an old, dear friend of many of ours has died from his injuries. Telanus Sarwa was hard working, loyal, a good man, a dear friend, brutally attacked by men who hated us for no reason other than our genetic origins and our religious beliefs. Sol and Telanus have been in a hospital on Legallis for almost a week now. Today, Telanus lost that battle."

A murmur rose from the crowd, a mixture of sadness, anger and confusion, as Joram watched. Aron's heart sank under the weight of sadness for the loss Tela and Davi must be feeling. He would go to them as soon as he could. Then Joram spoke again.

"The time has come to do as our forefathers, the Israelites did. They sought deliverance from God who sent a great leader, a former prince, to guide them out of Egypt to freedom. Our great prince, Davi Rhii, already helped us win that battle. But the fight is not over. We are not truly free. And the time has come to change that—to claim the freedom we believe is the right of all men and women! To pack up our families, take to the stars, and find a new home for our people; to make our own exodus. I will go. Who will join me?"

Several shouts of agreement came from the crowd and Joram raised his arms in the V of triumph. Hands raised and the crowd began to chant. "We will! We will!"

Uzah appeared ready to leap for the podium. Aron reached over and squeezed his arm, shaking his head as their eyes met. On a system-wide broadcast, they could do little except wait.

Joram reveled in the crowd's response, waving his fists in the air for several minutes before speaking again. "I have a message for you, High Lord Councilor; the same message Moses gave to Ramses. Hear me now: Let my people go!"

"Let us go!" Joram led the crowd in the new chant as the fervor seemed to catch fire until the majority had joined in. Aron, Uzah, Matheu and a few others remained silent, forcing smiles but shifting anxiously. Aron felt like a helpless animal frozen under a hunting party's spotlight. The can had been opened before the eyes of the whole world, and Aron had no idea what they could do to close it again, or if they even could.

"Let us go! Let us go! Let us go!" The words echoed around him as Aron's heart sank deeper and deeper with every passing minute.

Chapter Eleven

The doctors and nurses moved around Telanus like ants on a picnic. Tela just stood there stunned, clasping her father's hand as they moved around her. She'd been chatting with her father moments before. He was telling her how proud he was of her and how happy he'd been to have her back, when he just stopped mid-sentence, his breathing became a rasp, and then his head collapsed on the pillow, and his chest stopped moving. Davi knew right away he was gone, but Tela refused to accept it, yelling for the doctors and nurses to do their job and save her father.

Then the doctor turned, shaking his head as his staff whisked past and out the door. "I'm sorry. We did all we could."

Davi felt as if he'd had the wind knocked out of him. Tela just sank down on the chair beside the hospital bed, head against her father's chest as she sobbed and held tightly to his cold hand. Davi caressed her back and hugged her from behind, but she pushed him away. Sol, Lura and Miri watched in silent vigil from nearby, but none of them knew what to say. Then the news alerts flashed on the monitor overhead, broadcasts of ceremonies on Vertullis and Legallis and around the system for The Returning. The fact that Telanus was returning to his God on that day didn't escape Davi. It gave the words a whole new significance. But all that was still lost on Tela.

Finally, she took a deep breath and looked up at Davi's parents.

"I can't believe he's gone."

Their faces creased with pain as they nodded. "We know, dear. We're so sorry." Lura's voice cracked as tears rolled down her cheeks.

"He's been a lifelong friend," Sol added. Davi knew they'd come to think of Tela as a daughter, and he turned his eyes away from them as he fought back tears.

"I just got him back," Tela rasped, her voice almost a whisper.

"Oh, Tela, if there was something I could do..." Miri's voice cracked as she said it.

Tela stiffened, her face reddening with rage. "Well, you can't. None of you can. And no false solaces either. They murdered him in cold blood. Those bastards stole my father from me twice! And I can't forgive it. Ever."

Davi winced as blades sheared his heart with her every word. "Tela, at least we know he's at peace with our Lord."

Tela whirled, scowling at him. "Peace? You talk of peace? There can be no peace as long as men are monsters! I'm sick of the Boralians! Sick of being treated like I have no value. Sick of always having to be honorable and forgiving and kind to a people who have hated us for generations and done all they can to bring us harm, to destroy our people!"

"They've made an honest effort at peace, living side by side, Tela—"

"You grew up on the inside, the highest echelons of their society. I can understand how it would be difficult for you to accept things; to see things as they are. But I didn't, Davi. I grew up at the bottom and had to claw my way. And half of that, I had no parents to help me. No one to love me through."

Davi winced at the reminder, but he couldn't deny the truth. His life had always been much easier than that of most Vertullians.

"You have us now. We all love you." Lura stepped forward hesitantly but stopped at Tela's stare.

"You love me. And it's wonderful. And I love you. But it's not enough. I am done. Done following their orders. Done treating them like equals. Done being civilized. I hate every one of them! They are not equals! They are animals! They are criminals! And I swear to you, I'll do all I can to make them suffer as I have!"

Miri's lips pursed as she hurried over to close the door to the hallway. "Tela, I don't blame you for feeling this way. If I were in your shoes, I would, too. And I tell you, I've seen a lot that's disappointed me in my own people of late. But remember where you are. Getting arrested for treasonous threats will not bring your father back."

"Yes, Princess Miri! Forgive me, your royalness!"

Davi spun, his breaths catching in his throat as he sought to control his temper. "Don't treat her like that! She's right. She's trying to protect you."

"I don't want protection—from her or anyone else! Especially no Boralian!"

"She didn't do this!"

"Her family led the oppression of my people for generations! That's historical fact! And no matter how kind Miri has been, she can't erase that!" Davi cringed at Tela's every word. There was no point arguing. What she'd stated were facts. And even though Davi and Miri had dedicated themselves to reversing that legacy with every day they had left, they'd never be able to do enough to erase it.

Sol reached over to clasp Davi's shoulder, his eyes brimming with sympathy. "If it weren't for Miri, our people wouldn't have the freedom we have now," Sol said. "I wouldn't have my family! You wouldn't have seen your father again."

"And I'm grateful for her part in that. Really, I am. But my father's dead at their hands. And I just can't act like I don't see them for who they are any more."

Davi took deep breaths, waiting for his heart to stop beating against his ribs. "If you need us, we're here. Take the time necessary to go do what you need to. I know you don't mean all that."

Tela jumped to her feet, her fists balled as she pounded them into Davi's chest. "Don't tell me what I need! You don't give me orders in our private lives, Davi Rhii!"

"I didn't mean it like that. I thought we were partners."

Tela scoffed. "Partners? Me, your stay-at-home little missus while you go out and fight to protect, risking your life for the people who killed my father?" She sighed and frowned, her nose and mouth crinkling with disdain. "That sounds really equal. No thanks!"

Davi wanted to snap back. He'd never thought of her that way. Her piloting abilities had been part of what attracted him to her in the first place. But instead of arguing, he threw up his hands. "What do you want then? A personal war against an entire system?"

"I want my father back!" Then Tela sank to her knees in sobs as Miri and Lura hurried toward her. Sol watched from his hospital bed as Davi stepped back, knowing nothing he could say or do right now would make a difference. He hoped he was right—that she truly didn't mean what she'd just said. He couldn't bear the thought of losing her. Time would lessen her pain and make her regret her words. She had to. He needed her.

Manaen cringed as Xalivar entered his chamber and slammed his datapad down on the desk, then whirled around, his fists clenching at his side. His master scanned the small room, comparable to a closet in Xalivar's own chambers. It was adorned simply with only a desk, bed and chair and old military-issue crates for storage of Manaen's few belongings. A single terminal occupied the desk, allowing Manaen to be proactive in seeing to his duties and Xalivar's every need. A single reflector pad hung overhead from loose wires, casting shadows along the walls as it swung back and forth.

"I trusted you and you failed me!"

"I delivered the message as you sent it, my Lord."

Xalivar's eyes tightened as he searched Manaen's eyes for any sign of betrayal. Manaen simply relaxed and stared back. "Xanthis and Italis alone sent actual leaders. The Andorians and the Plutonians sent mere 'representatives.'"

"The Lhamors came."

"Representing themselves! And they alone accepted my offer. Do they forget who I am?"

Manaen held back a smile and shook his head. "It's not that, my

Lord. But they expressed doubts." *They know exactly what you think of them. They are not the fools you assume them to be. Do you really expect to fool them with your rhetoric?*

Xalivar's scowl deepened. "About what?"

"Whether you can be trusted."

Xalivar scowled, his fists clenching and unclenching as Manaen waited for the explosion. "Trusted, you idiot?! They are in little position to doubt me! None of them have known the power or borne the responsibility I have!"

With that, Manaen knew he'd chosen the right course. He'd tolerated years of abuse. And Vibryd was right. It had to stop. He lowered his eyes in pretend humility. "Of course, my Lord, but you are no longer High Lord Councilor."

Xalivar spun, causing Manaen to step back for fear of being struck. Xalivar had never physically harmed him, but he wouldn't assume anything when his boss was in this agitated state. His master instead just stared out the window at the desert beyond. "It is *I* who needs fear trusting *them*, not them me! Without me, they will lose everything!"

"I tried to convince them, my Lord. Perhaps Tarkanius' offer came first."

"Tarkanius made an offer?" Xalivar turned back to face him. "I never heard of it."

Was Xalivar really unaware? The story dominated the nets. Did he really depend on Manaen to tell him? This could be useful. "It's been on the broadcasts today. There seems to be some confusion regarding the location, however."

Xalivar had reached the desk before Manaen finished speaking and was already turning on the terminal to one of the major nets. The announcers rambled on with speculation about the High Lord Councilor's major meeting the following week. "Xanthis? Eleni 1? Idolis? Where's it being held?"

Manaen shrugged. "I learned of it as you are, my Lord."

Xalivar cursed. "What good are informants if none of them keep me informed?" He slammed his butt down into the chair and began fiddling with the terminal on his desk, sending e-posts to various sources, Manaen assumed.

He stood still, watching Xalivar unravel. So many feared his power and unrelenting confidence. If only they could see him for the weak man he really was.

"Don't disappoint me again. Dismissed!" Xalivar's eyes never left the terminal.

Manaen wondered how long it would be before his master realized he was in the majordomo's chambers. It didn't matter. He preferred to go elsewhere when his master was in such a mood. He turned and smiled as he hurried toward the door. Betraying his master had inspired great fear. But no more. He'd done what he must. And so far, it was working.

Tarkanius sat with Simeon, Kray and Qai in his study, watching the broadcasts with growing amusement. Their plan had worked perfectly. The networks were going mad speculating about all the different locations leaked for Tarkanius' meeting with alien leaders. None had the real story, and yet their reports revealed everything to Tarkanius and his friends. Of the thirty-seven members of the Council, twelve were now under suspicion, including the several Tarkanius and Simeon had most suspected. "Elal, Hachim, Niger—they're no surprise."

Despite his prior suspicions, Tarkanius felt relief at having further proof. While Kretzu's testimony would have been sufficient at a trial, it was reassuring to know the Lord hadn't just passed blame off as revenge or other ulterior motives. Still, the joy and pride he'd experience when he'd first joined the Council were all but erased. Now his service had become just work. He wondered if it would ever be the former again?

Simeon nodded. "But a few others are. The Council will be weakened by this for decades, I fear."

"We must arrest them, for the good of the Alliance," Kray said.

Simeon and Tarkanius nodded. "Of course. And we will. But it will make us all look bad in the process." Tarkanius sighed. "Once our service was honorable, prestigious."

"It's still got the prestige," Qai said. "It's the honor that needs restoring."

"If we replace them with good people, it will all be forgotten in five years," Kray said.

"Yes. Provided the Alliance survives," Simeon added. They all exchanged worried looks and Tarkanius sank back in his chair, resting his face in his hands. Five years was forever in politics, and, with all that faced them, the burden weighed on his heart.

"Do we have enough men we can trust to execute the warrants?" Kray asked.

Tarkanius nodded. "Let's hope the corruption hasn't spread that far. The military are still sworn to serve at my command." Those officers who stayed, at least. The defections left them all tainted and suspect.

"With the rest of the Alliance torn at the seams, one has to wonder." Kray shrugged.

"I'll send Rhii, Brahma and Noa. They can be trusted." Tarkanius looked at each of them for agreement, his eyes meeting theirs. One by one they nodded. "I know of a few others as well."

"Use a mix of Boralians and Vertullians. We don't want just Vertullians on this." Simeon stared out the window as he said it. He and Tarkanius shared a sadness in all that was happening. They had tried to discuss it earlier but found it hard to explain. It was not the Alliance they'd hoped for in their youth, nor the one they'd imagined when joining the Council. And neither had confidence he knew how to fix it.

"Who first?" Qai asked.

Simeon and Tarkanius exchanged a look. Simeon clearly deferred to his friend's office. "Niger and Elal. Hachim will be so afraid, he might surrender on his own. The others can be gathered after they are secured."

Simeon's face showed resolve. "I agree. Niger and Elal are the most dangerous."

"Perhaps it would be wise to send more than three men," Qai said.

Tarkanius shook his head. "We'll allow them the dignity of a quiet arrest until they force us to change plans. We're not out to humiliate them. Publicity of the arrests will come soon enough and will harm us as much as them." The press would elevate it on their own, and Tarkanius refused to do anything to further stain the legacy of his reign.

"Might it help for one of us to accompany the officers?" Kray looked back and forth between the two leaders, but both shook their heads.

"They'll know soon enough who we are," Simeon said. "Let's not tip them off while there's risk of endangering ourselves further."

Tarkanius sighed. "It's a sad day for our people. Perhaps tonight prayers and libations would be in order." He'd been praying a lot lately, and, to his surprise, it had helped calm him and give him focus if nothing else. Were there really gods or a God up there?

"With Joram calling for an exodus, we may already be too late to repair the damage," Kray said, shaking her head.

"We have to try," Tarkanius said. "Even those who wish to enslave again recognize the Vertullians as vital members of this community. Our agricultural industry would fall apart without them. We'd have few mechanics for our star ships." The thought of it terrified him. The loss would be devastating on levels most couldn't comprehend, including Tarkanius. Just trying to imagine all the scenarios it would affect sent his mind spinning. It had to be averted at all costs. Having one-third of the human population of the entire system depart for good seemed impossible just from logistics, but gods help the Boralians if it happened somehow. His eyes met Simeon's and he saw that his friend shared his alarm.

"The ramifications are frightening for us all," Simeon agreed.

"Where could they go? It would require an enormous fleet." Qai clearly thought the idea was ridiculous.

"More importantly," Simeon said, "many lost their lives bringing us together. We cannot give up without a fight."

The others nodded. "Agreed."

"May the gods protect us and give us wisdom." Tarkanius raised both hands, palms upward, as he said it, as if in prayer. The others nodded. "Send the warrants."

Kray nodded. "I'll issue them at once in the name of the Council." She and Qai hurried off as Tarkanius and Simeon stared at each other again.

"If we are wrong about them, we cannot change course," Tarkanius said.

"Why have you any doubts? It's clear they've broken our trust." Simeon looked resolved. Tarkanius envied his confidence.

He closed his eyes and turned away again. "That doesn't lessen the heartbreak."

Neither spoke again, both lost in sadness that their years of work and dedication had now come to this.

⌗

"It's getting out of hand." Uzah shook his head as he paced the control room. "I understand his anger. A lot of people share it. But this is turning serious."

Aron nodded as Matheu watched from a desk nearby. "We can talk to him again. Maybe he's had time to cool down." His own emotions were hard enough to control. Seeing Uzah lose it, he realized how on edge they'd all become. Joram was inciting the people daily, and, with every passing hour, the effects multiplied. People protested by skipping work, boycotting Boralian businesses and goods, even pulling their children from schools or Boralian-funded community programs. All it would take is one incident of Boralians striking back to fan the embers into a full-on flame, and Aron feared the outcome.

"Cool down?! Look!" Uzah motioned to the monitor which showed the third rally in as many days, a crowd of thousands, with Joram raising his arms in triumph.

"He's always been a reasonable man. Surely he can see the difficulties his proposal creates." But the new Joram was anything but reasonable. Talking with him was like conversing with an iron wall. It went nowhere.

Matheu cleared his throat. "He's a politician. Logistics are someone else's concern. He's all about ideals."

"The best ideal I can imagine is living here in peace with the Boralians," Aron said.

"I wonder if that's even possible now," Matheu said.

The entire room grew silent as Joram appeared in the doorway, smiling, surrounded by his entourage of aides and supporters. He saw them and waved, moving across the room, shaking technicians' hands and greeting them as he passed their stations. Some looked wary, while others looked thrilled to see him. His movement would soon threaten government order more directly, Aron feared.

"Oh, great," Uzah muttered, "he brought friends."

Just watching him, Aron marveled at the transformation. Joram's selection as planetary Governor had empowered him, but since the attack and growth in number of his supporters, Joram had become a different man. His posture, even his smile and eyes had changed.

"Uzah! Aron! Matheu! How are you my friends?" Joram quickly pumped their hands, beaming at them as he joined their circle. Matheu stepped from behind the desk to shake. "You asked to see me?" The Governor scanned their faces, each in turn.

Aron and Uzah exchanged a look, then Aron nodded. "Yes. Can we speak alone in the conference room?"

Joram shrugged. "I have nothing to hide from my team."

"Private government business. They don't have clearance." Matheu's voice was firm.

Joram sighed and nodded. Matheu led the way with Joram, Uzah and Aron following. Joram remained casual, as if he had no suspicion they were about to confront him, but Aron knew he was smarter than that. When they were inside the conference room, Matheu keyed the lock behind them, waiting as the door closed.

"What's this about?" Joram asked as they took seats around the table.

"You've created quite a movement," Matheu said.

Joram laughed. "Just like-minded people coming together around a common cause."

"And what is that cause, Joram? To destroy our people?" Uzah offered Joram a cold stare. The Governor blustered and looked surprised.

"Let's all keep our heads, please," Aron said, raising a palm to gesture for calm. "We're old friends. We know how to work together."

"This old friend is doing his best to undo all we've fought so hard for," Uzah said as he shot Aron a look.

"Undo what? Years of abuse? Suppression? Betrayal? Come

now, Uzah. The Boralians have proven they can't be trusted." Joram leaned back in his chair, his eyes full of confidence.

"Do you honestly believe we can relocate one-third of all humans in this system? The number of ships alone is monstrous to consider!"

"God is on our side, Uzah. Where's your faith?"

Uzah's fist slammed the table as he stood and began pacing. "Where's yours?" Joram just held Uzah's stare, the smile locked on his face.

Aron raised a hand, drawing their attention. "Let's all take a deep breath, okay?" He felt himself tensing even as he said it. Even he was struggling to keep his emotions in check. "Faith in God doesn't mean we can just stand by and not take appropriate action."

"Exactly." Joram nodded as if he'd meant that all along.

Matheu sighed. "Bankrupting ourselves to take our people on a fool-hardy quest to the stars hardly sounds like appropriate action." Even the General's own emotions were apparent now.

"You'd prefer we stay and continue to enjoy our host's abuse? Let them kill us off one by one?"

Aron took a deep breath and reminded himself this was a new Joram. The old one of polite reason had been replaced. Reasoning with a herd of Gungors might be easier. "Joram, even you can recognize the difficulties your proposal creates. You've been in leadership long enough to understand logistics."

Joram shrugged. "There are always ways, Aron." Aron and Matheu stared at him, waiting, while Uzah continued to pace. "We'll get a meeting with the High Lord Councilor and negotiate." He said it as if it were the simplest concept in the world.

"Negotiate with what?" Uzah said, whirling to meet Joram's eyes. "We lack the resources to pay for ships and fuel, let alone provisions. You're talking about a journey which could potentially last years."

"And save thousands, if not millions, of our people's lives."

"We could die of starvation, face unknown enemies, pirates. What makes you think this journey is any safer?"

"God delivered the Israelites. I believe He'll deliver us." Joram spoke with the fervor of an evangelist, not an experienced politician.

Uzah looked aghast. "Our people aren't even united around the idea. All you're doing is creating further division and increasing the security risk in the process!"

"Security's your job, Uzah. Mine is to lead the government. Let's not forget our places."

Uzah growled and began pacing again.

"We all have to work together, and always have," Aron said, his voice cracking as his own frustration showed. "Be reasonable, Joram. We're having this discussion out of concern for the best interest of our people."

"You mean to tell me you honestly believe the best interest of our people is to continue living with a people who hate us?" Joram leaned forward as his eyes met Aron's. His smile faded and his eyes looked sad. "I expected you of all people to understand, Aron. Your whole adult life you fought to free us from their tyranny."

Aron nodded. "Not to exchange tyranny for exile and foolhardy decisions."

Joram scowled and scooted back his chair. "I am not a fool."

"No, you never have been. But your emotions have gotten the best of your reason. Please. You must stop and think through the full implications here."

Joram scooted back his chair and stood. "I've heard enough."

"We're on the same side," Matheu said.

"Really? You stood there as they beat you, killing your friend, for nothing but just your presence, did you?"

"We've all lost friends to their hands over the years, Joram," Aron said.

Joram raised his hands in dismay. "And when shall we demand that it stops, Aron? When?"

The others watched him in silence. After a moment, Joram turned and marched to the door, pressing the lock and disappearing as soon as the door cracked enough to let him through.

Uzah sighed and leaned against the wall in a corner of the room.

"We need to pray for him," Aron said. "And for ourselves. We handled that badly." Aron put his face in his hands.

"It's past the point of prayer, Aron! Go talk with Tarkanius. Get him to refuse to meet with Joram." Uzah's eyes were locked on

Aron.

"I'll do what I can, but in the end, I fear it's a confrontation that can't be avoided." Aron took another deep breath then scooted back from the table and headed for the door. The world was going crazy around him, spinning out of control more each day. And he'd never felt so hopeless.

The Squadron briefing room rippled with tension as Davi arrived from the officer's briefing. The pilots had split into opposing groups. Davi spotted Dru, newly called back from the Academy, with Brie, Nila, Virun and Jorek. Command had called back anyone with flight experience to aid with the extra defense.

Dru smiled and waved. "Has the world gone mad while I was gone?"

"The only ones who are mad are the ones who think we should continue being pacificist against Boralian aggression!" Jorek said, angrily.

"You're standing in a Boralian military base!" Farien growled.

"What're you gonna do, bring us up on charges, sir?" Virun almost spat the words, staring at Farien as he said them.

"I'd have every right!" Farien looked ready to charge, but Davi stepped between them and shot him a look, pleading for calm.

"We're all on the same side here," Davi said, frowning. The last thing he needed was broken morale. They had enough to handle with civilian pilots fighting each other, protestors, and increased duty hours already adding stress.

"Oh sure, take his side, Prince! We all know you both used to supervise our slavery!" Jorek yelled back.

Davi took deep breaths to control his anger as Nila punched Jorek in the arm. "Hey! That's Davi, okay? He has nothing to prove about loyalty."

Brie nodded. "He's helped all of us."

"So has Farien. He's served with us for six months." Davi's eyes panned them one at a time, offering his best stern look. "This bickering is pointless. Do you really want us to fight each other?

Don't we already have enough to deal with?" The others' eyes went to the floor with embarrassment. "We're all in a tough enough spot. Let's not forget who our friends are."

"How's Tela?" Brie asked.

Davi sighed. "She's angry, heartbroken. She'll be on leave 'til all this is over."

"You can't blame her; the way those bastards murdered her father!" Jorek growled.

"We should make them all pay!" Virun added. The two looked pleased with themselves.

"Enough!" Davi stared at Jorek and Virun, taking several breaths to calm his rising anger. "I understand your anger. I even share it. But there's a time and place and this is not it!"

Both looked down at the floor.

"Is there anything we can do?" Nila looked up, her tanned face filled with grief.

Davi shook his head. "Stay rested, stay focused and stop fighting. Each of us has the right to make our own choices when the time comes. If you can't do your duty, I want your resignation immediately. Otherwise, shut up!"

"Captain!"

Davi turned to see Qajuan standing in the doorway, grinning widely. The young Xanthian's jumpsuit matched his blue skin. "I got those radios installed as requested."

Davi nodded. "Thanks. Just the two cockpits?"

Qajuan shrugged. "I can do them all if you want."

Davi waved dismissively. "No, no. It's not official. Just a little extra initiative, I thought would be helpful. Thanks for hooking it up so fast."

Qajuan chuckled. "Hey! It's my job, Captain!" Davi smiled back. Quajuan had really taken to his new duties, especially proud to be on the legitimate side of things for once. "Be safe out there!" And the Xanthian was gone. Davi had secured him a job helping the mechanics, who'd found the youth's ability to acquire hard-to-find parts quickly at fair prices came in handy, even when government requisitions were involved.

"What's he talking about? Radios?" Yao shot Davi a puzzled look.

"I had two civilian radios installed so we can monitor broadcasts and other traffic. We don't always get the latest when we're on long patrols and these days it seemed prudent to have more information."

Yao smiled. "Your cockpit and who else's?"

"Mine and Farien's. Should be enough." Davi turned to the Squad-ron. "We're on eighteen and off six for sleep cycle for the next week. That means no time off, people. So get your heads in order and get your ships prepped. We leave in three hours."

Groans filled the room. "A whole week?!" Virun shook his head.

"So much for escaping the Academy. At least they gave us time off!" Dru caught sympathetic looks from the others.

"Don't tell us the Academy's made you a pansy," Virun teased, ruffling Dru's hair.

"And Farien's still second in command, don't forget it," Davi reminded them, scanning their eyes for objections. They all nodded somberly as Farien smiled. "Dismissed."

"Who's a pansy?" Dru hurried to catch the others as they filed from the room.

As the others broke into chatter and cleared the room, Davi grabbed Farien's arm. "Take it easy. Everyone's confused and scared right now."

"I'm not the enemy!"

"I know that, and so does Yao. We've got your back. But antagonizing them won't help."

Yao patted Farien on the back. "You antagonize us enough already."

Farien rolled his eyes. "I was just trying to remind them of their duty. If a senior officer had overheard—"

Davi sighed. "I know. But you come across unfriendly."

"Unfriendly? Please. Just because I'm serious about my work..." Farien looked insulted.

Yao laughed. "You love to argue more than anyone we know, man."

"Only when I'm right." His eyes twinkled.

Davi chuckled, rolling his eyes back. "When have you ever

thought you were wrong?"

"It's rare, yes. But when it happens, I apologize."

Davi and Yao slapped him on the back as they exchanged amused looks. "Just do your best to stay professional and not rile them up, ok? We have to work together no matter what's going on between our peoples."

"Do you think the Vertullians will actually leave?" Yao asked.

Davi shrugged. "It seems impossible, but people are angry. I hope the politicans can find a more sensible course."

"Want me to go knock some sense into them?" Farien scrunched his face up like a street fighter.

"Gods, no!" Yao said as he and Davi grabbed Farien's arms and yanked them back behind his back. "We're protecting society from everyone else, but who'll protect them from him?"

Farien grinned. "I was only kidding!"

Davi and Yao exchanged a look and laughed, letting him go. Farien pulled free, rubbing his arms as Davi said: "Now come with me. We have an arrest order to execute."

"An arrest order?" Yao raised an eyebrow, but Farien looked eager.

"Straight from the Palace. I'll explain on the way." Davi turned and headed for the door as his friends hurried after him.

Xalivar had kept to himself since the failed conference with alien leaders, strategizing, trying to devise a plan that would remind everyone with whom they were dealing. A plan finally came into shape the night before, his mind waking him as it came into focus. He immediately began composing the briefing he was about to deliver to his leaders. He smiled as he entered and saw Dek, Lucius and Pres sat around the table with Obed, waiting. Things were finally going to move to the next level. Xalivar would declare himself again as a power in the Borali system in a way history would long remember and no citizen would ever forget.

"Gentlemen and Lady," he nodded to them as he moved around the table to take his seat at its head. "A monumental moment is upon us. We are about to make history in a way that will change our people's destiny ...forever!" He watched them a moment as their eyes met his, calm yet determined, anxious to follow where he'd lead. Even Obed's face held anticipation. "As you know, Tarkanius has called a conference with alien leadership at which we suspect he will enlist their partnership in his plans for defense. Great effort has been made to conceal its location. But my sources have confirmed the true destination. That conference is our target. We will take out the High Lord Councilor himself and as many others as we can in the process. Cut off from leadership, the Alliance will fall into chaos, and I will move in to provide the leadership they need to reunite."

"Reports are flying in of destinations all over the system. How can your source be so certain?" Dek's questioning eyes met Xalivar's.

Xalivar smiled, raising his datapad and typing the code to send his brief to the leaders' own datapads. After a few moments, datapads beeped in unison as it arrived and Xalivar watched their faces as they started reading.

"Tertullis?" Surprise registered on Lucius' face. "Would Tarkanius risk straying so far from the safety of his military command knowing a threat exists?"

Xalivar smiled. "It's Tarkanius who's behind the false reports, no doubt. He's so confident he's got us fooled, he hasn't even bothered to worry about safety."

"It could be a trap or a decoy," Pres suggested.

Xalivar shook his head. "My source is on the security team. His loyalty to me goes back to before the slave rebellion. Both he and his father owe me their careers."

"They'll have defensive forces there," Dek said.

"And it will be all too easy to destroy them," Xalivar said. "They don't expect to be found and won't be diligently awaiting us. That gives us the element of surprise." He had it all sorted out and nothing could sway his confidence now.

"Without knowing the numbers and make up of that defense, it's impossible to prepare a plan of attack," Dek said.

Trust, Admiral. Is your faith in me so weak? "The plan is to take out all defensive forces and execute the High Lord Councilor and anyone else present at the conference. As the Alliance falls into disarray, we move in."

"And if the Council opposes you?" Obed asked.

Xalivar chortled. "Tarkanius is sure to invite key allies to attend the conference. Anyone remaining who dares to object will be executed." He shot Obed a look to assure his rival he truly meant anyone.

"Even if the force defending the High Lord Councilor is not significant, we'll be greatly outnumbered," Pres looked to Dek and Lucius for support.

Dek nodded.

"Tarkanius will employ worker forces for his defense, to send a message to the Vertullians," Xalivar said. "The others who remain, after those forces have been destroyed, are loyal to you and the Admiral, General. And you will command them."

"When they discover where we've disappeared to, they may not follow." Pres' doubt was starting to get on Xalivar's nerves. She'd been so strong of late. Had her former weakness returned?

"You will make them obey, General. You do know how to command your men, yes?" Xalivar stared at her, unrelenting, until she sighed and nodded, ashamed. Xalivar grinned. "Diagrams of the attack plan have been provided. Study them well and come to me with any questions or suggestions. Double the training and make sure your people are ready. Failure will not be tolerated."

The Generals and Admiral stood as their fists formed in salute. "Yes, my Lord."

Xalivar smirked as they turned and hurried for the door. He felt Obed's cold stare on the back of his neck and ignored him. Let the man grow impatient. *This is my moment!* When the door slid shut behind the military leaders, he slowly turned. "You have doubts?"

"What if it's a trap?"

"I already told you—"

"I heard, and, nonetheless, you're trusting an officer who still serves the High Lord Councilor with the safety of our army, Xalivar."

"My people are loyal! And the army is mine, Obed! Not yours!

Never forget that. You may feel free to stay here and cower, if you wish."

Obed shook his head. "I will serve as commanded, my Lord."

Xalivar stared at him in silence for a moment, then: "Good. You disappeared, Obed. Were you off beating discipline into your problem-child son?"

"Bordox will obey," Obed said, his face tensing with anger.

"Then have him report to me. I want to be sure those instructions are understood this time. No more mercenary activities."

Obed looked ready to protest, but then his face relaxed. "As you wish."

Xalivar waved an arm dismissively and turned to look out the window. He heard the door slide open and footsteps as Obed departed. He was alone again. *You would betray me, old rival. I can sense it in you. But you are the one who will be betrayed.* Memories of their past conflicts flashed through his mind and he laughed at the reminder of so many victories. *No one can defeat me. This is my destiny.* The Vertullian rebellion was a fluke, a mistake. If his people had supported him, it would have been put down. They needed to see the consequences to recognize their need for Xalivar's leadership. When he was back in control, they'd be thankful and more loyal than before.

"All right, what's the plan?" Farien turned and joined Yao, looking at Davi as they rang the bell at the tower where Lord Niger kept a ground floor apartment. Amidst an elite grouping of residential high rises near the city center, the twin suns glinted off its shiny exterior, lending it a glow. "Home to the rich and mighty," it seemed to say. Today one of their number would fall.

"He's not gonna like this," Yao said.

"He should have considered that before he betrayed our people," Davi said as the door slid open to reveal a dark-skinned woman with her hair up. Her eyebrows rose in a question mark as she stared at them with concern.

"We're here to see Lord Niger," Yao said.

"My Niger's in his study and can't be disturbed right now," the woman replied, Davi searched his mind for her name—Abena, if he remembered right.

"I'm afraid he'll have to be," Davi said, extending his datapad.

Abena's expression changed to confusion. "What's this? A warrant?"

"It's from the Palace, ma'am," Yao said. "I'm afraid we really need to speak with your husband right away."

She scowled, shaking her head and stepping back inside, ripping the datapad from Davi's hand as she did. The door slid shut.

"Great! That was perfect!" Farien rolled his eyes.

"You would've done better?" Davi shot him a look.

Farien guffawed. "I always do better, Rhii. I think you've forgotten some of your diplomatic skills since you got demoted from Princehood."

Yao chuckled as Davi made a face. Then the wall beside them exploded in a shower of crumpled steel, broken glass and smoky dust. All three ducked and reached for their blasters, spinning around as their eyes panned for the cause of the blast. Six men approached up the street on Skitters, blaster rifles recharging with a whine. Davi recognized one of them as Major Valenti Broks.

"They're after me!" Davi called. Diving into a roll, he came up on his feet again; firing in the middle of the street. As soon as the blasts left his pistol, he took off running toward the corner. He caught a glimpse of the Skitters dodging to avoid his blasts and those Yao and Farien fired after him; then he was around the corner, searching the street for a place to hide. The smell of sulfur and melting metal filled the air amidst clouds of dust and debris.

"What do we do now? They outnumber us and we're sitting Gungors on foot." Yao said as they joined Davi, running up the street as fast as their feet could go. They heard lasers whining and a pole next to them exploded as a blast landed. Two more singed the sidewalk to either side of where they ran.

"Does this remind you of Xanthis?" Farien asked as Davi reached an intersection and scanned the traffic for an air taxi.

"There!" he said, pointing as a taxi rounded a bend a block

down and headed in their direction.

"A taxi?" Farien asked as they followed him, running toward it.

"Yeah, it's empty. Taxi!" Davi waved his arm and jumped into the street as the tires squealed from the cab-bot's hurried efforts to bring the vehicle to a stop.

As soon as it stopped, Davi raced for the door, pulled it open as servos squealed in protest, and jumped aboard.

"Good evening, sir. Need a cab?" The cab-bot inquired.

"Yes, thank you," Davi said and ripped the cab-bot free of the wheel, disengaging the autopilot as his friends joined him.

A klaxon sounded as a computer voice scolded: "Violation! Violation!" The sound of the Skitters drowned it out as more rifle blasts landed outside.

"Where'd those guys learn how to shoot?" Farien's face crinkled with disdain.

Yao laughed. "Why are we taking a taxi? Skitters are faster."

"With cab-bots driving, yeah. I outraced Bordox, remember?" Davi accelerated as he said it, throwing his friends toward the rear seats. Recovering, they quickly strapped themselves in and slid down the seats, seeking shelter from the lasers. "Don't just relax. Lay down some cover."

"What?" Farien looked confused as Davi reached over and flicked three buttons on the dash. The side windows whined and slid down. His friends took the hint and aimed their blasters as they passed the Skitters, firing repeatedly and forcing the men to duck and dodge as Davi spun around a corner and headed onto an on-ramp for the airoad overhead.

In moments, they'd merged into heavy traffic.

"I'd rather be on patrol," Farien grumbled.

"Are you kidding?" Yao teased. "All through graduation you complained about your boring assignment. Finally, you get some action and you want a boring patrol?"

"Haven't we had our fill of action lately?" Farien said as the Skitters appeared behind them, closing fast. "Here they come!"

Davi had spotted them in the mirrors. "Keep 'em busy for me."

Yao and Farien began firing back the way they'd come, doing their best to target the Skitters and miss the civilian traffic. The

Skitter riders returned fire, despite civilian vehicles and pedestrians moving between them.

"There are too many civilians," Yao said.

"Just scare 'em for now. I'm hoping it slows them down."

"It's not working," Farien said as another explosion rocked the air taxi.

Just then, two civilian air cars shook from explosions at their rear and swerved into each other. Davi cursed to himself and swerved off onto a ramp, cutting off an intracity shuttle. The driver shot them a stern look as Davi accelerated onto the ramp, waving apologetically. They had to get out of this traffic before innocent people died.

Davi hugged the wall of the ramp and zipped past cars lined up at a flashing red signal. "Hang on!" He waited just long enough for his friends to grab on, then slid out and did a ninety-degree turn onto the tail of a large, slow-moving delivery barge. The rough jostling of the taxi was sure to leave them all bruises, but he braked just in time to avoid the barge, then glanced back and forth between the mirror and the road ahead, waiting for an opening.

The air taxi rocked with explosions again as the Skitter riders closed in and began firing their rifles. The back window exploded inward as more bolts singed the sides and top.

"This isn't working!" Farien yelled as he fired several blasts toward the Skitters over the tops of civilian cars waiting behind them.

Davi saw the civilian drivers' terrified faces in the mirror. Then the next lane was open. He accelerated and slid over, racing forward and around the delivery vehicle. He heard explosions and cursing as the Skitter riders found themselves blocked, then he ducked around the next corner, hoping to lose them.

"Well, Niger's seeming pretty guilty to me now," Farien said.

"You think?" Yao teased.

The Skitters were back on their tail in moments, firing at them from both sides as Yao and Farien ducked and then stuck their heads back up and fired back.

"You said you could outfly them, Rhii! We're about to die in here!" Farien cursed as a blast tore up the seat beside him.

Davi rounded another corner and zig-zagged the air taxi in and out of traffic toward a large freight yard with huge metal containers, lifts, and other equipment scattered around. Entering the yard, he scooted past the obstacles and ducked the air taxi in between two shipping containers.

"Maybe we can get lost in here," Yao suggested.

Davi shook his head. "The Major's been after me for a while. He won't be taking any chances."

Suddenly, an explosion flashed behind them and a chunk fell off a building back toward the street they'd entered from. Davi spotted Skitters zigzagging in and out of the obstacle course as he navigated.

"What now?" Yao asked.

Two Skitters moved to flank him, so Davi began swerving the air taxi left and right, forcing them to drop back. "Perhaps a change in tactics." Then he slammed on the brake and let the Skitters shoot past. "Pick them off!"

Farien and Yao fired at the startled riders as they peeled off to the side, but a blast from Farien's blaster damaged one of their engines. The rider limped away, smoke curling up from the back of his Skitter.

Three other riders opened fire to their rear as yet another shot out from the alley where he'd hidden and raced up alongside again. Davi swerved toward him, and they began switching positions as they dodged around other vehicles and obstacles, entering a new street from the shipping yard.

"I have an idea!" Farien called to Yao. "Duck!"

He and Yao ducked as the fourth rider dodged around another taxi and slid in next to the window just in time to pass a public transport. The rider sneered as Davi snuck a peek back at him, then Farien popped up, leaned out the window and grabbed the rider, pulling him into the taxi. The Skitter skidded out from under him as he lost control and Farien released him, letting the man fall away right in front of the public transport at full speed. His limp body fell to the pavement below.

"Gods, Farien, where'd you learn that?" Yao asked, looking at him with amazement.

Farien shrugged. "Improvising. Here they come!"

Four Skitters raised up, one carrying the rider whose Skitter Farien had disabled.

"Okay, Yao, your turn. Don't leave this all to me."

Yao scoffed, shooting Farien a look as Davi laughed. "Told you, you were having a good time."

Farien grinned.

The four riders began firing their rifles. They'd clearly changed settings because the bursts were a constant stream, raking across the roadway in front of them, tearing into everything they touched. The public transport swerved to the side, smoke rising from its engines. Two private air cars burst into flame and swerved off to wreck into vehicles on either side. A civilian on a Skitter screamed as he fell sideways and crashed into the transport. Then the blasts were raking the air taxi.

"They'll tear us apart!" Yao warned.

"Hold on and get those blasters ready!" Davi called back, then glanced in the mirror to ensure that his friends had secured themselves handholds and put the air taxi into a one-eighty turn and headed straight for the Skitters. The Skitter riders kept up a raking fire across the front of the air taxi, dodging out of the way at the last second.

As they came alongside the taxi, Yao and Farien fired dead on, sending two riders to the pavement.

"Three down!" Yao called.

Davi chuckled. "I think we're getting good at this." Davi raced around another transport and took the next corner in a sharp arc, moving through skyscrapers. Only Valenti Broks and one other rider remained.

"You have a plan, don't you?" Yao asked.

Davi nodded. "Just follow my lead." It was rough, but he was making it up as he went.

Yao hollered as a blast shot through the window and struck him in the arm. He dropped his blaster and sank down in his seat.

"You okay, Yao?" Davi called, glancing back to check on him.

"He's fine. Keep your eyes on the road!" Farien fired randomly out the back at the approaching Skitters as Davi said a prayer for his friend then slowed the air taxi.

"What are you doing?" Farien asked.

"Part of the plan," Davi said.

The Skitters raced up again, the riders firing streams from their rifles again.

"Get ready to jump," Davi called.

"Jump? Where?" Farien looked confused and startled.

"You go right, I'm going left," Davi said. "Now!" He slammed the air taxi's brakes on and locked them with a button, then drew his blaster and dove out the window, rolling and firing. Moments later, he heard Farien firing from the other side. The riders skidded to a stop, aiming their rifles as the blasts missed them. A laser beam shot out the back of the stopped air taxi which looked a total mess. It hit the Major's companion dead in the chest, causing him to fire his rifle. Major Broks jumped clear as the rifle beam tore his Skitter to bits.

Davi landed on his feet and raced toward the Major, Farien close behind. The Major struggled to raise his rifle, but a blast from Farien hit him in the arm. He moaned.

Davi stuck his blaster in the man's face. "Why me?"

"Gods curse you, Rhii!" the Major spat.

Farien slammed him in the face with the butt of his blaster, leaving blood streaming from a smashed nose. "He asked you a question."

"He killed my brother!"

"Your brother?" Davi and Farien exchanged a look. "In the Battle of Vertullis?" Davi stared at the man, trying to recognize any soldier he'd battled. Too many had been unknown pilots in distant ships though.

"In an alley on Vertullis. Executed him!"

The Sergeant?! "It was an accident. He was attacking an innocent girl."

"A dirty slave whore!" The Major's feet flew up kicking at them, forc-ing Farien and Davi to dodge to the side. The Major reached for his rifle again, rolling over and aiming for Davi. Davi and Farien fired at the same time, hitting the man square in the chest. His rifle fired, but the beam shot over their heads.

Then the Major fell back, rasping for breath. "You'll pay!" he gasped and fell still. Davi struggled to refill his lungs, winded, as Farien kept his blaster tight on the Major. Was he really dead? After a few minutes, they both relaxed and turned back to find Yao.

Chapter Twelve

Why am I here?" Hachim choked out as light from the large reflector pads overhead glistened off his skin, blinding Aron through the one-way glass. Sweat dripped off the arms of the chair as it soaked through Hachim's robe. After twenty minutes alone in the interrogation room, he looked like he'd fallen into a lake. Tarkanius and Aron shook their heads, and Aron was thankful the glass covered the odor. They watched through the one way glass as Major Zylo stopped across the table from the sweaty Lord, staring at him.

"You know why," Zylo said.

Hachim coughed. "I've done nothing wrong."

"So you always sweat this much when you're innocent?"

Hachim grabbed the towel Zylo tossed across the table at him and began wiping the exposed flesh of his face, brow, neck and arms. "It's hot in here."

"I'm perfectly comfortable." Zylo sat in the seat across from him and leaned back, watching as the Lord cleaned himself. "You're gonna need a new robe."

"What is this about? You have no right to detain me without cause!"

Zylo nodded, then slid a datapad across the table, watching as Hachim set down the towel and began to read.

"Conspiracy? Assassination?" Hachim's eyes darted up from

the screen. "I had nothing to do with it."

"You knew about it."

Hachim shook his head. "If you could prove it, you'd have already arrested me." He smiled smugly.

Zylo laughed. "You're in an LSP interrogation room and you think you're not under arrest?"

Hachim's eyes darted around. "I've done nothing to warrant it."

Zylo didn't react. "The Alien Leadership Summit."

Hachim's eyes raced down the screen to finish the charges. "What about it?" Hachim slid the datapad back across the table and shot him a confused look that wasn't very convincing.

"What's the location?"

"That's classified for the Council."

"I have clearance, trust me. I'm on the security team."

Hachim hesitated, then melted under Zylo's stare. "Idolis."

Zylo shook his head. "Buzz! Wrong answer. And it was all over the news."

"So? I am not the only person privy to that." Hachim leaned back in his chair, attempting to appear bored, but Aron saw the fear in his eyes. And Zylo saw it, too.

Zylo chuckled. "Yes, you were."

Hachim looked at him again, startled. "What?"

Zylo nodded, smirking. "Each Lord was given a different location."

Hachim frowned. "A different location? They can't hold the Summit in more than one place…" His voice trailed off as the implications sank in. Zylo raised a brow as their eyes met. "Lies? A trap?"

"A security precaution. How many people did you tell?"

Hachim shook his head. "No, I'm innocent. I'm not going to tolerate this abuse." Slowly, he stood from his chair and took a step toward the door.

Zylo leapt up and shoved Hachim back into the chair. "Sit down and start answering." Hachim winced, grabbing his shoulder and looking of-fended at the treatment. Zylo casually returned to his chair. Aron was amazed by his performance. "Now!"

Aron looked at Tarkanius, wondering if it were time for them to join the interrogation. Tarkanius shook his head. "No. Let him suffer."

"Then their fate will be yours." Zylo shrugged and turned to casually stroll toward the door. Hachim's eyes widened.

"It was Niger's idea," Hachim began. Zylo turned back as Hachim's shoulders sank with his weight in the chair.

The days after Telanus' funeral were hard for everyone but, for Davi, in particular, it was a living nightmare. On his first break from the round-the-clock patrols, he'd come back to Miri's apartment to check on Tela. At least she was talking now. Before, she'd just stayed alone in a room, crying or silent. But she was civil to the others. With Davi, she became as electric as a thunderstorm.

"I understand that you're hurting. I understand you hate those men for what they did. But it's not all Boralians."

Tela spun around and slapped him hard across the face. "Don't justify them to me!"

Lura started toward Davi but, Sol held her back, shaking his head.

"It's not me, either!" Davi rubbed his cheek where it was red and tender from her attack.

"You're the one still defending them—both here and in your cockpit. Serving those monsters as an officer! I'll file my resignation this afternoon!"

Did she mean that or was it a bluff? Davi couldn't read her well anymore. "You can do that, if you wish. Throw away your military career. I still hope for a peaceful solution to be found."

"Peace?! With those monsters?! Our abusers?! Murderers!" Tela raised an arm like she meant to slap him again, but he stepped back. "I don't know who you are anymore!" She whirled and ran down the hallway toward the room again as Lura rushed to Davi, caressing his cheek.

"Are you okay?"

Davi nodded. "What's wrong with her? We used to be in love."

"You still are," Sol insisted. "Grieving does strange things to people."

Davi shook his head. "It's hard to love someone who keeps offering such abuse."

"Can you blame her for being angry?" Miri asked. Davi turned to face her. Miri looked more weary and older than Davi ever remembered seeing her, like she'd aged overnight. "I've seen a lot of things that disgusted me over the years done by my people, but now...this is the end for me. I can no longer defend them. If this is who they are, I'm ashamed to be Boralian. I can no longer respect or defend them."

"But it's not everyone, Mother! It's a few idiots on the street! The majority of Boralians are good, decent people. You know that! They supported our fight for freedom. It's a big factor in why Xalivar was overthrown!"

Miri shook her head with unusual fervor, her lips tight and thin as she raised her hands in protest. "The last few months I've seen hatred on a level I'd never imagined." She blushed a bit as she noticed Lura and Sol watching. "I'm sure your people have seen far worse, but I'd never seen it firsthand. Even when I was in prison, they treated me differently. Now there's no respect. No honor. It's unacceptable! I can't stay here with them!"

Davi groaned. Had all the women on this planet gone crazy? "What? You're leaving now too? What—joining Joram's circus? The star act—Princess Miri, Boralian convert? As if people will even accept you!"

"If they won't, I can go somewhere alone. Either way, I won't be here. Won't be a part of a people so depraved." She'd always been emotional, but the words stung. Despite his own anger at the Boralian's behavior, the change in Miri startled him.

"This is our home, Mother! For generations now! Where would we go? Where would you go?"

Miri shrugged. "There are many star systems. Many planets with human populations. The borders of our galaxy are far beyond the two suns that grace our sky, Davi."

"I've seen that, Mother. I've been to the edge of the system and back. The number of ships it would take to transport a third of the human population...the amount of supplies, food...and, speaking of food, Vertullis is the main agricultural supplier in the system...it would cause a mass crisis. Maybe starvation!" The implications sunk in even as he listed them and Davi felt flush with emotion.

"That will be Tarkanius' problem and that of the Council, Davi. The Vertullians must do what's best for them."

"We can live here in peace. I know we can." Davi looked at Lura and Sol for support. Sol didn't react but Lura nodded, hopeful. "I'm not leaving yet."

"That's your choice. It will sadden me if you choose to stay, but I know I must go." Miri said, with a firmness Davi had never heard from her.

Davi's shoulders sank as he lowered himself onto a couch. "And you two? Are you leaving also?" He looked at Lura and Sol.

"We don't know yet," Sol said. "But it'll be hard to stay."

Davi put his face in his hands. He'd never felt so defeated. Despite all the people who'd chased him and threatened his life, this was worse. His family was falling apart before his eyes, and he felt helpless to interfere. "If we leave, Xalivar has won. Do you realize that? We'd be letting him win."

"If he wants it so bad, let him have this place," Sol said, his eyes sad. "It hasn't been good to us." A moment before, Sol had claimed they were still undecided, but now he sounded convinced. Even gentle, kind Lura had a hardness on her face he'd never seen.

"We've never really known peace here," Lura agreed.

"Mother, not you, too," Davi said as his eyes met hers. "I need you."

Tears flowed from Lura's eyes as she nodded. "We need you, too, Son. But we can't force you to accompany us."

"We won't even try," Sol added.

Davi raced through the arguments in his head, searching for something convincing to make them change their minds. "Joram has no plan... limited resources. The other leaders aren't with him. It may not happen."

Sol nodded. "We're prepared for that."

"So you'll go anyway?"

Sol shrugged. "We haven't decided yet."

"It's just something we're thinking about," Lura said, looking at Miri. "And discussing."

Davi frowned, looking at Miri. "You let those two get to you, huh? Miri and Tela? I love you all, but I don't understand this!" His chest grew tight, and he needed fresh air. He stood, brushing off Lura's arm as she reached for his hand.

"Please, Davi. Don't go." Miri's eyes pleaded as he reached the door.

Davi just shook his head and pushed the button, stepping through as the door slid out of the way and marching down the hall toward the lifts. He needed to get away; needed time to think. It was all overwhelming, and he'd had no rest. He glanced at his chrono. He had a security meeting about the peace summit in less than an hour. Great! No time to rest yet. *God, please let this meeting be short!* He entered the lift and rode down to the street, hoping to at least get some Talis before the meeting started.

Xalivar watched his men assembling from a balcony high above. His face was a mask, yet inside he swelled with pride. To lead an army again—he reveled in the power. The Fist of Xalivar, he'd taken to calling them in private. Soon, they would demonstrate his might for the whole system. The has-been, deposed leader would be ruler again.

As Lucius and the other leaders finished the roll call, Xalivar turned and made his way down the stairs from the balcony to the dais, where they awaited him. The troops stood at attention, uniforms pressed and polished, not even a hair out of place. The only movement he observed from them was that of their eyes following his every motion. As he stepped onto the platform, he nodded to each of the leaders, then turned and stepped to the microphone at the front.

"Gentlemen and Ladies, our finest hour is approaching; the

moment when we will together stake our claim that our people must be restored to their former greatness. I led you well for years, my family for generations. And now, once again, I will lead you to victory. We fight together for the restoration of the Alliance we hold dear. Generations of our ancestors gave their lives to defend it, to preserve it. And now we must do the same. A terrible disease has infected our populace and the leadership. They have been led astray, and like doctors, we must wipe out the virus and restore them to health. Our weapons are the medicine, their rebellion the infection. We will tear them down and sew them up again, reuniting us in the process of destroying this menace. You've already proved your honor and dedication. You've worked hard for this moment. And finally, it is here. I commend you, I thank you on behalf of future generations, and I commit you into the hands of the gods!" He smiled as he raised his hands in the V of victory. The troops erupted into cheering and applause, the Generals and Admiral joining them.

It was then Xalivar realized Obed and Bordox were missing. Where had they gone? He had ordered that everyone be there. And where was Manaen? Up to some miniscule task which could wait, as usual, no doubt. Anyone with any recognition would not miss such an important moment. Oh well. Manaen was expendable as all aliens and slaves were. Soon enough, he'd be rid of them all. Not even Manaen's usefulness would protect him when the time came.

"Get good rest, my friends," he continued as he lowered his arms. "Tomorrow we have a meeting with destiny. We must be well prepared." He smiled, panning the assembly, then turned and nodded to the leaders. As they stepped forward to dismiss their troops, Xalivar started up the stairs again. He would find Obed and Bordox and make sure he reminded them of their place in this. He didn't trust them, all the more for their recent mysterious activities. But they might still be useful. And when they weren't, they too would meet tragic accidental deaths. He thought of Miri and Xander. *I hope they send you, Nephew. It would be good to face you again and watch you die!* He chuckled as he walked, seeing Manaen at the top of the stairs.

"Have you no sense of history, Manaen? This is a great moment for all our peoples!"

Manaen bowed, eyes focused on the floor. "I'm sorry, my Lord. I was attending to the dinner you requested."

"Very well then, I hope it meets all my specifications. I want to remember this night well."

"Of course, my Lord," Manaen said as Xalivar reached the top of the stairs. There was something off about his majordomo these days, something in the eyes Xalivar couldn't quite place. He had been watching him closely but still uncovered nothing. *What is it, my old friend? Will you betray me? Have you already?* He knew that one way or another he would find out. He always did.

Pres stood next to Admiral Dek as they watched their troops break formation to return to their quarters. Dek looked so handsome in his dress uniform. It would be odd to fight others in the same colors. They'd add ribbons to the shoulders to allow them to distinguish their own people, and their fighters and ships had special transmitters to emit a beacon as well. But where face-to-face combat was required, her troops would feel as if they were fighting their own. It would be hard, but she'd done all she could to prepare them. Now she wondered if she'd prepared herself.

As the last of the soldiers filed out, Dek turned to her and nodded. "The moment has come."

She smiled. "Yes, Admiral, we go to war again together."

"You've done well, General. You should be very proud. I am very proud of you."

For a moment, Pres couldn't form the words to respond. He was proud of her? She struggled to come up with what to say. "Thank you, Admiral."

He smiled back. "I've watched you triumph over great difficulties for many years, and I want to express my admiration and gratitude for your service to us all."

She couldn't bring herself to meet his eyes. "I've only done what any loyal citizen soldier would do, Admiral."

He shook his head. "You've distinguished yourself. There is no need for modesty, among friends. It is an honor to serve with you, Pres." He turned and extended his hand.

Pres hesitated a moment, then extended her own and took his firmly, shaking it. His warm, firm grip on her hand sent shivers through her. She had to focus just to breathe and then force words out. "I'm honored to serve with you as well, Dek."

"When this is over, I hope you will finally have a chance to return to a normal life."

She did her best to hide her shock at the suggestion. "Retire?"

"Do you not want more than this, Pres? A family perhaps? A normal life?" He glanced at her with a tenderness she'd never seen from him.

She steeled herself, repressing the tears forming at the corners of her eyes, and shrugged. She hadn't ever given it much thought. In truth, she'd never found a suitable mate, not until Dek. "I am happy with my career."

He released her hand and smiled again. "Of course. But don't make the mistake I have and live your life only for the Alliance. There's more out there. You should take the opportunity to discover it."

"You don't think Xalivar will have need of us once he's restored to power?"

"Perhaps, but arrangements can always be made."

"I cannot imagine a life not in service." She stopped herself before she admitted she meant a life without him by her side. What would she do if she couldn't see him every day? Did he ever think about her the way she thought about him?

"The Alliance is not all there is for someone like you. You can make your own piece of history. You deserve it. I want that for you. It's something I never had."

You could have it, my dear Dek...with me. For a moment, she almost confessed; almost told him everything on her heart, but then Lucius approached. "Well, we have a dinner to attend. I believe our Lord is waiting."

Dek and Pres both nodded. "We are honored, of course," Dek said. He looked at her, offering his arm in a gentlemanly manner. Another thing he'd never done before. Maybe he did have feelings for her.

But then he started walking, pulling her gently along and the moment passed. They followed Lucius up the stairs to the balcony, where Manaen greeted them with a nod and led them inward toward Xalivar's chamber. Would she ever get a moment to express how she felt to him? Maybe she'd find one, once this was all over.

🏰

Obed and Bordox ate dinner in a small clearing just outside the compound. It was their last dinner as father and son before the fighting began and Obed said he wanted their time together to be fruitful without distractions. As they sipped Idolian wine, Obed smiled. "Bordox, I'm proud of you."

Bordox coughed, struggling to avoid spitting out his mouthful of wine. "Father?"

Obed nodded. "I know I'm hard on you. But you've distinguished yourself as a fine, dedicated officer. And I know you'll only go farther in the future."

"Me?" *Who are you and where's my real father?*

Obed frowned. "Don't act so modest, my son. We are alone here. You have as much pride as I had at your age. I see that. That's why I'm hard on you. You cannot let pride control you. You have to rise above it or it will become your downfall."

For a moment, Bordox recalled an article he'd read about scientists developing bots with human skins. Could they have cloned his father somehow?

"This is an important moment, not just for Xalivar, but for our family, Bordox. We have an opportunity at last to set things right."

"Of course, father." Bordox watched him warily. His father looked more at peace than he'd seen him in years.

Obed reached over and put a hand on Bordox's wrist. "You must control your anger and focus on our goal."

"The destruction of the Rhii family is always on my mind."

Bordox swallowed another sip of wine. Starting with his insolent rival, of course.

Obed shook his head. "This is bigger than the Rhii family. Your obsession with revenge cannot interfere with what must be done."

"If Xander Rhii is there, he's mine, Father. He will not live to stand in my way again."

Obed sat his glass down and reached for some fresh bread and Gixi jam. He spread the purple paste on the brown crust with a knife and watched his son. "The time will come. But this moment is about so much more. We have the chance to finally correct the history of our family and change its future."

Bordox sighed. This was a clone or his father had lost it. "We have no support, Father. Do you honestly believe they will elect you in Xalivar's absence?"

Obed's eyes widened and Bordox could tell he was struggling with rage. "Watch your tongue with me."

"I speak only the truth. I mean no disrespect. But for my whole life, it's all you've thought about. Sometimes we have to set realistic goals; focus on things we know we can do."

Obed chuckled. "A son lecturing his father?"

"I am no fool, Father."

"You act like one!" Obed slammed the bread down on the small table, angrily.

So much for being proud of me. "Why? Because I dare to question you?"

"Because you fail to consider anyone but yourself!"

Bordox jumped to his feet and began pacing as his own rage swelled. His father had always treated him like a burden, brushed him aside. Yet Obed called him selfish? *You have no idea, Old Man!*

"The world does not revolve around you, Bordox!"

"Nor does it revolve around you, Obed!"

Obed's mouth dropped open at the use of his name. "How dare you use that tone with me?"

"I'm surprised you even remember my name! My whole life you've treated me like a weed to be plucked and thrown aside; like a pack you were forced to carry, instead of a blessing given you by the gods! How many times did you humiliate me? Mock me? Put me down?" Bordox fought the sudden urge to strike his father. It would be so easy to pound him into ground at this very moment.

"I told you. That was to humble you. Keep your pride under control." Obed's eyes never left his son's.

"What about your pride, Lord Obed? If I have pride, I never got it from listening to you! You treat me like nothing!"

Obed stood and faced him, brushing dirt off his legs. He remained eerily calm, despite his anger. "I have done everything I can to give you the best. I worked hard to provide your food, clothes, education. You have no appreciation!"

"Neither do you! I don't follow your orders! And I won't follow Xalivar's either! He has humiliated us enough! Starting with allowing that slave to live in the castle that should have been ours!"

"That slave was raised there against my knowledge!" Xalivar's voice boomed from the shadows, and both Bordox and Obed whirled with surprise in the direction from which it came.

Xalivar stepped forward, the light hitting his face as he smiled. "Plotting against me. That explains your failure to accept my dinner invitation. I suppose it also explains your recent absence, your secret trip to Estrela." He stood smiling as he watched their faces. "Did you really think I would not know? I have many friends, many sources. And I always knew I needed to watch you."

Obed shook a finger at Xalivar. "No. That was a business trip. I still have properties, my family's future to secure."

"If it was legitimate, why hide it from me?"

Bordox watched his father, but Obed said nothing and Bordox could see Xalivar knew the answer. Now Xalivar turned his eyes on him. "You wish my nephew dead? Fine! Kill him! But if your quest stands in the way of mine, you'll die too!" Xalivar pointed a finger in warning and waved it at Obed. "Your family has no legitimate claim to the throne. Your grand-father gambled it away to mine like it was nothing!"

"My grandfather was drunk! Yours took advantage!" Obed slammed his hands against his side in anger. It hadn't been as easy as Xalivar said. The throne couldn't be gifted in such a manner, but when the Council learned of Obed's grandfather's behavior, they deposed him and a vote awarded it to the Rhiis. Disrespect for the office and his duties, they'd said. Dishonor toward the Alliance. Bordox fumed just hearing of it. Given Xalivar's family's behavior, it was a mockery!

Xalivar laughed. "Utilizing weakness is how the strong prevail. Survival of the fittest, I believe our Old Earth ancestors labeled it. If your family is weaker, it is not the Rhiis who bear the blame!"

"We will see who's weaker!" Obed looked ready to commit violence himself now. The eerie calm of before had disappeared.

Bordox couldn't help himself. He started to laugh. Both Lords turned to glare at him. "You sound like children. It's amusing."

"You dare speak to me like that?" Xalivar's fists clenched at his side.

"Who? A deposed Lord? Thrown out by his own family? You speak of strength as if you have any. You've mocked my father all my life. And what have you done to prove yourself better? Our family's support helped make you strong! How easily you forget!" Bordox smirked, enjoying the anger his remarks prompted.

Obed stared at Bordox, and, for a moment, Bordox actually caught a glimpse of what might be real pride in his eyes.

"Leave! I want you both off this planet and out of my sight immediately! If you value your lives!" Xalivar pointed at Bordox. "And there will be no place for you in the new Borali Alliance. All your property will be claimed by the state. If I allow her, your mother may fly to meet you."

"You've not heard the end of it," Obed warned, shaking his finger again.

"Next we meet, one of us will die!" Xalivar shook a fist at them. Obed grabbed Bordox's arm before he could respond and rushed him away through a door leading back inside the compound.

The assembly took place in a park near the Iraja starport, the largest such clearing in the entire city. It had not been a park when the Boralians ruled, but the area's buildings were decimated during the fighting between the Worker's Freedom Resistance and the Alliance, and the new Vertullian government had moved quickly to relocate affected Boralian proprietors. They'd been given their choice of prime locations elsewhere and had been assisted while they settled in, while the old area had been converted for use as Iraja's largest park, a central gathering place with gazebos and an outdoor amphitheatre which was being used for the assembly. The crowd was several thousand. As word had spread of Joram's movement through broadcasts and conversations in bars and restaurants, interest had grown, and, today, Joram had promised some surprise announcements.

Miri could feel the anticipation of those around her as she waited backstage. Would they boo her as so many had in the past few months? Or would they accept what she was about to do and applaud her? The rejections by her own people still stung but not as much as the anger and bitterness of the bombing at the preschool or Telanus' death. Still, excitement filled the air around her as the crowd chattered amongst themselves. They were of many races and backgrounds, united in common belief. They looked just like so many Boralian crowds she'd faced over her lifetime. The commonalities were so evident that she couldn't fathom any longer how anyone could fail to see it. In a mixed crowd of the two peoples, it would be a challenge to tell them apart.

She watched stage hands going about their business as she scanned past them for Tela. She was out there somewhere amongst the crowd. How would she feel about Miri's presence? It was too late to ask her and too late to turn back. She hoped Tela could accept her. Miri treasured Tela's opinion more than anyone else's. Tela was like the daughter she'd never had. Had she really meant the hateful words she'd said to Miri or was it all in anger?

"All ready?" Joram asked as he appeared beside her.

She'd been so focused on the crowd, Miri hadn't heard him approach. She nodded and smiled. "Yes, of course."

He laughed, smiling and patting her forearm. "Don't be nervous. They may have bad associations with your name from the past, but you also raised our great hero and having a Boralian support our cause only lends strength to it."

"I'm just worried about Tela."

Joram's eyes searched the crowd. "Where is she? Out there? Why's she not here with you?"

"She's still dealing with her father's death. She doesn't want anyone Boralian near her. It's been most painful, as I'm sure you understand."

Joram nodded, and, for a moment, looked sad. "That anger serves us now, but the time will come to let it go and move on. She'll come around, I promise you." He grinned at her.

"I'm sorry for what they did to you."

"It was not you. I know your heart and your honor well, Miri. I do not hold you responsible." He reached over and clasped her hand, squeezing it gently with his own.

"Thank you."

He took a deep breath, releasing her hand. "But we must begin. Just relax while I introduce you." He offered a reassuring look, then headed up the stairs to the platform as the crowd's chatter turned to applause. Raising his arms in the V of victory, he greeted them with a broad smile and waved.

"Hello, my friends," Joram said and motioned for them to quiet down, then waited before continuing: "Twenty-seven years ago today, a great tragedy was perpetuated against our people, only a few miles from here. Barbaric forces from our age-old enemies, those who had long oppressed us, brutally attacked our brothers and sisters who sought to improve working conditions in a revolt against mistreatment. Let these memories serve as yet another reminder that the time has come for us to bid the Boralians 'goodbye.'" He stepped back as the lights faded and screens overhead lit up.

Miri's eyes turned toward the screen, but the images flashed through her mind instead. After all, it was she who had released these images to the world after discovering them hidden in her family's vault, concealed by her brother for over two decades. Leaking them to the media had helped bring Xalivar's downfall. The images and accompanying sound had haunted her ever since.

On the video, people yelled and screamed as lasers fired all around them. Alliance soldiers, led by Xalivar in full military uniform, mowed them down again and again in lines, bodies falling into piles in large pits dug in the earth. As the first row fell, the next stepped forward to the same position until they fell on top of the others. The numbers of slaves shown were endless. It was shocking, gruesome, unforgettable!

Miri clamped her eyes shut, trying to shut out the images, to end the suffering. She heard gasps and grumbles from the crowd as those assembled watched and became engraged. The noise rose in volume to a loud buzz by the end. Joram just stood on the stage, in the shadows, waiting. When the video finished, the lights faded back up, spotlighting him.

"Today, we are fortunate to have the woman responsible for finally ensuring that footage became public. She might have been the last one you'd have expected to release such damning evidence, but Miri Rhii is anything but predictable." The crowd mumbled at the mention of her name. "Raised in the Royal Boralian family, she risked everything because she believed we were being wronged and the time had come to set things right. The release of the Delta V evidence helped inspire a movement, even amongst Boralian citizens, in support of our freedom and greatly aided our fight. Please welcome with me, Miri Rhii."

With that he applauded and the crowd joined in, some reluctantly, as Joram turned toward Miri, motioning for her to join him on the stage. As soon as Miri stepped into the lights, the tenor of the crowd's reaction changed. She heard shouts of protest and even booing as the applause faded. Joram made jagged cutting motions beside her and the lights faded again as videos filled the screens overhead.

Miri glanced over at a stage-side monitor and saw herself surveying the banquet room where Danae had taken her to speak that horrible day. There she was being applauded, and then she spoke, her smile projecting such warmth. When was the last time she'd smiled like that?

"Good afternoon, my friends, it's so good to be here with you today and share with you about some new friends who are now part of us." On the video, she saw herself pan the crowd as she began with her speech. A few moments later, her onscreen self paused as new applause broke out around her from most of the tables. The bored onlookers toward the back remained indifferent.

Then, on the video, that deep voice came from the shadows in the back: "Not hard enough, and not long enough, I'd say."

Miri watched herself struggle to maintain her composure as her eyes sought the speaker. As the taunting continued, she saw herself glance over at Danae for reassurance, but Danae looked lost. Then Miri stepped back from the podium, her face filled with shock and sadness. The Miri on screen winced at every word, pained, and Miri relived it all over again. As her host rushed forward and Danae comforted her, the video disappeared and the lights faded up again.

Miri felt relief as Joram took to the podium again. "She has suffered on our behalf, my friends," Joram said, his voice filled with emotion. "Whatever you think of the past and her family's leadership of the Alliance, Miri Rhii has proven herself our ally and friend. And let's not forget the man she raised her son Davi to be. We all remember him as a hero in our fight for freedom. Please. Let's honor him now by hearing what she has to say."

The crowd remained silent this time as Joram watched them. After a moment, he smiled and motioned for Miri to step to the microphone. She did.

Her voice cracked as she tried to speak. Clearing her throat, she took a deep breath and tried again. "No words would be enough to tell you how sorry I am for the past; the way you were treated at the hands of my ancestors and my people. I make no excuses for that now. But know that I recognize it for the wrong that it is. And I did take action to help end it. Unfortunately, there are many who refuse to let it end. The time has come for you to seek the life you deserve in a new place. And I'm here to tell you today, that if you will let me, I'd like to come with you and start a new life for myself there, too, with my son and his family."

The crowd stared at her. She could see their uncertainty. Then a woman near the front spoke: "How do we know you don't come as a spy; to help the Boralians track us, so they can conquer us again?" Several grunted in agreement.

Miri saw a jostling in the crowd and stepped back from the microphone, fearing violence. She saw that someone was making his way to the front, then Tela appeared and came to the front of the stage. The young woman stared up at Miri for a moment, then pulled herself onto the platform and came to stand beside Miri.

"I vouch for her," Tela said.

"Who are you?" the woman hollered.

"Tela Tabansi. My father was Telanus, murdered by our oppressors in the attack on Joram in Legon." The crowd silenced, staring at her with respect and awe. "I've known this woman for eighteen months. She's been like a mother to me. She is no spy. And she's not a liar. You can trust her. Her honor is as great as that of her son. If she asks to join us, I assure you, she means what she says." Tela turned to Miri and smiled, then walked over and embraced her. Miri sniffled as tears formed in her eyes. Hugging back, they both cried for a moment, tears flowing onto each other's robes. She saw on Tela's face that she'd meant every word. It was better than an apology. They were family again and Miri knew that it would take a lot more to separate them again.

And even as they embraced, Miri felt the whole energy around her change. Glancing over Tela's shoulder, she saw a warmth in the eyes of those assembled which hadn't been there moments before. All of a sudden, she not only had their attention, but, with Tela and Joram's endorsements, she had the beginnings of respect. For the first time in months, Miri felt like there might be some place where she could belong. She squeezed Tela's hand, then wiped her tears on her sleeve and turned back toward the microphone. She had many words to say. It appeared they would listen.

Davi discovered Zylo's involvement with Tarkanius' plans at the final pre-summit leadership meeting. Zylo greeted him like they were old friends, but from the moment he saw him, Davi had a bad feeling. He'd not forgotten the tour Zylo took him on, when he'd first arrived to his station on Vertullis, nor Zylo's attitude toward the workers, or his involvement leading troops on the ground against the Worker's Freedom Resistance. Having him involved in a top secret summit so vital to restor-ing peace put Davi on edge, and he made a mental note to investigate. But first he had to get back to his room for a quick power nap before the next patrol.

As he exited the tunnel connecting the civilian starport with the military one, he spotted a familiar face at a terminal in the military comm center. Zylo sat alone in a cube, looking intently at the terminal as he typed. Coming so close after final discussions about the secret summit, Davi's spine tingled.

"What's the matter, Captain?"

Davi turned to see Qajuan smiling at him. "Hi, Q. Nothing. Just off to catch a nap."

Qajuan turned, following Davi's eyes to Zylo. "Old friend or old enemy? You don't look pleased to see him?"

"He's not a pilot." Davi said, turning his eyes back to Zylo.

Qajuan nodded then pulled a datapad from the pocket of his jumpsuit and walked to a terminal on the wall. He fiddled with some cables for a moment and then his fingers raced across the keypad. After a moment, he handed the datapad to Davi.

"What's this?"

Qajuan smirked. "What your friend there is seeing."

Davi shook his head, worried. "You tapped into a military comm center?"

Qajuan shrugged. "I have all kinds of skills. Do you want to know what he's doing or not?"

Davi sighed and took the datapad. The message appeared incomplete but Davi recognized the coordinates and time of the planned summit. Scanning it over, he couldn't figure out who the recipient was. "He's revealing the location of a top-secret meeting."

Qajuan shrugged, taking the datapad back. "He hasn't sent it yet. Hold on." His fingers danced across the keys again as his face took on a satisfied grin. "There."

Inside the comm center, Davi saw Zylo's face turn to

frustration. He grumbled at the terminal, then slammed a fist against it before logging out and yelling at the attendant. Davi drew his blaster and stood ready.

"Going somewhere, Major?" he said as Zylo stepped into the corridor.

Zylo turned, surprised. "Rhii. Why are you pointing that at me?"

"You're under arrest. Suspicion of treason."

Zylo scoffed. "For what?"

"That little missive you just tried to send."

Zylo's face took on a confused expression, but Davi saw the fear in his eyes. "I don't know what you're talking about." Zylo tried to remain casual, but stiffened in spite of himself.

Qajuan cleared his throat and waved the datapad he'd now disconnected from the terminal on the wall. Davi and Zylo looked at him questioningly. "I transferred it here."

"Transferred what?" Zylo frowned, growing annoyed.

Davi kept his eyes locked on Zylo as he answered. "Your message. The High Lord Councilor might find it very interesting."

Zylo spun and ran. Davi spun with him, disabling the safety on his blaster as he did. Zylo stopped as he heard the hum. "It's not what you think."

Zylo turned back, looking defeated. Davi hurried toward him. "You can explain that to Tarkanius."

Zylo's shoulders sank as Davi grabbed his arm. "Thanks, Q."

Qajuan nodded, amused as Davi keyed the comm and requested an LSP air car to take them to the Palace. He hoped it wasn't too late to undo whatever damage Zylo had already done.

As soon as they arrived, Tarkanius' majordomo escorted them into the throne room.

"What's this about?" Tarkanius said, his face filled with concern as soon as he saw whom Davi was escorting. Davi quickly pulled the e-post up and handed Tarkanius the datapad. Both he and Zylo stood silently as the High Lord Councilor read the screen. His shoulders sunk and his brow creased as his eyes took in the words.

"Is this what I think it is?" Tarkanius looked shocked. Davi nodded. "Can you explain this, Major?" Tarkanius turned to Zylo.

Zylo shrugged, cool and relaxed. "I was sending information to one of the men on the security team."

"The time and coordinates? Wouldn't he already know?" Tarkanius stared at Zylo, but the Major refused to meet his eyes.

Tarkanius looked at Davi. "Who's the recipient?"

Davi shook his head. "I haven't traced it yet sir."

Tarkanius turned back to Zylo, frowning. Davi saw his eyes darken with emotion. Tarkanius motioned to Davi. "Your blaster, Captain."

"Sir?" Davi looked at him. Was Tarkanius asking him to draw?

Tarkanius wiggled his fingers. "Give me your blaster, please, so I can execute the Major for treason."

Davi drew the blaster, choking back a laugh as he handed it to the High Lord Councilor. Zylo leaned back in his chair, curious but still calm.

"I'm tired of people suggesting I'm weak. Perhaps this will change their minds." Tarkanius pointed the blaster at Zylo as the Major's eyes widened in surprise.

"My Lord, this is a misunderstanding—"

"The misunderstanding was my notion that you could be trusted, Major," Tarkanius said, his voice full of anger. "Shall I tell your wife the truth?" His intensity surprised Davi.

Zylo scoffed. "You won't shoot me."

Tarkanius swung around like a lightning bolt and slammed the blaster up under Zylo's chin, knocking his head back. Zylo looked as shocked as Davi was. Then Tarkanius shoved the blaster hard against Zylo's forehead, holding him in place. "Try me."

Zylo wobbled as his legs failed him, and he toppled off the chair to his knees. "Please, my Lord..."

"I need a better answer," Tarkanius said as he stiffened his arm and held the blaster to Zylo's forehead. "Lord Hachim has been effusive in providing information. You can join him and earn leniency, or I can find out what it's like to kill."

Zylo remained silent. Tarkanius shoved the blaster harder against his head, leaving a mark. As he did, his eyes met Davi's. For a moment, Davi thought he might have to interfere, but then the High Lord Councilor winked. Davi saw Tarkanius' majordomo's shocked expression and coughed to stifle a smile.

Then Zylo began filling them in on Xalivar's plans.

🐚

Miri arrived home from the rally, feeling exhilarated. After Tela's endorsement, the Vertullians had been rapt at her every word, applauding her like one of their own. Several rushed to greet and shake her hand afterwards. For the first time in a long while, Miri felt like she mattered. Knowing Tela still respected her just made it better.

A light flashed on her living room terminal. Message waiting. After pouring herself a cup of Talis, she sank, exhausted, into a chair beside the terminal and logged on.

To: MRhii@Federal.emp
From: Unknown

My dearest sister,

My long-awaited reunion with dear nephew Davi appears imminent. As you can imagine, I await it with bated breath. I only wish you could be there to join us. Perhaps our reunion will come at his funeral. Something to look forward to, no doubt!
Your loving brother,
Xalivar

Miri's throat tightened as her elation turned to fear. Davi was a strong warrior but for Xalivar to be so confident, she knew her brother had a plan. She had to find Davi and convince him not to go. She couldn't bear to lose him or anyone else at the hands of Xalivar or his ilk. It wasn't their fight anymore. Why couldn't Davi see that? Joram had convinced her: an exodus was the only option. The Vertullians had no chance but to cut ties and start over somewhere else. She had to convince Davi some-how. Sipping her Talis, she typed in commands for a comm line to his quarters.

Chapter Thirteen

What's going on?" Davi asked, confused as he and Farien forced their way through the crowd at the military hangar. Crews and mech-bots scrambled to prepare the fighters for launch as people circled around them waving signs and chanting. "Not our fight!" one sign said. "You are free!" said another.

Yao appeared beside them in a brand-new blue flight suit, carrying his helmet. "Protestors. Vertullians. Guess who's in charge."

Farien pushed through the protestors with a shove, drawing angry stares. Davi and Yao followed, hurrying to catch up. Before Davi could say anything, they turned a corner and spotted Miri and Tela at the head of the column. As soon as they spotted him, the women smiled and rushed to meet him.

"Davi!"

He fought the urge to hide. "What are you doing here?" He did his best to look pleased to see them but inside he felt anger rising.

"You don't have to go. It's not our fight." Tela put a hand on his arm.

Not our fight? Who are you? What happened to make you forget all we fought for? He resisted the urge to shove her hand away. "I have a duty to all citizens," Davi said.

"They're not your people anymore," she said.

"They'll always be my people." His eyes met hers, and he saw a flash of anger at his words. He'd grown up amongst the Boralians. They'd been good to him much of his life. He'd always have friends and family amongst them. How could she expect him to just turn his back and throw that away?

"Don't go, Davi," Miri added. "Don't risk your life for people who wouldn't risk theirs for you." Both women's eyes pleaded with him as he brushed off their hands and moved past.

Hearing that from Miri stung. Unlike him, she'd always be Boralian by birth. She was one of the reasons he felt so attached to them. "They've risked their lives for me dozens of times. Many are my friends. I made an oath, and I'll honor it."

"Don't you understand?" Tela pushed him gently, then stepped into his path. "They don't consider us their equals. They've murdered so many of our people. We have to stand up to them." There was something in her eyes, a haunted look that diminished their usual sparkle, almost like looking at a stranger.

"If we don't stop Xalivar a lot of innocent people who had nothing to do with the murders will be hurt." Davi gently pushed past her.

"Don't do this, Davi. Please." Miri begged. "If we lose you—"

"Mother, you of all people should understand why I have to go," Davi turned back as Miri shook her head, tears rolling down her cheek. "He's done you enough harm. Don't let him destroy you."

"So you've already decided he's going to win?" Davi turned to where Farien, Yao and the rest of his Squadron stood waiting, helmets under their arms. "Pilots to your fighters. We have a mission to complete." They nodded and pushed through the protestors, hurrying for their crafts.

"So we don't matter then?" Tela's arms went to her hips as she frowned at him in anger.

He cursed inwardly, wishing their emotions had no effect on him. But his heartbeat boomed in his ears. Why couldn't they listen to reason? "I care about you both very much. You're why I'm doing this."

Tela shook her head. "Ignoring us is not showing us you care."

Davi sighed and gave them each a quick kiss on the cheek. "You're not yourselves right now. I'll be back and we can talk then."

"Don't bother!" Tela whirled and stormed off as Miri stared at him sadly.

As Davi climbed the ladder to his cockpit, he glanced back at them and smiled. "I love you, Mother. Take care of her for a bit."

Miri just stepped back toward her group then pumped a fist in the air. "It's not your fight! It's not your fight!" They began chanting with her as he turned his attention back to his ship and slipped inside.

In moments, the fighters launched.

Xalivar watched from the bridge of his command ship, *Tarragon*, General Lucius at his side, as the armada formed up around them. It was a ragtag group, for sure, not the usual sight one would expect from a Boralian armada, but then, they'd put it together piecemeal, and strength was all that mattered. The combined firepower would be more than enough. Just a few hours. He could already taste the victory. The whole bridge smelled of it. Oh, how Tarkanius would be surprised. He chuckled at the thought. This was just the beginning; still, a day long awaited had arrived.

Admiral Dek issued orders as technicians chattered around them. Consoles beeped and lights flashed. Data flashed across the screens of monitors and scanners. The various ships' captains acknowledged their orders as Dek coordinated everything with ease. Pres and her men were aboard several ships prepared to land on the planet's surface as soon as they arrived at Tertullis.

Xalivar hadn't gone to war in decades. Adrenaline rushed through his veins as he took deep breaths and smiled. He looked around him. Manaen waited a few feet away from his Lord, ready at a moment's notice. Xalivar remembered standing beside his father and grandfather on the bridge of an old battleship as they conquered the slaves; the pride he'd felt at being with them. How proud they'd be seeing him today! The family honor would soon be restored. "It's a beautiful day for a battle, isn't it, Lucius?" Xalivar asked.

Lucius nodded somberly. Always so serious when it came to his duty. "Yes, my Lord."

Dek strolled toward them, nodding as he stopped a few feet away. "All ships are in position and awaiting your orders, my Lord."

Xalivar cleared his throat as Dek motioned to a comm tech nearby. The tech hit a button and a panel lit up, indicating the fleet channel was open. "My friends, thank you for joining me in this moment of triumph. Victory will soon be ours. You have shown great honor in your loyalty. And I honor you in my thoughts as we go forward into battle. Fight well. Our people's future depends on it. May the gods be with you."

He glanced around again as all those on the bridge watched him closely. Slowly, he raised his fist over his head. "Fleet, away!"

One by one the ships launched into FTL on a path to Tertullis. Xalivar's heart raced and he cackled with delight.

"Lord Niger, in the name of the High Lord Councilor and the Council of Lords, you are hereby placed under arrest for treason and murder," Simeon continued, reading the charges.

Lord Simeon himself led the LSP in the arrests. The first took place at a residential tower where Niger kept an apartment. He knew Davi and his friends had been attacked there earlier and took extra security in case. But Niger answered the door alone and, despite his wife's protests, was taken into custody with little fuss. To Simeon, it seemed almost like he'd been resigned to it. His name had already been leaked to the news as a suspect. And the man looked tired and defeated. Simeon found himself a little disappointed.

Lord Elul drew a blaster as soon as Simeon and the LSP officers entered the restaurant where he was dining.

"Lord Elul, you must stop this right now. We're here under

the full authority of the Council and the Palace." Simeon's eyes met Elul's in a cold stare.

For a moment, Simeon feared innocent civilians might get caught in the crossfire, but then restaurant staffers interfered— two men tackling Elul from behind and pinning his yelling form to the floor as the LSP men moved in and restrained him. Elul cursed, his voice booming, but at the moment he resembled more of a bratty child.

"You can't do this! I've done nothing! You have no proof!"

"We have sworn statements," Simeon answered as he bent to retrieve the fallen blaster.

Altogether, it was quite humiliating, made all the more so when some of the innocent civilians snapped photos which later turned up on the news. Simeon chuckled at that. Elul's pride would be permanently scarred, but given his likely sentence of life in prison for treason, it wouldn't matter much.

Simeon was relieved when it was over. LSP squads all over the planet were making similar arrests. He'd made it a point to be present at the arrests of the two Lords lest they try any political power moves with the LSP. Simeon witnessed both arrests in their entirety, so there could be no false claims or charges made by either suspect.

As he arrived back at his apartment, he wondered how Kray and Tarkanius were faring with their own responsibilities in the mission. Attack was imminent. He hoped their forces would prevail. If not, perhaps he would be the one to wind up with the life sentence. Ironically, he already felt like he had one.

Xalivar returned to the *Tarragon's* bridge after a brief meditation period to watch his fleet's arrival at Tertullis. He'd hardly relaxed at all, despite his best intentions, because his mind raced with the anticipation of his return to power. Images of the throne room and his triumphant return to the Palace filled his head. A glorious restoration of the honor of the Boralian Alliance would follow. *Ah, the satisfaction which shall be mine in avenging myself!* The thought of his enemies' suffering made him laugh. They should have known better than to oppose someone of his caliber. Men like Xalivar didn't lose.

Admiral Dek approached, interrupting Xalivar's thoughts. "My Lord, we're arriving at the planet now."

Xalivar smiled and nodded as they both turned and watched the star field normalize as the ships slipped out of FTL one by one and into formation again.

"Jamming on. Shields on full," Dek ordered as techs rushed to comply.

Tertullis glowed with a purple hue as they approached, and Xalivar saw a familiar gray shape. The High Lord Councilor's flagship, *Alcazar*, orbited the planet surrounded by her usual escort—two Borali destroyers, three squadrons of fighters, and two light cruisers. There was no sign of reinforcements, no indication that they expected anything but a routine visit. The Boralians still thought their conference was secret. Xalivar chuckled. He'd already won.

As he watched, Admiral Dek and General Lucius issued orders and the fleet dispersed into attack formations; the ships hauling ground troops slipping off toward the planet's surface. The Boralian ships began realigning as fighters abandoned the fleet and hurried to intercept Xalivar's force.

"Shall we offer them a chance to surrender, my Lord?" Lucius asked from his station between the scanners and comm stations.

Xalivar chuckled. "We'll show them the same mercy they showed me, General. Launch the attack."

"All ships, fire at will," Dek announced over the fleet comm channel.

Fighters burst from their mother ships, hurrying to intercept their incoming enemy counterparts. The larger ships began laying down a barrage of fire. Three VS28s exploded within a few seconds as the lasers found their marks. In moments, they'd be in range of the larger Boralian ships.

Xalivar turned to a panel on the rail nearby and punched a button. General Pres appeared on a small monitor. "Yes, my Lord."

"General, our victory is at hand. Securing the location is your priority. Except for the High Lord Councilor, eliminate anyone who gets in your way."

"By your command."

Xalivar chuckled as Pres turned and the screen went blank. Who'd have thought he'd be relying on a woman to command ground forces in his lifetime. Pres was capable. He'd never have allowed her to take command if she weren't, but still, Xalivar had instructed Lucius to stay in constant contact with her and ensure nothing went wrong. Women were weak. His own sister had demonstrated it clearly. They were too emotion-al to be trusted fully in such situations. But Pres had more than proven herself so far, and he expected she'd do well. If not, her time of service would be over along with her life. He could almost smell the adrenaline as men and women raced around him, performing their duties. Those seated sat on the edge of their seats, their eyes locked to screens and consoles, their brows furrowed with extreme concentration.

A blaring klaxon rose above the din. Xalivar whirled and looked at Dek and Lucius for answers.

"Incoming ships, my Lord," Dek offered as he stared puzzled at the scanners. He glanced over at a nearby tech.

"Boralian, Admiral. Four light cruisers, five destroyers and a flagship just slipped out of FTL behind us," the tech said with alarm as he punched commands into his console.

"What?! They had no idea we were coming!" Xalivar scowled at his commanders, demanding answers with his glare, but they were too busy assessing the situation to reply.

Davi shifted in his seat and loosened the strap on his helmet. His head was already starting to sweat. His Squadron had circled the High Lord Councilor's escort for an hour by the time Xalivar's armada appeared. Immediately, he issued the order and the fighter groups sped toward the incoming craft. "Shields on full. Battle ready. Fire at will."

"They're not even reacting," Virun remarked.

"They don't know what we have planned for them," Jorek said with a laugh.

"Focus," Farien said, all business. "There's still enough of them to do real damage."

"Oh yes, master Boralian," Jorek replied, voice dripping venom.

"That'll be enough! We're on the same side here and we all have to work together!" Davi took a deep breath, lowering his voice as he realized he'd been yelling into the comm. Tensions remained rife and he'd been struggling to keep his Squadron unified and morale high.

"This is our chance to take out all that resentment on Xalivar. He caused all this." Yao was one of the few who'd stayed above the tension. The Squadron members enjoyed his company, especially his tales about Farien and Davi in their wild younger days. Yao seemed to enjoy the attention. And since he and Dru were add-ons, he'd insisted on them working together as wingmen, despite Davi's reservations. Neither had spent much time in a fighter cockpit in the past year. Still, both were skilled pilots and Davi needed them. With the tensions already raised, he was reluctant to rattle things further by breaking up existing teams, so he acquiesced.

Dru laughed. "I wish he'd come out in a fighter and give us a fair shot."

Davi heard the smile in Nila's voice. "Xalivar's always preferred to let others do his dirty work."

Davi's scanner beeped and he saw blips appear behind the oncoming armada. Help had arrived. He wished he could see the look on Xalivar's face now.

Aron stepped off the freighter *Cordelia* with the rest of the High Lord Councilor's entourage at the starport on Idolis, where the alien leadership waited to meet with them. Idolis was a bold choice. Known for their loyalty and dedication to serving others, many Idolians served high officials, including Xalivar, so having a meeting on their planet would be public knowledge quickly.

However, with the precautions of no advanced notice of the meeting's purpose and Tarkanius' surreptitious arrival on a freighter, the High Lord Councilor still hoped to keep things low key as long as possible.

Tarkanius strode confidently into the large hangar the advance LSP team had cleared for their meeting and greeted each leader in turn. Pharah walked beside him as interpreter, as much for appearances' sake as practicality. It had been Pharah's idea, since he'd been the ambassador to recruit leaders for the conference. Aron was grateful to have such a smart, kind man helping them.

The humid hangar smelled like the depot on Vertullis where he and Sol used to work—sweat mixed with chemicals and industrial cleaners. Effort had been made to make it presentable, and Aron knew it looked nothing like this on a normal working day. Any starships and mech-bots had been cleared out, along with most of the equipment and supplies. It was an amazing feat for a few hours' notice, but the LSP men were that good. As a result, the site lent the conference a more official, pristine air.

The building vibrated under foot, one of the small tremors Idolis was known for this time of year, influence from Charlis as the smaller sun was at its nearest. A sweet scent filled his nostrils as Idolian servants arrived with pitchers of water, juice, Talis and other beverages and a selection of sweet rolls, pastries, cookies and other delights. They distributed these evenly around the table where the leaders sat, serving any who asked, then quietly slipped away.

Tarkanius raised a hand, and the chatter died down. "Friends, welcome. It's good to be with you." He smiled warmly. The aliens smiled back, at least their approximations of it. Despite being on the Council, Aron had yet to venture so far outside the radius of the inner system. The only aliens he'd encountered were those who came to official functions or served the government. Amongst the twenty or so in attendance, there were a few races represented whom he had never seen outside of datapad histories. His senses delighted in it. *Ah, the diversity of your creation, Father. How wonderful you are!*

Various aides sat in a ring a few feet behind them, circling the table, ready at a moment's notice to assist those they were there to serve. Takanius motioned and his majordomo punched codes into a datapad. Datapads around the table beeped as the leaders each received a copy.

"Friends, today will be a great day in the history of the Boralis system, I assure you. I'm here to tell you that the time has come for us to become one people—joint citizens—with joint determination reflecting our joint interests. I'm here to invite you to participate fully in government. And to assure you that we will work with you to create a unity few of us would have every dreamed possible before."

Aron watched the leaders' faces as they took in Aron's words, some listening through electronic translators; others relying on aides. When the High Lord Councilor finished, most of them looked delighted, at least in their eyes. Would they accept his sincerity after years of being ignored, mistreated, used by other High Lord Councilors? Aron felt a burst of hope rising within. For the first time, it looked possible.

Uzah coordinated ground troops from his armored Floater as the battle unfolded, in constant communication via monitor with Lord Kray and General Matheu on the bridge of the Borali flagship *Reliance*. She had arrived just after Xalivar with a fleet of ships and quickly engaged the enemy from behind, but Uzah and his troops had been waiting on the surface since before Xalivar's armada arrived. General Grif and his Boralian forces accompanied the High Lord Councilor to his rendezvous, leav-ing Uzah, Matheu and Kray to coordinate this ambush.

Platoons of men surrounded the starport in Cree, the Tertullian's industrial port, the leaked location of Tarkanius' summit. When the enemy landed outside the city and moved in, his men had attacked from their positions as soon as they'd come in range. Explosions dotted the horizon now, punctuated by clouds of smoke and the whirr of lasers. He'd already spotted General Pres, who was leading the attack. Uzah had always admired her intelligence and dedication to duty. It was unfortunate to have to face off against her now. Her soldiers seemed highly skilled and numerous. Uzah wished he'd brought a dozen additional platoons. But if Matheu and the air forces were successful, he wouldn't need them. He just had to hold out long enough.

"Can you hold your position?" Lord Kray asked.

"For a little while, yes," Uzah replied. "They're strong and they outnumber us, but if you are successful, it won't matter."

"We'll be successful," Kray replied. "All else depends on it." She and Uzah glanced toward Matheu, who remained his stoic self, his face giving away nothing.

He offered a curt nod. "We took them by surprise. I'm expecting reinforcements soon. They should be enough to assure victory. He had greater numbers than any of us anticipated."

"Perhaps we all relied too much on military discipline and our own sense of loyalty," Kray said.

Uzah sighed. "Clearly times are changing and so must we."

"If enemies were predictable, there'd be no wars," Matheu answered. "Military cannot function without discipline and loyalty. Fortunately, enough still believe in those things to join our cause."

Explosions rocked the Floater and Uzah grabbed a rail to hang on as men jostled around him. "I have incoming fire. I'll be in touch again." As the screen went blank, he glanced back to the battle and spotted Pres' troops with artillery on the rooftops. He opened a comm channel to his field commanders: "Get men to take out those artillery banks. We need to hold the high ground at all costs!"

After the WFR's fight, Uzah had hoped he'd never have to face battle again. He'd had enough of it in his lifetime, including the disastrous Delta V incident. *War is a game at which no one wins.* Already, sulfur mixed with human sweat tinged the air. He softly offered a prayer and then called out orders changing the coordinates of his column to avoid the artillery.

General Pres appeared poised and confident in the monitor even as explosions rocked her Floater and flashed in bright yellow and orange smoke behind her. Xalivar, Dek and Lucius convened with her from *Ta-ragon's* bridge, keeping up to date on the battle.

"Have you made it to the conference location?" Xalivar asked, look-ing for any sign of weakness. Their success depended on her troops on the ground.

"We're getting closer, but their resistance is concentrated in the surrounding area, so we're still fighting our way through," she said, eyes confident.

"Your men outnumber theirs and our ships outgun them," Dek said. "It's a matter of time."

The *Alcazar* and its accompanying cruisers were lightly armed. They'd been designed to evade attack with great speed, not enter into battle. So that left only the eight destroyers, four light cruisers and a flagship against Xalivar's twenty ships plus fighters. In sheer firepower, he'd already won. "Indeed. A great day we can savor." Xalivar smiled. "I can't wait to see Tarkanius in his defeat. Prepare my shuttle for the surface."

"My Lord, it's not safe," Lucius protested. "It would be better to wait until we've secured the planet."

Xalivar whirled to face him. "I decide when and where I go, General. Prepare my shuttle. It's obvious we're going to triumph and I want to savor the look on Tarkanius' face." He relished it even as he said it. Once Dek moved the *Tarragon* closer to the planet, the shuttle could hide behind its mass. The fighters would be too preoccupied with each other to respond in time.

"We'll take him alive and hold him for you, my Lord," Pres said.

"I plan to be there to watch," Xalivar said. He motioned, and Dek hurried off to issue the orders for the shuttle preparations.

"Shall I accompany you, my Lord," Lucius asked.

Xalivar shook his head. "You're needed here to wrap things up securely. You have my complete trust. I know you won't disappoint me." Xalivar nodded toward the monitor, and Pres then turned away to converse with Lucius.

"He's taking an awful risk," Pres said.

Lucius sighed. "It's our job to protect him, and we shall do what must be done."

Davi raced his VS28 in between and back out of the mass of fighting ships. Explosions jostled him in his seat and sweat soaked his flight suit. The past ninety minutes had been some of the most intense fighting he'd ever seen. Pilots were being shot down left and right. So far, he hadn't lost anyone from his Squadron, but, with the firepower they were up against, he feared that wouldn't last. Brie kept tight on his wing, with Nila and Farien, Virun and Jorek, Yao and Dru and two other pairs working as coordinated teams in their attacks.

"We can't even break free to attack the larger ships," Brie groused. "The air's too thick with fighters."

The larger ships had moved into close contact, Borali and rebels fighting side by side against each other. "They'll have to fend for themselves for now," Davi replied. "We have to concentrate on staying alive."

"So many lost already," Nila said, her voice soft.

He hoped his people could hold their emotions in check. As exper-ienced as they were, the losses were devastating. Another Squadron had lost half its members. At the present rate, Davi knew they couldn't hold out for long.

"Are we actually losing this?" Virun sounded dismayed. "We need those reinforcements."

Lasers exploded in a blinding flash of oranges and reds outside his blastshield. Davi spun his ship into a dive as he keyed the comm. "The General sent the call. They'll be here." He glanced at his scanner to see Brie diving alongside him. Both spun in an arc and came back around straight at the enemy ships, firing a barrage of blasts straight at them as they came in range. Brie's blasts decimated a fighter's wings and sent it spinning off into space. Davi's shot out another's engine and it limped hurriedly away to safety.

Davi switched off the Squadron channel and sent a call to

Reliance. Lord Kray and General Matheu appeared on the screen. "We need some help out here."

Kray nodded. "Hang in there, Captain. More ships are coming."

"We need to eliminate those fighters, so you can help Uzah on the surface," Matheu said.

"We're losing men like Gungors at a shooting range," Davi said, gritting his teeth as he fired at another enemy fighter passing into range. "Uzah will have to fend for himself a while longer."

Matheu nodded. "He's holding out for now."

Stoic even in battle, Davi envied the General for once. He spun his ship again to evade an enemy fighter attempting to get on his tail. "Can your ships do anything to help with these fighters?" He saw Brie shoot up from underneath and blast the enemy's underside, startling the pilot, who dove up and away.

"We fire on them whenever they come in range," Matheu said, eyes dropping to check a monitor as he spoke. "But they're as preoccupied with you as you are with them for the moment."

"Perhaps you can distract them." Davi glanced over as Brie slid up alongside and gave him a thumbs up and a big grin.

Matheu nodded. "We'll see what we can do, but mines and torpedoes would damage as many of your ships as theirs. Do your best, Captain."

"And be careful," Kray added. Then the screen went blank.

Davi sighed, switching back to the Squadron channel as another explosion flashed off to his right. "We're on our own a while longer. Use guerilla tactics if you have to. Just don't get shot."

"I think we're all on the same page on that one," Dru said with a laugh.

"Good to have you back with us, Dru," Nila said.

"I wouldn't have missed this for anything." He let off a rebel yell over the comm. Davi cringed as he turned down the volume then lined up another enemy fighter in his sights and fired.

Miri circled in front of Iraja's Starport with the other protestors as

Joram stood at the center, cheering them on. Many carried signs bearing phrases like: "Let my people go," "We quit," "Not our fight," and "We're Free." Joram wanted those Vertullians still cooperating with the Alliance to see that their people didn't support their dedication to the oppressors. The location was perfect, just outside the military hangars near the depot where Sol and Aron had worked for decades before Davi was born. The protestors were a hodgepodge of men, women and youths of all ages, shapes and sizes. They were dressed from casual to formal, some having come directly from work or on a lunch break. If Joram had his wish, they would have quit their jobs to join the movement full time, but people had to eat and not everyone had the same resources.

"Let us go! Let us go!" The chant continued like a mantra around her, a cacophony of voices, who'd been saying it so long it had become a mishmash rather than a unified call.

Miri saw Tela across the circle with her placard reading "Not Our Fight." They'd had no news of the battle, despite Miri's regular checks of her datapad. Tarkanius had enforced a news silence to protect the secrecy of his ruse. Still, she knew someone was getting reports. If she could sneak away long enough, she might be able to find a friend in the military and get the status. She said a silent prayer to the gods to keep Davi safe.

A cold wind tousled her hair. A mass of clouds had settled overhead, only adding to her somber move. The planet was moving into fall now and with the changing colors of the foliage came changing weather. It wasn't an ideal day for a protest. Joram didn't even seem to have noticed.

As she turned to circle back to the other side, following the woman ahead of her, Miri spotted two familiar faces approaching. Lura waved as she and Sol stopped outside the line. They stared at Joram, who hadn't noticed them yet. Miri waved back, questioning them with her eyes. Both looked tired and worried. Miri made a decision and slid out of line, moving toward them.

Lura embraced her as she drew near. "Miri! We're worried about Davi. There's no news."

Miri nodded. "I haven't gotten any either. There's a blackout at Tarkanius' orders." She turned to hug Sol.

"We thought maybe Joram could help," Sol said, nodding toward the marchers as he hugged her back.

Miri glanced over at the protestors. Joram was patting people on the back and offering words of encouragement. A man slipped through the line and approached the Governor—some kind of messenger. She'd seen him cross the lines several times that morning. From his business attire, close-cropped blonde hair and tanned skin, Miri assumed he must be one of Joram's aides. The two men conversed silently a moment as Joram scanned a datapad the messenger handed to him. Then Joram smiled, nodded, and the messenger hurried away again. As he did, Joram noticed Miri, Sol and Lura. Smiling, he stepped through the line and hurried toward them.

"Sol! Lura! So glad you've finally decided to join us." He shook their hands with fervor, smiling. "It's a great day for our people."

Sol and Lura nodded, not sharing his elation, but Joram didn't even notice. "We came hoping you could help us, Joram." Sol's eyes met the Governor's.

"I'm helping all of us by leading this movement." Joram's jolliness didn't miss a beat.

"We've heard nothing on the fighting," Lura burst out. "Just a little news. Surely with your connections—"

"It's not our fight." Joram waved dismissively. "We serve our oppressors no more."

"Our own people are fighting with them in this," Sol said. "If Xalivar wins, it will mean great danger for us."

"Which is why we must leave and make our home elsewhere," Joram said, still unsympathetic to their concerns.

"Please, Joram, we've known you so long," Lura pleaded, placing a hand on Joram's arm. "It's our son out there!"

His eyes glowed with fervor. "A grown man who made his choice. What will yours be?" Despite her agreement, Miri wanted to slap him.

The messenger returned and motioned to Joram. "Excuse me," Joram said when he saw him. "The blackout applies to all of us I'm afraid. I have important matters to attend to."

More important than the feelings of your friends? Miri fought to control her anger. She believed in Joram, but his coldness toward her friends had her temperature rising. She started toward him, listening intently as she drew near.

"How long until we know for sure?" Joram asked.

"It's imminent from the military reports," the messenger answered, then clamped his mouth shut as he saw her watching them.

Miri's fury exploded as she rushed toward them. "Not our fight? Yet you've been getting regular reports all morning." She grabbed for the datapad, but the messenger yanked it out of reach and stuffed it inside his coat.

"This is government business," Joram said with a frown. "Not civilian, Miss Rhii."

"Don't talk to me like that," Miri scolded. "My security clearance is still as high as or higher than yours. I have knowledge of things you don't."

Joram motioned toward the circling protestors as the messenger hurried off. "Your duty is with the others. Please. We must get back to work here."

"Not until you tell us what news you have of the fighting," Miri said as Sol and Lura reacted to her words and hurried over.

"You have news?" Lura looked hopeful for the first time since she'd arrived.

"I told you, the blackout is for all of us," Joram turned to walk back toward the protestors, but Miri grabbed his arm.

"I heard what your messenger said about military reports," Miri said, squeezing his arm until he winced. "Tell us right now. What do you know?" She moved forward, her face inches from his.

Joram yanked his arm free of her grasp and stepped back, looking ready to snap at her. But then, seeing their faces, he sighed, hesitating a moment before: "We're losing men left and right. I have no word of specific personnel. But the battle is all but lost." Then he spun and hurried back to join the circling protestors.

Lura's shoulders sank at the news and Miri felt her own panic rising. Her heart thundered in her chest. Sol put an arm around his wife to comfort her, but both couldn't even manage to meet Miri's eyes. "I'm sure he's fine," Miri said. "He has to be." She said it as much to reassure herself as Sol and Lura.

Lura nodded. "We'll be praying in the chapel." Sol reached out and grabbed Miri's hand, and they walked off together toward the Starport. Miri didn't know what to do. She didn't share their religion. But yet, she was consumed with worry. How dare Joram keep this from them! She stood there watching the protestors as she offered her own silent pleas to the gods to protect her son.

The Tertullian Ambassador, Adoo Kwase, was the first to ask: "What happens if we align ourselves with you and you lose?"

Tarkanius handled the issue with poise. "We can't lose. That's why we need your help. The future of our entire system and all of us with it depends on victory." Aron resisted the urge to shout "amen."

The High Lord Councilor scanned the faces around the table—Italites, Regalians, Xanthians, Idolians—every planet in the system was represented. Red, purple, green—eyes of every shade, skin tones too. Some appeared almost human, like the Xanthians and Tertullians; others were more clearly alien. All spoke Common well, but most had accents. None used a translator—as diplomats all went through years of language training. It was a necessity given the ruling race's past refusal to compromise in dealing with them. Electronic translators could malfunction or be accused of being inaccurate or even get it wrong. Direct communication avoided issues and the rulers of the Boralians had a long history of deliberate mistakes against other races. No one could afford to take chances.

"I know you've been mistreated, marginalized, ignored. It's time for that to change. We changed it for the Vertullians, now we extend the same invitation to you. Come alongside, work with us, help us make this system strong and united. It can't survive unless we do. Help us defeat Xalivar and leave a past riddled with misrule behind." Tarkanius' eyes made it clear he meant every word.

A fruity Idolian incense floated past Aron's nose. Famous for its calming effects, the incense was clearly intended to aid the civility of the present proceedings, but, although their voices remained business-like, the leaders themselves dripped with tension.

The Xanthian ambassador, Quatol, spoke next. "You seem to be a different man than the type we are used to. Yet you cannot live forever. What assurance would we have that the one who follows you won't go back to the old ways?"

"The assurance that history and tradition rule the hearts of men as strong as love and fear. If we start now and integrate completely, by the time a replacement comes you will be able to help in selecting him. And you will have the power to stop him from taking back your rights."

"It's an awful lot to promise," Quatol said, clearly doubtful of Tarkanius' ability to pull it off. The Xanthians had tentative relations with the government, which is why their planet had such successful black markets. They had long flaunted their rebelliousness before the system but always paid their taxes and otherwise followed the laws, cooperating when needed. So the government hadn't bothered to crack down on them. Quatol was one of the older ambassadors here, so Aron suspected his personal feelings were stronger than most of the others.

"If we don't try, it will never happen," Tarkanius leaned back in his chair. "This system is home to all of us. Don't you want the same rights as everyone else?"

"We serve the same rights as every other race," the Idolian ambassador, Kanaan, said. "You came here, took over our planets, called us 'aliens,' despite the fact that we were born here. And now you talk about rights? We were born with such rights, but that didn't stop you."

Tarkanius nodded. "And I'm sorry for it. Sincerely. Which is why I want to change it."

The alien ambassadors kept their eyes on Pharah and Aron

through-out the meeting, as if trying to read their minds. It made Aron self-conscious about every gesture or reaction he made, but Pharah seemed at ease. He cleared his throat from the seat beside Aron and smiled, panning the faces around the table. "We have an opportunity here, an opportunity unlike any we've had before. Some, like me, have been given extraordinary chances and worked closely with the Boralians. I can assure you there are good people among them. Most of them, in fact, are good. You can build a relationship of mutual respect and trust, but it takes all of us to do it, and we all face risks in doing so."

"We trust you, Pharah, but you have lived among these people so long, you have a soft place for them," Adoo said. "We have to keep perspective here."

Pharah nodded. "Ask Lord Aron. His people were more mistreated than any of us, and yet he is willing to work with them." Pharah turned and smiled at Aron, a sparkle in his purple eyes.

Aron well understood their concerns, because he'd shared them once himself, but Tarkanius had earned his trust and leaders like Simeon and Kray inspired hope as well. He nodded. "The majority have been very supportive. Until the efforts of Xalivar and his agents inflamed old anger, we were living peacefully and quietly together. Hatred is taught, and a hard thing to unlearn, but we can do it if we work together. Combined, we'll equal their numbers. And if we're all united, we'll be a force to reckon with."

"What of the movement amongst your people to leave?" Kanaan asked.

Meeting the eyes of each ambassador in turn, Aron spoke slowly, choosing each word. "Political movements of all sorts arise. I'd rather see us stay. But to stay, we need support. And having you on our side would make a big difference." Aron truly believed it, even if he doubted Joram and his followers would ever change their minds.

"You're giving us much to think about," Adoo said, sitting back and rubbing his chin as he thought. Several aides leaned in to whisper to their Ambassadors, reading off datapads. Aron had heard no reports of the battle, but he hoped it was going well.

The last thing they needed was negative reports to influence the ambassador's decisions.

Uzah sat in his Floater atop a rise looking down at the devastation his troops were enduring. Explosions launched men into the air before his eyes, their screams mixing with the rumbling as debris, blood, flesh and foliage flew around them. If help didn't arrive, and soon, he'd have no choice but to withdraw.

He typed a code into the comm and watched the monitor flicker as Kray and Matheu appeared. "We're running out of time. I need air support or it's over down here." An explosion boomed in the valley behind him, punctuating his words.

"We don't have anyone we can send you," Matheu said, shaking his head.

"Free up three or four, or I'm calling for a retreat," Uzah answered, firm in his resolve. He knew Matheu wouldn't refuse help if he could spare it, but still, this was an emergency, and he needed to impart the urgency to the others in command.

"We'll find someone," Kray replied. "Hang in there!"

Uzah nodded as he heard a whistling overhead and quickly dove out of his Floater to the ground. The Floater exploded into flames behind him. Dirt clods slapped his head as he felt grass ricochet off his bare neck. He motioned to his driver and aides, who'd also made it out in time: "Let's hope they send those ships!"

Davi circled around and blasted two fighters as they stayed locked on Farien's and Nila's tails. Brie fired off her own lasers and the ships finally exploded into fireballs of orange, yellow and red.

"Thanks, Cousin!" Nila called.

"That was way too close," Farien added.

Davi saw streaks of black on the fuselages of both fighters. No one in his Squadron had gone undamaged at this point, not even himself. In a couple cases, pilots were lucky to still be flying. He'd have sent them back for repairs if he had anyone to replace them.

Davi signaled Farien as he came alongside and they switched to a private channel. "We can't hold out like this much longer. Suggestions?"

"Do you have a white flag?"

Davi chuckled. "Think Xalivar would honor it?"

"Oh yeah, he's always seemed really merciful to me."

Davi smiled. "At least Yao and Dru are holding up better than I thought."

"We need relief, or we're done for. All of us." Farien sounded as exhausted as Davi felt.

Davi nodded. "Matheu promises they're coming."

Farien sighed. "Maybe you should ask that God of yours to speed them up. Too many already dead."

Davi sighed and said a quick prayer silently as Farien slid off to rejoin Nila, and Brie closed up in formation on his own wing. His comm beeped. "Hang on. Command's calling." He switched channels, and Matheu and Kray appeared on the monitor.

"We need some ships to provide air support on the ground," Matheu said right away.

"We're not exactly rolling in extras."

"Can you spare two or three?" Kray asked, her eyes pleading.

Davi's ship rocked as an enemy's lasers exploded just right of his blastshield window. "Sure. Why not? We're already dying out here." He sighed. "Sorry. I'll find somebody." Clicking off the comm, he glanced down at his combat computer. Its calculations dutifully warned him they were outgunned and outnumbered badly with no chance to win. He spun in an arc to chase down the enemy who'd engaged him, while mentally running through his Squadron to decide whom he could spare.

"Is my shuttle ready?" Xalivar stepped out of the lift onto the *Tarragon's* bridge and strode toward Admiral Dek and General Lucius as they watched the scanners.

The officers exchanged a look of concern then turned to face him. "My Lord, it's still very dangerous," Lucius said.

"Great men gain through great risk," Xalivar said. "Pull out so we can get through to the planet."

Dek nodded. "Of course, my Lord. Still, perhaps you could wait a few more—"

"I've waited a year, Admiral! I will wait no longer! My victory is now! I want Tarkanius' surrender delivered in person. Tell them to be ready to depart in five minutes." Xalivar turned and marched back toward the lift, headed for his quarters, and then the landing bay. He heard Dek and Lucius issuing orders behind him and smiled. At least, they knew when to shut up and obey. He needed more men like that.

The protestors' lines were thinning. It was obvious and Joram looked annoyed. Miri kept marching, but even she was tempted to leave as she watched another couple headed for the Starport.

"Where does everyone keep disappearing to?" Tela asked, slipping up beside Miri.

"The Chapel, I think. Lura and Sol are leading prayer for those fighting."

"I thought we were protesting this fight?"

Miri turned and searched Tela's eyes. "You don't mean that. You have friends out there, including Davi."

Tela stared back a moment then her shoulders sank as she sighed. "I know. But this has kept my mind off of it."

"I appreciate the loyalty of those who remain," Joram said through a loudspeaker, as he launched into another speech intended to inspire and motivate them. As he rambled on, Miri realized the words that had once lit a fire in her now left her numb.

She halted and held a hand out to stop Tela. "I can't keep doing this. I want to go pray too." She didn't know who she'd pray to. She didn't share their faith, but being with them would comfort her. And she wanted to comfort them as well.

Their eyes met, and Miri saw the worry Tela was trying so hard to hide. Reaching out, she clasped the young woman's hand and squeezed. Tela's eyes softened and she nodded. The two women slipped from the line together, ignoring Joram's angry stares, and hurried toward the Starport after the others.

With Jorek and Virun providing air cover for Uzah's troops, Davi found his Squadron stretched thin. Another pair had been sent back to *Reliance* for repairs after suffering unsustainable damages, leaving Davi and Brie, Farien and Nila, Yao and Dru and the remains of two other squadrons to fight. Being spread out over a large area made covering for each other increasingly difficult, if not impossible, requiring them each to face twice as many targets as they'd faced before.

Farien's rebel yell came over the comm, followed by Nila's. "That's two more, Captain!" Davi could sense his friend grinning from ear-to-ear.

"Never thought we'd be shooting down VS28s with our own," Nila commented. "Still feels good when they're the enemy."

"Yes, it does," Farien laughed.

"Try and stay focused despite your enjoyment, okay?" Davi teased. He noticed a blip moving away on his scanner and turned to look. The *Tarragon* was moving out of range and pulling away from the fighting.

"Where's *Tarragon* going?" Brie wondered.

"I don't know," Davi said.

"Just let me finish cleaning up these fighters and I'll give them the attention they deserve," Farien said as he and Nila swooped in for another run against oncoming enemy fighters.

A flash from the *Tarragon* caught Davi's attention, and he turned again to see a shuttle launching. *They're launching a shuttle in the middle of battle?* It was the kind of small shuttle used by dignitaries and important businessmen. Now he knew why the flagship had withdrawn. Someone was trying to get down to the planet's surface.

"Do we intercept that shuttle?" Yao's voice came back over the comm.

Davi glanced up and saw Yao and Dru circling back. They were between him and the *Tarragon*, easily within range of the shuttle.

"It's got to be someone important," Dru commented. "Xalivar?"

"Xalivar's too scared to put himself at risk like that," Yao said.

"Unless he thinks he's already won," Brie suggested.

"Whoever it is, they're on the wrong side, and last I checked we were still fighting," Farien said.

Davi hesitated, wanting to go himself, but his computer put him too far out of range to catch it. Then an explosion rocked his fighter again and his eyes searched for the source. Two black stealth ships, like they'd encountered off Eleni 1 a month past, appeared against the starfield, cannons blazing. He fired back and knew he'd never make it. "Take them out, but keep clear of the *Tarragon's* weapons."

"We'll be careful," Dru said.

"Dru, stay with me," Yao answered, already focused on the mission.

As he and Brie exchanged fire with the stealth fighters, the two wing-men peeled off and headed for the departing shuttle. The *Tarragon* was between it and the fighters as the shuttle arced toward the planet below.

Bordox and his assassins snuck almost to the edge of the battlefield unnoticed, their small, dark fighter-sized craft blending in with the star-field. There were so many other ships, the scanners would confuse them and he fired off decoys to add to the confusion as they drew near. It didn't take him long to locate Xander's squadron, and then it was just a matter of watching behavior before he spotted Rhii himself. Xalivar could try to keep them out of this fight, but it wouldn't happen. Obed had sent them to sabotage Xalivar's ship and give him an in with the Council as an ally again, but Bordox had a debt to settle first.

He almost couldn't sit still as they moved around the edge of the battlefield toward the *Tarragon* together. Adrenaline had his heart racing and his head felt light, almost as if he were floating inside the cockpit. As they drew near to Xalivar's ship, he spotted a shuttle heading for the planet and two VS28s racing to intercept. The perfect distraction!

"Go after that shuttle!" he ordered his men. "It must be someone important."

As the assassins turned off to comply with his instructions, Bordox veered off and headed for Rhii.

"W'ere 're you going?" his wingman called into the radio.

"To deal with an old friend, just hold position and follow my lead."

"Our ord'rs—"

"I know what the orders are! I'm in charge! Now shut up and follow me!"

Stupid Lhamors! They'd served a purpose, but he couldn't wait to be rid of them. They refused to just shut up and follow orders! They didn't respect him any more than anyone else, but he'd show them all! This was it! His moment of triumph. And no one could spoil it for him now.

Circling in, he brought Rhii's VS28 into his sights and let loose a bar-rage of fire.

Yao let Dru lead the way, keeping a close eye on their proximity to the *Tarragon*. The larger ship's cannons could blast them to bits if they got in range, and Dru seemed to be cutting it close.

"Watch it, Dru! Change your angle, or you'll have those cannons on you!"

Dru adjusted course. "Fear not, Prof, I'm on this shuttle." Dru sounded as tired as Yao felt, but Yao was determined. He hadn't ever been in battle. He'd seen lots of friends die, even shot down a couple classmates. War was as horrible as he'd expected but they had to win. Everything depended on it.

The shuttle spotted them and shifted course, arcing back

upward slightly. Dru and Yao stayed on its tail.

"Fire and get out! They're headed back toward their—"

Dru and the *Tarragon* both fired simultaneously. Dru's lasers singed the shuttle, but then the cannon blasts struck his engines. In moments, he was spinning out of control toward the planet.

"Dru!" Yao spun his fighter but saw there was nothing he could do. The young cadet's fighter disappeared into the planet's atmosphere and turned back to the shuttle. "I lost Dru!" He fumed in silence, rage building as he hoped the young cadet could land safely on the surface.

Tensing in his seat as he focused, he aimed himself for the shuttle, hoping to come upon it at an angle that kept him out of range of the cannons.

"Forget it, Yao, it's a trap!" he heard Davi warn over the radio.

Then his scanner flashed as it locked on target and Yao fired. He immediately arced his trajectory to head back out. Moments later, his own ship rocked with explosions. The cannons had gotten his right engine. He felt his ship lose power.

The shuttle arced back, clearly deciding Yao was no longer a threat. It was headed for the planet again.

"Pull out, Yao!" Davi ordered.

Yao made a decision. "Negative. I'm taking this guy out."

He turned his fighter and put his remaining engines to full, racing after it.

"Hang on, Yao, we're coming!" Farien called.

But Yao knew help couldn't get there in time. Then his ship rocked again. Another blast from the flagship. He hadn't realized he'd flown back in range when he turned after the shuttle. His ship slowed as he lost another engine, but he was still faster than the shuttle. The *Tarragon* was turning in pursuit. Whoever was on the shuttle was that important. And no matter what, Yao was going to make him pay. His fingers clamped tighter around his controls.

Davi and Brie swooped and dove, exchanging fire with the stealth fighters, while also dealing with whatever VS28s paid them any mind. The fighting was pure chaos. It took intense focus just to fly, let alone lining up targets and firing off the cannons.

"Who are these guys?" Brie wondered aloud.

"Xalivar must have done more than rely on stolen Boralian ships," Davi replied as he dodged oncoming fire from the lead stealth ship.

Davi's hands tensed on his controls as he spotted Farien and Nila racing to assist Yao, enemy fighters hot in pursuit. It wasn't like Yao to be so aggressive. Maybe the loss of Dru and so many others had him on edge. The *Tarragon* turned in pursuit. "The *Tarragon's* chasing a fighter? Who's on that shuttle?"

"Whoever it is, I'm on them," Yao said. His voice sounded oddly cold. The exhaustion must be getting to him.

"No! Pull out and get to safety!" Davi ordered.

"Just one more shot, first."

Davi fought the urge to race over and protect his friend. He couldn't get there in time. Explosions rocked his right wing and he turned his attention back to evading and led Brie in an arc onto the tails of the fighters chasing Farien and Nila instead.

A stealth ship stayed tight on Davi's tail.

"These guys are starting to piss me off now," he said.

"You get ours, we'll take care of yours," Farien said as Davi lined up on the fighter giving his friend a run for his money. Glancing quickly over, he saw Brie lined up on the other. Just a few seconds and they could take off to help Yao and let Farien and Nila knock the stealth fighters off their tails.

Davi and Brie fired just as the *Tarragon's* gunners took out Yao's last engine.

Yao fired at the shuttle and missed.

"Yao!" Davi cringed as sweat dripped down and stung his eyes. He blinked it away as he heard:

"It's too late. One option." Yao sounded resigned.

"What do you mean? Just eject." Davi accelerated, desperate to help his friend.

Instead, Yao turned sharply and angled at the shuttle. The shuttle tried to evade, but Davi saw the angle was too sharp. They were going to crash. And then he realized it was intentional.

"No, Yao! Wait!"

Both ships went up as they collided, disintegrating into minute particles in a flash of orange and yellow light. The shuttle and Yao's fighter both gone in seconds.

"Yao!" Davi heard himself scream, but it was like he was somewhere else. He blinked, hoping the sweat fogging his eyes had created an illusion. But Yao's fighter and the shuttle were nowhere to be found. Davi tried to shake off his numbness, but he couldn't grasp it. Yao was really gone.

Alarms sounded in his cockpit and he checked his scanner—a huge mass of incoming craft. In moments, the computer identified them. The Borali fleet was here. The tide of the battle had just turned.

"All squadrons return to base," Matheu's voice ordered over the comm. "All squadrons return to base."

Davi saw Farien and Nila turn and head back for the *Reliance*. Then Brie did the same. Davi froze, still trying to come to grips with what had happened. It couldn't be true. Yao couldn't be gone.

Bordox watched the fighters explode and saw Xander's VS28 wobble. He had him lined up almost perfectly, then two other VS28s circled back and tried to get on his tail.

"Fall back and deal with those two while I handle these," he ordered his wingman.

"Your fath'r instruct'd—"

"Stop quoting my damn father to me!" Bordox fired but missed as Rhii's fighter suddenly dove. Then the VS28s behind him were firing as his wingman obeyed and fell back. Bordox had his hands full and lost track of Rhii while he responded. He launched into a steep climb, firing decoys to confuse the battle scanners. Decoys hadn't been employed in decades, but that made them all the better, since modern combat equipment wasn't designed to handle them. The two VS28s shots went wide, following the decoys.

Bordox whooped and turned back to look for Rhii when a shot came from his right and exploded one of his engines. He cursed and turned to see one of his own stealth fighters firing on him.

"What are you doing?!" he screamed. "It's me, you idiot!"

"Your fath'r instruct'd us to disabl' you if you deviat'd from orders," one of the Lhamors answered. The stealth ship fired again, narrowly missing Bordox's other engine. He swerved right into an arc.

"Stop! Damn you!" He was cut off as his other engine failed, and his ship was floating under no power.

"Orders." The Lhamor replied. His wingman appeared on his right side and the other stealth fighter on the left. They used the fighter's tractor beams to lock on and led him off toward the planet away from Rhii. Bordox spotted the other stealth fighters lining up around them for cover.

Pres heard a whistling overhead. Turning in her Floater seat, she saw a damaged VS28 spinning toward them. "Get us moving! Now!"

Her driver reacted with surprise but slid the Floater into gear.

"Hurry!" She motioned toward the incoming fighter.

Her driver's eyes widened with panic, and she was pushed back in her seat as the Floater shot forward. Just in time. The VS28 exploded behind them, leaving a crater in the ground.

"Get us out of here!" She ordered as the comm beeped.

"Code seventy-seven!" Lucius said as he appeared on the monitor, looking shaken and disheveled. "ASAP!"

"Full retreat? Why?" Pres couldn't believe her ears, but she'd never seen Lucius looking so frazzled.

"No time to argue. A whole Boralian fleet is here. Pull out and get back now! We're leaving!"

The monitor went dead as her mind raced. She didn't have time to save all of her men. How could she abandon them? Her driver was already turning back toward their ships.

Pres' fingers raced to send codes through the computer to her men.

He'd had to push his engines to get there, but Davi reached the spot where Yao's fighter had been and slowed his ship, stunned. The enemy fighters paid him no mind as they responded to the arrival of the Boralian fleet. He ran his scanners through the paces searching for any sign of his friend. But it came up clear for VS28s. Just the *Tarragon* and her cruiser escorts remained there. He couldn't believe his friend Yao was gone. It couldn't be. Tears streamed down his face so fast he could barely see his controls. He felt numb and struggled to breathe. Who was on that fighter? Who was responsible? The family necklace weighed heavy against his chest. He thought of the images on it: laborers, soldiers, farmers and priests—those were the people he was fighting for. And they were more than just his flesh and blood. Yao was family, too. In pure rage, he screamed and accelerated straight for the *Tarragon*, targeting her engines.

Ignoring his computer this time, he made mental calculations. "This is for Yao!"

Then the big ship accelerated, her FTL engines lighting up as she took off like a streak and disappeared.

"Nooooo!" Hands clenched around the controls, Davi unleashed his weapons at her as he raced through her exhaust trail, but there was nothing he could do. Both Yao and the *Tarragon* had disappeared.

Epilogue

The footsteps echoed across the hangar as the aide ran toward the table. Aron wasn't the only one who looked up and took notice, despite the intensity of the ongoing conversation. An Idolian aide approached Kanaan, leaning over to whisper in his ear. Aron watched the ambassador's face for a reaction. His face went from disbelief to amazement to shock in a matter of seconds. Then the aide stood, waiting for a response, but the ambassador only waved him away.

"If we had some sort of guarantee," Quatol was saying. "Good faith only goes so far, Lord Tarkanius."

"The whole world has changed," Kanaan said, as if he could bear the secret no more, the news burst from him.

Everyone at the table turned, puzzled. "You have something to add?" Adoo asked.

Kanaan gave only a slight nod, still in shock. The news must be something very serious. "Xalivar is dead."

"What?" Tarkanius looked stunned. The others appeared uncertain. What was he talking about?

"Killed in a shuttle near Tertullis, during the battle. His troops have fled. Many pilots died. One gave his life to destroy the shuttle."

Xalivar dead?! Could it really be true? Everyone reached for their datapads, typing as furiously as Aron did, searching for information.

"How do we know Xalivar was aboard?" Quatol asked the question hanging unanswered in most of their minds.

"A shuttle from the *Tarragon* headed to the planet in the midst of a battle where Xalivar believed this conference was being held. Who else would be aboard?" Kanaan's voice was more confident.

"We must know for certain," Adoo said.

"Preliminary battle reports are frequently inaccurate," Pharah said, nodding.

"Xalivar's troops have fled in fear," Quatol said with a pleased smile as he confirmed the news. "They are defeated."

"It is a glorious day!" Kanaan exclaimed, smiling now too as he transitioned from shock to glee.

"News we've hoped for many years," Adoo nodded.

"We must know for sure," Tarkanius cautioned. He still looked stunned as his aides buzzed behind him, working to obtain fuller reports.

"If this is true, we are in," Quatol said.

Kanaan's head bobbed vigorously. "And we as well."

Adoo watched them as several other representatives joined the chorus. Finally, he cleared his throat. "We echo their sentiments. Let us hope the news proves true."

Tarkanius glanced at Aron, amazed by the turn of events. "We will gather the data and ascertain its truthfulness as soon as possible, of course." He sat back in his chair as an aide handed him a cup of hot Talis. Tarkanius sipped slowly. Aron knew exactly how he felt. Xalivar's death would ensure a new beginning, a new age of certainty for everyone. Much of the chaos might end just from the news. Protestors would lose their will. Their hopes would be dashed, while, for those on the other side, hopes would be renewed. It was a remarkable moment.

Aron closed his eyes and offered a prayer for peace.

Word had reached them at the chapel within two hours. The flagship *Tarragon* had fled. The Boralians had won. A few other ships had been captured, but several got away along with part of the forces on the ground. Still, there'd be a lot of courtmartials for treason in the near future.

The news of Dru and Yao's deaths was a shock. Dru had come through training with Tela, helped with the Resistance. It was like losing a brother, and Yao, he'd become beloved quickly. She could only imagine how Davi must feel. But had Yao really taken out Xalivar? If it was true, it made him a certified hero. He'd saved them all!

She thought back on all of the tension between Davi and her over the past few months. She'd really been hard on him, and, reflecting now, she wasn't sure why she'd been so emotional. Certainly the reunion with her father had reignited old fears of abandonment and loss and feelings of protectiveness as well. That Davi wanted to protect her, given their relationship and his own recent reunion with his parents—especially his own father—now made some of her reactions seem inconsiderate and selfish. Most of it, they could have talked through, if she'd just made more effort.

She said a joyful prayer of thanks to God for the news of Davi's safety and the victory of the Boralian forces. But with Yao, Dru and other friends lost, Davi would now face the very feelings Tela herself had been wrestling with. She promised herself she'd help him through it. They could help each other. The relief and happiness which flooded her heart upon hearing he was alive reminded her how much she loved him; how much she still wanted the future they'd dreamed of together. Yet her throat tightened and her heart ached for the pain she knew he was experiencing now.

That night, she gathered with Davi's family and other families as the first wave of troops returned to Legallis' starport. Davi and Farien couldn't even meet her eyes. Nila and Brie hugged and cried as they stepped off the shuttle. Everyone who'd fought looked devastated from more than mere exhaustion.

Tela's eyes met Davi's and he fell against her, weeping. She wrapped her arms around him and wept with him. Lura and Sol and Miri moved in to lend support, whispering words of encouragement. Each embraced Davi in turn as he cried. It dawned her that she was no longer alone. For years, she'd grown used to depending on no one but herself yet here she was surrounded by family, even after Telanus' death.

"I'll miss them, too, Davi," Tela managed to say. It had been so long since she held him that she'd forgotten how comforting it was. She pulled him closer, knowing he needed her right now as much as she needed him.

Sol hesitated a moment, glancing at Miri. "Is it true about Xalivar?"

Davi's eyes grew sadder. "We think so. Unconfirmed but the flagship left right after." He glanced at Miri. Tela knew both still cared about Xalivar despite all that had happened.

Miri nodded and forced a smile. "Then they're heroes and they've saved us all! Long live the memory of Yao and Dru!"

"Yao and Dru!" Others around them heard and picked up the call. Soon everyone in the hangar was shouting it out like a mantra. Tears dried forgotten on cheeks as frowns became smiles and pride filled the eyes of everyone present. Except Davi.

"I ordered him to pull out. He wouldn't listen."

Tela pulled Davi's head against her shoulder again. "People do what they have to in battle. He wanted Xalivar."

Davi nodded. "I just can't believe he's gone."

"Thank God for your victory," Sol said, and reached out to squeeze Davi's arm.

As the news of Xalivar's death spread around them, some cheered, others laughed, everyone's moods brightened. Tela hoped the official confirmations proved it to be true.

She focused her concern on Davi.

"Thank God you're safe," she said as she held him.

"Amen." Lura caressed Davi's back and shoulders.

There'd be time to sort it all out tomorrow. It was a day they'd never forget, but they'd find a way through. And for the first time in weeks, Tela felt hopeful.

Glossary

Agora—One of Vertullis' two moons.

Auto-bot—Prototype robot created to perform basic human tasks.

Barge—A smaller transport used primarily to carry loads between neighboring planets.

Boralis—The larger of two suns in the solar system.

Bots—Robots designed to perform tasks formerly assigned to humans.

Cab-bot—Bots designed to drive air taxis and interact as tour guides with passengers.

Charlis—The smaller of the solar system's two suns.

Chrono—Watch.

Council of Lords—The elected body that works with the High Lord Councilor to lead the Borali Alliance.

Courier Craft—Round, silver craft designed to carry supplies and papers between planets in the solar system with light speed drives.

Daken—Large, blue, predatory birds, coveted for their beautiful feathers.

E-post—Messages sent over the computer, like e-mail. Usually sent via computer terminals or kiosks in public places.

Feruca—A black fruit with a thin skin and soft pulp.

Floater—A floating platform with two seats facing a control panel at the front which moves by manipulating the air underneath to float above the ground. The largest floaters have benches to hold as many as twenty troops—more if ten stand in the middle. Smaller models are typically designed for four or five passengers.

Gixi—A round, purple fruit grown in orchards on Vertullis and Italis with a delicious, tender pulp and sweet juice.

Gungors—Six-legged brown animals with yellow manes raised for their tasty meat.

High Lord Councilor—Leader of the Borali Alliance, elected by the Council of Lords. The post typically passes down through members of the same family until the Council decides new blood is required.

Iraja—Capital city of Vertullis.

Italis—Ninth planet in the solar system, home to the Lhamors.

Jax—A blue and oblong fruit with crispy pulp and a bitter taste, which becomes tart and sweeter when boiled; often used as an ingredient in salads.

Legallis—Seventh and largest planet in the solar system and capital of the Borali Alliance.

Legon—Capital city of Legallis and headquarters of the Borali Imperial government.

Lhamor—Native to the planet Italis. Lhamors have green-scaled skin and disproportionally large, orange eyes and four arms, the lower two extending from either side of their large, round stomachs, parallel to the arms which extend out of their shoulders above them.

Lords—Elected members of the Council of Lords, usually of high bloodlines from the upper echelons of Legallian society.

Mech-bot—Bots used as mechanics in starports.

Off-worlder—Person not from the same planet as a person calls home.

Plutonis—The 12th planet in the solar system, an icy world suitable only for natives and the Qiwi antelope. Also the location of the Borali Alliance's outermost post, Alpha Base.

Presimion Academy—The Borali Alliance's leading school for future military leaders located on Eleni 1, one of Legallis' largest moons.

Qiwi—Antlered creatures native exclusively to Plutonis, with dark brown fur and white spots lining either side of their spines. Waist high on most humans, qiwi have four long legs ending in black hooves. Their antlers can grow up to forty centimeters out from their skulls.

Quats—Striped creatures with long tails similar to Earth's cats but larger, like Cocker Spaniels.

Regallis—Thirteenth planet in the system, habitable only because of its development as a major indoor resort.

Royal Shuttle—Smaller version of the shuttles (see description below) reserved for the Royal family and their guests.

Serve-bot—Bots used for serving patrons in bars and restaurants.

Shuttle—White personnel transport with light gray interior. The cockpit has two black chairs facing a transparent blast shield, surrounded by controls, and is separated by a bulkhead from a passenger compartment containing four rows of seats—two lining each exterior wall and two back-to-back down the center. Each has its own safety harness. Intraplanetary models operate without lightspeed capabilities, while interplanetary models are equipped with ultra-lightspeed drives.

Skitter—One-man ground craft that operate on a system allowing it to fly above the planet's surface, higher than a floater. Sleek and fast, skitters are easy to maneuver through trees and other obstacles and are known to handle much like Imperial VS28 starfighters.

Talis—A warm beverage brewed from beans grown on Vertullis—somewhat like the old Earth beverage, coffee.

Tertullis—Eighth planet in the solar system, home to tall humanoids similar to humans except for their orangish tinted skin and purple eyes.

Transport—Larger craft used to transport supplies, food, and other loads across the solar system.

Vertullis—Sixth planet in the system and home to the humans known as workers, the only slaves in the solar system.

VS28—Sleek and black starfighters with snub noses and three wings—two longer wings out of each side, and a third shorter wing extending vertically above the fighter's four engines. Each bears its squadron's insignia, and a few bear names given them at a pilot's indulgence. They have laser cannons on each wing as well as in the nose. The cockpit lay beneath a gray, transparent blast shield through which the pilot can see the stars in space around him.

WFR (Worker's Freedom Resistance)—An organized resistance formed by workers on Vertullis to seek freedom from the Borali Alliance's rule.

Workers—Residents of Vertullis, and age-old enemies of the Legallians; they live and work as slaves for the Borali Alliance.

Acknowledgements

The idea for this story came to me when I was a fifteen-year-old science fiction fan living in a small Kansas town where it sometimes felt like dreaming was the only way out. Over the years, I lost my original notes, but the idea in my head and the names Xalivar and Sol stayed with me as well as the opening line "Sol climbed to the top of the rise and stared up at the twin suns as they climbed into the sky." I revised it a bit when we did the Author's Definitive Edition for Wordfire in 2015 and again for this version, cleaning up some typos, missing words, logic flaws, and repetitive words. But for the most part, it is the first novel I wrote—imperfect and an example of a less mature, established author than I am now.

I made that choice because ultimately a writer can only go back and fix his flawed works so many times before it loses any meaning, and this book took me twenty-five years to write and I wrote daily through some of the toughest trials I've experienced in my life. So this book you hold in your hand is a victory in many ways, and I'm still proud of it and what it accomplished for my career (giving people an experience similar to the first *Star* Wars and making Honorable Mention on Barnes and Noble's Year's Best Science Fiction of 2011) and hope you'll enjoy it and share it with others.

Thanks go first to Lost Genre Guild for inspiring me to try writing for *Digital Dragon* and to T.W. Ambrose for encouraging me to write more space opera stories, and then agreeing to publish them. An abridged version of the prologue to this novel first appeared in *Digital Dragon*'s May 2010 issue.

Secondly, thanks go to fellow authors like Blake Charlton, Ken Scholes, Jay Lake, Mike Resnick, Leon Metz, Moses Siregar, and Grace Bridges who have supported, encouraged, and advised me time and time again, no matter how silly my questions were or how many times they'd heard them before. Special thanks to Blake and Grace for taking time to read and offer more specific advice to help me grow as a writer and to Mike Resnick for advice in figuring out this crazy business.

Thirdly, thanks to first readers and friends like Larry Thomson, Tim Pearse, Jeff Vaughn, David Melson, Todd Ward, Mike Wallace, Andrew Reeves, Chris Zylo Owens, and the members of the FCW-Basic Critique Group for actually seeming to enjoy my writing even in its roughest form and for giving me feedback which helped me to improve it greatly.

Fourthly, thanks to friends like Charlie Davidson, Aaron Zapata, Mark Dalbey, Nelson Jennings, and Greg Baerg, who, along with some of the guys above, have helped me escape from behind the desk and keyboard and laugh a little bit when I needed it.

Fifthly, thanks to Vivian Trask, Randy Streu, Jen Ambrose, Paul Conant and Darlene Oakley for their editing and advice, Anthony Cardno for proofing the latest iteration, the El Paso Writer's League for encouragement and fellowship, and Mike Wallace for the science of the Boralis solar system. Thanks also to Jeana Clark for the solar system map which brought it to life for me.

Thanks to you, the reader. I hope you like it enough to come back for more and check out my John Simon Thrillers and other works.

Thanks to God for making me in His image and giving me the talent and inspiration to do this and continually opening the doors. I look forward to seeing what's behind the next ones.

About the Author

Bryan Thomas Schmidt is a national bestselling author editor and Hugo-nominee who's edited over a dozen anthologies and hundreds of novels, including the international phenomenon *The Martian* by Andy Weir and books by Alan Dean Foster, Frank Herbert, Mike Resnick, Angie Fox, and Tracy Hickman as well as official entries in *The X-Files, Predator, Aliens Vs. Predators, Joe Ledger, Monster Hunter International,* and *Decipher's Wars.* His debut novel, *The Worker Prince,* earned honorable mention on Barnes and Noble's Year's Best science fiction. His adult and children's fiction and nonfiction books have been published by publishers such as St. Martins Press, Baen Books, Titan Books, IDW, Blackstone, and more. He lives in Ottawa, KS with his canine bosom companions, Louie and Amelie, and four cats.

Website/Blog: www.bryanthomasschmidt.net
Twitter: @BryanThomasS
Facebook: www.facebook.com/BryanThomasSchmidt
Goodreads:
goodreads.com/author/show/3874125.Bryan_Thomas_Schmidt

**To sign up for
Bryan Thomas Schmidt's
Author Newsletter
and get a free short story,
go to bit.ly/3yE13Kt**

www.ingramcontent.com/pod-product-compliance
Lightning Source LLC
Chambersburg PA
CBHW050516110726
47899CB00005B/1473